W9-CAU-024

ASHES AND LACE

Song of Erin No. 2

Other Books by B. J. Hoff

Song of Erin series
Cloth of Heaven

An Emerald Ballad series
Song of the Silent Harp
Heart of the Lonely Exile
Land of a Thousand Dreams
Sons of an Ancient Glory
Dawn of the Golden Promise

The Penny Whistle
Winds of Graystone Manor

Song of Erin 2

B. J. HOFF

ASHES *and* LACE

Tyndale House Publishers, Inc.
Wheaton, Illinois

Visit Tyndale's exciting Web site at www.tyndale.com

Copyright © 1999 by B. J. Hoff. All rights reserved.

Visit B.J. on the Web at www.bjhoff.com

Cover art copyright © 1999 by Aleta Jenks. All rights reserved.

Author's photo copyright © 1996 by Bill Bilsley. All rights reserved.

Designed by Catherine Bergstrom

Unless otherwise indicated, Scripture quotations contained herein are taken from the *Holy Bible,* Revised Standard Version, copyright © 1946, 1952, 1971 by the Division of Christian Education of the National Council of the Churches of Christ in the United States of America, and are used by permission. All rights reserved.

Scripture quotations marked NIV are taken from the *Holy Bible,* New International Version®. NIV®. Copyright © 1973, 1978, 1984 by International Bible Society. Used by permission of Zondervan Publishing House. All rights reserved.

Scripture quotations marked NLT are taken from the *Holy Bible,* New Living Translation, copyright © 1996. Used by permission of Tyndale House Publishers, Inc., Wheaton, Illinois 60189. All rights reserved.

Library of Congress Cataloging-in-Publication Data

Hoff, B. J., date
  Ashes and lace / B. J. Hoff.
    p. cm. — (Song of Erin ; #2)
   ISBN 0-8423-1479-2 (sc)
    1. Irish Americans—New York (State)—New York Fiction. I. Title. II. Series : Hoff, B. J.,
date   Song of Erin ; #2.
PS3558.034395A95 1999
813´.54—dc21   99-33318

Printed in the United States of America
05   04   03   02   01   00   99
8   7   6   5   4   3   2

ACKNOWLEDGMENTS

With special thanks:

To Ken Petersen, my editor, for more grace and long-suffering patience than I deserve and for always pushing for the best instead of "good enough."

To Ron Beers, whose walk of faith, integrity, and kindness is an inspiration for us all.

To Travis Thrasher, who always does so much more than what he needs to do and does it with a cheerful heart entirely. (He is really three people, but no one knows this except his authors.)

To Anne Goldsmith, who seems to have developed an Irish sense of humor and a high tolerance for technologically challenged dinosaurs.

To everyone at Tyndale House, a publisher who so beautifully and clearly defines *Christian publishing*.

To my family, for putting up with me and loving me in spite of myself.

And to those special friends—you know who you are—who prayed me through the fire . . . one more time. *Dia linn!* (God bless us!)

B. J. Hoff
1999

....

PART ONE

Like Gold in the Fire

I go east, but he is not there. I go west, but I cannot find him.

I do not see him in the north, for he is hidden. I turn to the south,

but I cannot find him. But he knows where I am going. And when he has

tested me like gold in a fire, he will pronounce me innocent.

JOB 23:8-10, NLT

Between Destiny and Despair

Roll forth, my song, like the rushing river
That sweeps along to the mighty sea.

JAMES CLARENCE MANGAN

ABOARD THE *PROVIDENCE*, ON THE ATLANTIC,
LATE SEPTEMBER, 1839

The bunk creaked as Terese Sheridan turned to look at the little girl beside her. Although it was still long before dawn, the child was awake, staring at Terese with those large, still eyes that seemed to hold a river of sorrow. At their feet the girl's younger brother slept, though fitfully.

Already the children had been marked by the voyage. The girl, Shona, had become frighteningly lethargic, showing no interest in anything except for her little brother, Tully. As for the boy, he had developed a cough that seemed to deepen with each passing day. And packed in as they were among countless others who carried all manner of sickness and ague, there was no telling what they might yet come down with.

Again Terese shifted, hoping to ease the ache in her back. The berths were little more than wooden shelves nailed to the wall, with nothing to cushion the constant, bruising impact as the ship rode the sea. There had been no thought that they would need to bring their own mattresses, and so they had come with only minimal bedding, this provided by the Orphan Friends Society. Their first day out, Terese had tried to soften the bunks by lining them with blankets, but the nights were too cold to lie uncovered, and so they now faced interminable weeks of the punishing bare berths.

By the time they had been at sea a week, some of the steerage passengers had taken to calling the *Providence* a "coffin ship." An apt description if ever there was one, Terese thought. It was like a dungeon, this stinking hole: cold and dark, the air foul with the stench of aging timbers, bodies crammed too tightly together, and human waste. In the dim, unventilated quarters, the sounds of light snoring or women weeping mingled with the moans of those who writhed on their bunks in the throes of sickness and the prayers of those still strong enough to storm heaven in search of deliverance.

And always there was the relentless, sickening pitch and roll of the ship.

It only made their cup more bitter still that they had never been meant to travel in steerage at all! Brady had thought to spare them that much at least, arranging, through the sponsorship of his brother's newspaper, for proper cabins in second class for Terese and the children.

By the end of their first day aboard ship, however, they had been herded off to steerage like cattle, the officer in charge viciously driving them below with a few other "filthy peasants" who had straggled on board after them.

Terese had screamed at him, had even tried to shove her way past him to plead their case with another officer, but the lout easily threw her off, strong-arming her and the children below, where they remained, virtual prisoners with the rest of the poor souls packed in around them.

Terese had existed in a state of barely contained fury ever since, daily blaming Brady for spurning her, for not being man enough to claim responsibility for the child she carried, for not going aboard with them to inspect their accommodations—indeed, she blamed Brady for every imaginable grievance, even for the disgusting food and vile water.

Unable to lie still any longer, she rose, stepped away from their bunks, and stared at the mass of bodies stretched out in all directions. A familiar feeling of confinement, of being caught in a trap and abandoned—cut off from everything and everyone except the underworld of this ship—threatened to overwhelm her. The dank hull of the ship seemed to close in on her, and the passengers sprawled wherever she looked made her want to scream at the futility of her situation.

She almost thought it would be easier to make her way up to the deck and fling herself into the sea than to endure this cursed existence another day. So wretched was she, so nearly defeated with disillusionment and despair, that she might have done just that had it not been for the babe she carried and the two young orphans dependent upon her.

Instead she forced herself to turn her back on the squalor all around her and, squeezing her eyes shut, hugged her arms to herself so fiercely that she shook with the very effort. She reminded herself once again that with every day that passed in this hellhole, she was putting the misery of her past in Ireland behind her.

Unexpectedly, the voice of Jane Connolly, the poor crippled

woman whose brittle facade had concealed a surprisingly compassionate heart, rang through Terese's mind like the wail of the wind, and she lifted her hand to study the gold ring on her finger.

On the night before Terese's departure, Jane had not only added an extra week's pay to Terese's wages but had astonished her with the gift of a solid gold *Fede* ring—the faith ring of the Claddagh, once worn by Jane and then by her daughter.

But the gift had not been given without a chilling admonition. . . .

"Wear it to America," Jane had said of the ring. *"Wear it . . . and remember me and the Claddagh. . . . Remember Ireland. For Ireland is not only where you come from, Terese Sheridan—Ireland is what you are."*

Jane was wrong! Ireland was *not* what she was. Ireland was her past, a past as dark, as cold and bitter, as the bowels of this accursed ship.

With her back still turned to the abominable reality of steerage, she reminded herself that Ireland was behind her, while America—her future—lay ahead. All she had to do was survive this pit of perdition, and she would be free to begin a new life.

And survive it she would. Whatever it took.

If God allowed it . . .

The whisper in her spirit chilled the heat of her resolve like an icy waterfall. The farther they put out to sea, the more difficult it became to hold on to her already tenuous faith. She could almost feel it slipping away from her, like the waves in the wake of the ship. There were times, usually in the dead of night when the sounds of suffering all around her were heightened by the groaning and creaking of the old ship, when she feared that God might have abandoned her altogether.

What if, because of her sin with Brady, God had turned his back on her for good? What if there *were* no future for her and her child, only an unremarkable death in this squalid hole before she even reached the harbor of New York?

The thought made her shudder, and in spite of her determination not to give in to her circumstances, she was suddenly afraid. She began to tremble, her entire body racked by one seizure of chills after another.

Oh, please, Lord, I'll not be denying that I deserve your punishment, but my babe is innocent of any wrongdoing, he is! Won't you please help me to survive this horror and give my child something better?

Sweet Savior, at the end of this nightmare, let there be a new life waiting, a future for the both of us, in America!

1

A Most Respectable Man

It's the jewel that can't be got that is the most beautiful.
IRISH PROVERB

NEW YORK CITY, EARLY NOVEMBER

Jack Kane sat in his office at the *Vanguard,* pondering, not for the first time, at what point his fascination with Samantha Harte had deepened to love—and exactly what he was going to do about it.

It was an autumn-apple-crisp Monday morning. The past week, typical of New York, had been wet and gray, but today seemed to promise at least a glimpse of late fall as depicted by the poets: brisk and clear and golden.

Jack's mood was almost light, if somewhat distracted. He had more than enough work to keep him busy the rest of the day, yet he seemed incapable of concentrating on anything but Samantha.

How had things come to such a pass?

He had scarcely touched the woman, after all, other than an occasional clasp of the hand. The one act toward her that might possibly have been construed as something more than merely a harmless, friendly gesture had occurred weeks ago, when he'd come treacherously close to kissing her: an impulsive move and one quickly halted when Samantha virtually recoiled from him. Ever since, Jack had almost religiously exerted his self-control when they were together.

A priest could not have been more restrained.

But hang it all, he was no priest, and for all his earlier intentions to be nothing more than her employer and her friend, he was more bedazzled by the woman than ever!

He had managed to maintain his self-imposed discipline not merely because he was determined to win her trust—although that was at the heart of it—but perhaps just as much because he feared he might frighten her off altogether. Although Samantha had told him hardly anything about her previous marriage, she had at least confirmed Jack's suspicion that she'd been mistreated. How badly, or what form the mistreatment had taken, he didn't know—perhaps never would—for Samantha was obviously either unwilling or unable to speak of it. In fact, she had seemed to indicate that she hadn't even confided in her parents.

On one level Jack longed for her confidence—he coveted her trust, if not her affection. Yet at times he felt something akin to relief that she had kept her silence, for he wasn't at all sure he could handle the truth.

He could not bear the thought of Samantha's being hurt; indeed, he cringed at the very idea. The few times he had allowed himself to wonder about the circumstances of her marriage to Bronson Harte, a treacherous kind of fury would invariably rise up in him. Perhaps he was better off not knowing the details.

He couldn't help but wonder if this might not be a form of

cowardice, but then again, he had no doubt but that if Samantha *should* ever choose to unburden herself to him, he would be quick to listen and even grateful for her confidence.

The truth was that he desperately wanted Samantha to trust him, no matter what it took to achieve that trust.

He wanted her to trust him. He wanted her to need him.

And he wanted her to marry him.

Jack sighed and leaned back in his chair. He was in a bad way, no doubt about it.

He found himself wondering if his exemplary conduct was having any effect at all on Samantha. Was he only deluding himself that his campaign to win her over was actually working? He could never be quite sure what to make of the woman.

She had a way of looking at a man, Samantha did, that seemed to peel right past any and every layer of subterfuge while revealing nothing of her own emotions.

More than once Jack had been struck by the discomfiting suspicion that she was only too well aware of the effort required of him to play the gentleman. And while he might not go so far as to say she found his attempts amusing, on occasion she would regard him with a certain quirk of the eyebrow that made him wonder if she wasn't simply biding her time, expecting him at any moment to trip over his newly cultivated respectability.

He let out another long sigh of exasperation, but he couldn't quite suppress a smile at the thought that he was going to see Samantha today. Indeed, if all went well, he hoped to see her later this morning and again tonight.

His mood brightened considerably at that point, and he pushed away from the desk in anticipation. This could be a very important day in his life, and he didn't want to waste another minute before getting on with it.

Samantha had been expecting Tommy Ryder with the day's copy, so she wasn't surprised when someone rapped on the door a little after eleven.

Tommy was late, which meant that she would have to really push in order to have the proofing ready for the afternoon pickup. Even so, she felt no real annoyance, only a mild relief when the boy finally arrived.

Her smile quickly fled, however, when she opened the door to find not the youthful messenger from the *Vanguard* but the *owner* of the *Vanguard*.

"Jack!"

He stood there, tall and dark, filling the doorway like a lean black bear. Under one arm was tucked the day's copy; in his free hand, he held a small bouquet of fall flowers.

Samantha stared, her gaze going from his slightly smug smile to the bouquet. Flustered, she couldn't seem to find her voice.

Even now, after months in his employ and despite the odd—and often confusing—sort of friendship that had developed between them, Jack's presence still unnerved her.

To say the least.

His smile widened, as if he found Samantha's discomfiture highly gratifying. "It seems that I'm your messenger boy today," he said smoothly, extending the bouquet. "May I come in, Samantha?"

Samantha stared at the bouquet without making a move to accept it. "Oh—well, actually, I don't know that that would be a good idea."

She thought she had long since passed the time when Jack Kane—or any other man, for that matter—could make her stammer like a schoolgirl, but even as she struggled to regain her composure, Samantha felt her mind go to mush.

She reminded herself that she was *not* a schoolgirl—indeed would soon be turning thirty—and she could think of nothing less becoming to a mature woman than to suddenly start behaving like a mindless chit.

She supposed she *should* invite him in; despite the difficulties of their relationship, he was still her employer, after all. But if her landladies downstairs, the Misses Washington, should learn that she had allowed a man inside her apartment, even for only a moment, they would be scandalized.

She suddenly realized that Jack was watching her with a decidedly amused expression, as if he knew exactly what she was thinking.

"No doubt you're anxious about offending your delightful landladies," he said. "You needn't worry. I believe the dears actually find me rather charming."

Samantha stared at him.

"Oh, I met Miss Rena and her sister on the way in," he said, as if in answer to her unspoken question. "They were bringing in the flowers from the stoop—they seem to think we'll have frost tonight, you see—and I offered to help. I explained that my call is rather urgent and strictly business, and they were most understanding. And very helpful," he added, still smiling cheerfully.

"So, you see, Samantha, it's perfectly all right to have me in. We'll leave the door open, of course, but I assure you that both Miss Rena and Miss Lily have the utmost confidence in me. Apparently, I look every bit the gentleman to them."

He looked, Samantha thought worriedly, like a *pirate*. A pirate in a perfectly tailored suit, as it were, and with a white posy in his lapel.

But a pirate all the same.

Again Jack extended the bouquet, and this time Samantha practically yanked it out of his hand. "All right, then, I suppose you might as well come in."

"Why, thank you, Samantha," he said, making a quick little bow and then breezing by her. "I was hoping you'd ask."

2

A Small Hint
of Rebellion

*Something there is in the virtuous heart
that rebels if a thing is unfair.*
ANONYMOUS

Inside, Samantha put the flowers in water, at the same time groping for something to say that didn't sound altogether banal. Jack had followed her to the kitchen and, after placing the copy on the table, stood leaning casually against the sink as he watched her arrange the bouquet.

When he reached across her to inspect a wan-looking blossom that looked out of place among the others, Samantha almost stumbled in her haste to step away. He lifted an eyebrow but said nothing as he moved to reposition the drooping flower with great care, gently plucking a leaf or two before bracing it between a couple of larger, healthier blooms.

He straightened and turned back to her with a smile. Only then did Samantha manage to drag her gaze away from his hands.

"The copy is late, you know," she said abruptly, cringing at the waspish tone of her own voice. "I'll have all I can do to be finished by two."

"Well then, why don't I just stay and help?" he said, making a move as if to shrug out of his suit coat.

"No!" Samantha blurted out, more sharply than she'd intended.

Again one dark brow lifted as he hesitated, half out of his coat.

"I mean—that's not necessary." Her words spilled out in a rush as she fumbled to conceal her discomfort. "It won't be all *that* late. Besides," she hurried to add, "I wouldn't want you to get news ink on your suit."

He studied her, his eyes glinting with something Samantha couldn't read. "If a little news ink bothered me, I'd be in a terrible fix, now wouldn't I? May I?" he said, not waiting for her reply before slipping the rest of the way out of his jacket and rolling up his shirtsleeves. "Do stop fretting yourself, Samantha. I'll just give you a hand with this and take it back to the office with me."

With that, he sat down at the table and started in on the top sheet of copy. "Besides, there are some things I've been wanting to discuss with you. That's the real reason I'm here, as it happens."

Samantha would have raised yet another objection, but the words lodged in her throat. It occurred to her that her small, cozy kitchen suddenly looked even smaller—cramped and almost suffocating—with Jack's long legs stretched out under her table and his dark head bent over the work at hand.

They worked without speaking for several minutes before Samantha broke the uncomfortable silence. "I should have thanked you for the flowers. They're very nice."

"You're welcome," he said, not looking up. After a brief pause, he said, "One of the reasons I wanted to see you was to ask a favor, if I might."

Samantha glanced up from the copy.

"I'm a bit concerned about Cavan's sister and the Madden tykes. You recall that they're due to arrive any day now?"

Samantha did remember, of course. As a part of her various job responsibilities, she had begun weeks ago to make the necessary arrangements for Terese Sheridan and the two orphaned children who were traveling with her.

Jack's newspaper, the *Vanguard,* had begun to publish a series of articles about the Irish immigrants arriving in the States in ever increasing numbers. Written by Cavan Sheridan, each article focused on a specific individual or family and the circumstances that had precipitated their immigration, as well as the difficulties that might await them when they arrived in America. Already the series had attracted considerable interest around the city, even throughout the state. As a result the *Vanguard's* subscriber list had begun to expand—and Cavan Sheridan had won his first byline.

Samantha had been only too pleased to be involved in this unprecedented project, a project that had actually been Cavan Sheridan's idea. In addition to the stories themselves, the paper had committed to financing the featured immigrants' passage and assisting in their resettlement. Samantha's duties included meeting the new arrivals at the harbor and then helping them with their living arrangements and employment possibilities while monitoring their situations as they adapted to their new country.

The fact that one of the first arrivals would be none other than Cavan's sister—his only surviving family member, in fact—merely added to the importance of the project for Samantha. Cavan was her "star" student from the night classes she taught among the immigrant settlements. From the beginning he had stood out as particularly gifted. He had a fine, quick mind and an aptitude for painting pictures with words that was unrivaled even by many of the city's more experienced newsmen.

The young Irish immigrant had actually been responsible for Samantha's position with the *Vanguard*. Initially employed as Jack's driver and stableman, Cavan had brought the proofreading job at the newspaper to Samantha's attention, at the same time bringing *Samantha* to Jack Kane's attention.

At first Samantha had resisted Jack's insistent efforts to hire her, largely because of his notorious reputation. By now, however, she had come to count her job with the *Vanguard* as one of the best things that could have happened to her. She enjoyed the proof-reading, enjoyed even more the editorial assignments Jack had lately begun to send her way. And the additional responsibilities she would soon assume with the immigrant resettlement project only added to the job's appeal. As far as Samantha was concerned, she couldn't have custom designed a job with more advantages or one with fewer drawbacks.

Except, perhaps, for the man who had given her the job.

She glanced over at Jack, saw him watching her, and realized he was waiting for some sort sort of response from her.

"I'm sorry?"

"I asked if you'd mind keeping tabs on the harbor while I'm gone."

"Gone?"

He looked at her. "I'm leaving for Philadelphia Wednesday, re-member?"

There was no accounting for the sudden but undeniable twist of disappointment that coiled through Samantha. He would be away for only a few days, after all, but for some reason she felt an almost painful emptiness at the prospect.

"I'd forgotten. Your meeting with Mr. Poe."

He nodded. "I'm to meet with him on Thursday and, depending on how that goes, possibly once or twice more before I come back." He paused, watching her. "I don't suppose you've changed your mind about coming with me."

Samantha felt the heat rise to her face. "You know I can't possibly do that. Please don't mention it again."

"It would be entirely proper," he said reasonably. "You'd be traveling as my assistant."

Samantha had the feeling he was deliberately baiting her. She was appalled by the fact that for an instant she had actually caught herself wishing she *could* go with him.

"I hardly think it would be seen as proper," she said, forcing herself not to rise to his bait. "And I'd rather not discuss it any further. Now, shouldn't we try to finish the proofing if you want it for today's edition?"

He feigned a sigh of disappointment before turning his attention back to the copy. "You concern yourself too much with what people think, Samantha."

She made no reply. Minutes later, she changed the subject to safer ground. "You've still had no word from the ship, I take it?" Samantha asked after a moment.

He shook his head. "The Sheridan girl is to send a message by one of the runners from the harbor as soon as they pass quarantine. So far there's been nothing. I assume the ship hasn't anchored yet, but I'd like to know for certain. You'll recall that Brady said the two children weren't in the best of health."

Samantha nodded. Shona and Tully Madden were two Irish orphans whom Jack's brother had submitted for sponsorship, at the same time arranging for Terese Sheridan to oversee their welfare during the crossing. Apparently, both of the children had been in rather poor health when the arrangements were made.

"Wouldn't there have been something in the arrival notices if the ship had put in?" she asked Jack.

He made a dismissing motion with one hand. "You can't count on those. They miss more than they list. It's occurred to me that they might end up in quarantine once they arrive. We'll need to keep check on them."

Samantha looked at him. "Oh, Jack, I'd hate to think of those children being held at Tompkinsville. It's such an awful place."

"'Tis that," he said, making a sour face. "In any event, you'll stay in touch with the harbor while I'm away?"

"Yes, of course. But shouldn't you ask Cavan instead of me? He's already been haunting the docks for days. I'm sure he's desperate to see his sister after all these years."

"He is," Jack agreed, "but he won't be back from Albany until the weekend or possibly Monday. Bill Worth is down with the grippe, so I sent Sheridan up to the governor's mansion in his place to find out what shenanigans Weed's been up to this month."

Samantha saw his expression turn even darker. Jack's dislike for Thurlow Weed and his Whig politics was no secret.

"I don't mean for you go to the harbor alone, mind," he went on. "Until Sheridan gets back, one of the lads from the paper will drive you."

Samantha didn't argue. She had no desire to frequent New York Harbor by herself.

They finished the proofing within the next few minutes, and Jack leaned back in the chair, stretching his arms out in front of him. "You see—right on schedule," he said, watching Samantha. "Have supper with me tonight?"

Samantha glanced away for fear he would see how much she wanted to accept.

"Please," he put in quickly.

"Jack—"

"I missed lunch. We'll have an early meal. We can go to the club, if you like."

Over the past two months, Samantha had had supper with Jack on three or four occasions, each time at the Portico Club, an unpretentious midtown eating establishment, off the beaten track. No one there was likely to recognize either Jack or Samantha.

Samantha knew it was in deference to her reputation that Jack always suggested the club when he asked her to supper. While she was touched by his caution on her account, she resisted the idea that her reputation could be irrevocably damaged simply by dining out with a man society happened to deem "unacceptable."

It was actually Jack who continued to "protect" her from scandal. Left to herself, Samantha would probably have ignored the gossipmongers and gone wherever she pleased with *whomever* she pleased. But he insisted that for her sake they be discreet, and she supposed his way was best. At least this way her mother—who was as sensitive to society's approval as Samantha was *not*—needn't be subjected to the sort of notoriety that seemed to hang over Jack like an ugly thundercloud.

For a long time now, Samantha had questioned the rumors that so relentlessly dogged Jack. There was no denying that he had a "past," as her mother was fond of pointing out. Nor did he seem inclined to conceal that fact from Samantha. He had actually made reference to his earlier gambling habit once or twice, for example, even admitting that he'd won most of the purchase price for the *Vanguard* in a marathon round of blackjack.

But at the same time, Samantha believed him when he said he no longer indulged in the vice. I gambled because I was set on making a lot of money fast," he had once told her matter-of-factly. "When I discovered I had a streak of luck about me, I went for higher stakes. But once I had what I wanted, I quit. It was never that much fun, in truth. It was simply—" he shrugged—"a means to an end."

As for the rumors that he was a notorious womanizer, Samantha had no way of knowing how factual they were. She *did* know it was all but impossible to walk into a room with him without being aware of his effect on women. Even the gazes of the more "respectable" matrons invariably followed him. Jack was a startlingly tall man, uncommonly handsome, with a definite air of power—perhaps even a certain ruthlessness—that seemed to make the very air in the room crackle with excitement.

His conduct toward Samantha was unfailingly irreproachable. Oh, he never entirely lost the roguish air that clung to him like a playful shadow. And his manners might be slightly rough edged, his speech blunt and even harsh at times. But he was obviously determined to be the soul of propriety with her, and most of the time he carried it off quite well; indeed, his mien with her often bordered on old-world *courtly*. On occasion Samantha found herself hard pressed to conceal a touch of amusement at the effort she speculated this sterling behavior might require of him.

Mostly, however, she was moved by his attempts to gain her approval, even though she suspected that if she were to press, he would cheerfully admit to being the reprobate he was rumored to be. He almost seemed to take an unaccountably grim sense of satisfaction in not contradicting his questionable reputation. In fact, it was this that kept Samantha from dismissing the gossip about him out of hand. In spite of the way he conducted himself with her—and in spite of an undeniable attraction for her—she had to admit that Jack could conceivably be the ruthless, cold-blooded infidel the rumors held him to be.

Her mother obviously believed, even seemed to relish, the worst of the stories, haranguing Samantha at every opportunity with comments to the effect that "that awful man you work for" was nothing more than an Irish thug whose success had been ill gotten and whose reputation was an absolute disgrace.

What if her mother was right?

Well, what if she was?

Whatever Jack might have been in the past, with *her* he had never been anything but a gentleman—kind, courteous, perhaps even overly protective of her. In most of the other areas of her life, Samantha had overcome the tendency to perform according to her mother's convention-bound expectations. Why shouldn't that hard-won independence extend to Jack?

Abruptly she turned to him. "I'd like very much to have supper with you tonight," she said before she could change her mind. "And why don't we try somewhere besides the club for a change?"

He stared at her for a long moment. Then he smiled, his dark eyes holding her captive as he caught her completely off guard with his reply.

"What I would really like, Samantha, is to have dinner with you at my home. I confess that for a long time now I've fancied the idea of seeing you at my table. I don't suppose you'd consider it?" He paused only an instant before adding, "It would be altogether proper, I promise you. My housekeeper would be there, as well as Mrs. Flynn, my cook. We wouldn't be alone. Not at all."

Samantha studied him, already questioning her impulsiveness yet intrigued in spite of the clamoring of her better judgment. This was the last thing she'd expected. And yet he suddenly looked so eager, so hopeful, she found herself loath to refuse.

"I . . . that hardly seems fair to your cook, to invite a guest on such short notice."

Jack waved off her concern. "Mrs. Flynn routinely cooks for half a dozen or more every time she fires up the stove. She cannot seem to help herself. I do my part, of course, to digest her bounty, but even a greedy Irishman has his fill sooner or later." He grinned at her. "I can't think of anything that would please her more than knowing she has a legitimate license to overdo. Besides—don't you ever get tired of dining alone? I know *I* do."

When Samantha continued to hesitate, he glanced around the kitchen, saying, "I've been in *your* home now, and I should like it very much if you would visit mine." He leaned forward, reaching across the table to lightly touch her hand. "You would honor me, Samantha."

There it was again, that unexpected, almost quaint touch of humility that seemed so out of keeping with the air of utter confidence he usually exhibited,

Apparently, this was her day for acting on impulse.

"I . . . all right. But I'd have to make it an early evening, you understand."

The light that suffused his features somehow seemed to make years drop away. He was suddenly animated, almost boyish, as if he had just been given a delightful gift.

"Aye . . . yes, well . . . that's grand then! I'll send Ransom around for you close on seven; how would that be? And of course he'll drive you home whenever you say."

Samantha smiled at his pleasure, at the same time trying hard to suppress her own.

3

Shadows of the Heart

I sat with one I love last night.
GEORGE DARLEY

Jack's house—if such a sprawling old mansion could actually be reduced to the word *house*—was both a surprise and a study in contrasts.

From the first moment she entered, Samantha was both intrigued and somewhat confused by the splashes of ostentation that she would have thought foreign to Jack's nature. Her initial sense of the house was a disturbingly oppressive feeling of *gloom*. Most of the furnishings were dark and massive and heavily ornate. Yet there were also touches of restrained elegance as well—simple, but classic and in excellent taste. She found herself wondering which extreme was more in keeping with Jack's character.

The enormous entrance hall was almost garish with its crimson silk damasks and gilded wall hangings. But the massive mahogany staircase was absolutely splendid, solid and unyielding yet exquisitely carved with a certain grace in its rise all the way to the third story. Its overpowering presence and stately strength somehow reminded Samantha of Jack.

The dining room was immense, its table nearly spanning the length of the entire room, flanked by tall chairs, a large sideboard, and a china cabinet that appeared more in keeping with a medieval castle than a house on Thirty-Fourth Street. The room was just barely saved from vulgarity by the collection of lustrous silver, delicate china, and crystal that graced the table, all in unembellished, tasteful patterns.

Being in Jack's home, eating at his table, fueled Samantha's curiosity about the deceased Martha Kane. What had she been like, Jack's tragic wife who, according to Amelia Carver, had died childless while still in her twenties, leaving Jack in bitter despair at her passing? Had she chosen the more tasteful objects in this cold, dreary room? Had it been Martha who embroidered the scrolled *K* on the white dinner napkins?

Did Jack still miss her, still grieve for her?

Samantha dismissed the questions by reminding herself that the answers were actually none of her business. Yet she couldn't quite shake the image of Jack sitting here, dark and silent and alone in this enormous, echoing room with only his memories to keep him company. The thought wrenched her heart with such unexpected force that she actually flinched, her fork clattering against the plate.

She looked up to find him watching her. "Ugly, isn't it?" he said, taking in the room with a quick sweep of his hand.

Flustered, Samantha glanced away. "No, no, of course not. You have a very impressive home."

"It's grotesque," he said, seemingly indifferent to the fact as he took a bite of cheese soufflé. "Most of this stuff was already here when I bought it. I always meant to make changes but never seemed to find the time. I often think about selling the place, moving into something a bit less—formidable." He flashed a quick smile. "I must say you brighten up the old horror with your presence."

Unnerved by the warmth of his gaze, Samantha again looked away from him, feigning interest in her dessert. "You didn't exaggerate about Mrs. Flynn's cooking. Everything was delicious."

The truth was that she had scarcely tasted the food at all. She had eaten most of the roast pork and baked apples without any real appreciation of flavor.

"I'll tell her you were pleased," Jack said dryly, as if he knew very well how little attention she had actually given to the meal.

Silence hung between them for a moment, until the housekeeper, Mrs. O'Meara—"Addy," Jack called her—came back into the room, one of several appearances she'd made throughout the evening.

"Didn't I tell you we'd be well chaperoned?" Jack said under his breath.

Samantha had to smile. The housekeeper's intention *had* been almost amusingly obvious as she continued to come and go, even after the final course of the meal had been served.

"Mrs. O'Meara would seem to take very good care of you," Samantha said after the woman had again left the room.

"Ha. 'Tis *you* the outrageous woman is looking after, you can be sure."

Samantha studied him. "You don't fool me, you know. The two of you badger each other terribly, but I can tell that you're actually quite fond of her."

His dark brows drew together in a mockery of a frown. "Yes,

well, you so much as breathe a word of that to our Mrs. O'Meara, and my life will be pure misery from this night on."

"It strikes me that she already knows her position is safe."

He shook his head. "I don't know what I'd do without her, and that's the truth. But she'd be at an utter loss if I didn't give her a bit of grief on a daily basis."

Samantha laughed at his wry expression. "How long has she been with you?"

"Forever," he cracked, then added, "A long time, as it happens. In between ruling my life and running my household, she also helped to mother my brother and sister."

Samantha remembered that Jack's sister, Rose, was a nun in New Jersey, while his younger brother, Brady, was still in Ireland, working on the immigrant series.

"How long does your brother plan to stay in Ireland?" she asked him now.

He made a sour face. "I'm beginning to think he means to take up permanent residence there."

"And you don't like the idea?"

"Troublesome rascal that he is, I find that I miss him. And Rose as well. But there was no dissuading either of them once they set their heads to what they wanted."

Samantha saw something in his eyes at that instant—a flash of regret or even sadness—that tugged at her heart. Not for the first time, she wondered how much Jack actually enjoyed the wealth he'd accumulated, the power and influence he wielded.

What had motivated him to attain such heights? She knew he had emigrated from Ireland when he was still a boy. The rumors about his past claimed that he had launched his publishing empire by sweeping floors at a small print shop. Now he owned one of the country's most powerful newspapers, as well as two large, prestigious publishing houses. Yet he couldn't be much past forty, if that. His astonishing level of success had to have come in a relatively brief span of years. Either he had been incredibly fortunate in his dealings—or incredibly driven.

How much of his ambition had been for himself, she wondered, as opposed to a desire to provide a better life for his younger siblings?

Even the harshest of Jack's critics were inclined to allow him a certain grudging admiration. He had, after all, achieved a stunning level of success with nothing more than his wits, a cavalier kind of courage, a great deal of hard work, and—according to Jack himself—a considerable amount of good luck. Yet in spite of his prosperity and power, Samantha had never sensed any measurable degree of happiness or contentment in him. To the contrary, she was beginning to believe that his success had gained him little more than a self-imposed loneliness and a deep, barely concealed anger.

Almost from the first, she had sensed the quiet rage in him, the darkness that seemed to lie never far from the surface of his emotions—a darkness that could be explosive, Samantha suspected, even frightening. In fact, she couldn't quite shake the feeling that there was a side to Jack's nature that, once unleashed, could easily turn ugly. While she had never actually seen him lose control, had never been the recipient of his legendary temper or scathing sarcasm, she had heard more than she cared to about the verbal assaults that reputedly could be venomous, if not downright cruel.

Yet she found it difficult—nearly impossible—to reconcile the rumors with the man who had been so exceedingly kind to her. In spite of the undeniable attraction between them—and the tension resulting from that attraction—they had managed to become friends. Good friends, as it happened, and at a time when Samantha *needed* a friend. Jack's kindness to her, his consideration and en-couragement, had been like a balm to her sorely wounded spirit.

Because of this, perhaps she tended to dismiss the sordid stories about him too easily. But she simply did not care as much about his past, about the man he might have been, as she did about the man he was with *her*—the man who had befriended her and who seemed so quick and willing to tolerate in her even what he could not hope to understand.

How, then, could she do less for him?

Besides, who knew better than she about the darkness of the human soul, the shadows lurking in the secret places too deeply hidden for the world to ever see? And who was she to judge Jack for what he was *rumored* to be when she had learned firsthand how appearances could deceive, how easily darkness could conceal itself behind a mask of goodness and light?

⚜

He still could scarcely believe she was here. When he'd extended the invitation he had literally held his breath, anticipating her refusal. Then, when she astonished him by accepting, there was no describing the wave of unreasonable pleasure that had washed over him.

Watching her now, Jack was acutely mindful of the conflicting emotions Samantha set off in him. Her very presence seemed to turn him from a badly jaded forty-year-old man into an awkward, inarticulate schoolboy. Surely the pleasure he took from simply being with her bordered on foolishness, if not utter lunacy. Why, every time he was with the woman, he had to fight back a grin as idiotic as that of the village simpleton!

But even as he struggled to control this annoying streak of boy-ish eagerness, he was almost painfully aware of the same strange, uneasy sensation that invariably gripped him when he was with her: the feeling that by simply coming too close to her, he might somehow *tarnish* her.

She had a light about her, Samantha did, a soft light of loveliness and goodness of which she seemed entirely unaware. It was a quality that both endeared her to Jack and at the same time served to restrain him from acting on his growing desire for her.

With Samantha he felt as if he had been somehow openly tarred with every mean, reprehensible thing he had ever done, for her and all the world to see. At times his very skin seemed to crawl with the awareness of the dark that lurked within him, the mire that had attached itself to him, and he wished he could physically peel away the layers of contamination so that he might be more acceptable, more decent, more *worthy* of her.

⁂

They moved to the study for coffee, and here Samantha found yet another marked contrast in decor. Immediately she was more comfortable with her surroundings, for there could be no mistaking Jack's influence. Spacious, but not so cavernous and oppressive as the dining room, the study seemed more a retreat. It was a peaceful room, she decided: restful, like a kind of sanctuary, with its green damask-covered walls, its fine, sturdy furniture of rosewood and leather, and the aged, honey-rich paneling.

Every wall but one held bookshelves crammed with volumes that appeared well used. On the single plain wall hung an assortment of opera and theater posters, many of which, Samantha noticed, had been signed by some of the leading performers of the day.

They sat by the fire, at opposite ends of a somewhat worn sofa, a small table in front of them. Jack watched her as he drained the last of his coffee. "You still haven't told me whether you think I should publish Poe," he said, setting his cup on the table.

Samantha gave him a quizzical look. "I'm hardly qualified to offer an opinion on whom you publish, Jack."

"In truth, Samantha, you're probably more qualified than I on that very subject. Now, tell me what you think. I've come to trust your instincts."

Samantha took a sip of her tea, trying to ignore the flush of pleasure his words stirred in her. "I thought you'd already decided to publish Mr. Poe's latest work."

He shrugged. "I may try to strike a deal with him. Once I'm certain I want to." He traced the line of his mustache for a moment. "I'd not be the one to argue Poe's genius. But genius or not, I find his work almost too—" He stopped, as if the word he wanted eluded him.

"Dark?" Samantha supplied.

He looked at her, nodding slowly. "Aye, there's that. I'd take him for a very sad fellow, even troubled. Have you read him?"

Samantha had, and although she appreciated Poe's formidable skill, for the most part she found his work too dreary for her liking. "I've read his poetry, mostly. And a few pieces of his shorter fiction."

"What about the novella?"

Samantha set her cup on the table, shaking her head. "I think even Mr. Poe must not have taken that particular effort too seriously. Frankly, I thought it a bit silly."

"Not one of his better efforts," Jack agreed. "He has a rather odd background, doesn't he? For a writer, that is. He was actually at West Point for a time, did you know that?"

"He was court-martialed at the Academy," Samantha pointed out. "And it's rumored that he brought it on himself deliberately, to spite his godfather, or some such foolishness."

Jack shot her a look of surprise. "How on earth would you know that?"

Samantha shrugged. "Mr. Poe's life hasn't exactly been a closed book."

Jack slanted a look of pained disbelief at her unintentional pun. "That was awful, Samantha. So, then, what else do you know about him? Apart from the scandalous stuff, I mean. I've already heard that business about his marrying his thirteen-year-old cousin."

"Actually, she was almost fourteen, I believe." Samantha hesitated, reluctant to further the gossip she'd heard, yet understanding Jack's need to know as much as possible about a prospective writer. "It's said that he drinks. To excess, though for Poe that might not be all that much. Apparently, he's of a rather delicate constitution."

Jack turned, settling himself against the arm of the sofa as she went on.

"It's not that he drinks all the time," she explained. "In fact, he seems to have long periods of sobriety."

"Let us hope that this is one of them," Jack said dryly, crossing his arms over his chest.

Because of Jack's own past, Samantha was hesitant to mention the next piece of information. She chose her words carefully. "I've heard that he also gambles rather a lot. But either he's not very good at it or not very lucky." She paused. "So I've been told."

Jack leaned back as if he were starting to enjoy this. "Samantha, you never cease to amaze me. Where do you get your information, if you don't mind my asking?"

"My mother," Samantha said matter-of-factly. "She's a veritable treasure trove of gossip."

Jack grinned. "Perhaps I should offer *her* a job."

Samantha couldn't help but smile at the thought. The very

mention of Jack's name was enough to strain Angela Pilcher's strait-laces to the breaking point. Her mother tended to relegate Jack to the same level as foreign sailors and opium eaters.

He poured himself another cup of coffee from the pot on the table. "Incidentally, I haven't forgotten the appointment with your Mrs. Shanahan and Avery Foxworth. We'll get that taken care of after I return." He paused. "I suppose you're still set on being there?"

Samantha nodded. "I think Maura will be more at ease if I'm with her."

"I expect you're right. But I'm still not sure why you want me there."

Samantha hesitated, then said carefully, "I hope you don't mind too much. But I suppose in this case it's *I* who would be more comfortable if *you* were there. I don't know Mr. Foxworth at all."

Jack arched an eyebrow. "Really? I was under the impression the two of you had met. He knows who *you* are."

"I can't think how," Samantha said, frowning.

Jack gave a thin smile. "Well, you may have forgotten, but Foxworth hasn't. In any event, he thinks you're exceptionally attractive. I gave him no argument on that score, of course."

Flustered, Samantha avoided his gaze while trying to think of a way to return the subject to Maura Shanahan. Back in the summer, the woman had shot and killed her husband, who had apparently been beating her and threatening the children. Samantha had good reason to believe that Mrs. Shanahan had acted in self-defense and out of fear for her children.

One of those children was a little newsboy for whom Jack seemed to hold a particular fondness. To Samantha's surprise, he had not only supported her interest in the matter but had gone so far as to retain his own attorney for the court case.

"I know it's presumptuous of me," she said, "asking you to take time out for something like this, especially as busy as you are. Maura Shanahan is just another immigrant in trouble, after all—a common enough occurrence. But with the trial about to begin—"

"Samantha—" Jack leaned toward her, his eyes glinting with faint amusement. "You needn't apologize. I don't mind in the least. You seem to forget that I'm just 'another immigrant' myself." He moved a little closer to her and took her hand. "Besides, if it's important to you, it's important to me."

Samantha felt the heat rush to her face. "I don't want you to do this for *me,* Jack!" she blurted out, keenly aware of the warm strength of his hand covering hers.

He pulled back a little but didn't release her hand. "And don't I know that well enough?" he said with a long sigh. "It would be a terrible thing entirely if you should somehow feel beholden to me."

"It's not that—"

"It's exactly that," he said bluntly. "And we both know it. Our . . . 'friendship'—" Samantha winced at the sardonic edge he gave the word—"would never survive your feeling obligated to me. Nor would I want you to feel put upon. But, woman, you do make it devilishly difficult sometimes for me to supply a bit of help."

"I'm sorry, Jack," Samantha said, meaning it. "I suppose I've been so intent on making my own way that I'm not always as gracious as I ought to be when a friend does me a favor."

He was watching her closely, an expression on his face that she couldn't quite identify. Whatever it was, it made her uncomfortable.

With his hand still holding hers securely, he closed the remaining distance between them on the sofa. "The thing is, Samantha," he said, his voice much lower than before, "I don't want to be your friend. I want to be your husband."

Samantha stared at him in total shock. The firelight flickered, dappling his face and softening his strong features. He was smiling a little, clearly aware that he had stunned her, yet obviously expecting a reply.

Samantha forced herself to meet his gaze. "You're joking, of course."

He gave a slight shake of his head and lifted his eyebrows. "You know I'm not, Samantha. I think you also know I'm in love with you and have been for some time."

Samantha glanced away. "Then I think you're just trying to rattle me," she said, trying hard for a lighter tone. "You do seem to enjoy doing that, I've noticed."

"Samantha, look at me," he said, increasing the pressure on her hand.

She heard the slight hoarseness in his voice. Somehow she managed to drag her gaze back to him, and when she did, she saw that he was not teasing her at all, that he was deadly serious. Her heart slammed against her ribs, and she couldn't seem to get her breath. "Jack, I don't know what you want me to say."

She was aware that she had edged as far away from him as she could and was now pressing against the arm of the sofa.

"I should think that would be fairly obvious. What I want you to say is *yes.*" The searching look he gave her seemed to arrow right to her soul. "Samantha," he said softly, "don't draw away from me. Not this time."

His grip on her hand tightened even more, and slowly, with great gentleness, he began to pull her toward him, bringing her as close . . . no, closer . . . than she had ever been to him before. She could see the unyielding line of his jaw, the faint silvering of his black hair, and the reflection of the fire in his dark eyes. She could actually feel his breath on her face, tinged with the faint scent of clove she had come to associate with him when he hadn't been smoking one of his cigars.

She thought that he would surely kiss her, but other than holding her hand, he made no move to touch her. He simply sat there, his eyes going over her face, then capturing and holding her gaze. "Marry me, Samantha."

A surge of panic shot through Samantha, but only for an instant. As she watched him, she could see nothing in his eyes to be afraid of. To the contrary, she sensed that the only threat to her at this moment was her melting heart.

"Jack, please don't do this—"

"Look at me and tell me you feel nothing for me but friendship."

It took everything she had to look away from him. In the end it was the intensity of his gaze, the sheer, almost overwhelming force of the look in his eyes—the *power* that virtually hummed from him—that enabled her to resist him. Jack was a man used to getting anything he wanted, she reminded herself as she tugged her hand free of his grasp. It wouldn't do to let him believe, even for a minute, that just because he wanted *her*, anything could come of it.

"Jack—*please!*"

The look of surprise that now went over his face only confirmed that he had not really expected her to resist him.

It occurred to Samantha, with some sense of irony, that the very aspects of Jack's personality that most likely enabled him to achieve whatever he fixed his sights on were the very traits that served to turn her away from him. If she wasn't exactly afraid of his strength, the force of his will, his driving self-confidence that made him believe he could bend any situation—perhaps any *person*—to his control, she was at least intimidated enough by it all to back away from him.

Mustering as much composure as she could, she stood. "I—should be going. It's after nine."

Jack studied her for a long, tense moment, then, almost as if he had read her thoughts, gave a reluctant nod. "If you must," he said, slowly getting to his feet.

"Don't take offense, Samantha. Please? I simply can't pretend any longer that all I want from you is friendship."

Samantha deliberately kept her gaze averted. "Just promise me we won't speak about this again. It's an impossible situation for me, Jack, it really is."

"Nothing," he said, his voice the low rumble she had come to recognize as an indication of his resolve, "is impossible, Samantha. Nothing." He stopped, and with one finger tipped her chin up to make her meet his eyes. "I won't raise the subject again for now. But eventually . . ." He shrugged, his meaning clear.

At the front door, she waited while he helped her with her coat. "Do you mind if I ride along while Ransom takes you home?"

"I—suppose not," Samantha said, aware of his hands lingering for perhaps a moment too long on her shoulders. "But it's not necessary."

He squeezed her shoulders lightly, then turned to shrug into his topcoat. "But I want to," he said. For a long moment, he stood looking down at her. "Samantha," he finally said, "thank you."

Samantha gave him a questioning look.

"For coming tonight," he explained. "It meant a great deal to me, your trusting me enough to come to my home."

Only then did it strike Samantha that she *did* trust Jack, in spite of all the very real reasons she probably *shouldn't*. Even now, after the discomfiting scene in the study, she found it impossible *not* to trust him, or at least his affection for her.

But at the moment he was standing much too close, and Mrs. O'Meara seemed to have disappeared. Samantha was keenly aware of his dark handsomeness, his almost black eyes searching hers. Her throat tightened, and she took an involuntary step back from him.

Nothing registered in his expression, no sign that he had noticed, other than a slight tightening of his jaw as he turned away from her to open the door. Outside, he took her arm on the way to the carriage, but it was purely a courteous gesture, impersonal and even perfunctory.

Samantha knew that she had hurt him, and for an instant she wanted to touch him, to take his arm and tell him she was sorry. Sorry she couldn't be what he wanted her to be, couldn't give him what he seemed to want from her. She almost wished that she dared tell him that she *did* care for him, perhaps cared too much—and that was why she couldn't possibly be anything more to him than a friend.

Instead, she allowed him to take her to the carriage. They ventured nothing more in the way of conversation than polite small talk for most of the drive home. When he had delivered her safely to her door, he merely gave her that quick little mocking bow that was his way, leaving her with an aching sense of disappointment—and an unaccountable feeling of loss.

Jack would have flatly denied that he was sulking. But the truth was that all the way back to the house, he had to struggle to keep from doing just that. He recognized that part of his dark mood had to do with the fact that he was simply not accustomed to being rejected. The more common scenario had *him* doing the spurning, not the other way around.

But he had been rebuffed all right, and with enough firmness that his pride was still smarting. He had backed off the instant he'd seen her eyes go cold with that familiar closed look of withdrawal. It would have been a fatal mistake to press her, and he'd known it.

But what Samantha most likely did *not* know was that a challenge had never yet sent him packing. To the contrary, a bit of a struggle served merely to raise the stakes, so far as Jack was concerned.

His mood lightened somewhat as he pondered his next move. The first thing was to retrench and consider where he'd miscalculated. Samantha wasn't the type who simply wanted to be coaxed. When she said no, she meant just that. At the same time, he found it difficult to believe he'd been reading her wrong all this time. She was attracted to him, and he knew it; before tonight he would have said it was *more* than attraction.

Perhaps he'd been rash in springing the idea of marriage on her so abruptly, without a proper job of courting beforehand. But hang it all, he had *tried* to court the woman, hadn't he? Samantha didn't make it easy for a man, after all, with that wall she kept so squarely in place most of the time.

Well, and what about that wall? The thing to do was figure a way to break it down, wasn't that so? If his memory served him correctly, he'd tumbled more than a few walls in the past.

Granted, he knew more about breaking down business opponents than a woman's resistance, but it all called for strategy, didn't it? And even if he said so himself, he did know a little something about strategy.

Indeed.

4
What Kind of Welcome?

We came to the city in search of a dream,
but the high gate to hope was closed against us.
CAVAN SHERIDAN
FROM *WAYSIDE NOTES*

STATEN ISLAND, NEW YORK, NOVEMBER

Terese Sheridan had spent her first two weeks in the United States
in a quarantine hospital.

Tompkinsville, as it was called, sat on a hill across the river from
New York City. Terese and a host of others from the *Providence*
were taken there in a skiff and dumped on the beach like bags of
rotten potatoes. The grounds were virtually littered with immigrants. Entire families huddled together: men with gaunt faces and
angry expressions, women with frightened eyes, and restless, fretful
children in raggedy clothing. All manner of languages could be

heard, but mostly Irish or else English that was laced with a thick Irish accent. Some seemed to have set up camp as if they anticipated making their homes there.

Their arrival in America had been a nightmare from the beginning. Terese and both of the Madden children, Shona and Tully, caught cold the last week of the crossing. By the time they arrived in the harbor, their coughs sounded severe enough that after a hasty examination, the medical inspectors pronounced the three of them as "possibly consumptive" and ordered them to be quarantined for an indeterminate length of time.

Terese tried to protest, but the officials ignored her claims, refusing to even read the letter from Brady's brother, which clearly stated that she and the Madden children were under the sponsorship of the Kane newspaper—the *Vanguard*.

Subsequently she, Shona, and Tully were pressed back into the line. As they stumbled forward, Terese heard one of the men mutter an aside to his companion. "Filthy Irish rabble! They wash up on the docks like starving rats with their dirt and disease and expect to be treated like royalty! I'd send them all back to their miserable pigsty island if it were up to me."

Furious, Terese would have turned and flown at him had she not glanced down over herself, then at the children. The sight of their shabby homespun clothes and her own faded dress and worn-out shoes stopped her where she stood. Even the fine emerald cloak Brady had given her back in Ireland was soiled and crushed from weeks aboard ship. She had made an attempt to tidy the children upon their arrival, but Tully's nose continually needed wiping, and there was a rip in the hem of Shona's dress. Shame coursed through her as she realized they looked no better than the rest of the woeful souls traveling with them. No wonder the Americans treated them with such contempt.

Now, close on two weeks later, they were still at Tompkinsville, and fear had begun to seep through her every waking hour. Not long after dawn, she sat on the sagging, lumpy cot that served as a bed, thinking about their situation and trying to figure a way out of it.

The humiliation of being confined to such a dismal place would have been bad enough if she had been ill. But she was *not* ill, and her resentment and frustration at the injustice of their predicament had begun to eat at her like acid.

She couldn't imagine how the people from the *Vanguard* would ever find them. They wouldn't go on trying forever, sure. How long would it take before they simply gave up, thinking them lost or perhaps assuming they had never sailed at all?

And then what would she do? How could she possibly manage on her own, with two frail children to drag along and Brady's child growing bigger in her belly every day?

No, *not* Brady's child, she corrected herself. She must not forget the story Brady had concocted for her, the tale he had already written to his brother. She must remember that so far as Jack Kane was concerned, her condition was the result of having been raped by an unknown attacker. Brady had insisted it was the only way, that his brother was sure to withhold any hope of assistance if he knew the truth.

So she and the Madden children had become a part of a much larger program, initiated by the Kane newspaper. A few carefully chosen individuals and families would be the subjects of an ongoing series published by the paper, and thereby provided the means to start a new life in America.

More than anything else under heaven, Terese wanted the opportunity for that new life, and so she would keep the bargain with Brady. She would stick to their story, no matter what.

Aye, well, little matter about the story if there was nary a one to hear it!

She had to find a way out of this place and get back to the harbor. She *must!* If need be, she would even take the children into the city in search of Jack Kane and his newspaper. But to stay here seemed an almost certain end to her plans—if not certain *death!*

She glanced at the youngsters who lay dozing on the next cot. The girl, Shona, was listless and wooden, almost as if she took no notice at all of her surroundings. But it was the boy who concerned Terese even more. His fever seemed never to abate. By now it was raging almost out of control, and his cough was so deep and hard it pained her to hear it.

This place—this *hospital*—was in truth little better than a prison. They were packed in among hundreds of other immigrants, many of whom seemed desperately ill. In fact, Terese lived in dread that she and the children would contract some sort of terrible disease from the other poor wretches before they could make their escape.

Just yesterday she had heard that there was typhus among them. In cold terror, she had squeezed a place for herself and the children in a corner across the room, but there was no real protection in such cramped quarters.

She had begun the voyage with no end of resentment at being saddled with the responsibility of two orphaned children, and strangers to her at that. At some point during the crossing, however, she had actually begun to feel a certain fondness for her young charges. The girl, Shona, was a sad little thing whose eyes were already old with untold sorrows. But her brother, Tully, was different. Fragile as he was and crippled from a severe case of frostbite, the small boy was invariably cheerful and tried to boost his older sister's spirits at every opportunity.

Her growing affection for the children only made their present circumstances that much more difficult. If she could have man-aged to remain indifferent to them, perhaps she might have been able to break free of this accursed place and strike out on her own. As it was, she felt trapped and frightened not only for herself, but for the two young ones as well.

At times she allowed herself the hope that surely someone from the newspaper would be searching for them by now and would show up any day to take them out of here. On the heels of this thought, however, came the stark reminder that a man as rich and important as Jack Kane would not likely go to much trouble for a trio of raggedy strangers.

Terese turned on her side, away from the children, her mind still groping for a solution to their plight. Her condition could no lon-ger be concealed. Although she was still lean everywhere else, her swollen midsection blazoned the fact that she was with child. She felt awkward and extremely vulnerable.

And ugly.

In frustration, she ran a hand through her hair—what was left of it. She had been forced to submit to having her hair cropped upon their arrival at the quarantine center. To rid her of lice, the officials claimed.

Terese had protested, had even tried to break free and run once she learned their intention, fiercely protesting that she did not have lice. They had ignored her entirely, dragging her back to the chair and threatening her into submission.

"*All* the Irish have lice," the fish-eyed matron had sneered, giv-ing Terese's hair such a vicious yank that she cried out. "Bugs breed in your filth. Now sit down and hush your impudence, or I'll have you *tied* down. You're in America now, and if you want to stay here, you'll obey the rules. You can be sent back, you know."

In the end, Terese had had no choice but to sit and be sheared like a sheep. Later that night she wept for the first time since leaving Ireland. While not exactly vain about her hair, she had not cut it for years, and it had grown long and thick with a heavy natural curl.

It would grow back, she reminded herself, dropping her hand away from her head. She wouldn't look like a poorly thatched roof forever.

But Terese could not forget the way she had felt, watching them lop off her hair and then sweep it up into a dustpan like a pile of dead leaves. It had been not only her hair that had been lost to her that day. They had taken something else from her, something that went much deeper than what Brady had often called her "shining glory."

Aye, her hair would eventually grow back, but in her heart of hearts, Terese could not help but wonder how long it would take to recover her self-respect.

5

A Meeting in the Marketplace

A vulture preys upon our heart;
Christ, have mercy!
RICHARD D'ALTON WILLIAMS

THE CLADDAGH, CO. GALWAY, WESTERN IRELAND

Roweena caught her breath at the sight of Brady Kane near the far end of the quay. He seemed intent on something at one of the other food stalls, and her first inclination was to gather her baskets and flee the marketplace before he saw her. But she needed to sell more of her brack and breads if she was going to take Evie to the auction later, as she'd promised. So instead of leaving, she simply turned her back, hoping Brady wouldn't notice her in the crowd.

It was a mild morning for November. The fog was already clearing, and the sun showed signs of breaking through the clouds soon. Roweena's spirits had been high until now. At the sight of Brady

Kane, however, confusion and doubt had set in, combined with a niggling sense of guilt that threatened to steal her earlier cheerfulness.

She could all too easily imagine Gabriel's displeasure if he should happen to see her with the "troublesome Yank," as he was wont to call Brady. Although he hadn't strictly forbidden her and Evie to stay away from the American, there was no doubt but what he expected them to do just that.

After Terese Sheridan had left the Claddagh, her shame a secret known only to a few, Gabriel had explained about the affair with Brady Kane that had left Terese with child. Although his features had been set in a careful mask, there had been no mistaking the fact that he was deeply troubled about the situation.

Some thought Gabriel a hard man, but Roweena knew better. While he seldom showed his deepest feelings, he was nevertheless a man of sensitivity and great compassion. Roweena sensed that he carried a heavy burden for Terese Sheridan and for the American artist also, to whom he had opened the door of their home.

Her own heart still ached, not only for the island girl, who must have loved Brady Kane very much to surrender to him in sin—but for Brady as well. She found it difficult to reconcile the man who had behaved so dishonorably toward Terese Sheridan with the same lively, spirited artist who had been nothing but kindness itself to her and wee Evie.

Although Gabriel had made it clear enough that he did not trust the American, at the time Roweena had thought he was simply being overly protective, as was his way where she and Evie were concerned. For herself, she found it difficult to imagine Brady as anything but the fun-loving, good-natured soul he appeared to be: thoroughly American yet possessed of a genuine affection for Ireland—especially the Claddagh—and its people.

Unfortunately, his affection for Terese Sheridan had turned into something else, something deceitful and debasing.

After everything that had happened, Roweena no longer knew exactly how she felt about Brady. There was no mistaking *Gabriel's* feelings, however. Even now, months after the trouble, he remained unrelenting in his attitude, so much so that Roweena knew she would be going against his will simply by speaking with Brady Kane.

This, too, made her very sad, although she had encountered him no more than two or three times in recent months, and each time in the marketplace, surrounded by people. Even so, guilt suffused her after each meeting, for she knew that Gabriel would be sorely disillusioned—perhaps even angry—if he should happen to come upon the two of them together.

She had long sensed Gabriel's disapproval of the American's attentions to her. Yet for her part Roweena could not bring herself to believe that Brady Kane meant her any real mischief. There was something in the way he looked at her that was kind and even careful, something that hinted of a tenderness belying any casual motives or deviousness.

But she sensed there was no convincing Gabriel of this, and she had no heart to go against his wishes if she could help it. So how was she to manage the unavoidable encounter with Brady without incurring Gabriel's disapproval or causing Brady further indignity?

He had seemed genuinely hurt by Gabriel's scathing rejection and subsequent notice to stay away from their home. Apparently, Gabriel had even gone so far as to advise that perhaps Brady should avoid the Claddagh altogether.

The American artist's outrage had been fierce and explosive when he managed to catch Roweena long enough to tell her of Gabriel's pronouncement. "He's not your *father* after all!" he stormed. "Why do you allow him such control over you?"

What she could not make Brady understand was that while Gabriel was not a *father* to her—although in truth he was exactly that to Evie, indeed, the only father the child had ever known—he was much more than a guardian: he was also her closest and dearest friend. It seemed that any attempt she made to defend Gabriel only angered Brady even more.

She drew in a long breath and turned slightly to check his whereabouts. At that same instant, she realized that he had seen her and was now striding briskly in her direction. Quickly, Roweena turned and began to retrieve her things, intent on avoiding him if at all possible.

Something akin to sadness clenched her heart with the reminder that the time was almost certainly coming when she would not have to worry about running into Brady, for he would be going away. He had spoken often enough about traveling the country, making his pictures for his job back in America. He had never had any intention of staying in Galway, after all, and by his own admission, he had already lingered longer than he'd planned. Surely his work would soon be finished, and then he would leave.

But long after Brady Kane had left Galway, she would still be here. She and Evie and Gabriel.

Gabriel . . . how often had she secretly wished that he would look at her as Brady did, with gentleness and warm affection? But it was not to be. Even now, after all these years, it seemed that to Gabriel she would always be a child—a somewhat helpless child in need of a protector.

He had been faithful and diligent in his self-appointed role as her guardian from the time she *was* a child, and so perhaps it was only natural that in his eyes she had *remained* a child. It was not what she wanted from him—in truth, she didn't know exactly what she *did* want from Gabriel. Perhaps to have him look at her and see her as she really was, rather than as the lost, terrified wee girl he had taken under his care so long ago.

One thing she *did* know: she would give much if he would only lose the closed, guarded expression he invariably wore when he was with her.

At times Roweena almost envied Evie her childishness. With Evie, at least, it seemed that Gabriel could be lighthearted, even playful. But with herself he was all seriousness—kind and even tempered but never carefree, never really open or demonstrative.

Foolishness! How dare she hope for more than she already had! Hadn't Gabriel provided her with a good home, a shelter? Hadn't he taken care of her when she'd been unable to take care of herself? When others had thought her odd or even mad, Gabriel had found value in her. More than likely, he had saved her from certain destruction.

He had been brother and friend to her, as well as her teacher. It had been Gabriel who taught her to read, to figure, even how to speak, despite her inability to hear sounds. And always, he had tried to instill in her a sense of adequacy and self-worth.

Gabriel was a good man, a *godly* man. Of course, he would not conduct himself like other men—he was not *like* other men. He was . . . larger. Finer. And she had no right, no right at all, to be longing for anything more than he had already given her. Certainly she had no right to cheat him of the respect to which he was entitled. So if he preferred that she not keep company with Brady Kane, then she would not.

But obviously there was to be no escaping the American today. By the time she had gathered her baskets and prepared to leave, Brady had almost reached her, his dark gaze locked upon her as if to demand that she acknowledge him.

Brady's heartbeat quickened as he increased his stride, determined to make his way to Roweena before she could run from him. He had seen the look in her eyes, the sudden confusion and indecision as she watched him approach. He wouldn't have been surprised had she tossed her baskets aside and bolted down the quay.

Gabriel had really done a job with her. For months now, every time Brady had come upon her, she appeared half afraid of him, as if she thought he might attack her like a mad dog in the streets!

At the back of his mind, the thought occurred to him that it might not be Gabriel's doing that accounted for Roweena's behavior. Maybe the bad business with Terese had left her with so much contempt for him that she simply didn't want anything to do with him.

Roweena was hard to read, to say the least. Even before all the trouble, he had never quite known what to make of her—her excessive shyness, her furtive looks, her unmistakable devotion to Gabriel.

When it came right down to it, Brady didn't know what to make of his *own* behavior where Roweena was concerned.

He had never played the fool for a woman before. There had never been any need. Women liked him, and he'd always found it easy to attract those who caught his interest.

Roweena was attracted to him, too—he was sure of it. In spite of her shyness, those enormous gray eyes of hers held something besides indifference, or he'd be a monkey on the moon.

But getting her to *act* on that attraction was another matter entirely. Between Gabriel's heavy-handed meddling and Roweena's own reserve, he was beginning to despair of ever managing more than a hasty exchange in the middle of a crowd.

For the first time he could remember, Brady found himself

wanting more than a casual fling, more than just the excitement of a brief affair. He wanted to *know* this girl, wanted more than a few stolen hours of passion with her. Without understanding why, he found himself wanting to know everything about her: what accounted for the frightened look that sometimes darted across her face, what went on in her silent world, what her dreams were, what made her happy.

She evoked something in him that no other girl had ever tapped. Sometimes he was almost overcome with the desire to draw that fragile form into his arms, to protect her, to take care of her.

He was struck by the nasty reminder that Roweena hardly needed *him* to take care of her, not with the mighty Gabriel breathing over her shoulder with fire in his eye.

But Gabriel wasn't here now. And even at this distance, Brady could see Roweena watching him as if there were no one else around. For one breathless moment, he felt as if he would drown in those eyes, and he knew an insane need to somehow capture her so she couldn't run away from him ever again.

He was closing in on her, looking neither left nor right, when he slammed into an old woman trying to hoist a sack of potatoes onto her back. Brady hit her hard enough that the potatoes went flying, bumping over the cobbles and scattering everywhere.

Impatient, Brady muttered an apology and shoved past the woman more roughly than he might have at another time.

To his surprise, the old biddy caught the hem of his coat, stopping him. She was a good head shorter than Brady and probably didn't weigh ninety pounds, potatoes and all, but she went at him like a harpy, haranguing him in the Irish, stabbing a gnarled finger in his face with every word.

People were staring now, and Brady felt his face heat with anger.

"I *said* I was sorry!" he snarled, bending to help scoop up some of her precious potatoes. After a moment, he left the rest to the sour-tempered old woman and took off at a half run, still intent on catching up with Roweena.

❧

At the edge of the marketplace, Gabriel watched the whole thing. He had been about to go and help Roweena carry her baskets home when he saw the altercation between Brady Kane and Maire Fahy. He continued to watch as the American hurried up to Roweena and took her by the arm.

Blood rushed to Garbiel's head, and he took a step in their direction, then stopped. Roweena would not thank him for playing the watchdog in her behalf.

In truth, he had not come to the market to spy on her but to purchase some fabric and ribbon for both Roweena and Eveleen, so they could sew new dresses for the festival. Happening upon her and the American had been pure coincidence.

He was close enough to see Roweena's expression change as Kane stood speaking to her. At first she had appeared uncertain, as if she might have wanted to run from him. Now, however, she was smiling a little.

Whether the encounter had been accidental or not, she looked as if she were pleased to see the persistent American, Gabriel observed, trying to ignore the ache in his throat.

Aye, Kane had her attention now. She was watching his lips in an effort to understand his words.

The temptation to confront them was like a pressing shove at his back. But what end would it serve? What could he do? Accuse them of deception? Chastise Roweena for disobeying his wishes? She was twenty-seven years now, a woman grown. She was no

53

child to be scolded; Kane, no schoolboy to be bullied. He had no right to issue demands to either of them, though he had admittedly done just that with the American rogue.

With Roweena, he had simply informed her of his wishes, asking her to voluntarily abide by them. But he had no taste for trying to force her to comply. She would be hurt. She would not understand.

He wasn't certain *he* understood. Oh, Kane's shabby treatment of the Sheridan girl and the shirking of his responsibility were reason enough to want him well away from Roweena. But there was more to his own hostility than that unfortunate affair, Gabriel knew.

From the beginning, there had been something about the American artist that had set him on edge. He had never quite trusted the young wag. Even though he hadn't actually disliked Kane, at least not at first, he had invariably felt an uneasiness about him.

Watching him with Roweena now, he felt it again. Was it merely a measure of reasonable caution—the fear that he would ensnare Roweena, in all her innocence, with his sweet talk and attentions? Kane was young and handsome, after all—the kind who seemed to have no trouble charming women. And there was Roweena, infinitely lovely and completely innocent—good through and through. But oh, so vulnerable, so easy to deceive.

Another possibility asserted itself on Gabriel's mind—a vile thought, and one he had shrunk from until now. How much of his distrust and growing dislike for the American was born of his own barely controlled jealousy?

Jealousy?

It was an ugly thing to face, but there it was. He had loved her forever, cherished her as he might have a beloved sister when she was but a frightened child under his protection and throughout the years of her growing up.

But somewhere along those years his love had begun to change, had taken on a different complexion, a depth he'd felt bound to conceal, lest he drive her away from him.

He had no illusions about what he was to her. Roweena loved him in her own way, he knew. But as a guardian, a surrogate brother, perhaps, who had virtually raised her from a wee wane to womanhood. Her feelings for him were true and strong, feelings of trust and devotion and certainly affection. But hardly the affection of a woman who loves a man.

No doubt she would be shamed if she were ever to learn that his devotion to her was anything more than the brotherly concern she believed it to be. She might turn against him. She might even leave him.

And how would she manage then, on her own? How would she survive, alone in her silent world?

With a heavy sigh, Gabriel watched the two a moment more, the bitter admission of his jealousy a hot, tearing blade ripping through all his preconceived motives and noble intentions. Perhaps it was time he admitted the truth and stopped trying to dance around it, even if the truth made him nearly ill with self-disgust.

All that aside, he wasn't yet convinced that jealousy alone accounted for his growing aversion toward Kane. There was something more, something maddeningly elusive, and he knew it would give him no peace until he discovered its nature.

He resolved to set about doing just that without further delay. He meant to find out exactly who Brady Kane really was and what he was doing in Galway.

After another moment and one last, hard look at the couple in the marketplace, he turned and walked away.

6

Uneasy Lies the Heart

The best lack all conviction, while the worst
are full of passionate intensity.
W . B . Y E A T S

Disgruntled by Roweena's resistance, Brady left the marketplace in
a huff. The fact that she wouldn't so much as take a walk with him
foiled any hopes he might have had of breaking down her defenses.

Given half a chance, he was certain he could bring her around
and make her see that he wasn't the dragon Gabriel had undoubtedly made him out to be. But first he had to figure out a way to get
her out from under the big fisherman's hawk eye for more than a
few minutes.

By the time he left the Claddagh and headed back into the city,
he was in a thorough sulk. The day had lost its appeal. He had no
interest in doing anything or going anywhere.

The idea of being trounced by a deaf girl and a surly fisherman who fancied himself some sort of feudal overlord grated on him more than he liked to admit. It occurred to him, though not for long, that the smart thing to do would be to simply give it up. Forget about Roweena, get out of Galway, and get on with the work he was supposed to be doing for Jack.

No doubt that was what he *ought* to do, instead of mooning around like a lovesick schoolboy over a girl he'd never so much as kissed . . . never so much as held *hands* with!

Never before had he been in such a state.

He tried to tell himself it was simply the thrill of the chase, that he wasn't all *that* infatuated with her. Hadn't he always been more interested in the girls who played hard to get?

But Roweena wasn't playing games—he doubted very much that she would even know *how*—and he despised himself for even thinking of her in such a way. The truth was that he had really come to care about her. Even though he'd scarcely seen her for weeks, every effort to put her out of his mind invariably failed. He had feelings for her he couldn't begin to understand, feelings he found almost frightening. But clearly, she was having no part of him—whether purely by her own choice or because of the cantankerous Gabriel, there was no telling.

By the time he reached his apartment building, he was fuming: at Gabriel, for the man's insufferable heavy-handedness; at Roweena, too, for allowing Gabriel to dictate her life as he did; but most of all at himself, for playing such a fool over Terese that he might have spoiled any chance he could have had with Roweena.

He stamped up the steps, the thought of Terese fueling his anger. It seemed to him that he'd taken all the blame for that to-do, even though he wasn't convinced that Terese had been entirely innocent. In fact, now that enough time had elapsed for him to gain some perspective, Brady wondered if the girl hadn't planned to deliberately entrap him.

She hadn't exactly made any secret of the fact that she expected some sort of commitment from him once they'd been intimate. A commitment that he had been unwilling to give. When he made it clear that he had no intention of taking her with him on his travels—much less on his return to the States—well, perhaps she'd thought a baby would change his mind.

He no longer saw her as an innocent, instead was beginning to believe that she might have set out to deliberately seduce him for her own purposes. And a big part of Terese's purposes, he had always known, was to get to America.

Ah, well, she was gone and that was that. And they would both be all right, so long as she didn't do anything to arouse Jack's suspicions. Brady had sworn her to secrecy, and he didn't think there was any real need to worry about her slipping up. Terese was too clever to be careless. Still, he'd feel better when he knew for certain that Jack had bought their story.

Only then would he really breathe easy again.

With that thought, he put Terese behind him for once and for all, poured himself a drink, and turned to the need at hand, that of deciding what *he* was going to do. He knew he ought to be leaving Galway soon; it was getting more and more difficult to justify his extended stay to Jack. But every time he thought about leaving, Roweena came to mind, and he found himself delaying once again.

He knew he *had* to leave before much longer. Jack wasn't going to keep up his wages indefinitely, not without getting something for his money. If he began to suspect that Brady was lying to him, he wasn't past cutting him off cold, with no warning.

No one bamboozled Jack Kane, not even his brother. A few had tried—and paid a treacherously high price for it.

No, he would have to make a move soon, and to that end he needed to be deciding where to go. Up to Westport, perhaps, and then Sligo. But instead of getting out his maps and drawing up an itinerary, he plopped down on the bed with his drink, giving in to an increasingly familiar pall of inertia.

More and more these days he found himself feeling like a ship-wrecked sailor stranded on an island that was quickly being eroded by the sea. He knew he had to get off the island or eventually drown, but because he couldn't see anything in any direction except more water, he simply continued to sit where he was, watching the waves move in on him.

Up until now Brady had seldom had any problem making decisions. In fact, Jack had often accused him of making them *too* easily, too casually, and it was true that he didn't always trouble himself much about the consequences of his actions. Once he decided on a thing, he simply did it.

Lately, though, he seemed to haggle over every little thing, changing his mind, then changing it again. Something as basic as choosing the subject for a sketch could bring him to a total halt for hours, until he got so frustrated he would discard the entire idea.

He didn't know what was going on, but he *did* know he'd better be doing something about it or he was going to ruin himself with Jack.

For the moment, however, he would just have a quick snooze, then get up and go to work. First thing, he'd decide on his next stopover, then set a date to leave.

Soon, he told himself again. It would have to be very soon.

Brady's last thought as he drained the glass of whiskey and finally drifted off to sleep was of stumbling backward in a futile attempt to escape a towering, fast-encroaching wall of water.

Gabriel waited until the table had been cleared, the dishes put away in the cupboard, before sending Evie out to play and indicating to Roweena that he wished to speak with her.

He noticed that she kept her eyes averted as she sat down at the table across from him. He touched her hand once to get her attention, and she looked up, watching his lips closely as he began. "I saw you with Brady Kane at the market."

A faint stain blotted her cheeks, and she glanced away for a second or two before looking back at him and nodding.

"'Tis not a good idea, Roweena. He is trouble, that one, don't you understand?"

As always, she focused her full attention on his lips until he had finished speaking, then seemed to consider her reply with care.

"He came up to me," she finally answered, signing with her fingers but speaking the words as well, as Gabriel insisted that she do. Her voice was halting, the words coming slowly but remarkably clearly, given her deafness. "What was I to do?"

He had always found her voice pleasant to the ear. Others no doubt thought it somewhat strange, since she spoke with the lack of inflection common to those who could not hear. Perhaps it was because he had worked so hard and so long with her, teaching her to speak. It had been a laborious, often frustrating process for them both—but a vastly rewarding one as well. She did not seem so locked out of his world once she could form words, and he no longer felt at such a disadvantage in trying to communicate with her.

At this moment, however, he almost dreaded what he might hear from her. He realized that she was studying him with an expression that hinted of anxiety, and he found himself suddenly impatient with her for being so . . . careful . . . with him.

"I'm not angry," he said, reassuring her. "I simply don't want you hurt, don't you see? I don't trust Brady Kane, and you shouldn't either."

He was surprised to see the look of sadness that crossed her delicate features. For a moment he thought she was about to weep.

Instead, she nodded as if to say she agreed, then lifted her gaze to his. "Please don't . . . worry, Gabriel," she said. "Perhaps I'm not as . . . foolish as you think."

Dismayed, Gabriel reached to take her hand, then stopped himself. "I have never thought you foolish, Roweena," he said, holding her gaze. "I mean only to protect you."

Again she nodded, looking down.

"Roweena?" Gabriel leaned across the table and tipped her chin with one finger to get her attention. She looked up, but he was unable to read her expression. "Do you care for this man?"

She frowned as if she didn't understand.

"Do you have—*feelings*—for him?" He heard the thickness of his own voice, felt apprehension spring up in him like a bitter weed when she deliberately looked away without making any response to his question.

His mouth dry, Gabriel again reached to turn her face toward his. "He is not the sort of man who can be trusted. You must see that."

He felt himself shrink under the searching gaze she turned on him.

"You always say we are not to . . . judge others, that we . . . must try to see them as . . . the Savior sees them. With tolerance . . . and forgiveness."

Her words seemed an indictment of sorts, and Gabriel found himself at a loss. "That's so," he said gruffly, fumbling for the words to explain himself. "But there will always be those who take advantage. I'm not suggesting that you judge Kane, simply that you be cautious."

Her dark gray eyes never left his. "But . . . you are judging him, Gabriel. Are you not?"

He tensed still more. "Kane brought much trouble on the Sheridan girl with his lack of restraint. And he continues to sneak his way past me to you. That would seem to speak of a nature that cannot be trusted. I will ask you again to stay away from him. For your own good."

Her mouth tightened, and for a moment Gabriel thought she was going to argue with him. But at last her features softened, and she gave a small nod of assent. "I will . . . try," she said. "But what am I . . . to do when he happens upon me in the marketplace? Would you . . . have me run away then, like a mindless child?"

Now it was Gabriel who turned away without an answer, even though he silently admitted to himself that indeed, that was exactly what he would have her do.

If only it could be that simple.

7

Between Friends

Two are better than one. . . .

ECCLESIASTES 4:9, NIV

That same evening Gabriel made a rare visit to an out-of-the-way tavern in Galway City. Although he wasn't one to frequent such a place, the man he was looking for did.

He had no way of knowing whether Ulick was anywhere in the area, but he could leave word with Phelim Lynch, the owner, that he was looking for him. As soon as he entered, however, he spied the wild shock of silver hair and the drooping mustache of his old friend.

Ulick was sitting at the far end of the room in front of a cold fireplace with two other weathered seamen. The room was dim and uncrowded. It smelled of dampness and ale and cooked fish. Only a few men were seated at tables, their faces solemn as they huddled over their pints.

Ulick looked up and, seeing Gabriel, gave a one-sided grin. At the same time, he made a sharp jerk of the head as if to order his companions away. By the time Gabriel reached the table, the other two men had scraped their chairs back and, with nothing more than a brief nod in his direction, ambled off to a table near the bar.

Ulick motioned Gabriel to one of the recently vacated chairs. "Your gob would sour new milk, Gabriel Vaughan. Have Lynch fetch you a jar to lighten your load."

"'Tis your poison, not mine, Ulick. I came to talk, not drink."

"Sit down then, you great oaf. As you know, I take pleasure in both."

They spoke in the Irish, in low tones: two men who had known each other too many years to count and whose conversation needed no embellishment.

"So then, Gabriel, what is on your mind? It would appear to be heavy, whatever the nature."

Gabriel took the chair across from him, and Ulick waved the aproned owner away.

"You have some time, do you, Ulick?"

"I have nothing else," the other said, watching Gabriel closely. In contrast to the brown, leathered face, Ulick's eyes appeared so pale they might have been glazed with ice. "You have a reason for asking after my time, I expect."

Gabriel gave a nod and got right to it. "I'm wanting some information on a man. He claims to have been born here, in the city, and I'm curious about his people—who they might have been, if he's telling the truth. I thought that if anyone would know, you would, or, if not, you could find out."

Ulick turned his glass around in his hand. "Who is this man?"

"Brady Kane," said Gabriel.

Ulick lifted heavy brows. "The American who does the drawings? He was born here?"

"So he says." Gabriel paused. "I wouldn't stake much on his word, though."

Ulick nodded. "I heard he brought trouble on one of the island girls."

"He did that." Gabriel's mouth tightened.

"And then he packed her off to America."

"There is quite a story in that. I didn't get the whole truth, I expect, but what the Sheridan girl told Jane Connolly was that Kane had connections of some sort with a big newspaper in New York. Supposedly this newspaper was paying passage for some orphaned children to go across and offered to pay the girl's way as well, if she would tend to the orphans during the voyage. That's all I know about it, but I suspect there's more."

Ulick quirked one corner of his mouth, and the heavy mustache lifted. "The Yank's connections must be good ones. You think the story was put-up?"

Gabriel shrugged. "I don't know, and what's done is done, so that part of it isn't my concern." He stopped, uncertain as to how much he wanted to tell his old friend.

Ulick set his glass on the table and waited.

"'Tis Roweena I'm thinking of," Gabriel finally offered. "Kane won't leave her alone, though I've done everything but threaten him to warn him off."

"Then he is a fool as well as a rake," said Ulick with a laugh. "Few men would want to bump heads with you, had they their wits about them."

"The coals of my temper have cooled considerably, man," Gabriel said, his tone gruff. "I, too, was a fool in my youth."

"Ah, and isn't every man?"

"As for Kane," Gabriel went on, "the boy is not an easy one to dislike. All the same, I've never trusted him. And less now, after the bad business with the Sheridan girl. I don't want him anywhere near Roweena."

Ulick's expression turned thoughtful, and he nodded, slowly. "What is it, then, Gabriel? What are you thinking, that you might learn something to discourage him for once and all?"

In truth Gabriel didn't know what, exactly, he was hoping for. "Kane keeps his silence about himself. Too much so, it seems to me. He tells little, other than that he lives in New York City, and he has an older brother. Supposedly, he earns his keep by making drawings for newspapers in the States. He claims to be in Ireland on some sort of 'special assignment.' I expect he told the Sheridan girl more, but if that's the case, she kept it to herself." Gabriel leaned across the table a little. "I don't know quite what I'm looking for, but I intend to keep him away from Roweena by any means I can find. I'm wondering if there isn't a reason for his telling so little about himself. You know the city better than any man and can find what I want faster than I could. Will you help me?"

Ulick traced his heavy mustache with one finger. His expression was dubious. "It seems to me you might accomplish more by simply knocking the laddie about some. If you've not the taste for it, I know a pair of lads who would do the job. A good thrashing ought to get the Yank's attention, wouldn't you think? Perhaps even persuade him to leave Galway altogether."

The suggestion turned Gabriel's stomach, and he shook his head. "That's not my way, Ulick. For now, all I want is information."

Ulick gave a shrug. "As you say, then. So this Kane—do we know if that's his real name?"

"There's no telling. But I've no reason to think otherwise."

Ulick shifted his bony frame in the chair a little and cupped the back of his neck with one hand. "All right, then. We'll start where we are. *Kane . . . MacCathain* or *O Cein,* that would be . . . let's see, now. . . ."

Ulick went on muttering to himself for a moment, then glanced up. "Has he by any chance mentioned when he went across? How old he might have been when he left Galway?"

"No, I told you, he has little to say about himself."

They went on that way for a few more minutes, Ulick throwing out possibilities and more or less thinking aloud, with Gabriel unable to provide any real assistance.

Finally, Gabriel stood. "I must get back. Come to the house or send a message anytime. I'll be waiting."

Ulick seemed to scarcely notice his leaving, so engrossed was he in the puzzle Gabriel had presented him. "I'll be going over to Dublin soon for a few days, to visit the boy and his wife," he said after a moment. "Not for long, though. You'll hear from me, sooner or later."

Hoping it would be sooner rather than later, Gabriel turned and left the tavern.

8

Encounter with Darkness

Know thou the secret of a spirit
Bow'd from its wild pride into shame.
O yearning heart! I did inherit
Thy withering portion with the fame.
EDGAR ALLAN POE

PHILADELPHIA

Jack made no attempt to conceal his study of the man seated across
the table from him. With some effort, however, he had managed to
conceal his impatience with the self-important Mr. Poe, suppress-
ing the inclination to suggest that the morose, albeit esteemed,
writer grow up and cease his whining.

He had met Edgar Poe only once before, nearly two years ago
while Poe was still staying in New York. He seemed to have
changed little. Jack knew he was no more than thirty, though the
writer had a haggard, discontented look about him that made him

seem much older. Poe was a small man, a somber, delicate sort, with an unusually broad forehead and uncommonly sorrowful eyes. It occurred to Jack that Poe looked every bit the tortured genius he was rumored to be.

He also looked not altogether well. Poe's complexion had an unhealthy pallor, emphasized by the man's apparent proclivity for black: black frock coat, black cravat, black gloves. Poe's hair was also dark, his gray eyes intense; taken together with his attire, the appearance of the man was strangely spectral.

They had met at the oyster house over an hour ago, and so far the writer had done little more than pick at his food, elaborate on his misfortunes, and undermine with a blistering tongue a number of his literary contemporaries—including Washington Irving, a personal favorite of Jack's.

"Overrated," Poe commented now, summarizing his poor opinion of Irving. "Greatly overrated."

Jack said nothing. It had already occurred to him that Poe's arrogant dismissal of his peers might be born of envy, perhaps even resentment. His own sales weren't all that impressive; Poe was notorious for his financial woes and had, in fact, faced jail on more than one occasion for his bad debts.

Jack reminded himself that he had not come all the way to Philadelphia to let himself be provoked by a troublesome writer. Poe had distinctly expressed interest in publishing with the *Vanguard* or one of Jack's other publishing interests, such as Perriman and Ware. Poe's work was well-enough regarded that Jack had thought he ought to at least explore the possibilities.

So far this evening, however, Poe had exhibited little interest in a professional relationship with *any* of the Kane publishing enterprises. To the contrary, he seemed bent on conducting himself like some sort of a literary lion being pursued by a runny-nosed newsboy.

Jack was used to being patronized by the aristocrats in the literary community. Although he had become fairly adept at concealing his feelings, there had been a time when some of the more supercilious among the elite had managed to make him feel like a clumsy Irish peasant, out of his class and over his head.

These days, however, it took more than a pretentious author to put him at a disadvantage. His years in publishing had taught him that many of the brightest stars of the literary galaxy, no matter how eminent or highborn they might be, actually lived in dire financial straits. Indeed, some, like the notable Edgar Poe, seemed to exist in near poverty much of the time. So while the blue bloods might raise their eyebrows at his Irish commonness, they almost never turned up their noses at the smell of his money. He'd warrant that in that regard Poe was no different from the rest.

By the time dessert was served, he had grown impatient with the man's posturing; in fact, he wasn't at all sure he even wanted to bother with him.

With no further delay, he came to the point. "Well, Mr. Poe, let me just explain what I'm looking for, and you can give me a yes or a no as to whether you're interested."

Ignoring Poe's somewhat huffy frown, Jack scooped up the last bite of his sugar-cream pie before going on. "I'm looking for material I can serialize in the *Vanguard,* preferably over a period of weeks. An adventure story, perhaps—something on the high seas, for example, with plenty of action and lots of excitement. Something to keep people buying the papers."

Poe regarded Jack as if he had suddenly sprouted a horn in the middle of his forehead. "You're not serious, of course."

"I am entirely serious."

Poe lifted a pale hand to finger his cravat. "I don't write . . . *serial fiction,* Mr. Kane. I assumed you were familiar with my work."

"Oh, I'm well acquainted with your work, Edgar—you don't mind if I call you 'Edgar'?—but tell me, how does your work *sell?*"

"I beg your pardon?" Poe's mouth twisted downward, as though he had caught a hint of a bad odor.

"Your work," Jack said. "Does it sell well for you?"

Poe's features seemed to constrict. The fingers on the cravat trembled slightly. "I don't write simply for profit, Mr. Kane."

Jack saw the unsteadiness of the white hand, the uncertainty in Poe's mournful eyes. "Be that as it may, Edgar, I am obliged to *publish* for profit. So, you see, I'm wondering if you wouldn't like to try your hand at something different, perhaps a large adventure story, as I mentioned earlier. Something with a hero in jeopardy, a defenseless lady and a great deal of excitement. *And*—" Jack deliberately emphasized his words—"*a happy ending.* In other words, a story that would have subscribers eager for the next edition. I'm willing to pay very generously for that kind of story if you can give it to me."

Poe was still looking at him with something akin to distaste, but Jack thought he detected a glimmer of growing interest as well.

"As I said, I'll pay well for the right material," he pressed. "Are you interested?"

It was Jack's observation that Poe was *very* interested, all right, but was unwilling to admit to it. His impatience with the man grew.

Poe crossed his arms, hugging them to himself, as he fastened his eyes on something just above Jack's head. For his part, Jack took the opportunity to study the writer even more closely. For the first time, he noticed that, despite Poe's distinct impression of breeding and Byronic airs, the man had a certain indefinable seediness that didn't quite square with the image he obviously meant to project. There was a strange sense of interior *decay* about Edgar Poe that Jack found unsettling, to say the least.

"I find myself wondering if I should be insulted by your offer, Mr. Kane."

Jack shrugged. "It's not actually an offer, merely an idea. But I'm curious as to why you'd be insulted. As I recall, you contacted *me*. I'm simply trying to figure a way this might work for both of us and make you a bit of money in the process."

Poe's eyes flashed. "I do not hire myself out to the highest bidder, sir. I have a certain reputation to maintain in the literary world, as you must be aware."

Jack placed his fork carefully on his plate and leaned back in his chair, looking Poe directly in the eye. "I can't think your reputation would be impaired by getting your work out to a larger audience, Edgar. Certainly it wouldn't hurt your bank account."

"Really, Mr. Kane—"

"Why don't you call me 'Jack,' Edgar?"

"I'm not accustomed to discussing my bank account—*Mr. Kane.*"

"Sorry, Edgar, I meant no offense." With some effort, Jack kept his tone casual. "I confess that *I'm* not accustomed to dealing with men who are insulted by the subject of money. Most of them find the idea of getting paid for their labors fairly appealing. Especially," he added with a considerably harder edge in his voice, "those with families to support."

Poe started to rise from his chair. Jack watched him in silence. By now he was relatively certain he was wasting his time and even more convinced he wanted nothing to do with this man. Poe seemed unable to let go of his insufferable pride, and Jack had neither the patience nor the inclination to coddle him to a decision that would salve his ego.

Besides, something in the man put him off, genius be hanged. He thought Poe might be a little mad; he was almost certainly more than a little foolish.

But Poe had apparently changed his mind about leaving. Looking everywhere but at Jack, he slowly lowered himself back into the chair and sat examining his dessert plate.

Jack decided to make one—and only one—last attempt to get past the man's pride. "Though it may surprise you, Edgar—coming from a peasant like myself—I think I can appreciate your commitment to quality in your work." At Poe's skeptical glance, Jack gave a rueful smile. "Oh, the *Vanguard* prints its share of sensationalism, of course, along with the usual tripe—got to keep that segment of the population satisfied so we can pay the bills. But I make it a point to offer something better as well—not just through the paper but by way of my publishing houses. That's why I'm here."

He paused, again sensing more than a grudging flicker of interest from the other. "Let me be perfectly frank, Edgar. I've read your stuff"—he saw Poe's mouth tighten—"your *work,*" he amended, "and I think you're a man capable of writing what I'd like to publish. You're more clever by far than most of the writers I've worked with, and despite your somewhat grisly choice of subject matter, you do spin a grand tale."

Jack paused, ignoring the other's surly expression. "The thing is, Edgar, I happen to think you could pen just as fine a story using a less morbid tone than is your custom. Something . . . brighter, perhaps. More acceptable to the *Vanguard's* readers than what you usually write. No less gripping, of course, but possibly less . . . depressing. More wholesome, is what I'm getting at."

Poe shook his head. "Considering your reputation, Mr. Kane, I find your request somewhat puzzling. You hardly strike me as the kind of man given to the sort of pedestrian drivel the religious element so admires."

Jack inwardly bristled. There was something about having his reputation called into question by a man like Poe that set his teeth to grinding. But he managed to give a casual shrug, saying nothing.

"I do not subscribe to the sort of artificial prattle you seem to want," Poe went on, his tone less pedantic now, even somewhat rambling. "I don't believe in . . . happy endings, Mr. Kane. Therefore, I do not write them."

Jack leaned his elbows on the table, steepling his fingers and regarding Poe with growing annoyance. "I'm not personally acquainted with too many happy endings myself, Edgar, but that doesn't mean they don't exist—or *can't* exist, at least in a story. And I'm certainly not suggesting that you write—*drivel*—for my readers. Quite frankly, I respect them more than that. But I see nothing artificial about stories that contain at least a touch of hope to mitigate the despair. A bit of light to relieve the darkness, if you will."

He sat watching the somber Poe for a moment. "Forgive the observation, Edgar, but I can't help thinking that you're quite a young man to take such a dismal view of life."

"What has age to do with anything?" Poe said, lifting a languid hand.

"Perhaps nothing. But aside from age, you're a bright, gifted fellow with a lovely young wife, a home, a fine education—and the means of earning a highly respectable income from doing something you apparently enjoy. As for myself, I admit to being the worst of cynics. But I can't help wondering what would account for your preoccupation with such dreary, macabre subjects."

Poe looked at him as if considering how to reply. Then, without warning, he launched into a bitter tale of misfortune that should have moved Jack—and ordinarily would have, had the man not been so obviously engulfed in self-pity.

He already knew about the "premature loss" of Poe's actor parents, his alienation from his foster father, his ongoing problems with poor health and indebtedness. But so far as his poor health and even poorer finances were concerned, a great deal of Poe's difficulties in both areas seemed to be the products of his own excesses.

By the conclusion of Poe's diatribe, Jack's patience was at an end. All he could think of was getting away. He felt an almost desperate need for fresh air and light; at the same time, he wondered why he found the man across from him so oppressive.

At one time or another over the years he had had dealings with some thoroughly unsavory characters, a number of which were almost certainly as odd as Edgar Poe and a sight less gentlemanly in their conduct. He had trafficked with felons and traded with fools, rubbed elbows with thieves, and risked his own skin countless times in New York's most abysmal slums—including the vile Five Points—just to ferret out the facts for a story. By now he had surely encountered the very dregs of humanity and should have been inured to just about any manner of corruption.

Given all that—not to mention that he wasn't exactly the salt of the earth himself—why did the decadence he sensed in Edgar Poe strike him as so particularly offensive, even as the man himself seemed to hold an eerie kind of fascination?

In that instant Jack's eyes met Poe's, and what he saw there shook him like a blast of winter wind. It was as if something in that dark and haunted gaze threatened to draw him in and trap him in a vacuum from which there was no outlet. In some bizarre way that set him to trembling, he recognized looking out at him something that appeared treacherously familiar, yet terrifyingly alien.

At that moment he realized that the darkness he sensed in Poe might well be but a reflection of the darkness that inhabited his own spirit.

Thoroughly chilled, Jack decided that this meeting was at an end.

And so was his interest in publishing the "tormented genius."

He would leave Philadelphia tomorrow. He suddenly found himself not only excessively eager to be away from Edgar Poe but more eager still to be with Samantha. He craved the light of her, the sweet . . . *goodness* of her. Perhaps he could figure out a way to see her again before the meeting with Foxworth next week.

He had every intention of renewing his proposal in the near future—the *very* near future. This time, he would be more convincing.

And more resistant to any attempt on her part to turn him down again.

His decision made, he brought the interview to a close as speedily as possible without being unnecessarily rude. He couldn't be sure, of course, but it seemed to him that Poe was every bit as anxious to part company as he was.

It was as if, he thought grimly, like had recognized like and could not abide the resemblance.

9

In the Harbor

November's wind is a lonely song.
ANONYMOUS

NEW YORK CITY

Cavan Sheridan's reservations about bringing Samantha to the harbor could not have been more evident. Even now, after nearly an hour on the docks, he was obviously still wishing he had come alone, his strained expression clearly signifying that a lady had no place in such surroundings. But Samantha's new duties required that she meet any immigrants traveling under the *Vanguard*'s sponsorship, and she felt it particularly important that she present herself to their first arrivals—especially since Terese Sheridan, Cavan's sister—was one of them.

Cavan returned from Albany on Saturday morning, sooner than expected, and had arrived on Samantha's doorstep that same afternoon, explaining—with obvious reluctance—that "Mr. Kane had left instructions" for him to escort Samantha to the harbor if and when she wanted to go.

So far, their excursion had proved futile. Inquiries of harbor officials had yielded only the disturbing news that the *Providence* had actually docked over two weeks ago. Yet, there had been no message to this effect from any of Jack's sources, no word from Terese Sheridan and the Madden children. Consequently, there was no way of knowing their whereabouts.

As they stood looking around, trying to decide what to do next, Samantha pulled her heavy coat more tightly about her. It was bitter cold on the docks. A stinging drizzle had settled over the day, and a harsh wind was blowing off the water. Despite the inclement weather and their lack of success, however, she was glad she hadn't let Cavan come alone. He was obviously shaken and apprehensive about his sister's well-being.

On impulse, she lay a reassuring hand on his arm. "Try not to worry, Cavan. We'll find them. We'll keep looking until we do."

He managed only the lamest of smiles. "'Tis just that we don't know where to begin."

"You said Jack—Mr. Kane—had employed someone on the docks to send word when the ship put in, a Mr. Hoey?"

Her voice was almost drowned in the pandemonium of their surroundings: the loud clamor of men shouting in foreign tongues, mothers and children wailing, dockworkers clanging metal against metal as they loaded and unloaded cargo—all was noise and mass confusion.

But both of them heard the familiar voice behind them clearly enough.

"You might have at least brought along an umbrella, Sheridan."

Samantha and Cavan spun around at the same time to find Jack standing directly behind them, a faint smile belying the rebuke in his tone.

"Jack!" Samantha blurted out his given name before she thought, but Cavan Sheridan seemed not to notice the familiarity. "I thought you weren't coming back until Monday."

She found herself hard pressed to conceal her pleasure at the sight of him. He stood watching her, one dark eyebrow crooked, the familiar quirk of a smile on his face in response to her surprise. As always, he wore no hat, indeed had not even bothered to open the umbrella he carried, and so his head and shoulders were slick with rain.

With a flourish, he now opened the umbrella and held it over Samantha.

The way he was looking at her, as if he had been away for months and was virtually starved for the sight of her, made her heart turn over.

"What—why did you cut your trip short?" she said, struggling to regain her composure, at the same time trying to ignore the way his black eyes continued to hold her gaze.

"I found myself impatient to get back," he said quietly, still watching her.

His close scrutiny and the warmth of his tone disarmed Samantha's attempt to formulate a cool response. At the same time, the memory of his proposal only a few nights past struck her unexpectedly, threatening to snap the already frazzled thread of her self-control.

Fortunately, Jack turned his attention to Cavan Sheridan for a moment. "I saw your report from Albany. Fine job."

Cavan flushed noticeably under his employer's approval. "Thank you, sir. I hope it's all right that I came back sooner than we'd planned. Nothing much seemed to be going on, so there didn't seem any point in staying."

Jack waved off his explanation. "That's fine, though I may be sending you off again soon."

Cavan frowned, and Samantha sensed that he would be reluctant to go anywhere until his sister had been found. "Where might that be, sir?"

"Connecticut," said Jack.

For a moment Cavan's face registered only bewilderment. "I . . . ah . . . don't believe I know where that is, sir."

"Well, you may be finding out soon enough. There's been some sort of slave mutiny on a Spanish ship. For some reason, the Navy seized the entire vessel and towed it to Connecticut. Sounds as if there's going to be quite a fuss. The abolitionists have gotten involved somehow, and who knows what's going to come of it? I don't have any of the details yet, but could be we'll want in on the story. But we'll talk about that later. What of your sister and the little ones? Any word?"

"Apparently, their ship put in two weeks ago," Cavan replied.

"Two *weeks* ago?" Jack cut a glance to Samantha.

She nodded. "We haven't been able to find out anything about Cavan's sister or the Madden children. None of the officials we talked with were any help. We were just about to look for the other gentleman you told us about—Mr. Hoey."

"Hoey's no gentleman," Jack said absently, turning to glance around. "But he usually knows most everything going on about the harbor. That's why I use him now and then."

A few feet away, a boy with a filthy face and wearing a coat two sizes too large was perched on his haunches, fishing a string through the cracks of the wharf. Jack got the boy's attention with a sharp whistle, then palmed a coin from his pocket and held it up.

The youth, who looked to be no more than eight or nine years old, dropped his string and came running.

"You know Hoey, lad?" Jack asked him.

The boy nodded, his eyes locked on the coin in Jack's hand.

"Fetch him for me, then, and this is yours."

The child stretched a hand for the coin, but Jack held it out of reach.

"Ah, no—first you bring Hoey to me. And be quick about it, mind! If I have to wait too long, you'll not get a cent."

The boy took off at a run, the tops of his oversized boots flapping about his thin legs. Jack turned back to Samantha and Cavan. "Hoey's a runner—one of the older boyos," he said, his expression dark with distaste. "A real master of the trade, Hoey is."

Jack's look of contempt mirrored Samantha's own feelings. She knew about the runners who infested the docks, a low breed who earned their subsistence by fleecing unsuspecting immigrants right off the boat, many of them the runners' own countrymen. These unscrupulous creatures would actually board the ships, virtually overwhelming the bewildered immigrants, hawking their services either through ingratiating spiels, or, more often, sheer intimidation. Under the ruse of arranging "decent lodgings at reasonable rates," the runners would quickly manage to seize an entire family's baggage and belongings before leading them off the ship and out of the harbor.

Almost without exception, runners worked for unprincipled men who owned some of the most disgraceful tenements and boarding houses in New York. Once he had maneuvered a band of immigrants off the docks, a runner would proceed to one of his employer's tenement buildings, where the new arrivals would be packed into dark, filthy rooms with other victims of their deceit and charged exorbitant rates for quarters scarcely fit for animals.

Jack gestured that they should move back a ways, under the shelter of a warehouse overhang. "You shouldn't have come out today," he said, raking a hand through his wet hair as he turned to Samantha. "'Tis a wretched day entirely."

"I'm not as frail as all that," Samantha said. "Tell us about your visit with Mr. Poe."

His shrug and sour face said it all. "As you see, I wasn't inclined to spend a great deal of time with the man."

"What happened?"

Jack shrugged. "Let's just say that Mr. Poe and I seem to have decidedly different viewpoints on the publishing process."

"I see," Samantha said after a second or two.

He gave a wry smile. "But you still want to know all about him."

In fact, she did. She had come to realize that Jack's perceptions of human nature could be chillingly insightful, if at times almost brutally cynical; she was learning more and more to trust his judgment. Still, even though some of Poe's work repelled her, and the more lurid stories about the man appalled her, she could not help but be curious.

"I promise a thorough recounting over supper," he said.

Samantha looked at him.

Still smiling, he darted a quick glance from her to Cavan, then went on, making it clear that both of them were included in the invitation. "I thought I'd take the two of you to Guiliardo's, if you're free. It would seem to be perfect weather for something a bit spicy."

Samantha knew she should say no; she'd been seeing far too much of Jack lately. But she had seen the way Cavan's eyes brightened at the idea, and no doubt he could use some cheering up after the disappointment of the day.

Besides, the truth was that *she* wanted to go. It would be an opportunity to hear about the meeting with Edgar Poe, without any concern that Jack might raise the troubling subject of marriage again. Cavan's presence would guarantee an impersonal atmosphere.

As for Cavan, he hesitated only a moment, as if to gauge Jack's sincerity. "Perhaps I should be getting on back—"

Samantha was relieved when Jack waved off his uncertainty. "Nonsense. Mrs. Harte wants to hear about my meeting with Poe, and I want a briefing on your trip to Albany. You'll have supper with us." He stopped, inclined his head toward Samantha, and said, "That is, if you're free?"

Just for an instant, caution renewed its war with an unsettling desire in Samantha to be with him. As seemed to happen more and more frequently these days, caution lost the battle.

"Yes, that would be nice," she said. "And of course you'll come, Cavan. We know all about your passion for Italian food."

Cavan gave a weak smile, but it was obvious that he was still distracted by concern for his sister—as well he might be.

Samantha turned back to Jack. "Can you think of anywhere else we should look?"

She stopped as a rumpled, wizened little man in a tattered sweater and a stovepipe hat trotted up to them, the raggedy child Jack had sent off a few moments before at his side.

This would be Hoey, she presumed.

The man doffed his hat and bowed so low he almost chinned himself on the planking. "At your service, Mr. Kane!"

Jack tossed a coin to the boy who had fetched the runner before turning to the strange little man. "I seem to recall that you were going to send word the day the *Providence* dropped anchor."

The man nodded vigorously.

"The ship put in two weeks ago, you little monkey! Why wasn't I told?"

The runner gaped. "Two weeks ago? Why, I didn't know, sir!"

Jack nailed him with a black scowl that made Samantha cringe. "You were to keep a sharp eye out for certain passengers I described; isn't that so?"

"Indeed, Mr. Kane! But as luck would have it, I was sick for a time, don't you see."

Jack waved off the man's attempt to explain. "Hah! Sick, is it? I know you, Hoey; more than likely you've been in your cups since the day I gave you the money."

The wiry runner seemed excessively nervous under this cross-examination but again made an effort to defend himself. "Now, Mr. Kane, sir, I'm not a drinking man, and that's the truth! The ship must have put in while I was indisposed. Sure, you can't blame a man for a bad stomach, now can you?"

For the first time, Samantha got a glimpse of Jack's legendary temper. With one hand, he gripped the lapels of Hoey's coat, practically lifting the bantam runner off his feet. "'Tis not a smart idea to take my money and not give me what I paid for, Hoey! And now that I think of it, I believe we have had this discussion before."

"I'm on it right now, Mr. Kane, I swear to you! I'll have the information you want yet today, I will! No later than tomorrow for certain!"

When Jack still didn't release him, Hoey's eyes bugged until Samantha felt almost sorry for him. Jack was twice again the size of the little runner, after all. And why had he paid the man in the first place if he didn't trust him?

"Jack."

If he heard her, he pretended not to, though he did finally release the frightened Hoey. "I'll expect to see you at the *Vanguard* first thing in the morning, and no later. You'd best be there well ahead of me, mind, and with the information I want. Understand?"

Hoey nodded so violently he nearly lost his ridiculous hat. "But, sir—Mr. Kane?"

Jack's eyes narrowed.

"It—it occurs to me," the little man stammered, "that these passengers you're expecting—if they weren't met when they put in and you've had no word of them, they might be at Tompkinsville—the quarantine hospital."

Jack seemed to consider the idea, then gave a nod. "It's possible." He jabbed a finger in the air at the runner. "You hotfoot it over there yet today, d'you hear? Ask after a girl named *Terese Sheridan*. As I told you, she'll be traveling with two youngsters by the name of *Madden*. See what you can find out."

Hoey shifted from one foot to the other, obviously eager to get away. "I'll go right now, Mr. Kane! This very minute. And I'll keep on the situation until I find them."

"First thing tomorrow, Hoey, don't be forgetting it."

"First thing tomorrow it is, Mr. Kane! You can count on me, don't you know?"

Jack gave him a murderous look, and the man went scurrying down the dock.

Samantha watched him go, then turned to Jack. "Why don't we just go to Tompkinsville ourselves?"

Still scowling, he turned toward her. "I'd hardly be taking you to that miserable pesthouse, Samantha. Besides, let the little soaker earn his money."

"I imagine I've been in worse places than Tompkinsville," she said mildly.

"Not with me, you haven't," he snapped, his tone and the look in his eyes making it clear the subject was closed.

"Is it a bad place, this Tompkinsville?" Cavan said, speaking for the first time since Hoey had come on the scene.

Jack exchanged a look with Samantha. "It's a kind of hospital," he said, "a place where they detain immigrants who are ill when they come into the country.

"Brady did say the Madden children weren't all that well," Jack continued, in an attempt to spare Cavan further alarm. "It could be that they've been taken to the quarantine center for a time. Just until they're found fit."

"Please don't worry, Cavan," Samantha put in. "We'll find them." But even as she spoke, her mind went to some of the more harrowing stories she had heard about quarantine facilities. There had been frequent attempts on the part of some of the city's politicians and concerned citizens to have the place razed on the premise that it was a health hazard.

For the most part, Samantha thought the concern about quarantine stations was probably justified. Some of the tales about such places were the stuff of nightmares. Silently, she hoped Cavan's sister and the children had somehow managed to find their way to a decent lodging house rather than being held at Tompkinsville.

From what she knew of quarantine hospitals, Jack's reference to Tompkinsville as a "pesthouse" might actually be too kind.

10

A Bitter Hope

There is always hope for those who will dare and suffer.
JAMES CLARENCE MANGAN

Terese stood at the top of the hill behind the quarantine hospital, her eyes averted from the trenches where numberless dead had been buried—one of the most recent being wee Tully Madden. The child had died in the night, finally surrendering to weeks of fever and a cough that would have devastated a man grown.

Terese had watched the tyke die, her own insides wrenching at the sound of the death rattles in his throat—a dreadful sound and one she remembered all too well from the time when her own mother and sisters lay dying. She swallowed, biting down hard on the acid taste of a grief she did not want to feel, telling herself she could not afford to expend what strength remained to her on the death of a child she had hardly known. And yet she *did* grieve for the sunny-faced little boy who had deserved so much better than a painful death in a mean, cruel place among strangers who had not even noted his existence.

She glanced over at the boy's sister. Shona had not uttered a word since her brother's death. Even after the attendants took away the small, wasted body for burial, the girl had remained speechless, weeping silently for her brother. Now her pale features registered no emotion at all.

Terese feared for her. The girl had been frail when they started the voyage, and by now she was little more than a shadow. But it was her mind that concerned Terese most. Throughout the crossing, Shona had spent entire hours without speaking, staring straight ahead with a vacant gaze as if she had no real awareness of her surroundings.

Ever since their arrival at the quarantine hospital, she had withdrawn deeper and deeper into herself; at times she hardly seemed to be breathing, so quiet, so listless had she become. Only her little brother had managed to rouse her from her peculiar soporific state now and again.

But with Tully gone, Terese could not think what would become of the girl. For that matter, she didn't know what was to become of either of them unless she could somehow manage to find a way out of this abysmal death trap.

But perhaps she *had* found a way. While standing at the grave site, a plan had begun to form in her mind, a plan that might just mean escape from this miserable island. It would mean stealing, and Terese had vowed never again to resort to such an act—especially in light of the fact that only months ago she'd very nearly landed in a Galway *gaol* for stealing a basket of bread.

But which was the greater sin, she wondered, stealing a piece of paper or ignoring a chance to save a child's life—and perhaps her own in the process?

She shifted her poke—the sack that held her meager belongings—and glanced down at Shona. The girl stood clutching her own small satchel close to her chest, her eyes glazed in the familiar numb expression. Although she appeared to be studying the trenches of fresh graves before them, Terese questioned whether she actually saw anything at all.

After a moment Terese turned from Shona to watch a throng of people descending the hill. These were passengers from another ship, the fortunate ones who, having passed a final medical inspection, had just received their tickets to freedom. As they hurried along, many waved their precious papers of escape—the papers that would allow them to leave the quarantine center and enter the city. At the same time, an even larger group—new arrivals—were making their way *up* the hill.

Terese's mind raced, her mouth going dry as her gaze locked on a woman and a young, ginger-haired girl trying to jostle their way through the band of immigrants hurrying down the hill. With one hand, the woman gripped the girl's arm, while in her free hand she held the same papers of release as most of the others.

The two looked to be having a difficult time threading their way through the crowd. Terese's gaze traced a line from the papers in the woman's hand out toward the docks. She hesitated only a moment before grasping Shona's hand in hers, anchoring the girl at her side.

"Come on," she said, her voice low as she began to move toward the crowd. "Hurry!"

The ground was mud-slicked from the cold rain that had fallen the night before, but Terese took the hill at a near run, stumbling more than once in her haste as she pulled the wooden Shona along beside her.

When they reached the others, Terese wedged herself and the

girl into their midst with little effort, snaking through the crowd until she was directly behind the two she had singled out. The woman was bone thin and shabby, clad in little more than rags; the girl was even more wraithlike than Shona. Heart pounding, Terese swallowed hard, then in one swift, lightning move kicked out, smacking the woman in the backs of the legs with enough force to throw her off balance.

The woman cried out, her feet flying out from under her, the passes sailing out of her hand as she fell. The others around them either didn't notice or didn't care, going on down the hill as Terese, dropping Shona's hand, made a pretense of stopping to help the woman.

In the press of the crowd, she almost went down herself but somehow managed to scoop up the passes with one hand while pulling the woman to her feet with the other. She grabbed for Shona then, pushing herself and the girl quickly forward, squeezing their way through the others until they were almost at the front of the crowd and well on their way to the docks.

By the time the frenzied wailing rose far behind them, they were boarding the ferry for Manhattan, passes in hand.

⚜

With a silent, trembling Shona clinging to her skirt, Terese stood at the edge of the South Street port, looking out toward the ragged streets of New York. Her face stung, slashed by the frigid wind and driving rain. She was beginning to wonder if she would ever be warm again.

The scene in front of her was almost enough to drive her back to the quarantine station. The streets teemed with people, all of them hurrying and shouting, many in languages she had never heard before today. She saw peddlers pushing carts filled with rags, and other dark-faced men in tattered clothing hawking hot chestnuts, apples, and other delicacies. The spicy smell of food drifted out on the wind, and her stomach clenched in a fierce stab of hunger.

As she watched, arrivals from the docks meshed with the bustling crowds in the streets, some chattering loudly, excited; others scurried along, shoulders hunched against the elements, looking as apprehensive as Terese felt. The churning in her stomach was as much fear as hunger, and she fought down a surge of nausea. Panic pressed in on her as she considered the situation in which she had thrust herself and the girl at her side.

Here she stood, in a strange city in a foreign land, without so much as a familiar face or a recognizable landmark. She had no way of knowing what had happened to the newspaper people who were to have met them, no idea where to look for them, where to go . . . what to do.

Her attention was caught just then by two suspicious-looking creatures coming toward them. Brady had warned her about the runners, the unscrupulous leeches who preyed upon arriving passengers in an attempt to bilk them of their money and any other belongings. Instinct told Terese that the two heading their way might well be of this class of brutes.

One seemed little more than a boy, with a cheeky grin, a shiny coat, and an exaggerated swagger. The other was older and badly in need of a shave and probably a wash, from the looks of him. Both were eyeing Terese in a calculating way as they approached. The older man did not seem all that interested, no doubt because he saw no fine luggage or other signs of prosperity. The younger of the two, however, continued to appraise the length of her with eyes that made Terese think of a fish gutter.

"Can we help you and the wee miss?" The younger spoke first, his voice unctuous, his eyes still clinging to Terese's form, which in truth had filled out some with the child she was carrying. "Perhaps you're in need of directions or decent rooms to let?"

The two planted themselves in front of Terese in such a way that she suddenly felt trapped.

"Not at all," she said, forcing a note of confidence into her voice. "We are waiting for our friends, so you need not concern yourselves."

The two glanced at each other, and this time it was the older man who spoke. "Ah, so 'tis Irish you are then?" He cracked a gaping grin, and Terese could almost smell the rotten breath that surely emanated from that toothless cavern. "We are Irishmen ourselves and bound to look out for our own. Come along with us now, and we'll take you to safe lodgings where you can stay as long as need be."

Terese was aware that the two were closing in on them still more. Suddenly angry, she bared her teeth and made a slashing motion with one hand. "Didn't I say we're meeting friends? Now let us pass, if you please!"

The young one thrust his face only an inch or so from hers. "Ah, now, you needn't pretend with us. We're here to help you and your little sister, don't you know? We'll see you safely to the city and a proper place to stay. Here, now, let us help with your belongings," he insisted, making as if to relieve Terese of her sack.

"You'll be taking us nowhere at all!" she hissed at him, lunging sideways with Shona firmly in tow.

The younger of the two bounders was quick and blocked Terese's move, his maddening smile still in place even as a definite threat glinted in his eyes. "A comely lass like yourself alone on the city streets is an invitation to trouble itself! Be a clever girl now and come along with us. We know a fine boarding house where you and the wee lass can have a good meal and a warm bed for a reasonable rate."

"Are you deaf as well as ugly?" Terese shot back. "We're being met, I tell you! We are in no need of your *assistance!*"

With that, she surprised him by stamping on his foot, then hauling herself and Shona off at a fierce run.

The cobbles were slippery from the rain, and Shona was weak, stumbling and faltering as she went. But Terese was determined to put as much distance as possible between themselves and their pursuers. She kept going, her chest pounding as much from anger as exertion as she dragged Shona down the street beside her.

They didn't stop until they reached a narrow alley. When Terese looked back, she was relieved to see no sign of the runners. Apparently they had decided that two poor, hungry-looking girls were not worth their efforts.

With their backs to the entrance of the alley, they stood watching the mass of pedestrians pushing past. Finally, because she did not know what else to do, Terese took a tight grip on Shona's hand, and, with the girl snug at her side, slipped in among the crowd.

She had no thought of where they were going, no idea as to what to do next. She knew only the need to get away from the docks, to make her way into the city that beckoned.

They trudged down the street, so close to those hurrying by that they could overhear a jumble of conversations in different languages all at once.

Yet in spite of the host of strangers on all sides and the child clinging tightly to her hand, Terese had never felt more alone in her life.

11

A Futile Search

They brought her to the city
and she faded slowly there.

RICHARD D'ALTON WILLIAMS

NEW YORK CITY

It was Sunday morning before Terese and Shona finally reached
the forbidding brick building that housed the *Vanguard*.

They had spent the night huddled in the doorway of an abandoned warehouse. Once again Terese was more than thankful for
the emerald cloak Brady had bought her back in Ireland, for its
folds were generous enough to keep the chill from both herself
and the girl. The overhang of the building warded off the worst of
the rain and kept them fairly snug.

Even so, it had been a long, uneasy night. For the most part, the
few people who passed by ignored the two desolate girls in their

crude shelter. In the deepest hours of the night the city seemed to pulsate with strange sounds and even stranger inhabitants. Terese felt as if she hadn't been asleep at all, though in truth she had managed to doze some off and on.

She had awakened long before dawn with a fierce gnawing in her belly and a sick taste clinging to her mouth. By now they were both famished. They hadn't eaten since the day before at the quarantine center, a breakfast of thin gruel that wasn't enough to satisfy even a puny child like Shona.

They might have found the newspaper building the day before had they not gotten themselves lost numerous times. The directions gleaned from strangers had varied widely enough so that each route they followed led them to a different place. Finally, with darkness and a heavy rain settling thickly over the city, Terese had given up the search and sought shelter for the night.

This morning, with the help of a jolly pushcart vendor's directions, given in broken but understandable English, they had found the *Vanguard* building at last.

But the doors were locked, and from all appearances the building was empty.

Dismay swept over Terese as she remembered that this was Sunday. Of course no one would be working, even at such a big, important enterprise as the *Vanguard*.

For a long time, she stood staring at the building. Rain water had pooled in the cobbles of the street, and her *pampootas*—her homemade shoes—were worn so thin she might as well have been barefoot. But Terese was scarcely mindful of her wet feet. The only thing she could think of was the seemingly hopeless situation into which she had plunged them by her foolhardy act of stealing the passes and fleeing the hospital for the city. Now they truly had no place to go, no shelter from the bitter cold and rain.

But if they *hadn't* left the quarantine center, she reminded herself, they probably would not have survived another week.

Aye, but at least at Tompkinsville there had been a roof over their heads.

It was still raining when she led Shona around to the back of the building, in hopes of discovering an unlocked door. A few sodden sheets of newspaper were strewn randomly on the ground, as if the wind had blown them off the wagon parked nearby. A few feet away, two young boys were hunched over a barrel where something was burning. A thin ribbon of smoke snaked upward from the barrel.

The two boys eyed Terese and Shona with suspicion, and it occurred to Terese that she and Shona must look a fright by now. They were probably dirty, and their clothing was soaked from head to toe. But as she took in the boys' shabby apparel and pinched faces, she decided that these two would probably pay little heed to another's tattered apparel.

She tried to smile but felt it come more as a grimace. "Please, could we share your fire for a moment?" she said, grateful—not for the first time—that she had learned the English as her da and Cavan had insisted.

Neither boy made a reply, but finally the taller of the two—who looked to be eight or nine at most—gave a jerk of his head as if to indicate assent. He was a proud-looking little fellow, his worn cap set at a jaunty tilt atop a mop of red hair.

With Shona in tow, Terese wasted no time in joining the boys at the barrel. Whatever they were burning stunk of something vile, but Terese was too thankful for the warmth to mind the smell. "Would there happen to be anyone about this morning, do you suppose?" she asked, nodding to the building.

The boy with the cap looked at her, and Terese was caught off guard by the utter lack of childishness in his features. He might have been a tiny man, so hard were his eyes, so tight his mouth.

"'Tis Sunday," he said with a hint of a sneer.

"Aye, it is that," Terese shot back, irritated by his insolence. "But the two of you are here."

"We sleep over there," said the smaller of the two, pointing across the street where a another brick building stood, this one with a stairway crawling up its side. "Under the steps."

"'Sides," the older boy put in, "we've sold out of our Sundays."

Terese looked at him. His speech wasn't quite as thick with the Irish as her own, but not far from it. "Sundays?"

"The Sunday *papers,"* said the boy, looking at her as if she hadn't all her wits.

"You work here?" she said, hope quickening in her.

Again the redheaded boy watched her as if she were a fool. "Not *here.* We're *newsboys,* don't you know?"

"Newsboys?" For some reason, Terese seemed to be having a difficult time concentrating. Her head ached, and her hands and feet felt strangely numb, disembodied. Her own speech sounded slurred to her, and the boy with the red hair was staring at her as if he found her peculiar entirely.

"We sell newspapers," he said in a snide tone, as if he were trying to communicate with an eejit. "We work mostly for Black Jack himself."

"Black Jack?"

"What are you, then, just off the boat?" cracked the boy. "Black Jack Kane, of course. Him who owns the *Vanguard.* Mr. Kane, he don't let out his papers to just any boy. He picks and chooses those he knows he can trust." His chin went up a notch higher. "Like me and Whitey here. We got a better deal than most, don't you see? Most places, they make you pay for your papers right up front, no matter what. If you ain't got the money, you get no papers. But Mr. Kane, now, once he learns he can trust a boy, he'll dole out the papers for a few days without makin' us pay, if we're short."

Terese was only vaguely aware of the boy's spiel. She wasn't interested in his newspapers. All she cared about was finding Jack Kane.

"Your Mr. Kane—could you be directing us to his house, then?"

The two boys gaped as if she'd taken leave of her senses altogether. "Sure and you're daft, if you're thinking you can just march up to Black Jack's *house!*"

"Sure and I will be doing exactly that," Terese snapped, suddenly impatient with his cheek, "once you give me the directions!"

Both boys snickered. Again it was the older of the two who spoke. "Even if I knew where himself lived—which I don't—but if I did, and say I was to tell you where that is, wouldn't the coppers run you off the street? Old Black Jack, they say he lives in a fine big mansion somewheres uptown. You ain't likely to be finding much of a welcome there, I expect."

Terese was so numb from weakness that her ears were ringing. "Mr. Kane is expecting us!" she grated. "And you can keep a civil tongue."

The boy reached to give her a shove. "And *you* can find your own fire!"

Just then the back door of the building swung open to reveal a big, angry-looking baldheaded man. He poked his head out, then stepped the rest of the way into the street. "What're you boys up to now, hangin' around here on a Sunday mornin'? That you, Snipe?"

"Me and Whitey, that's right, Mr. Wall. We ain't up to nothing. Just warmin' ourselves up a bit, is all."

"Well, you can just be warming yourselves somewhere else! You know the rules—there's to be no pottering about once you've finished with your papers. Now get on with the both of you!"

The older boy cast a sly look at Terese. "Well, but wasn't we tryin' to help these girls, Mr. Wall? They're wanting Mr. Kane's home address. They claim that he's *expecting* them, don't you see?"

The bull of a man turned to glare at Terese. She felt Shona pull behind her, clinging to her skirt.

"What's this?" he snarled, his gaze raking Terese with undisguised contempt. "What the divil are you up to, girl?"

Nausea scalded Terese's throat. She could scarcely force a reply. "Please, sir," she choked out. "I need to find Mr. Kane. I need to find him right away."

The man shot her a look of outrage mingled with suspicion. "And what sort of business would the likes of you be havin' with Mr. Kane?"

The building behind the man had begun to sway, and Terese felt the street tilt crazily beneath her feet. "He's expecting us, and that's the truth."

"Oh, indeed?" The big man sneered, and planted his hands on his hips. "Expecting you, is he? Well, ain't that strange now, seein' as how he only left his office but a short time ago? Seems odd, don't it, that he wouldn't have waited, if he was *expecting* you?"

Terese groped for something to steady herself, found nothing, and staggered toward him. "He was here? We missed him?"

"He was. And he didn't say nothin' about two raggedy girls either."

Terese moistened her lips, struggling to get the words out. "If you'd just be telling me where to find him . . ."

"I'll be telling you nothing of the kind, you foolish girl! Whatever your game is, you'd best look elsewhere. Why, Black Jack Kane no doubt has scrawny little girls like you for supper!"

He made a move toward her, and Terese stumbled backward. For an instant, the man's hard features seemed to gentle. Then he began to spin crazily right in front of her, his mouth moving with words no longer audible as a storm of darkness hurtled toward him, sucking him up and out of sight before swallowing Terese along with him.

✦❦✦

Madog Wall—predictably dubbed "Mad Dog" by his cohorts—thought of himself as a hard man: hardfisted, hardheaded, and hard hearted.

No one was likely to disagree with him. He had earned his reputation as a formidable fighter by brawling on the docks before coming to work for Jack Kane, and he could still trounce a man twenty years his junior if the situation called for it. His stamina was legendary. No man had ever seen him swagged, and though he seldom engaged an opponent, everyone knew Madog Wall would never back down from a challenge.

What was *not* so widely known—indeed it was not known at all—was that although Madog coveted the reputation he had earned for himself and maintained it with deliberate effort, he nevertheless had his soft spots. His loyalty to Jack Kane, for example, was so fierce as to be blind, if not obsessive. Then, too, he harbored an almost maudlin weakness for the helpless—especially injured animals and abandoned or orphaned children.

When he saw the older girl's eyes roll back in her head, Madog lunged to catch her before she dropped to the street. At the same time, he caught a glimpse of the little one at her side, the thin face crumpled in bewilderment and fear.

As he caught the older of the two in his arms, her fancy cloak parted and Madog saw that she was in the family way. Was she the mother of the smaller lass as well? Surely not—she looked little more than a child herself!

The girl was unconscious entirely, limp as a rag doll in his arms. The little one had begun to wail—an odd, thin sound like that of a sick kitten—and tug at the older girl's hand as if she feared that she were dead.

Madog's wits failed him for a moment. Clearly, the two lasses were either ill or starving—possibly both. The little one was so thin her flesh appeared like paper drawn over her bones. And the unconscious girl in his arms, though she seemed not so frail, looked as though she might be bad sick. Her cheeks were flaming, and he could feel the heat of her even through that heavy cloak. And her with child!

A thought struck him, and he gave the girl a sharp look. But, no, surely Jack Kane would not be responsible for her *condition!*

Ah, no, of course not! There was little likelihood of the boss's consorting with a peasant girl.

So what sort of deviousness was she up to, then?

There was no thought of allowing her to get next to Mr. Kane, of course. If by some unimaginable chance the boss had actually been looking for these two, well, then, he would have stuck around until they showed up, wouldn't he?

What to do with them, then? They were none of his affair, these two shabby strangers.

He looked at the little girl and saw that she was shaking. Was she that cold, then, or simply afraid?

She looked directly at him, her gaze never wavering. Something in Madog softened in spite of himself. There was no call to be cruel to a wee one like this, after all.

As he stood looking around, it occurred to him that the mission over on Pearl Street would almost certainly take them in. That Dr.

Leslie, who ran both the women's dwelling and the house for the men a few doors down, was a good enough sort. It was said that he never turned a needy soul away.

Madog's gaze came to rest on one of the newspaper wagons pulled close to the door, then flicked to the wee girl who still stood watching him, a fist pressed against her mouth.

Finally, Madog heaved an exasperated sigh and jerked his head toward the wagon. "Come on then," he told the little one, hoisting the other girl more securely in his arms. "Let's get the both of you to shelter."

12

Faces in the Crowd

A man has often cut a rod to beat himself.
IRISH PROVERB

The choir had already begun their opening hymn when Samantha stepped inside the sanctuary. She had shed her coat in the closet at the entrance, but her shoes were dripping, her feet and hands chilled. She tried to ignore thoughts of a head cold as she slipped into a pew next to Cavan Sheridan, who smiled and motioned for the two youngest Carver children next to him to move down and make more room.

Rufus's oldest boy, Gideon, had come for Samantha in the church wagon, already packed with children from outlying neighborhoods. But the wagon leaked badly, offering little protection to its occupants, and Samantha was almost as wet as if she'd walked part of the way.

As she settled into the pew, Samantha promised herself—again—-that from now on she would put aside even more
from her wages until she could afford her own buggy. Jack was actually paying her quite handsomely; she should·be able to save an
extra dollar or two a week without any great sacrifice.

She glanced at Cavan Sheridan again, saw that his pleasant features showed definite signs of strain. Dark smudges under his eyes
plainly indicated that his concern for his sister had kept him up
most of the night. Samantha wished she could think of some reassurance to offer him, but what was there to say? They could only
hope that Jack's informant—Hoey—would turn up some word
before much longer.

She smiled at Rufus's and Amelia's two youngest, on Cavan's
right. The taller of the two, Ezra, was whispering something to his
brother, Tommy. Both stopped long enough to give Samantha a
sheepish grin when she caught their eye.

The church smelled of rainwater and mildew and was, as usual,
far too cold for the sake of comfort. The small woodstoves in the
front and back never quite managed to chase away the chill in the
drafty old building. Rufus sometimes joked that he kept it that way
on purpose to make it more difficult for certain members to doze
off.

But the choir was warming things up now with their lively rendition of a spiritual. Heads were nodding and shoulders swaying,
and Rufus looked animated and eager to begin as the song ended
and he approached the pulpit to greet his flock.

The Mercer Street Tabernacle had been Samantha's church
home for over two years, ever since she'd gotten to know Rufus
Carver, the preacher, and his wife, Amelia. She no longer felt the
need to explain to anyone why she had chosen to join a mostly
black congregation. It wasn't altogether due to the friendship that

had sprung up between her and Amelia Carver as they worked to-gether in the slum settlements, although in the beginning that might have accounted for a part of her interest. The fact was that in this place Samantha had found a genuine working out of the gospel of Christ, as well as the kind of unconditional acceptance of herself as a person, that she had never known within the cold stone walls of her former uptown congregation.

The little clapboard building on Mercer Street was not only a shelter, a haven to its people, but it was also a happy place, the kind of place where people *wanted* to be.

The friendliness and goodwill of the congregation, the soulful, stirring music, and Rufus's lively Bible preaching worked together to create an atmosphere that was both cheerful and worshipful. It seemed to Samantha that God must be very much in attendance here, and surely he enjoyed every minute of his time among them.

Not all the members were Negro, as it happened. Over the years, several of those who, like Samantha, taught and worked in the settlements—and others, like Cavan Sheridan—had found themselves drawn to the Mercer Street congregation. On any given Sunday morning, one could look out over the crowded pews, as Samantha was doing now, and see an increasing number of light-skinned faces among the regular members.

The one face Samantha wished she might find in their midst, however, was never there, nor, if she were to be honest with herself, was it likely that it ever *would* be.

But she could still hope. She could still pray. A mocking thought insinuated itself at the edges of her mind: that she was almost certainly praying for the impossible. Yet that scornful whisper could not completely drown out the quieter, gentler voice deep within her spirit reminding her that the God she loved and trusted was Lord of all things, even the impossible.

And so she had not as yet given up her heart's plea, had never completely ceased searching for that one special face—Jack's face—among the crowd.

⚜

For years now it had been Jack Kane's habit to work off his tensions or an occasional foul mood with a lengthy, brisk walk. When his mind was cluttered or his emotions in a jumble, he would simply start out walking and not stop until decisions were made or problems solved—or until he had at least managed to clear his head and lighten his mood a bit.

The weather had never been a deterrent. In fact, he actually found something rather cleansing, even invigorating, about a good walk in a driving rain or a winter snowstorm.

This morning was no exception. He had left the house in an almost desperate rush to get away from the pandemonium of his own thoughts. Addy's barbed remarks about his "heathen" ways—in other words, his neglect of the Sunday morning mass—had only thrown coals on the fire of his exasperation.

His hovering housekeeper meant well, and for the most part Jack tolerated her impertinence in areas where no one else would have dared to go. But this morning the woman had come very near to exhausting his patience.

In truth, this morning he seemed to *have* no patience.

After his walk he had taken the buggy as far as the office, where he'd waited in vain for Hoey to turn up with information on the missing Sheridan girl and the two orphans. When the little weasel hadn't shown, Jack had finally gone storming out of the building.

As much as he tried to blame Addy's meddling or Hoey's failure to show up for his black mood, he knew he was dissembling. He had risen from his bed before dawn feeling sour and edgy, and as the morning went on his disposition had only darkened.

His bad temper almost certainly had more to do with the events of the previous day than the morning's irritations. He had come back to New York eager to see Samantha, hopeful of spending the entire evening with her. Well, he had seen her all right, but not in the manner he would have chosen. They had spent most of the afternoon prowling about the harbor in the rain with Cavan Sheridan, trying to find news of the boy's sister, who seemed to have disappeared almost as soon as the ship put in.

At supper both Samantha and Sheridan had been too distracted to do more than peck at their meals while they fired questions at Jack about the possible whereabouts of the missing travelers. And to his great disappointment, there had been virtually no time alone with Samantha later on. To cap it off, when they called it a day, he'd come home to find that infernal letter waiting for him.

It was the first of its kind since last summer, during the time when Cavan Sheridan had taken a bullet in Jack's place—a bullet which had very nearly cost the boy his life. Before then there had been other threats—random ones mostly and seemingly unconnected—which Jack had discarded as the meaningless ravings of a lunatic or some hothead with an ax to grind. Even now he still wasn't convinced that any of the earlier letters had been related to the attempt on his life.

But this latest one was different. Written in a hand that would suggest a certain measure of literacy, it gave the sense of being carefully composed, its threat ever so much more chilling because of the lack of choleric raving that had been common to its predecessors. There had been such a cold precision about the whole thing, such a complete lack of emotion throughout, that Jack had found himself more troubled by it than by any of the others.

Supposedly the motive for the anonymous writer's umbrage had to do with the *Vanguard*'s current series of articles dealing with immigration—a series under Cavan Sheridan's byline, focusing on the individual stories of immigrants whose passage and resettlement were being sponsored by the newspaper. Certainly there was no denying the undercurrent of racism that ran through the writer's invective. There was also an obvious attempt to apply a tone of outrage against Jack's encouragement of immigration, "an odious practice that would eventually pollute the city and the entire nation with undesirables."

Yet despite the pervading bluster of bigotry throughout, Jack sensed there might be something else at work, something more *personal* behind the words. More disturbing still, however, was the fact that the malice was directed not only toward Jack himself but against the entire newspaper, along with Cavan Sheridan and anyone else who happened to be associated with the immigration project.

Quite possibly, it was the kind of grievance that could even extend to Samantha. She was a part of the resettlement program, after all.

The thought that he might have unknowingly placed Sheridan and even Samantha in jeopardy had kept Jack awake much of the night. No doubt it was also responsible for the knot of dread and hot anger building inside him now as he tramped the streets of the city in the rain.

He pulled the collar of his topcoat tighter against the cold sting of the rain, a wave of chilling isolation settling over him as he picked up his pace even more. The feeling of being cut off from everyone else was nothing new to him. He often felt himself to be a stranger in an entire city of strangers. Entire settlements existed side by side, so close that their cooking odors and the stench of their refuse often intermingled. And yet no one really knew anyone else. Each community lived within its own environment, its own boundaries. People came and went and sometimes intermarried but more often than not mated within the colony. Neighborhoods sprang up and died, but those who moved on often relocated only to build a new community in which the old traditions and customs—and insularity—were reestablished.

And so it went. And all the while no one really knew more than a few others outside his own small circle of existence.

Jack's sense of New York was not so much that of an enormous, sprawling city but of many *hidden* cities, a number of which were still unknown to him and perhaps always would be. Although as a newspaperman he was probably less confined to place, less limited by boundaries, than other men, he often felt as if there were vast communities of which he knew virtually nothing.

He had spent a quarter of a century in this city, had come to love it with a strange ferocity, loved it for its weaknesses as well as its strengths. New York was a city of great power and little patience. A place teeming with grandeur and riddled with squalor. A domain that glittered with opulence and reeked with decadence. A city of sinners and saints, barons and beggars, mystics and monsters.

And always it was a city of secrets.

In a little over two decades, Jack had managed to carve out his own small monarchy in this place, had established a dominion of sorts over the publishing business while gaining for himself, if not respect, at least the stature—and notoriety—inherent with that kind of success. He had friends, and he had enemies—and he liked to think he knew one from the other.

But did he? He was no longer quite so sure. Was it possible that somewhere among these secretive, violent streets an enemy lurked—perhaps one with a familiar face but with the soul of a stranger—who harbored a hatred intense enough to destroy not only him but everything and everyone he cared about?

Over the years he had fought and defeated many an adversary.

But they had been rivals he recognized, opponents he knew well enough to anticipate. This was different. A faceless foe would be harder to trounce.

That being the case then, what he must do was learn the identity of his nemesis.

At the same time, he had to warn Samantha and Cavan Sheridan.

He felt a sudden, almost feverish urgency to reach them. He knew where to find them, of course. At this hour on a Sunday morning, there was only one place they were likely to be.

As soon as he realized the direction in which he was headed, Jack was struck by a grim sense of irony. Both Samantha and Sheridan had been anything but subtle in their attempts to lure him to Sunday morning services at Rufus's church. Sheridan in particular was positively blatant in his efforts to see Jack "saved," whereas Samantha was more likely to drop a light-handed invitation every now and then.

Jack's response—routine by now—to their tactics was an off-hand allusion to the effect that, short of an act of Providence, they should not pitch their hopes too high on his behalf.

Now, as he approached the Mercer Street Tabernacle, his insides still humming with a sense of urgency to reach the two of them, Jack couldn't stop a thought of that "act of Providence" to which he'd so casually referred.

It occurred to him to simply wait outside until the service was dismissed, lest they get the wrong idea.

He had not quite reached the entrance doors when the sky opened in earnest and sent the rain pouring down in a fury. Jack stopped and looked up, scowling at the surprising force of the downpour.

After another moment and a wry mutter of resignation, he hurried up the front steps and made for the door.

13

A Shelter
from the Storm

Whence came you, pallid wanderer, so destitute and lorn,
With step so weak and faltering, and face so wan and worn?
ANONYMOUS: *A LAMENT*
FROM THE NATION

Terese felt herself surfacing through dark waters, floating back to awareness. She was cold, so cold her entire body was shaking in a frenzy. In spite of the trembling, her limbs felt leaden and useless, and a weight seemed to be pressing down on her chest, her breath coming in labored gasps.

Had the rain stopped? No. . . . She was inside, in a place she had never seen before . . . lying on a cot or a bed . . . and she was ill . . . hurting. . . .

She turned her head, and the mere effort sent a fierce pain shooting up the back of her skull. She blinked, trying to focus—and looked directly into the eyes of a lean-faced man who was stooped down on one leg beside her, watching her closely.

Terese shrunk back.

"Don't be afraid," the man said in a quiet voice. "You're quite safe. No one's going to hurt you."

He brushed a shock of sandy-colored hair away from his eyes and tucked the blanket more closely about Terese's shoulders.

"What . . ." Terese's voice sounded muddy to her ears, thick and unnatural. Her head felt the same way. She couldn't think of the words she needed to form a simple question.

The stranger smiled at her. "It seems you fainted," he said in the same quiet voice.

Fainted? Had she ever fainted before?

She couldn't remember. She remembered only a big man with a shining dome of a head and a gruff voice. And the rain . . . the cold, relentless rain . . .

"You were out for quite some time," said the man with the light hair. "How do you feel?"

Terese's mind was still scrambled. She found it impossible to think. Trying to ignore the pain in her head, she turned to look around her surroundings. The room was large, like a big meeting-house of some sort, and furnished with only single cots such as her own—perhaps twenty or more—and some small tables. Most of the cots were empty, but here and there a woman or child lay sleeping or staring at the ceiling.

"Where am I?"

"You're at the Grace Mission house. Mr. Wall brought you and the little girl here in a wagon, after you fainted. My name is David Leslie. I'm a doctor."

Terese stared at him.

She had never met a doctor before. She studied him, trying to take his measure. He did seem kindly natured, and he had a strong, open face that somehow invited trust. But she no longer trusted any man, doctor or no.

She glanced toward the foot of the cot and saw Shona standing there. The girl's features were drawn taut. She looked terribly frightened.

"Shona . . ."

"Ah, so that's her name. She wouldn't tell us. Is she your sister?"

Terese shook her head. "I've . . . been looking after her, is all."

After a slight hesitation, the doctor went on. "Well, she's all right, I think. She has something of a cold, but nothing serious. Someone will keep an eye on her until you're up and about."

He looked to be a fairly young man, Terese realized, and his dark blue eyes, though intense, appeared kind. But when he reached to put a hand to her forehead, she drew back.

He made a slight motion with his hand, shaking his head. "I'm not going to hurt you. Just lie still a moment, won't you?"

His hand on her brow was warm. Somehow it seemed to leave a chill when he took it away. Terese watched as he reached inside a small black case and withdrew a bottle, then poured something into a spoon.

"I want you to take this," he said, putting the spoon to her lips. "It won't taste very good, I'm afraid, but it will help you."

He put a hand behind Terese's head, helping her to sit up. A wave of sick weakness slammed into her with the effort, and she barely managed to swallow the vile-tasting liquid.

The doctor quickly eased her back onto the cot.

For a moment the floor seemed to tilt beneath her, and Terese thought she would pass out again. But she fought the nausea bubbling in her throat, knotting her fists and pulling in a deep breath, then another.

"What is this place?" she finally asked him.

He smiled again as he closed the black case. "Think of it as a shelter from the storm," he said. "A place to stay until you have somewhere else to go. You'll find it clean and warm—well, as warm as one could hope for from such a drafty old house."

He had an odd way of speaking: hesitantly, as if he might be somewhat unsure of himself, and his words came clipped and short, with a slight roll and a lift of his voice at the end. Even when he wasn't asking a question, it sounded as if he were.

He stood, and Terese saw that he was a fairly tall man, but slender and deep eyed. He had a way of leaning slightly forward that gave his shoulders a bit of a stoop.

She was so cold! She thought she would surely freeze to death. And it hurt so much to breathe! "What's . . . wrong with me?" she choked out.

He stood looking down at her. "You're very ill. I'm afraid you have pneumonia."

Pneumonia? Pneumonia was a death disease! It had taken the lives of her mother and her sisters.

"Am I going to die, then?" she asked him, fear churning in her stomach.

He frowned. "Not if I can help it," he said firmly. "Tell me, how far along are you in your pregnancy?"

Terese felt her face flame at this strange man's bluntness about her condition. She couldn't bring herself to look at him when she replied. "Six months—perhaps close on seven." She caught a breath. "Is—will the babe be sick too?"

"Not necessarily. And I'd caution you not to worry about that right now. Let's concentrate on getting you well, so you can take care of your baby." He studied her for a moment. "You're Irish, isn't that right?"

Terese nodded.

"And am I right in assuming that you haven't been here—in New York—very long?"

How long *had* it been? A week? Two? A month? Terese couldn't remember. Her head felt heavy and cluttered, like broken pieces of pottery about to fall free. He was asking her something else, and her mind fumbled to grasp what he was saying. But so consumed was she by the pain in her chest and the nausea driving through her in waves that she couldn't think of anything but how utterly wretched she was.

She felt herself turning hot as a furnace. Dizziness whirled around her, and she could scarcely make out the doctor's words as he went on. He seemed to be apologizing for his questions, for tiring her. "I'll let you rest for now," he said.

He went on to add something more, but his words were swept away by the sudden storm of hot, angry pain and sickness that came roaring in on her. His voice, then his face faded as Terese felt the churning black water close over her.

❧❦❧

David Leslie watched in dismay as the girl again spiraled down into a state of semiconsciousness. Even as he fumbled for the smelling salts in his case, he knew they would do no good. She was too deeply under, too tightly trapped in the delirium-clouded stupor of a raging fever.

He also knew the chances of losing her were great. Both lungs were afflicted. Her temperature was dangerously high, and she was obviously malnourished as well. From the looks of her and the little girl, neither had enjoyed an adequate meal for days, perhaps longer.

Her condition was all too familiar to him. Among the hundreds of immigrants he had seen at the men's and women's mission houses over the past few months, pneumonia was a common ailment, though certainly not the only one. Bronchitis, measles, scarlet fever, and the deadly typhus seemed to ride the backs of these foreign immigrants—especially the indigent Irish—like leeches.

He had saved a number of those he'd cared for—by God's grace and the benefit of his Edinburgh medical training—but he had lost almost as many. Pneumonia was especially treacherous for those poor travelers who came across on the "coffin ships." Trapped in the dank, cold bowels of steerage, with an utter lack of fresh air, proper food, and the means of keeping themselves dry and warm, they more often than not arrived dangerously ill—if they arrived at all. The Irish seemed particularly victimized by the unconscionable ship owners, who often packed in three or four times as many persons as should have been allowed, then fed them nothing more than slop and foul water for weeks on end.

David pulled up a stool by the girl's bed and again took her pulse, which was entirely too fast. Listening to her chest, he found almost no healthy sounds, but instead the whistling and the dreaded rattle that meant the pneumonia was advancing to the final, almost always mortal, stages.

He watched her for a moment. Her breathing was rapid and labored, her skin flushed an angry crimson.

"What's her name?" he said, turning to the young girl at the foot of the bed.

The child stared at him. She had said nothing since they arrived at the mission. David was beginning to wonder if she could speak at all when she finally murmured a single word.

"T'reece."

"*Terese*, is it?"

The girl nodded.

"What about her last name?"

The child looked at him, then shook her head.

The poor thing was clearly frightened half out of her wits. No telling what she had been through by now. David smiled at her, hoping to put her at ease. "And your name is *Shona,* isn't that right?"

She looked at him with those sunken, woefully solemn eyes, then again gave a hesitant nod of her head.

"Well, I expect you know *your* last name, Shona, now don't you?" David said lightly.

"Madden," she said softly after a moment.

"Ah. Well, Shona Madden, I'm going to go downstairs and fetch one of the ladies to help me. I'd like you to just come round and sit close by until I come back. All right?"

The child was obedient, he'd say that for her. Like a little marti-net, she walked around the cot and sat down on the stool, her eyes fixed on the girl named *Terese.*

David took a last look at his patient as well. Despite the fact that she was in the throes of a devastating illness, wasted by fever and malnutrition—and swollen with child—she was difficult *not* to look at. At her worst—for he couldn't imagine her being in a much worse condition—she was striking; at her best she must be absolutely magnificent. Even cropped and tangled, that russet hair was lovely. And when she'd first opened those shadowed, smoke-blue eyes, David had experienced a catch in his throat that caught him completely unawares. She was too thin by far, of course, disheveled, and frighteningly ill. But somehow none of that took away from her uncommon loveliness.

As he went downstairs, he found himself wondering again about the lack of a husband. She was wearing a ring—an unusual object cast in heavy gold. But it didn't appear to be a wedding band. Had her man perished during the voyage? Even the strongest weren't exempt from the ravages of an Atlantic crossing.

There had been no time to learn anything about her, really. And he suspected the child would be of no help, since apparently she didn't even know the other's last name.

Always, he wondered about their stories, these immigrants who risked so much to come to America. Sometimes they told him of whatever it was that had compelled them to break all ties with their past and begin new lives in a strange land.

Sometimes they failed to survive long enough to tell him anything.

His own parents had made this same life-changing decision; perhaps that fact accounted for his ongoing curiosity about other immigrants. In the case of Annice and Duncan Leslie, faith had been the motivating factor. David's father had heard a "clear call of God" to America when David and his brother, William, were still boys. Duncan Leslie's first congregation had been a dying church in Boston, which, by the time Duncan received a "new call" a few years later, had virtually doubled in membership.

Although his parents had long since retired and gone back to their home country to live, David had returned to Scotland only twice, to take his medical education in Edinburgh and to visit his parents on a later occasion. America was David's home, and he loved it: its sprawling expanse, its energy, its excitement, its people—especially the people, with their never-ending, fascinating diversity.

His own "call of God" had not been quite so clear as that of his father's, at least not in the beginning. He had known only that he was called to some sort of ministry and had for a time assumed that ministry would take place behind a pulpit. Only when he returned from Edinburgh and began to do some charity work in the tenement sections of the city did he finally catch God's vision for his life's work. Since then he had established four mission houses—two of which he still supervised on a daily basis—and trained two "Timothies" of his own, sending them out to launch similar missions, one near the harbor and the other in the notorious Five Points slum.

During the years that he labored as both physician and pastor, he came to realize that he was no more one than the other. His patients had become his church, a church without walls. They had also become his family. He had no real home of his own. Home was whichever mission house he happened to lodge in on any given night. With his parents back in Scotland and his brother, William, teaching in a New England college, there was no reason, after all, to maintain a home.

He could easily have slipped into a solitary, empty life, had it not been for his patients and others who passed through the mission houses. Most of the time, though, David would have said his life was anything but empty. He seldom indulged in introspection, and when loneliness crept in on him, he usually managed to deflect it by busying himself even more.

So far as he was concerned, God had granted him a full life, one blessed by a work he loved to do and a faith that had thus far sustained him through all manner of change and challenge. As he now approached his midthirties, however, the occasional thought of a home and family edged its way into his thoughts. Sometimes a particular event—such as coming upon the lovely but unfortunate young expectant mother upstairs—would evoke a yearning for something more that what he had.

Other times it was the bleak prospect of returning to an empty room late at night, with no one waiting to care whether he returned or not.

He hoped these longings didn't mark him in the Lord's eyes as an ingrate. At those times when loneliness crept in on him without warning he would remind himself that Christ, too, had lived a solitary life.

But wasn't it possible that even Christ had sometimes been lonely?

The thought came unbidden, catching David by surprise, and he found himself wondering if the Lord might not suffer similar pangs of loneliness and disappointment when his own creation, the children he loved beyond all understanding, drifted through their days with only halfhearted attempts to seek his presence, his fellowship—when they sought him at all.

The possibility caused David to take time out from his efforts and stop to offer a heartfelt prayer of loving thanks to his Savior, the one friend who *did* share that empty room late at night.

14

Tearing Down the Walls

The Pharisee's cant goes up for peace,
But the cries of his victims never cease.
JOHN BOYLE O'REILLY

Samantha was so astonished to glance over and see Jack—very wet, slightly disheveled, and obviously disgruntled—slipping into the pew beside her that she could do nothing but stare at him, speechless. Jack countered with a narrow-eyed, somewhat challenging look, as if daring her to show even the slightest hint of satisfaction at his appearance.

"Jack! What are you doing—"

Heads turned at her loud whisper, and Samantha felt her face flame.

"You invited me, remember?" he muttered a little too loudly. Again, people turned to look, including Cavan Sheridan—who broke into a wide smile at the sight of Jack—as did the Carver children and the widowed Sadie Brown at the other end of the pew.

"I—well . . . yes, I did," Samantha finally managed to choke out as he settled himself into the cramped space beside her. "I'm so glad . . . you could make it."

She tried to move down to allow him more room, but the pew was packed to capacity.

"You're drenched," she whispered.

One dark brow lifted a fraction. "It's raining," he said, straight faced. His gaze flicked over her. "As you've obviously discovered for yourself."

Samantha put a hand to her still damp hair, and his eyes followed her movement.

"I need to talk with you and Sheridan immediately after the service," he whispered, leaning closer. "It's important."

"Has something happened? Did you find Cavan's sister and the children?"

He shook his head. "Not yet. But there's something you need to know. Both of you."

At that point, an elderly black lady directly in front of them turned to scowl. Again, Samantha's face burned. But Jack merely shot the woman an engaging smile, at the same time giving Samantha a slight nudge with his elbow.

Rufus was just stepping up to the scarred wooden pulpit. The instant he spied Jack, his face broke into a wide, gleeful grin. For a moment Samantha thought he was going to delay the sermon and come barreling out into the congregation!

Instead, he delayed only another second or two, then launched into the morning message.

"*Brethren!*" he thundered. Every head snapped to attention, including Jack's. "This morning the Lord has laid it on my heart to speak to you about tearing down the *walls* of this church!"

Predictably, several people in the congregation glanced at the interior walls, then cast questioning looks at their large, usually jovial preacher.

"That's what I said, brethren. We need to tear down these walls!" Rufus made a wide, sweeping motion with one arm to encompass their surroundings. "Tear them down and take this church out of this old building!"

It took Samantha only a few seconds to realize where Rufus was going with his curious opening. She was pleased to note that, beside her, Jack seemed to be all ears.

Always direct, Rufus leaned over the pulpit and began to scan the faces of his congregation, as if to make eye contact with each of them, one by one.

"The Lord, he's made it clear that we've been sittin' in our pews long enough. It's time to quit hidin' behind these walls. We need to get out there in the world and find out what's been goin' on all this time we've been hunkerin' down in our warm, comfortable church building."

Samantha suppressed a smile. The slight lift of Jack's shoulders told her that they—and others—were likely thinking along the same lines: the wooden pews were anything but comfortable, and even with both stoves firing full blast, the building was never really warm.

But Rufus seemed not to notice his congregation's amusement. He was clearly a man with a message. "It strikes me, brethren, that we've been playin' church so long, we might just have forgotten what the real world out there is like. Well, today the Lord says it's about time we go find out!"

It wasn't that Jack had never heard Rufus speak before. He'd had occasion, if infrequently, to observe his old friend's ability to hold an audience and would thus have speculated that no sermon of Rufus Carver's would ever be boring.

What he hadn't expected was to find his interest so immediately and wholly captured by the subject of this particular message. At first he'd been intrigued to realize that the thrust of the sermon apparently had to do with one of his own personal grievances against the "institutional church"—be it the Roman church of his boyhood or an uptown society congregation. It had long been Jack's observation that most of the churchgoing crowd, at least those with whom he'd come in contact over the years, knew next to nothing about the "real world"—and cared even less.

When he realized where Rufus was heading, he could have no more shut him out than he could have ignored Samantha's disquieting presence beside him. Never mind that he felt much like the proverbial black sheep in the midst of the flock. In spite of his general feeling of not belonging, he settled back, frankly curious to hear what Rufus had to say.

And it seemed that Rufus had quite a lot to say.

"I want you to understand that I'm not just preaching to *you*, brethren. I'm preaching to *myself* here too. Because all of us, myself included, have been guilty of bein' so busy with *church* work of late that I fear we might just have lost sight of the *Lord's* work. We've been havin' such a good time with our suppers and our socials, been so wrapped up in our prayer meetings and our board meetings and our Sunday-after-service meetings that we haven't taken the time for meeting with the people—the folks who need what you and me already got. The *Lord!* People like the tax collectors and the trash collectors, the publicans and the prostitutes, the gamblers and the guttersnipes, and the godforsaken souls dyin' in the streets because we've been too *busy* to take the love of Jesus to them!"

Jack stared at the massive black man whom he had long counted as his closest friend as if he'd never seen him before. Rufus had just issued the same indictment on the camp who called themselves *Christians* that Jack himself had harbored for years now.

With the exception of a few—Rufus, obviously, for one, and certainly Samantha, for another—it seemed to him that many of the churchgoers who professed to be "imitators of Christ" gave rather poor imitations indeed.

From the little he knew about him—and it *was* little, he conceded—the man called Jesus hadn't just sat around singing hymns and looking pious and generally doing nothing. Jack wasn't exactly sure what he *did* do, for his education in spiritual matters was sorely lacking if not bordering on nonexistent. But according to those who claimed to know, Jesus had been a lot more than mere talk.

Rufus's voice abruptly jerked him out of his reflection. Startled, Jack felt as if his friend had been reading his mind as he went on with his sermon.

"Too often we act like we might catch some fearsome disease, were we to go among the *heathens* out there. But from what I can tell, the Lord, he didn't seem to be the least bit concerned about that. He made it his business to get to know all kinds of folks. He went to their houses. He sat down at the supper table with them."

Jack grinned at the thought of Rufus's fondness for a good meal.

Rufus was just getting warmed up, it seemed. "Jesus, he got to know people. Who they were, what their troubles were, what they needed—and more times than not, he pitched in with some help . . . . *before* he started preaching to them!

"The Lord, he was smart enough to know that people wouldn't pay much attention to what he had to say if they were hungry or sick or down-and-out. He knew they weren't goin' to care about what a fellow had to say unless they saw that that fellow cared about *them*.

"And something else, brethren—I don't know about *your* Scriptures, but I don't recall *my* Bible sayin' a whole lot about the Lord criticizing folks, much less *condemning* them. Fact is, the only ones I recollect the Lord ever condemning were the *Pharisees.*" Rufus paused, drew in an expansive breath, then broke into a big, broad smile as he added, "You know. The *religious* people. Like *us*.

"And I sure don't recollect his *ignoring* folks! He paid *attention* to people, the Lord did!"

Jack studied his old friend. He had often taunted Rufus—good-naturedly—that he could have been a rich man if he had chosen politics instead of a pulpit. But he had never realized before today just how accurate that observation probably was.

No matter how much he needled Rufus, however, he never doubted the conviction of his friend's heart. Rufus was exactly where he was meant to be, doing what he was meant to do—what he wanted to do.

In truth Jack knew beyond the shadow of a doubt that the big, jovial son of a slave, who now stood leaning on his pulpit and smiling on his people, was above all else a true man of God.

Indeed, if ever he had known such a man—a man of God— Rufus Carver was that man.

He hadn't the faintest notion what had set Rufus off this morning. Apparently, he'd had one of his "words from the Lord" and felt constrained to share it. As for himself, he had to admit that he felt a certain satisfaction in knowing that Rufus didn't necessarily equate *religious* with *Christlike*.

Jack would concede that his own contempt for the mealymouthed hypocrites who could quote the Scriptures at length but saw nothing whatsoever wrong with tearing children away from their parents and selling them on an auction block might be somewhat excessive. As was, no doubt, his disgust for those who saw no disparity between warming the pews every Sunday and charging impoverished immigrants obscene rent monies for rooms unfit for pigs the rest of the week.

Pharisees, Rufus had called them.

Jack's censure would have undoubtedly been a lot less charitable.

But what had captured his interest so thoroughly today wasn't the realization that he and Rufus apparently saw eye-to-eye in this regard. He was more intrigued by the portrait Rufus had drawn of a Christ who wasn't above rubbing shoulders with the infidels of his day.

Jack supposed his reaction to this bit of enlightenment might have something to do with the fact that he was an infidel himself.

In any event, this was a different view of the Christ he remembered from his mother and his brief experience with the church of his childhood. That Christ had been a suffering Savior, who, to Jack's childlike imagination, had seemed somewhat pale and wan, beleaguered and victimized by his accusers, then mercilessly nailed to a tree, where he died in agony. That Christ had been beyond his comprehension.

Another view, again almost entirely based on his boyhood recollection and to some extent the teachings of a few particularly tyrannical nuns, had been that of a stern rule maker, a kind of divine disciplinarian. Fiercely stubborn and independent even then, Jack had responded as he was wont to do with authority in general: with deep-seated rebellion and even a certain measure of animosity.

Perhaps if Martha had lived longer, he might have come to know *her* Christ better. Certainly the Jesus Martha had worshiped had been a more approachable Christ, albeit a compassionate, long-suffering one. But they had had so little time, he and Martha, and back then he had lived in a virtual frenzy, establishing the paper and amassing his fortune. Work had become his god. And after Martha's death, work had also become his salvation.

The Christ Rufus had spoken of this morning was unfamiliar to Jack, but he was not without appeal. This Jesus would seem to be a more *manly* Christ, someone who wasn't afraid to get his hands dirty, who valued Everyman and perhaps even enjoyed going into the midst of a crowd and getting to know them while making himself known to them.

He considered Rufus's frequent references to the fact that Jesus had been a great one for sitting down to supper with the worst of the worst. Now, Jack could say for a certainty that most of the Christians he had known would never dream of jeopardizing their reputations by having supper with Black Jack Kane. Yet from what Rufus claimed, Jesus had sat down at the table with some very shady types. Obviously, he hadn't been one to mind what other people said.

He thought about Samantha, about the night she had graced his table with her presence, how surprised—and delighted—he had been that she would dare to risk her reputation in such a way. For him.

The memory warmed his heart all over again.

And Rufus and Amelia—how many meals had he shared with them over the years? Countless times he had sat at their table and known himself to be the object of their affection and goodwill.

Yes, Jack decided, he thought he could almost believe in, even admire, a Christ such as the one Rufus had described.

The thought startled him, and he was almost relieved when Rufus again yanked him out of his musings, so foreign to his nature, with a rousing declaration that was surely meant to challenge the entire congregation:

"You are good people, brethren! Truly good people. But I think the Lord is telling us today that we're in danger of thinking ourselves *too* good, too *holy* to be of any earthly *good!* Seems to me we need to roll up our sleeves like the Lord did and commence to knock down the walls of this church building. We need to be taking our religion out there where it belongs—into the streets of the city, to the people! *Amen,* brethren?"

Jack actually jumped when the entire congregation issued forth a resounding communal *"Amen!"* He realized with great surprise that for a minute there, he'd been close to adding one of his own.

⁂

Samantha was keenly aware that Rufus had captured Jack's full attention. She had known almost the exact moment when he honed in on the morning message with the same intensity he seemed to bring to everything that engaged his interest. It was evident in the way he sat, unmoving except for an occasional flexing of his shoulders, his arms crossed over his chest, his gaze locked on Rufus in absolute concentration.

She made an effort to suppress the ripple of excitement coursing through her, warning herself not to make too much of this. Jack had already indicated that his coming here today had nothing to do with the worship service.

Still, she found it impossible not to be encouraged, at least a little, by his unmistakable attention to Rufus's words, enough so that she closed her eyes for a moment and breathed a silent but fervent prayer for him. God knew Jack's motives for coming, after all, and, if he chose, could use those motives to his own ends.

Please, Lord . . .

15

A Divided Heart

Dread has followed longing,
And our hearts are torn.
W . B . Y E A T S

GALWAY, WESTERN IRELAND

Outside, the evening was bitterly cold, but inside Brady Kane's
rooms, a fire had just been lit.

He couldn't believe he had missed something so obvious. Why,
it had been right under his nose all the time! Big Brother Jack
would have ragged him for not seeing the solution long before
now. And he would have been right.

"You'll catch more flies with honey than vinegar, boyo," Jack
would say.

He slugged down another shot of whiskey, a slow smile forming
as he studied the roughly drawn portrait in front of him. Yes, it was
really quite simple. Why had it taken him so long?

Since it seemed that the only way to Roweena was through Gabriel, it stood to reason that somehow the big fisherman must be made to serve as a door instead of a wall.

With an energy he hadn't felt for weeks, he began to tinker with the sketch of Roweena. One of many others by now, this one was exceptional, if he did say so himself, especially considering that he was working from memory, without a live model.

But then Roweena's image was so clearly engraved upon his mind—upon his heart—that he carried her with him, wherever he went. She haunted him, surrounded him . . . at times even seemed to obsess him. So excruciatingly clear was his vision of her that he thought he could have captured that exquisite face on canvas blindfolded.

He had drawn her as he'd last seen her, standing in the marketplace, the morning wind whipping her dark hair into a cloud about her face and wrapping her skirt around her bare legs. He reached out and with one finger gently traced her profile, smudging the line of her mouth and delicate jaw a little as he did so.

He took another drink, glancing down at the glass in his hand for a moment. It occurred to him that he was drinking too much of late. He supposed he ought to ease off a little.

Until lately, he had never had a particular fondness for the drink. On the other hand, he'd never shared Jack's disgust for it. To his way of thinking, the stuff was neither poison nor elixir but merely something to enjoy or not, as one chose.

Jack, however, called it the "poison of our people" and would have nothing to do with it. But then Jack tended to dismiss—or condemn—anything that didn't quite square with his own set of tightly held paradigms.

Brady was aware that he drank even more when he was alone; of late, that was often the case. Some claimed it was the solitary drinker who ended up in trouble, enslaved by his habit. Perhaps he'd best be a bit more careful. Just in case. He had never had much use for those ne'er-do-well weaklings who tossed their self-respect down along with the whiskey. He had no intention of becoming one of them.

Besides, he was going to need all his wits about him. There was a plan to be made, and he would have to be clearheaded entirely to devise it. Gabriel was no fool, not by anyone's measuring rod; it would take some doing to win him over.

He took a last, reluctant look at his now empty glass, then deliberately set it and the bottle—not quite empty—well away from his reach.

<hr />

Gabriel looked up with a faint smile at the sound of the child's laughter. Across the room, Roweena was soaping Eveleen's hair while the wee wane pulled foolish faces at her.

Roweena, too, was laughing now and mimicking her smaller charge. Once she bent her dark head over the child and hugged her in a spontaneous gesture of affection. Her embrace was returned by an immediate, hard clasp about the neck that splattered soap and water over them both.

Gabriel watched them for another moment from his chair beside the fire. They were like blood, those two; no sisters could be closer. Roweena cared for the child and hovered over her with a fierce protectiveness. As for the little one, she delighted in the attention. She also, for one so young, displayed an uncanny sensitivity toward Roweena's fragile emotions.

As he studied them, Gabriel thought he would be a fool to crave more from life than the contentment of times like this: a quiet night, a cozy cabin and cheerful fire, the reassuring sounds of the girls' laughter and play. He valued a peaceful hearth as much as any man and had no need for idle luxuries about him. Instead he had long sought, like the apostle Paul, to be content in any circumstance.

'Twas a treacherous thing, the tendency to wish for more than one had, and well he knew it. Yet of late, to his dismay, he would find his imagination wandering down forbidden paths, dreaming like a callow youth of things that could never be—pretending, if only for a few shadowed moments, that Roweena was his wife and the child their own.

It was at this place he now found his traitorous thoughts, and only by an act of deliberate will did he manage not to pursue his folly. He got up suddenly, so suddenly the chair scraped the floor with a loud screech, causing the child to whirl around in surprise. Roweena, too, upon seeing Evie's wide-eyed stare, turned to look.

An unexpected dart of annoyance stabbed at Gabriel. He gave a wave of his hand and started for the door. "It would seem," he said gruffly, "that if a man is to have some peace he must seek it outdoors. I will take some air until the two of you have tired of your foolery."

He slammed the door behind him with uncommon force, wincing at his own churlishness. Outside, the chill night wind slapped at him. He trudged off down the path, feeling the great fool, for, sure, wasn't his vexation in truth directed at himself and not at the two girls? He could only hope that Roweena would consign his odd behavior to nothing more than a fit of sour stomach or ill temper and not the surliness of a middle-aged man caught up in the futility of a secret, unrequited love.

The thought only served to darken his already black mood, and he went lumbering down the street like an injured bear.

The Claddagh was deep in darkness at this time of night. Most residents had retired at an early hour, and few dwellings showed any signs of light from within. But Gabriel, wide awake with his turbulent thoughts, trudged on through the cobbled streets, scarcely aware of the black night and the bitter cold.

From his own house at the eastern edge of the village, he had walked into the heart of the settlement, where a number of mud-walled, thatched-roof cottages converged. Gabriel stopped, his gaze scanning the small, primitive colony that had been his home for nearly two decades. There was little that could be seen. Here and there a dim stream of lamplight from one of the houses relieved the dark. But for the most part, he was surrounded by shadows and a deep, familiar stillness.

To some, no doubt, the remoteness and solitude of the Claddagh, especially at night, might be unnerving. To Gabriel, however, it had always been a place of peace. For Roweena, especially, it had offered a haven from a less kind world, where those who were different were often viewed with suspicion and even distaste. Here in the Claddagh, however, a deaf girl was not perceived as savage or mad—or accursed—but simply as "special." Here, among these simple folk, she had been accepted and made a part of the normal, daily life of the village, which was what Gabriel had sought for her when he first brought her here as a frightened child.

Roweena's mother had been little more than a child herself when a British soldier, drunk and ablaze with lust, had brutally taken her innocence. A few years later, Roweena, by then an achingly lovely but lonely child, was rescued from the same convent fire that killed her mother, who had sheltered among the nuns since her attack. Gabriel's deeply devout but elderly parents took the child in, but when they too passed away within months of each other, Gabriel assumed guardianship of the little deaf girl.

He had brought Roweena to the Claddagh to find peace from the ignorant fear and malice that might otherwise have destroyed her. And peace is what they had found—for Roweena, at least. During recent years, however, Gabriel had found his own peace more difficult to come by. His fierce sense of protectiveness for Roweena, his resolve to do what was best for her, seemed more and more often in conflict with his growing love for her, until of late he sometimes felt as if his very heart were being torn asunder.

More than once the desperation of his love had driven him to the very edge of declaring himself. But always he stopped, either out of fear that such a confession would repulse her, even drive her away from him, or, worse, that she might actually feign affection for him out of some misplaced sense of obligation. He simply could not bring himself to face either possibility. But recently he seemed to live with an encroaching sense of dread, a sick awareness that he was nearing a time when he would no longer be able to hide his true feelings. He felt trapped, much like a fox cornered on a great precipice, with a pack of slavering hounds at his back and the prospect of a bottomless fall if he jumped.

If Roweena were to learn the true nature of his love for her and be repelled by it—as she almost certainly would be—what would he do? Walk out of her life? And what would *she* do then? How would she manage in her silent, sheltered world, inexperienced and untrained as she was in any sort of skill required to sustain herself, not to mention her sometimes irrational fears, her excessive shyness and lack of knowledge of the world's hard ways?

If, on the other hand, he did nothing—if he should somehow manage to keep his secret—he might not die of it, but he would almost certainly grow more and more restless and contentious under the strain.

Either way she would surely come to resent him and finally despise him.

With a heavy sigh, Gabriel looked up. The night sky, thick and unyielding, without stars or moonlight to relieve it, seemed to mirror his spirit. He raked a hand through his hair, then dropped it to his side.

"What am I to do, Lord? What is your will in this? I can no longer see your way in any of it."

His whispered, anguished plea was met by silence, and he wondered if he had offended his God with his self-pitying reflections. Or did his love and desire for Roweena contain elements of an unholy lust he refused to confront?

"I am only a man, Lord, not a saint. I know my thoughts, my needs, are sometimes impure. But is my love for her such a bad thing? How can that be, when I cherish her so completely and wish nothing for her but good? I want to do the right thing for Roweena, but I live in dread of doing *anything* lest I make the wrong choice. I cannot imagine a life without her—and yet I would rather lose her entirely than bring harm to her. What shall I do, Lord? What am I to do?"

Wait. . . .

Gabriel expelled a shaky breath. "But do I wait in silence, Lord? Or do I unburden my heart to her and take what comes? Ah, Lord, you know the state I'm in! I am like a blind man who does not dare to move this way or that, for fear of falling to my doom!"

Dismayed, Gabriel pressed both hands to his temples. Was that what this was about? His weak, demanding flesh? Did it all come down to an older man's foolish desire for a younger woman? Had he been lying to himself all along, deceiving himself into believing that his love for Roweena was pure, that it transcended mere lust or the body's demands for fulfillment?

Was he really such a hypocrite?

Gabriel hugged his arms to himself, for one of the few times in his life feeling small and weak and utterly inadequate. The black sky seemed to descend and crowd in on him, engulfing him in a cloying, oppressive darkness.

He squeezed his eyes shut against the stifling sensation. Slowly, then, it began to dawn on him—a truth that he thought he had learned long ago. It seemed he had forgotten the need to surrender. Everything. In his own hands, his dreams, his needs, his wants, his highest hopes were but poor things of the flesh and easily tarnished or misused. In God's hands, they became holy.

He opened his eyes, the words echoing through him like a carillon. *Surrender. Surrender everything.*

His eyes filled with quick tears. "Aye, Lord . . . it seems I needed reminding, even now. Forty years I am, and yet I still forget. 'Tis your will, not mine, that I'm to seek. Always your will, Lord. No matter the cost."

For a considerable time, he stood there in silence, the bleakness lifting from his spirit, the night bathing him now in serenity rather than dread. Finally, he stirred and turned back toward the way he had come, leaving behind him, at least for now, his earlier feelings of loneliness and confusion as he started for home.

16

A Plan Conceived in Darkness

What lies within the dark of the heart,
What whispers the words of deceit?
ANONYMOUS

Brady had been awake all night, plotting. Even now, with the hour bordering on midday, he felt no need for sleep. He had spent the hours into late morning at the small table in his sitting room, sometimes getting up and pacing the floor, his mind and body pulsating almost feverishly with excitement and expectation.

It would work. He was sure of it. Once before he had ingratiated himself with Gabriel by coming to the aid of Roweena and Evie. Of course, that event had been totally fortuitous; he had simply encountered the two girls the night of the devastating windstorm back in January and helped them to reach safety. Even though Gabriel's acceptance of him had always seemed somewhat grudging, he had, for the most part, made Brady feel welcome in his home.

Until the situation with Terese.

Now he saw an opportunity to win Gabriel over again. If he played things right, the big fisherman would not only grant him his earlier acceptance, but perhaps even his approval—thereby removing the barrier to Roweena.

During the night, he had formulated a plan to achieve his goal. He had tried to anticipate everything. There must be no carelessness, no idle mistake—nothing left to chance.

Finding just the right help to see it through, however, might take some doing. It would take two men, just to be safe. He didn't know all that many fellows around Galway, especially the sort he'd need. But he knew the kind of place where he was likely to find them, and tonight he would go looking.

He went to the window and looked out on the street below, where a beggar in shabby clothes squatted, staring up at a priest who had stopped to converse. Two men in broad Connemara hats passed by without a glance at the priest or the beggar. Several women, probably on their way to market, hurried by, talking among themselves.

For a moment a faint stirring of uneasiness nudged Brady. Admittedly, the plan wasn't without risk. If anything should go wrong, there would be the devil to pay. But nothing *would* go wrong. He'd make absolutely certain the fellows he hired understood that they had to carry out the plan exactly as he instructed. It was simple, really. All they had to do was visit the house on a Thursday evening, when the girls were alone, with Gabriel gone to the meeting hall for whatever it was he did there on Thursday nights.

There would be enough time, probably more than enough. Brady had watched the house for nearly a month running, hoping—in vain—for an opportunity to be alone with Roweena. Gabriel was always gone for exactly an hour and fifteen minutes—seldom more, never less.

On two consecutive Thursdays, Brady had gone to the door and tried to coax Roweena into talking with him. Both times she had appeared badly flustered, almost frightened, so much so that she'd practically slammed the door in his face.

Even so, he continued to watch. He knew that Evie would come outside a few minutes before six to empty the basin, that she would dawdle in the yard for a bit—not long—mostly staring up at the evening sky or simply standing, unmoving, as if listening for the call of a night bird.

Brady felt certain that once he managed to carry out the first part of his plan, the second part could proceed without a hitch. To that end, he must make every attempt to convince Gabriel that he was properly penitent for his behavior with Terese, that he deeply regretted his actions and was making a genuine effort to redeem himself.

He hadn't deceived himself into thinking this would be easy. No matter; he would scrape and grovel if that's what it took. It wouldn't do to go ahead with the rest of the plan until he'd won Gabriel over. He *had* to soften him up before going any farther. His instincts told him it would be a vast mistake not to lay the necessary groundwork first.

This decided, it was all he could do not to rub his hands together in glee as he anticipated the all-important first step, which he intended to take this very afternoon.

Clearly, he was the last person Gabriel had expected to find when he opened the door. The big fisherman's eyes went as cold as ice chips as he took one look at Brady. Without blinking, he moved to close the door.

Brady caught only a glimpse of Roweena and Evie behind him, both wide eyed as they watched from beside the hearth.

He pretended not to notice and instead turned his full attention on Gabriel.

"Gabriel. I—would you just step outside for a moment? This won't take long."

Gabriel's craggy features remained rigid. Without speaking, he continued to chill Brady with that same relentless stare.

"Please, Gabriel? It's important."

Brady was careful to keep his eyes off Roweena, his expression properly solemn. Gabriel studied him for another long moment through narrowed eyes, as if to gauge his intent. Finally, with a quick, backward glance, he stepped outside, closing the door firmly behind him.

Brady gave a deep sigh. "Thank you. I was hoping you'd see me."

No response.

Brady met the frigid blue eyes with a steady gaze of his own. As he faced the towering, black-bearded fisherman, it occurred to him—not for the first time—that Gabriel almost seemed to step out of another time. All the giant needed was a kilt and a pike and he would have resembled for all the world one of the ancient warrior chieftains from whom every man in Ireland seemed to claim descent.

But it wouldn't do to let that ice-pick stare intimidate him or, even worse, provoke so much as a hint of defiance.

Brady reminded himself to adopt the proper note of remorse as he commenced his speech. "I have something that needs saying," he began. "I don't quite know how to go about this, but it's important to me that you understand."

The jaw lifted a fraction, but the cold stare never wavered.

"I've come to apologize," Brady said quietly, casting his own gaze downward. "For everything."

At the continued lack of response, he looked up to find the big fisherman still watching him with a poker-faced expression.

"I'm aware that you think poorly of me," Brady went on. "And rightly so. I've behaved in a—a despicable manner. But whether you realize it or not, Gabriel, your opinion matters to me. I had even thought we were friends once. I'd like to somehow regain your approval."

He could detect no sign of softening in the other, but he was determined to go on with this. "I just—wanted to tell you that I'm sorry."

Gabriel's gaze, still void of emotion, flicked over him. "You owe me no apology. 'Twasn't me you wronged."

The man's coolness was beginning to wear on Brady, and he had to force himself not to show at least some irritation. "True enough. Nevertheless, I lost your respect, and I deeply regret it." He paused, keeping his expression grave. "Well . . . that's all I came to say, that I'm sorry. I'll be going."

He actually turned to walk away before Gabriel could speak.

"What is it you want from me, man?"

Brady turned back, hopeful now. "If possible, your forgiveness. Nothing more."

Gabriel's close scrutiny was unnerving, to say the least. "As I said, you did me no wrong."

Brady fumbled for the right response. He knew he could spoil it all by going overboard; Gabriel was no fool. On the other hand, he thought he had at least managed to crack the big fisherman's defenses, and he was reluctant not to press the advantage.

"Perhaps not directly. But the fact remains that you trusted me, and I abused that trust." Brady paused for effect, even managed to make his voice catch a little as he went on. "Gabriel . . . I *am* ashamed of my actions with Terese. And while there's no reason you should believe me just yet, I want you to know I've changed. I've—done some growing up."

He met Gabriel's eyes with a look that he hoped was entirely open and without guile.

If the big fisherman had been moved in any way by Brady's speech, he gave no indication of it. The silence that hung between them was long and thick until, finally, Gabriel made a slight nod. "You have had your say, and you've been heard. I bear you no ill will."

It wasn't all Brady had hoped for, but he would have to be satisfied with it for now. It was a start. He returned the nod and extended his hand. "That's that, then. I'll be on my way."

Gabriel hesitated long enough to make the moment awkward before accepting the handshake. Brady forced himself to leave without further delay, but he was keenly aware of the fisherman's measuring gaze until he reached the end of the yard and turned for home.

⚜

Gabriel watched him until he was out of sight.

He was both puzzled and vaguely disturbed by Kane's unexpected behavior. The young American's words had seemed sincere enough, and he had not belabored the proffered apology. But had the regret been genuine? And why bring this sudden avowal of penitence to *him?* Why indeed?

It was not up to him to judge Brady Kane, although Roweena had accused him of doing just that. In spite of his personal reservations about Kane, he could at least hope that the young rogue was truly contrite, that he did indeed regret his contemptible behavior and meant to change his ways. There was no reason *not* to believe him, after all, though his previous conduct might make it a bit of a struggle.

Was it merely a disagreeable streak of cynicism in himself that made him suspicious of Kane's remorse?

There had been nothing concrete, nothing specific, in the American's professed self-reproach to make Gabriel doubt him. And yet doubt him he did. Those dark eyes, always so deep, so difficult to read, had seemed more shuttered than usual today. Try as he would, Gabriel had been unable to take Kane at his word. Nor could he dismiss the sense of uneasiness that still lingered, long after the lad had disappeared from view.

He knew that once he went back inside, the girls would expect an explanation as to what had transpired between himself and Kane. He made up his mind to offer only a cursory one. Unless and until he was satisfied that the American was indeed a changed man he would say nothing—absolutely nothing—that might serve to warm Roweena toward him even more. For whatever reason, he was uncomfortable with her believing that Brady Kane had undergone some sort of transformation.

He would reserve his opinion until this surprising—and, to his way of thinking, still highly questionable—change had been proven.

If it ever was.

17

Rogues' Gathering

One rogue knows another.
IRISH SAYING

GALWAY, WESTERN IRELAND

Brady found the men he wanted with surprising ease. He'd been discreet; it took only a few careful questions of one of the local tavern owners and a brief show of money.

By Monday night he found himself sitting down at a table in the Brown Sail, a pub he seldom frequented but knew of from its rough reputation. Across from him sat a duo who almost certainly had helped to establish that reputation.

The one called Biller was small and whip thin, with a beak of a nose and narrow, pale eyes that never quite met Brady's gaze. He seemed to be charged with energy. He was also openly hostile.

The second man, while not exactly cordial, wasn't as surly as his cohort. Oddly enough, however, Brady felt more uneasy around him than the other. Robuck was the only name he offered. He had red hair, thick and heavy, and he had obviously not seen a barber's chair in recent weeks. His face, broad and flat featured, was nearly as florid as his hair. The man was solid and wide, a burly sort. In New York he would probably have been called a thug.

Unlike his companion, Robuck had no problem looking Brady in the eye. In fact, his heavy-lidded gaze held such a mocking glint that Brady found himself looking away.

Neither was the sort he'd want to pal around with, that much was certain. But for his purposes, they would suit. Besides, his dealings with the two would be short lived.

"There can be no mistakes. No rough stuff." Brady kept his voice low but firm.

"So you've said," Robuck came back at him. "And why would we get rough? A wee girl, isn't it?"

"That's right. I just want to be sure you understand. You put a mark on her in any way, and you'll never see the rest of the money. Not a cent of it."

Biller scowled even more darkly at that, but Robuck merely flicked Brady an amused look. "Ah, now, there's no need to be getting riled, man. We heard you clear enough, and we'll do the job just as you want it done. No questions asked. And no roughness. But I'm thinking, seeing as how the task would seem to require such careful handling and all, we might need a bit more in payment than you're offering."

Brady flared. "I'm offering you plenty, and you know it."

Robuck's sneer returned. "Well now, that might be so, mister. But you're obviously a particular man, wanting things done just right. And quietly, as well. That sounds to me as if it's a very important matter to you, this thing you're asking of us. That being the case, then—another fifty. In your American money, of course."

Brady fumed, but they had him. He was paying not only for a hole-and-corner piece of work but for caution.

He was also paying for their silence.

"All right. Another fifty. But not until after the job's done and I'm satisfied. Take it or leave it."

"Oh, we'll take it," Roebuck said casually. "Now—as to when you'll be wanting the deed done?"

Brady expelled a long breath and proceeded to tie up the deal.

Gabriel knew it was too soon for word from Ulick, but each day he grew more impatient to hear if his old friend had learned anything about the American. Kane's behavior—the sudden apology, the uncharacteristic self-effacement, and the alleged desire to set things right with Gabriel—puzzled him.

There was something in the lad that made Gabriel almost wish that he had been wrong about him, that he could indeed trust this unexpected transformation. Yet the fact was that he did *not* trust it, had in truth never trusted Brady Kane—and still didn't. In spite of his suspicion—or perhaps because of it—he found himself increasingly curious about the American and each day now hoped for a visit or a message from Ulick.

This day, however, was nearly over. There would be no news tonight. After listening for a moment for the sound of Roweena's and Evie's slumber behind the curtain and offering up, as he always did, a quiet prayer for them, he went to his own bed.

He slept fitfully, waking often and abruptly, as if jolted from sleep by some unfamiliar sound or troubling dream. Once he heard an outcry from Roweena, followed by the predictable drowsy murmur from Eveleen. This was no unusual occurrence; since childhood Roweena had often cried out or even wept in her sleep. Always, the wee wane woke just enough to reassure her until they both fell off to sleep again.

But no matter how many times Gabriel had heard those night cries, they pierced his heart. He ached to think that Roweena had endured something that years later still troubled her peace of mind, even in her sleep. And every time it happened, he never failed to wish that he could go to her, hold her, and comfort her until her haunted dreams disappeared.

The thought that she might always suffer so filled him with an infinite sadness.

The thought that he could never be close enough to her to console her made him sadder still.

PART TWO

Too Close
to the Flame

Take no part in the worthless deeds of evil and darkness.

EPHESIANS 5:11, NLT

18

Looking past the Veil

Pulse of my heart,
What gloom is thine?
FROM
WALSH'S IRISH POPULAR SONGS

NEW YORK CITY

By Tuesday afternoon there had still been no news about Sheridan's sister and the children. At that point, Jack decided to get the police involved.

He sent word to Ed Boyle, a sergeant at the first precinct, including in his message any information that might help with a search. It could easily take days, Jack knew, if not longer, to turn up anything. If the city would ever stop dithering around and set up a harbor police patrol it could make all the difference in this kind of situation. As it was, he could only hope that the already overworked Boyle and a couple of his best men would be willing to look into the situation as a personal favor. Boyle owed him more than one, as it happened.

In the meantime he was doing his best to keep Sheridan busy. Jack had sent the boy on a story right after lunch—a murder at one of the dime museums in the Bowery. Although that wasn't exactly news in New York, Sheridan must have found enough to occupy him, since he hadn't yet returned to the office.

The lad was understandably downhearted. What should have been a happy reunion with the sister he hadn't seen for years had turned into a nightmare.

There was no way of knowing the girl's whereabouts or the circumstances of her disappearance. Jack's apprehension for Terese Sheridan and the orphaned tykes traveling with her deepened daily. The more time that passed with their not being found, the less likely it was that they *would* be found.

There was also the reality that because the Sheridan girl and the two children were the first immigrants to be brought over under the *Vanguard's* experimental resettlement program, it was vital to the project itself that everything go well. If the initial effort turned out to be a failure, it might well doom the entire venture.

He gave a long sigh, pulled away from his desk, and stretched. Beyond impressing upon Ed Boyle the importance of finding the missing immigrants as quickly as possible, he couldn't think of what else to do. For now, it was time to leave the office and pick up Samantha. They were scheduled to meet with Avery Foxworth and Maura Shanahan at the jail within the hour.

With Sheridan off on assignment, Jack decided not to drive himself but to take a cab instead. It was another wretched day—would this miserable cold rain never end?—and he didn't much take to the idea of driving when he could ride snug inside a cab with Samantha.

He took time to check his appearance in the closet mirror, running a hand through his hair and frowning at the dark shadow of beard already in evidence. Well, there was no help for it now. It had been a hectic day, with no time for anything but work. In truth, Samantha had seen him looking worse by now, but he still wished he'd managed to spruce up a bit.

Shrugging into his topcoat, he took the steps at a clip, whistling as he went. As always, the prospect of seeing Samantha had made him somewhat rattlebrained. He couldn't remember when he'd felt such conflict in his emotions. One minute he was cross as a bear, the next as sappy as a schoolboy. He certainly hoped his foolishness didn't stick out on him the way he felt it must. He never quite knew what was going to strike him next.

If nothing else, love certainly made a man one great mass of contradictions.

Perhaps she would have supper with him. Unless, of course, she happened to be in one of her "distant" moods, as he thought of those times when she seemed to withdraw from him for no apparent reason.

Ah, well, perhaps he could change her mind with a bit of Irish charm.

Though he wasn't aware of that particular ploy ever working with her before.

The meeting with Avery Foxworth, Jack's attorney, and Maura Shanahan took place in the "visiting room" of the jail.

In truth, the room was little more than a storage area, and a cold one at that. Samantha sat at a table beside Mrs. Shanahan, with Jack and Avery Foxworth directly across from them.

Jack had asked Foxworth to handle the Shanahan case as a favor to Samantha, who had taken a personal interest in the woman. He knew Avery found Samantha's involvement curious, her work among the immigrants notwithstanding. Few women of Samantha's station would care one way or the other about a hapless Irish immigrant woman in trouble with the law.

Maura Shanahan had shot her husband to death a few months past. According to her story, the man had abused her for years. On the day in question, he had allegedly beaten her with a gun, threatening to go after the children as well. Samantha was convinced that Mrs. Shanahan had simply snapped after years of horrific abuse and, in a state of terror, acted to defend herself and her children.

Jack was inclined to agree and had brought Avery Foxworth in to defend the woman. As it happened, Avery had suggested to Jack that he might be able to make some sort of a deal with the prosecutor, given the history of abuse. Jack had opted to say nothing to Samantha about this just yet, however, for fear of raising her hopes in vain.

The speculative looks his attorney had been giving Samantha since the start of the meeting clearly indicated that he was more than a little curious about her interest in the Shanahan woman's predicament. As for himself, Jack thought he knew what lay behind Samantha's determination to help Maura Shanahan.

After some months of getting to know Samantha, becoming friends with her—and falling headlong in love with her—he had no doubt but that she'd been caught up in this particular case because of her own history. By her own guarded admission, her deceased husband, the highly esteemed clergyman Bronson Harte, had beaten *her.*

Samantha never talked about her husband. But Jack was convinced it was Bronson Harte who was responsible for the pain that darkened those magnificent eyes and the closely guarded restraint she wore like a suit of armor. On the one occasion when he had confronted her about her marriage, she broke her silence only enough to confirm his suspicions. At the same time she made it perfectly clear there would be no further discussion of the subject.

More than once, the perverse thought had struck Jack that perhaps it was just as well Harte was dead. Otherwise, he might have been tempted to add murder to his already lengthy list of sins.

When he first admitted to himself that he was in love with Samantha, the idea had terrified him. He had loved only one other woman besides his mother and sister, and he had lost Martha to cancer after only a few years.

A succession of meaningless flings had followed—all brief, all unsatisfying. His lack of commitment had not been altogether deliberate. He had always found it next to impossible to trust anyone other than himself. The very idea of revealing his innermost heart to another human being evoked something akin to panic in him. Even Martha had accused him of being "shuttered," of closing certain parts of himself off from her and others.

After Martha's death, he simply couldn't seem to muster the interest in or the initiative for a new relationship. Instead he continued to drive himself harder and harder, reaching higher and higher, until eventually he knew no other way to live. For years now he had kept himself so busy there was little time for anything other than work. He had allowed no closeness, no intimacy, no real friendships with anyone, save Rufus.

Rufus was fond of saying he had seen the best in Jack and couldn't ignore it. But Jack thought the truth was that Rufus had seen the *beast* in him and *did* somehow ignore it.

He valued his friendship with Rufus Carver beyond telling, but there had been no inclination to extend anything remotely like it to anyone else.

Until Samantha. She had swept into his life with her quiet grace and haunted eyes before he knew what hit him, and he hadn't been the same man since.

He was mad for her. He wanted to take care of her, protect her, be with her. He wanted to lavish everything he had on her.

He wanted to marry her.

Jack flinched, then actually glanced around to make sure the others hadn't noticed.

He needn't have worried. Samantha's attention was concentrated on Avery Foxworth, who was outlining the legal options of the case. As for Avery, he couldn't seem to drag his gaze away from Samantha, even as he spoke.

A jolt of something primitive arced through Jack at a blistering speed. Shaken, he took a minute to recognize the feeling for what it was.

Jealousy.

It was an unfamiliar emotion to Jack. Indeed, he couldn't remember having ever experienced it before today. With Martha, there had been no occasion. Their courtship had been brief and uncomplicated; their marriage, the same. And although his reputation as a womanizer still dogged him—a reputation he found amusing for its very exaggeration—the truth was that no woman since Martha had meant enough to him to provoke anything as intense as jealousy.

Until now.

Unsettled, he glanced from Avery to Samantha, who seemed to be engrossed in the attorney's every word. Occasionally, she turned to give Maura Shanahan an encouraging smile, but for the most part her attention belonged to Foxworth.

In that moment, Jack couldn't help seeing her as Avery Foxworth undoubtedly saw her. Even with her glistening chestnut hair confined to that stuffy little bun at the nape of her neck, and in spite of the fact that she was dressed as always in an un-adorned—but exquisitely cut—suit, Samantha was a stunning woman. Her presence seemed to cast a soft glow even on the dingy visiting room.

Any man would be taken with her. Why should Avery be the exception?

Feeling increasingly edgy and out of sorts, Jack started to pull a cigar from his pocket, but stopped in deference to Samantha, who claimed to abhor the smell. He turned his attention back to his at-torney. Although he had retained Avery Foxworth years ago, he still didn't know all that much about the man. Like himself, Avery kept his own counsel, seldom revealing anything of a personal na-ture. Their relationship over the years had been strictly business, by mutual consent.

The man was a study in contradictions, the total opposite of his partner in the firm, Charlie McCann. Charlie was colorful, jolly, and unabashedly vulgar, whereas everything about Avery fairly shouted *breeding*.

Avery was British, and although removed from his native land for more than twenty years now, he had retained a slight accent, which Jack half suspected might be a deliberate affectation. Where Charlie was large and lumbering, Avery was slender and fine boned. Jack had never seen the man looking anything less than impeccably bar-bered and attired, while Charlie McCann was a tailor's nightmare.

The one thing the two partners held in common was that they were both, Jack was convinced, thoroughly corrupt—Charlie bla-tantly so, whereas Avery was careful to maintain the veneer of a gentleman—and one of integrity.

Jack almost grinned at the thought. Avery Foxworth was proba-bly one of the shrewdest, most resourceful men Jack had ever done business with. He was also quite possibly the most ruthless. As to integrity—an alley cat probably had more.

At the moment, he was more curious about what sort of impression Avery might make on a woman.

More to the point, a woman like Samantha.

Not a tall man—Jack probably topped him by several inches—Avery somehow *looked* tall and struck a sense of importance and power that didn't seem in the least practiced, though Jack suspected it was exactly that. He was probably in his late forties, only a few years older than Jack himself. If he was graying—and he most certainly should be by now, Jack thought peevishly—it was well camouflaged by the natural, sand-colored shade of his hair. He had a long, lean face. His eyes were an indefinable shade of gray, like cold slate, with an unnervingly intense gaze.

There was no denying the fact that he was a "well set-up man," as the Irish would put it, and while not exactly handsome, Jack grudgingly conceded that Avery Foxworth would probably hold a certain appeal for women.

Apparently, he was also eligible. There was a daughter somewhere, but to the best of his recollection, Jack had never heard tell of a wife.

He looked at Samantha, and the thought struck him that both she and Avery Foxworth bore that elusive air of refinement that someone like himself could never hope to attain; one was born to it, he supposed. Indeed, his attorney's enviable elegance only served to remind Jack of his own somewhat ungainly height and the callouses—and news ink—embedded in his hands. He had the long arms of a plowboy, the near swarthy skin of a Galway sailor, and while his own tailor was the finest in Manhattan, he had never quite lost the memory of the threadbare pants and run-down shoes he had once worn.

In truth, although he was obscenely rich, at times he still felt wretchedly poor.

And always, he felt thoroughly, blazingly *Irish*.

More irritable than ever, Jack reminded himself that he had come here today as a favor to Samantha, to lend a bit of moral support, as it were, not to wallow in his own shortcomings. Samantha seemed to think his presence might influence Avery to make a more vigorous defense on behalf of the Shanahan woman, and the very idea that Samantha would look to him for help of any sort went a long way in relieving his self-doubts. At least for the moment.

Of course, he knew Avery Foxworth too well to think he could influence him one way or the other, but if Samantha wanted him here, he was only too happy to oblige.

Given the way the conversation was going, he thought Samantha could rest her concern about Maura Shanahan. Avery clearly had a plan in mind.

"I've given you a rather detailed account of what *could* happen, Mrs. Shanahan," Avery was saying, "but it's by no means what I think is *going* to happen."

His well-modulated voice held an uncharacteristic warmth, Jack noted.

For Samantha's benefit?

"In my opinion," the attorney went on, addressing his words to Maura Shanahan but still watching Samantha, "I can bring an end to this unfortunate situation rather quickly. If you'll just sign this paper, Mrs. Shanahan, I'll take care of things from here. I've arranged a private meeting with the prosecutor, and I'm fairly certain that when he reads your statement and hears my assessment, he'll dismiss your case without a trial."

He handed the paper to Maura Shanahan without a glance, his gaze still locked on Samantha.

Jack knew a sudden, unreasonable desire to take a swing at him.

Again he told himself that Avery was surely not the first man to be smitten by Samantha's loveliness.

Indeed.

For the moment, he dragged his attention away from Samantha to Maura Shanahan, who sat staring at the paper in her hand with an absolutely dismal expression. Finally, she looked up. "I'm sorry, sir, I don't . . . I can't—"

Obviously, she couldn't read. Samantha moved to save the woman from further embarrassment. Gently, she took the paper from her, saying, "Here, Maura, this light is terrible. Perhaps Mr. Foxworth wouldn't mind explaining what it says."

She looked at Avery, who gave her a faint, knowing smile and nodded. "Of course. Briefly, Mrs. Shanahan, this is a chronicle of the circumstances leading up to the day of the shooting, as well as the events of the day itself. It gives an account of the long-term mistreatment you suffered at your husband's hand, both physical and emotional. It also details his threats and actions during the hours before you . . . shot him."

He leaned back, linked his well-manicured hands over his handsome waistcoat, and continued. "Clearly, you felt yourself and your children to be in grave danger of physical harm. He was threatening you. You were terrified, and you reacted. It was self-defense, pure and simple. I believe we'll have you back home in no time, without the delay and aggravation of a trial. For now, though, I'll need your signature."

Without looking at him, Maura Shanahan murmured, "I cannot write, sir."

Jack saw Samantha's eyes cloud with compassion as she touched the other woman's hand. "That doesn't matter, Maura. All you need to do is make a mark. I'll help you."

Her expression was dubious as she looked across the table at Avery. "I don't mean to question your judgment, Mr. Foxworth, but are you quite sure about there not being a trial? It would seem almost—too easy."

Avery Foxworth leaned forward, folded his hands on the table in front of him, and gave Samantha a look of steady earnestness. "I wouldn't mislead you, Mrs. Harte. I'm almost certain we'll avoid a trial. In the first place, Mrs. Shanahan's husband sounds as if he were a low sort all 'round."

Maura Shanahan seemed to wince at his words, but Avery appeared not to notice.

"If the shooting happened as she says," he went on, "I'm quite sure the prosecutor will conclude that the man got no more than he deserved and will then summarily dismiss the case."

Jack was surprised at the strength of the Shanahan woman's response. Her face tinted with emotion, she leaned toward Avery and burst out, "Why, it *did* happen the way I said! Don't you believe me, then?"

Avery Foxworth's eyebrows lifted a fraction. "It doesn't matter in the least whether *I* believe you or not, Mrs. Shanahan. My job is to make certain the prosecutor believes you. And I assure you, he will."

"But will he *care*?"

Samantha's voice was low and none too steady. Jack looked at her, saw the set line of her mouth, the tautness of her features.

"I'm not sure I understand, Mrs. Harte." Avery Foxworth's tone warmed considerably when he addressed Samantha.

"Are you quite sure the prosecutor will appreciate Maura's circumstances, that she *had* to act to defend herself and her children?"

The attorney smiled a little. "I'm afraid I can't vouch for the humanitarian instincts of the prosecutor, Mrs. Harte. But I *can* tell you not to concern yourself with the outcome of all this. It's a *fait accompli."*

As Jack watched, Samantha studied Avery Foxworth as if she were taking his measure and was none too certain she liked what she saw.

"Maura *is* telling the truth, Mr. Foxworth," she said firmly. "Her husband beat her for years. Viciously. The day she shot him, he was threatening to kill not only her but the children as well."

"I'm not questioning Mrs. Shanahan's story." Avery gave her a conciliatory smile. "If I gave that impression, I apologize. I'm simply trying to explain that what will count in the long run isn't so much whether the authorities believe her or are sympathetic to her but rather that they're aware of the caliber of her husband. The man was obviously a bully, so it's not as if we're dealing with any great loss. Once the prosecutor understands as much, he's not likely to initiate the expense and fuss of a trial."

Again Jack saw a cloud of anger darken the Shanahan woman's face, as if she resented this condemnation of her late husband. But it was Samantha's response to Avery's somewhat glib dismissal that took him aback.

For an instant he thought she was going to rise from her chair. Instead she gripped her hands on top of the table so tightly her knuckles went white as she faced Avery Foxworth. Her face was pale, her voice noticeably strained. "So whether or not a woman is to be believed—or exonerated—depends on the mettle of her husband? If he's a drunken boor, then her chances with the courts improve, but if he's a man of good reputation, the law might not be quite so sympathetic to her plight, is that it? Even if his offense is just as heinous?"

Avery Foxworth's gaze was speculative as he replied. "That

might be oversimplifying somewhat, but yes, it's probably a fair assessment of how things work."

As Jack watched, Samantha drew in a long, none-too-steady breath. He didn't miss the slight trembling of her chin and the sudden flush of color to her face that told him she was probably aware she might be overreacting and already regretted it.

He wanted to go to her, but of course he could not. He could do nothing but sit there and agonize for her, for the old, clearly unhealed pain that Avery Foxworth's rather callous summation must have evoked in her.

⁂

If Samantha hadn't realized her mistake right away, that she had reacted too strongly to Avery Foxworth's words, Jack's pained expression would have told her as much. She was aware, too, of the attorney's close scrutiny.

She felt the heat of embarrassment stain her neck and rise upward. Quickly, she fixed her gaze on her knotted hands atop the table.

Jack came to her rescue after only a second or two. "I think Mrs. Harte's concern in the matter is the same as mine, Avery. You really are convinced this won't go to trial?"

Samantha could have kissed his hand in gratitude for the way he managed to divert Avery Foxworth's attention away from her so smoothly.

At the attorney's nod of confirmation, Jack turned to Samantha with a faint smile. "I think you can rest easy, Mrs. Harte," he said, his tone one of careful formality. "As I may have told you, Avery—Mr. Foxworth—has represented me and the *Vanguard* for some years, and I can assure you that when he makes a judgment about some legal matter, he is almost always right on the money.

After hearing what he's had to say this afternoon, I feel certain there won't be a trial. So if you'll just make your mark on that paper, Mrs. Shanahan—"

He gave an almost imperceptible nod to Samantha, indicating that she should help Maura, then turned back to Avery Foxworth. "Mrs. Harte and I have another appointment yet today, so we need to be getting along. You'll contact us once you have final word?"

Samantha looked at him in surprise. He hadn't said anything to her about another appointment.

The two men shook hands as she showed Maura where to make her mark. Jack seemed altogether oblivious to Avery Foxworth's inquisitive glances in Samantha's direction, but Samantha was sure he noticed. For her part, she had been uncomfortably aware of the attorney's studying, appraising looks throughout the entire meeting. She had also observed the way his expression occasionally altered when he looked at Jack, though she was fairly certain Jack didn't notice. She wasn't quite sure what she was seeing in the attorney's gaze, but she almost thought it might be resentment. Once she even thought she'd caught a glimpse of overt dislike.

But to be fair, her impression of Foxworth might well have been colored by a few of his seemingly insensitive remarks.

In any event, she found herself suddenly anxious to leave and was only too grateful for that "other appointment" Jack had referred to, whatever it was.

19

An Unexpected Proposal

I had a thought for no one's but your ears.
W. B. YEATS

Outside, the gloom of early evening was drawing over the streets. It would be dark soon, and the raw wind and rain hinted of a bitter night ahead. The smell of the sea and the ever present stench of garbage mingled with the damp air to hang heavy over the streets.

Their cab was to return between six and six-thirty, but there was no sign of it yet. Even at this time of day, Broadway was still busy. The hooves of horses clopped over the wet streets, impatient drivers shouting or cursing the traffic, cracking the reins as they tried to push ahead of slow wagons or pedestrians pooling into the streets.

After Avery Foxworth had pulled away in his carriage, Samantha turned to Jack. "Thank you for trying to cover my blunder back there. I don't know what . . . came over me."

The softness and depth of understanding in his eyes as he looked down at her stabbed at Samantha's heart. "Don't fret yourself about it," he said gently. "I doubt that anyone noticed but me."

Samantha wasn't so sure, but she still felt embarrassed about the incident and had no intention of dwelling on it. Instead she changed the subject. "What was that about another appointment?"

The cab pulled up just then, and Jack took her arm as they began to walk. "It was just a way to get us out of there," he said, gesturing to the driver that he would help Samantha in himself. "Besides, I rather hoped we *might* have another appointment. For supper."

Samantha started to protest—they had been together entirely too much recently—but Jack pretended not to notice. Inside the cab, he caught her at a loss by sliding into the seat beside her, instead of sitting across from her as he usually did. Ignoring her scrutiny, he draped the lap robe about her, then rapped on the roof to signal the driver before turning back to her.

Unsettled by his closeness, Samantha edged toward the door as much as possible. She avoided his gaze as she clenched her hands in her lap and stared straight ahead. "Do you really think Mr. Foxworth can convince the prosecutor not to go to trial?"

"Avery can be a very persuasive fellow," Jack said. "I think it's safe to assume there won't be a trial."

"I do hope you're right."

Out of the corner of her eye, Samantha saw that he was still watching her. She felt the need to keep talking, to avoid that intense dark gaze. "Have you spoken to the police yet about that anonymous letter?"

Ever since Jack had told her of the recent threatening note, Samantha couldn't help but speculate as to whether it had been written by the same madman as the unknown assailant who had shot Cavan Sheridan—an unintended target—a few months past.

The thought of how close Cavan—and Jack—had come to trag-edy that night still froze her blood. Either of them might have been killed. As it was, Cavan had taken the bullet in Jack's place, but now it seemed that Jack was still in danger.

"There's been no time for that," Jack said in reply to her ques-tion about the police. "Besides," he went on with a shrug, "it's not as if they can do anything about it."

Samantha stared at him. "Jack, you can't afford to take this lightly! Someone is threatening you! You've already had one at-tempt on your life. Now this. You thought it important enough to warn Cavan and me," she reminded him. "Please promise me you'll not ignore this."

He eased his shoulders a little and passed a hand over the back of his neck. "I'm hardly ignoring it, Samantha. But I'll admit I don't quite know what to do about it. Except—" he turned toward her again—"it *has* occurred to me that perhaps I should keep my dis-tance from you for a time, given the nature of the threat."

Samantha tried to ignore the sick wrench of dismay his words evoked. It startled her—and troubled her more than a little—to re-alize how much she didn't *want* him to "keep his distance."

"Obviously, I'm not doing so well in that regard," he said wryly. "No doubt you've noticed that I can't seem to stay away from you."

Samantha couldn't look at him, instead made a pretense of smoothing the glove on her right hand. He had thrown her emo-tions into a turmoil. She was puzzled by his behavior, puzzled even more by her reaction to it. She thought she'd caught a glimpse of some sort of change in him this evening, at least in regards to his treatment of her. Not that she wasn't used to these unexpected shifts in character. The gentlemanly conduct Jack was usually so careful to maintain with her sometimes reverted to a lighter, al-most roguish—and blatantly flirtatious—guise.

Although she continued to discourage it, Samantha had reached the point where it no longer annoyed her—or flustered her—as it once had. This was just Jack . . . being Jack. She had come to suspect that the role of a rake he sometimes affected might be little more than a kind of protective veneer—that at the same time he seemed to be playing bold, he was actually withdrawing, instinctively arming himself against any genuine closeness or the threat of a serious relationship.

She sighed inaudibly. There were so many contrasting facets to Jack, she never quite knew what to expect. He could be droll or somber, carefree or intense. She was told he could be an impatient taskmaster, harsh and demanding. But according to Rufus and Amelia, he was also a model of friendship and something of a philanthropist. He had a relentless sense of humor, yet often seemed given to dark fits of melancholy. He loved flowers and the opera, and she had never seen him in a suit that wasn't impeccably tailored. Yet, on occasion he seemed altogether oblivious to the fact that he reeked of cigar smoke and his shirtfront was stained with news ink.

Jack had an iron reserve, she knew, a hardness about him that almost certainly would have warded off anyone who dared to come too close. He was distrustful, occasionally arrogant—at least on the surface—and openly contemptuous of society in general, New York's elite in particular.

He almost always had the last word, and it was more often than not a sharp-edged one. Samantha suspected he had a defense for any occasion, and even after months of working for him and spending more time with him than was wise, she was never quite sure when she was seeing the "real" Jack.

But it was at those rare times when he seemed to drop all the masks, like now, that she found him the most unsettling. These were the times when he seemed almost vulnerable, and in that very vulnerability, he somehow became more of a threat to her emotions.

In any event, something was definitely different about him this evening. And whatever it was, it was sending up warning signals at a dizzying rate.

"Samantha?" His voice was soft, and when Samantha turned to look at him, he was watching her with the same tenderness, the same softness she had seen in his gaze earlier.

Her throat tightened, but she couldn't seem to look away from him.

"Are you in a hurry for supper?"

"Jack, I really don't think—"

"I thought we'd drive around a bit first," he interrupted.

She knew she ought to go home. She had work waiting: papers to grade before her next night class, an article to proof before to-morrow's edition, and a number of other tasks that lately kept get-ting brushed aside.

"A drive would be nice, but—"

"Good," he said, his pleased expression clearly indicating the matter was settled.

Samantha didn't know whether to be annoyed with him or with herself.

After another second or two, he took her hand on top of the lap robe. Surprised, she almost pulled away—but didn't. For a time, they rode along in silence. Samantha wondered that she no longer felt threatened, as she once had, when Jack touched her. To the contrary, she found his touch strangely comforting, the strong clasp of his hand almost reassuring. Yet she would have thought that in light of his recent proposal—and her rejection—she would have felt distinctly ill at ease in such an intimate setting.

Darkness drew in on them now, and in the shadowed interior of the cab Samantha felt the strain and tension of the past few hours begin to drain away. When Jack again turned toward her, this time with a studying look, she was able to meet his eyes and even smile at him. "What?"

"I've always been somewhat intrigued with how comfortable you apparently are with silence," he said, his tone thoughtful. "That's unusual, you know. Most people seem to think they have to blather incessantly, as if they always have to be amusing."

"I don't amuse you?" Samantha teased lightly.

Something glinted in his eyes, then banked. "I would hardly describe your effect on me as amusing, Samantha."

Still puzzled by his odd behavior, Samantha frowned and turned a little to study him more closely. "Jack? Is something wrong?"

He didn't reply for a moment. When he did, Samantha was completely caught off guard. "What exactly do I mean to you, Samantha?"

She stared at him, her mouth suddenly going dry. "I—don't understand."

"I think you do."

His expression was unreadable. "Samantha—am I wrong in thinking that you have feelings for me? That you care for me?"

Samantha saw that he was deadly serious. Her heart slammed against her ribs, and she couldn't seem to get her breath. "I don't . . . I can't—"

She broke off, instinctively edging away from him a little.

"Tell me the truth, Samantha. Do you care for me at all?"

Samantha's gaze went to his hand on hers. Even through their gloves, she could feel the warmth of his touch. "Of course I do. You've—been a wonderful friend to me."

His clasp on her hand tightened, and his tone turned unexpectedly hard. "Don't do that, Samantha. Don't dissemble. I'm not talking about friendship, and we both know it. I'm not going to hold you to anything or expect anything of you—I give you my word. But I think you feel something more for me than friendship, and I need to hear you admit it."

Somehow he was clasping both of her hands now. He sat there, watching her, dwarfing her with his dark, powerful frame, and Samantha felt as if his eyes were searing layer after layer away from her soul.

She drew in a ragged breath. "I don't know . . . how I feel. Not really."

"Then will you permit me to say what I need to say," he asked quietly, "before it burns a hole in my heart?"

Samantha's head roared with warning, but something in his eyes told her that with or without her consent, he intended to speak.

She saw the rigidity of his shoulders relax, but he retained his firm grasp on her hands. "Just—let me speak my piece, if you will, before you answer me."

His jaw tightened, and although Samantha again felt a panicky urge to stop him, she hesitated too long.

"You already know that I'm in love with you," he began, holding her gaze. "I suppose if you hold the more common opinion of me, you might question whether or not I even know what it means to be in love. But I assure you, Samantha, I do."

Samantha's pulse began to hammer as he went on.

"I expect I've employed every known device to *not* love you," he said with a self-mocking smile. "But the fact is that I find myself in a hopeless state entirely."

"Jack, please—"

He shook his head to quell her interruption. "Let me finish. Please. I know you must think I have a colossal nerve. If I offend you, Samantha, I'm truly sorry. But I can't stop now. I have to finish this.

"Samantha—I've asked you once to marry me. And I confess that I had high hopes—unfounded, as it happened—that you would say yes."

His words were coming faster now, as if he felt compelled to say everything at once to allow her no chance to interrupt. "Well, I'm asking you again, Samantha. And this time I'm going to predicate everything else by saying what we both already know—that admittedly, I'm no great prize. To the contrary, you might just have reason aplenty to laugh in my face—or slap it—for my even *thinking* you might marry me."

Now Samantha *did* try to stop him, but again he cut her off. His words continued to spill out in a rush. In the darkness of the cab, Samantha's head was swimming, her ears thundering, and for a moment she had an insane urge to leap from the cab into the street. She hadn't expected this, not again, at least not so soon. Indeed, after she'd turned him down the first time, Jack being Jack, she thought his pride would have stopped him from raising the subject of marriage ever again.

Samantha thought she would strangle. Shaken, she had to stop him before he went any further, but she couldn't seem to get the words past the swollen knot in her throat. In fact, she couldn't seem to do *anything* but sit and stare at him as if she had suddenly been struck dumb.

This wasn't going the way he'd intended, Jack realized with a swell of agitation. Samantha was staring at him in what could have been either utter incredulity—or abject misery.

He had set out to deliberately make himself vulnerable, to appear less confident, less in control. He had already decided he would grovel, if necessary—though the thought made him grind his teeth—if that would help him win her trust and make the idea of marriage more appealing to her. Or at least less loathsome.

Obviously, he had been wrong. He seemed to have succeeded only in making himself appear pathetic and perhaps making an already awkward situation for her even more impossible.

He swallowed down his impatience with himself. He had to think. He'd been careless with both attempts to convince her to marry him; he saw that now. In short, he had assumed too much. Even if his instincts had been right, and she really did care for him, why had he been foolish enough to think a woman like Samantha—the very epitome of virtue and respectability—would willingly subject herself to marriage with a middle-aged Irishman with a sordid past and the presumption of a fool?

Small wonder she looked as if she might jump screaming from the cab at any instant.

He had made a blunder, and he knew it, blurting out his feelings like an adolescent and presenting himself as an importunate bumbler. He stared down at their entwined hands, watching with increasing annoyance at himself as she slowly withdrew from his grasp. He fiercely wished he could somehow retract everything that had happened during the last few minutes, but what was done was done.

Once again, it seemed, he would have to change courses. Fast.

Not looking at her, he uttered a short, dry laugh. "Well, perhaps the third time will be the proverbial charm."

He was surprised to feel a light touch on his sleeve. His head snapped up to find her watching him with those magnificent, shining eyes that never failed to make him go weak.

"Jack, I'm sorry."

He heard the distress in her voice and could have kicked himself for putting her in such an untenable position. But at the same time his hopes rose when he saw the way she was looking at him. "I apologize, Samantha. The last thing I wanted was to offend you—"

"Offend—" She seemed genuinely bewildered. "Oh no—no, you haven't offended me, Jack!" She gave him a tremulous smile, and he could almost feel the effort it took for her to manage even that. "Stunned me, perhaps, but not offended me."

Jack studied her. "I can't help the way I feel about you, Samantha. Believe me, I never expected this. I meant only to be your friend."

She shook her head, averting her eyes. "I never thought of anything like this either. Perhaps if I'd only realized sooner—"

She let her words drift off, unfinished.

Jack pulled at his fingers, cracking his knuckles. He suddenly felt coarse and common——a feeling he would have thought long forgotten, but one that occasionally tore at him when he least expected it. A feeling that never came without an accompanying wave of self-disgust.

"Well," he managed to say with a lame attempt at a smile, "there's no help for it now. It seems to me that the entire city must know how I feel. I can't look at you without gaping like a lovesick schoolboy."

She turned back to him, her expression one of dismay. "Oh, Jack! I'm sorry. But I thought you understood."

Jack groped to recover his control of the situation, which he felt rapidly spinning away from him. "Samantha, let me be altogether honest with you. I have no illusions about myself. I've never tried to deny what I am, and I've never tried to lie to you. I'm bitterly aware that you could have your choice from all number of respectable fellows—the veritable cream of society, I'm sure—who would be far more in keeping with your background and station."

He took a breath, then hurried on. "But for all I lack in that regard, I believe I could more than compensate in terms of—well, to be blunt, Samantha, I can give you just about anything you'd ever want! And it would be my greatest pleasure to do just that! Isn't that worth anything at all to you?" He paused, "Isn't it?"

To Jack's dismay, he saw that she was trembling, a look of extreme distress settling over her features. "Oh, Jack! Please try to understand! This isn't about you or the kind of man you are—and it certainly isn't about what you can or can't give me! This is about *me!*"

Jack stared at her in bewilderment. She looked absolutely miserable, and for the first time since he'd launched tonight's campaign, he began to realize that he might have done a terrible thing. Clearly, he had put her in an utterly wretched position. She looked as if she were about to weep.

"I was wrong to do this," he said, trying to ignore the painful tightness in his chest. "Somehow I thought—"

"I can't possibly marry you, Jack," she interrupted, almost as if she hadn't heard him. "Don't you see—I can't marry *anyone!*" She stopped, and the look of raw anguish that lashed her features hit Jack like a hammer blow. "That doesn't mean I don't love you—"

She stopped, her hand going to her mouth, her eyes widening as if she were stunned by her own words.

For an instant, Jack felt a surge of hope, and he reached for her again.

But she drew back, shaking her head. "I can't allow myself to . . . love you. I *can't!* Not after—Bronson."

Jack stared at her, understanding finally dawning as he saw the torment in her eyes. "Samantha—I would never—*never*—hurt you! Whatever happened between you and Harte, you can't think it would be like that with me. Surely you know me better than that by now!"

Jack was totally unprepared for the blast of bitterness that met his words. "I thought I knew Bronson Harte, too! But I couldn't have been more wrong!"

She fairly hurled the words at him. "You don't know what it was like for me! You couldn't possibly *imagine* what it was like! No, I can't believe you would ever hurt me. But then I never dreamed that *Bronson* would hurt me either."

She stopped, her voice breaking as she added, "As it was, he would more than likely have *killed* me—if he hadn't killed himself first!"

20

Samantha's Secret

Too long a sacrifice
Can make a stone of the heart.
W. B. YEATS

They sat staring at each other in what was clearly mutual astonishment. Jack saw that she had been taken as unawares by her extraordinary disclosure as he had been, hearing it.

"Harte committed suicide?" he said softly.

Samantha nodded. He saw her bite her lip, obviously struggling to keep her emotions in check.

"I'm sorry, Samantha. I didn't know."

Pain, sharply drawn, constricted her features and made her appear suddenly older. "No one knew," she said, her voice little more than a whisper as she looked away.

She had knotted her hands into fists, and Jack longed to cover them with his own. But he hesitated, not certain she would welcome any attempt to comfort her.

"How?" he finally said.

"Bronson had suffered from a heart condition for years." Her words sounded strangled. As she spoke, she began to clasp and unclasp her hands in a strange, awkward rhythm. "He took quite a lot of medicine. The note he left for me indicated that he'd deliberately taken a massive overdose with the express aim of ending his life."

Finally, she looked at him, and her stricken expression tore at Jack's heart. He wanted to take her into his arms and hold her. He wanted to heal her.

Instead, he sat unmoving, feeling utterly, miserably helpless. "You said no one ever knew. What about his doctor?"

She shook her head. "Ethan Carter—Bronson's physician—was also a close friend. If he suspected anything, he kept it to himself. He continually tried to convince Bronson to retire, to live a more sedentary existence, but Bronson ignored him." She glanced down at her hands and for a moment ceased wringing them. "In fact, during the last few months of his life he seemed to push himself even more relentlessly. When he died, the assumption was made that his heart had finally given out, and it probably would have, had he continued on as he had been. But it wasn't exertion that killed him."

She drew in a long, ragged breath, as if the disclosure had completely drained her of all her strength.

Jack studied her, sensed the effort she was making to keep from falling apart. "Why didn't you tell anyone, Samantha?"

She raised her eyes to his.

"Why the secrecy?" he said gently.

Her eyes flickered with what might have been painful memories. "At first, I suppose I meant to protect his reputation, his . . . name. Bronson was held in high esteem by a great many people.

And there were his parents to consider. They were good people, and getting on in years—they're both gone now—and Bronson was their only son. The truth would have devastated them. Losing him was a terrible blow in itself, but at least they were able to find comfort in . . . the kind of life he'd led, the good he'd done."

Jack felt an unreasonable stab of anger that she would go to such lengths to protect the memory of a man who had caused her such incredible anguish. Apparently, she sensed his resentment, for she shook her head slightly as if to ward off any objection he might make.

"Bronson *did* accomplish quite a lot of good, Jack. There are countless numbers of people who might never have found faith without his preaching, his writings—his attention to their needs." Her voice trembled as she added, "I've never understood how he could be such a saint to so many and yet be . . . as he was with me."

She wiped a hand across her eyes and slumped back against the seat. Her tortured look broke Jack's heart, and he wondered how she could have ever kept silent for so long a time about something that must have caused her such despair.

"I don't mean to rationalize or try to justify what he did to me," she said, averting her gaze. "It was a nightmare. But I finally came to realize that in the last few years of Bronson's life he was almost certainly—mad. The fact that he made me a victim of his madness was simply because I was the one closest to him, I suppose."

Her expression was one of acute misery, and Jack felt chilled by the thought of what she must have endured at Harte's hands. Again he longed to pull her to him and try to ward off the pain, the agonizing memories. But she was hugging her arms to herself now, her eyes glazed with a numb expression, her entire bearing one of stony self-control. He sensed it would be a huge mistake to try to encroach upon that rigid restraint, and so he forced himself to do nothing but wait—and listen.

"I was very young when I married him," she went on in a quiet voice. "Too young, no doubt, and too naive to recognize the warning signs. I was so—overwhelmed by Bronson, so in awe of him, that I was completely blind to the *darkness* in him. For a long time, he actually convinced me that it was . . . *my* fault, that I had somehow driven him to—"

She broke off, her face, her fragile composure, crumpling.

Fury at Bronson Harte clashed with a monumental sorrow for Samantha's pain, and Jack could no longer *not* touch her. Gently, he covered her hand with his, relieved when she didn't pull away. After a few seconds, she straightened and seemed to regain at least a remnant of calm.

It occurred to him that Samantha was more than likely the bravest—and unquestionably the most unselfish person—he had ever known, but the torment in her eyes at this moment tore him apart.

"Your parents—surely you told them?" he said, his voice raw with his own heartache for what she must have gone through. "Your mother?"

She visibly shuddered at the suggestion, and he gripped her hand a little more tightly.

"I could never have made my mother understand my marriage! Believe me when I say that it would have only made matters worse. Besides, I realize now that I wasn't merely protecting Bronson's good name or his family. The truth is, I was protecting *myself* as well."

Jack looked at her in disbelief.

"It's true," she insisted. "For months after his death, I was convinced that I'd failed him somehow. I couldn't shake the thought that there must have been something I could have done, some way I could have prevented my own husband's self-destruction. I blamed myself, and I suppose I thought everyone else would blame me, too, if they were to learn that Bronson had committed suicide."

Jack lifted one dubious eyebrow, and she hurried on, seemingly intent on explaining. "You must understand that everyone who knew Bronson admired him deeply, even *revered* him. He drew people to him, won their affection—and held it—by the sheer force of his personality. I can't really explain what it was in him—but he had a kind of power over people that was almost . . . frightening. I simply couldn't face the disappointment or the disapproval of his friends and followers. By the time I came to realize that there was really nothing I could have done, that perhaps I had been wrong to keep his suicide a secret—well, by then it was too late. I had been silent too long."

She paused, and Jack saw her shoulders sag slightly—a weary gesture that spoke more of dejection than fatigue. "Besides," she added in a near whisper, "I'm not at all sure anyone would have believed me."

The thought of what it must have cost her to live with such an abominable secret set off an ache in Jack that made him almost ill.

"What a remarkable woman you are, Samantha," he said quietly.

His praise seemed to embarrass her. She shook her head, turning away. "There was nothing noble in what I did, Jack. I was protecting myself as much as Bronson's memory."

Jack realized that she truly had no sense of her own courage, her innate decency. Not only that, but he wasn't convinced but that even now she still didn't blame herself, at least a little, for whatever Harte had done to her. Perhaps even for his suicide.

More incredible still, he was sure he had glimpsed, if only f instant, a genuine sorrow for the loss of the man who h likelihood brutalized her throughout their marriage. Sh for him, sorry at least for the tragedy he had made c

Shaken, Jack wondered how he could have ever hoped to win such a woman.

She had spoken of the "darkness" in Bronson Harte, triggering the unsettling awareness—not for the first time—of the darkness in *himself.* Indeed, he never felt that darkness more keenly than when he was with Samantha. One brief hour with her could somehow tilt the axis of his existence and set him to searching his soul, albeit unwillingly.

The faint, indefinable light that seemed to glow within her somehow brought the shadows in himself roaring to the surface. It was a singularly unpleasant, bewildering experience, much like that of a nocturnal animal who crawls out of the depths of a dark cave in search of the sun, only to find upon exit that the brightness brings such pain he must close his eyes against the very light he came seeking.

And yet he needed her. Needed whatever it was in her that spoke of something better, something finer than anything to which he could ever hope to aspire. He needed her goodness, her gentleness, her honesty.

He thought perhaps he needed her to survive.

Jack suddenly realized that she was watching him, her features strained and showing signs of fatigue even in the weak glow from the cab's lanterns. He glanced down at the slender hand enfolded in his, then met her gaze and held it. "I wonder . . . do you think you could ever trust me, Samantha?"

Her brows knit in a frown of confusion. "What kind of question is that?"

"The kind leading up to yet another proposal," Jack replied.

"Jack, *don't—*"

He lifted a hand to forestall any protest. "Wait. Hear me out. I think you love me, Samantha. If that's true, then perhaps I can eventually gain your trust. And if you can trust me—well, then, perhaps you'd consider marrying me."

"Didn't you hear anything I said?" she countered, her voice rising in pitch. "This isn't about you—"

"It *is* about me, Samantha," Jack broke in, tightening his clasp on her hand when she tried to pull away. "Of course, I heard what you said, and every word of it was like a knife to my heart. I can scarcely bring myself to imagine your going through such torment. Samantha—I would give everything I own if I could somehow wipe those years completely out of your memory, as if none of it ever happened."

She stared at him in what appeared to be confusion, but her hand had relaxed somewhat in his.

"That's a fiddler's dream, I know. Only a fool would think you can simply forget the past and go on as if it never happened. It *did* happen, and to my grief I expect you will wear the scars for a long, long time. But here's the thing, Samantha, and please let me finish: we *both* have a past we'd like to forget, yours through none of your own doing; mine—well, to my shame, mine *was* largely my own doing."

Her gaze never left his face as Jack went on, choosing his words with as much care as if he were on trial for his very life. In a way, perhaps he was. Surely he had never felt so desperate a need to convince anyone of anything as he did at this moment.

"What I'm trying to say, and making a royal muddle of it, is that I think we might be able to help each other, Samantha, even heal each other. In time."

She was studying him with an unnerving intensity. Once she seemed about to speak but stopped, as if she'd thought better of

By now Jack was gripping both her hands, as much to himself as to keep her from withdrawing from him.

"Samantha, I confess to you that at sometime in my

have done every despicable thing you've heard me accused of. But this much I can promise you: I will never, ever hurt you. I will never lay a hand on you in anger. I will never touch you—unless I touch you with love. My word on it, Samantha."

He watched her, searching for some slight crumbling of resistance, uncertain as to whether or not he detected any. "Let me try to explain something, *macushla*," he said softly.

She blinked at the endearment that had rolled off his tongue so easily, without thought. But when she made no move to pull away from him, Jack continued. "Samantha, hard as it may be for you to trust my word, I vow to you that if you'll give me the chance, I'll spend the rest of my life trying to be the kind of man you can respect. And trust. With all my faults, I promise you that I can be—I *will* be—a good husband to you."

Jack saw her tense and begin to shake her head. Yet he sensed that her earlier resolve had weakened, if only a little, so he kept a firm grasp on her hands. He *had* to get through to her. He had tried everything he could think of: He had attempted to charm her into wanting him; he had tried to make himself so vulnerable in her eyes that she would feel no threat whatsoever from him, no fear of him; he had even tried to win her on the basis of his wealth—what he could give her. And nothing—*nothing*—had moved her.

Now he would try to make her *believe* in him. Somehow, he had to convince her that she could trust him.

"Samantha?" he said quietly.

Her eyes stripped past every defense Jack had ever built for himself, and again a surge of hope rose in him. "Marry me, Samantha," he said, making no attempt to control the urgency, the desperation, behind his plea. He was beyond pride now, beyond any pretense of caution. "I don't care if you don't love me the way I love you. I can live for a long time on the hope that your love for me will grow. We can make a good life together, Samantha. I'll build you the house you want—you don't have to live in that ugly old horror of mine. We'll make a home, have a family—"

She uttered a low sound, much like a moan, stopping him cold. The stricken look she turned on him hit Jack like a blow.

"I can't have children," she said, her voice breaking.

Stunned, Jack stared at her. Almost instantly, he saw her withdraw from him, heard the door to her heart slam shut.

Jack struggled to conceal his shock, the wave of disappointment that came hurtling through him with her grim announcement. He knew that how he responded in this moment might well cost him any hope he'd ever had of winning her.

"All right," he said, somehow managing to keep his voice even as he looked directly into her eyes. "You can't have children. I didn't know that, Samantha. But it needn't make a difference. It *doesn't* make a difference. Not to me."

It was as if she didn't hear him. "I was carrying his child at the last," she said, the words little more than a broken whisper. "Not long before he—killed himself, he beat me so viciously, the baby died." She caught a breath that was more a sob. "After that, there was—I can't have children. Not ever."

Jack felt a boiling, savage hatred slam through him, and it was everything he could do not to explode with rage at what had been done to her. It seemed a monstrous twist of fate that he could not somehow make Bronson Harte pay for the evil he had inflicted on Samantha.

"Oh, Samantha, I'm sorry. I'm so sorry," he said lamely.

She looked at him. "So you see, I have nothing I can
You say it doesn't matter, but eventually it would. A
you ought to have children. You need a wife w'

more than I can. You should have a son to carry on your name, the newspaper—"

She broke off, her face a mask of bleak resignation.

Jack had not wept since Martha's death, and even then the tears had come sparingly, as if being ripped from him. But at this moment he had everything he could do not to give in to a fit of weeping.

He steadied himself, caught her by the shoulders and forced her to meet his gaze. "Samantha, you couldn't be more wrong! All right, I would have liked to have had children. And, yes, it was a disappointment to us, to Martha and me, when we didn't. But this is the truth, Samantha, and you *must* believe me: I can live without children. But I don't think I can live any sort of life from now on without *you!*"

He pulled her closer, and she allowed it, but he was careful to hold her gently. "You have spoiled me for ever going on as I was before I met you. I can't go back to that life, Samantha. Please, don't make me."

Suddenly she was weeping, the tears tracing a slow path down her cheeks. Racked by the sight of her pain, Jack gathered her into his arms, wrapping her in a careful embrace. "I'm sorry," he said, feeling as if he would strangle on his own words, tasting the salt of her tears as he pressed his lips to her wet cheeks. "I am so terribly, terribly sorry for what he did to you. Please, Samantha . . . *please* . . . give me a chance to heal you with my love."

Jack held her to him while the tortured sobs shook her slender body. He thought her pain would tear him apart. After a long time, he felt her shudder, then grow quiet in his arms.

"You haven't answered me, Samantha," he whispered.

She looked up, her gaze still clouded with tears.

"Will you marry me?"

She closed her eyes. "You don't understand," she choked out.

"I'm . . . *afraid*. I don't know. . . . I don't think . . . that I can ever be a wife to any man again! But it's not just that—"

"What, then?"

"Jack—you say we can heal each other. But we can't. Not really. No matter how much we might *want* to, we can't. Only God can bring that kind of healing."

He studied her. "And has he brought it to you?" he said bluntly.

She seemed to frame her answer with great care. "Not entirely. But in part, yes, he has. He's done something for me that I could never have done for myself, something I could never do for you." She stopped, then added quietly, "But *he* could."

Jack wasn't sure what kind of a reply she expected from him. This had always been an issue between them, this matter of her faith and his inability to share it. But he wouldn't deceive her, wouldn't try to make her believe a lie. All he could do was attempt to understand.

"What do you mean, Samantha?" he asked her. "What, exactly, has God done for you?"

He had seen her pain, after all, seen it for himself, had witnessed the torturous memories that still haunted her. What sort of healing was that?

"He's given me peace," she said quietly.

Jack studied her. "I don't always see peace when I look in your eyes, Samantha. I see suffering."

She flinched visibly. "God's healing doesn't always come quickly, or all at once. But it comes, Jack. If you open your heart to it . . . to him . . . it comes. I expect what you're seeing are the scars. Not the wounds themselves, but the scars they left on my spirit. Eventually—"

She looked away, and he saw her throat work as she stopp swallowed hard, then went on. "Eventually I hope even th will disappear."

189

Again Jack puzzled over a way to overcome this barrier between them. But this was one place where he could offer her nothing. Whatever hope he might have held for some sort of divine healing or true peace had burned to ashes long ago, if indeed he had ever known such a hope at all. Yet there was no denying that something about Samantha—something indefinable, but the very essence of everything she was—set off a yearning in him for *something more*, something he instinctively knew he could never buy or win on his own.

"I confess that I don't understand what you're talking about," he said. "But I believe life with someone you love has to be immeasurably better than life alone. I love you, and I want to be with you." He tightened his embrace, but only a little. "And I'm willing to try to learn to be—the man you need me to be in order to make that happen.

"Samantha—I won't give up. I'm going to keep right on trying to convince you to marry me. No matter *what* it takes. No matter how *long* it takes."

She started to protest, but he stopped her, pressing a finger to her lips and shaking his head. "I'm only asking you to think about what I've said tonight. Don't be too quick to give me a decision. Not this time."

She gave him a troubled look but made no more argument. Finally, Jack bent his head to search her gaze, and what he saw there gave him the courage to cup her face between his hands and gently kiss her on the forehead, then, even more gently, on her lips. Her eyes were closed, and there was a softness about her mouth that wrenched his heart. He touched her cheek, gently. She opened her eyes.

"Samantha," he said, "we'll make it work. Somehow. We will, I promise you."

They rode the rest of the way in silence, the only sound the clopping of the horses on the wet streets and the steady rain falling on the roof of the cab. Jack was content to simply hold her hand and breathe in her closeness.

❧❧❧

Hours after Jack had left her outside the door to her apartment, Samantha sat on the side of the bed, staring at the floor, twisting her hands in her lap. This was not the way a woman should feel after having just received a proposal of marriage from the man she loved.

That she *did* love Jack was no longer in question. She had known it for a long time, no matter how fiercely she might have tried to deny it to herself.

Nor could she refuse to face what she had only suspected up until now, that Jack cared for her, too, and cared deeply. He had said he loved her, and after tonight she would have found it difficult to question his sincerity; she had seen it in his eyes every time he looked at her, even with the awareness that she would come to him damaged and wounded—and barren.

Shouldn't she be feeling elation instead of this aching despair of the soul?

She had wept until she was too spent to weep any longer. The scene in the cab had apparently uncapped an old but still extant reservoir of pain, propelling it full force to breach her hard-won wall of self-defense. Tonight for the first time she realized how desperately she had needed to purge herself of the truth about her marriage and Bronson's suicide. Yet now that she had done so, guilt and regret had come gnawing at her like angry scavengers.

The enormity of what had transpired this night still shook her to the core. A confession of love, a proposal of marriage, and the fall of the stronghold where her darkest secrets lay buried had left her emotions in turmoil. Her head was pounding, as much from the chaos of emotion as from exhaustion. She knew she needed nothing so much as a full night's rest, knew just as certainly there would be no such peace for her tonight.

Somehow she mustered the initiative to drop to her knees beside the bed and attempt to pray. For a long time, words failed her. She could manage nothing more than to hide herself in the presence of God and let his peace settle over her, his comfort quiet her.

But gradually, as she felt the first faint stirring of renewal in her spirit, she was able to form at least a faltering entreaty, a plea for guidance. When her petitions were met by only silence, she reached to the night table for her Bible and began to pray through some of the dearly familiar verses that over the years had strengthened and sustained her when her entire world seemed to be crumbling.

Samantha knew that even if she were to eventually overcome her resistance—her *fear*—to the idea of marriage again, she could not lightly dismiss the Scriptural admonition to not be "unequally yoked with unbelievers." By his own admission, Jack professed only a "limited" faith of any sort and apparently had lived most of his life as an unbeliever. How could she even consider a proposal from him?

The Scriptures spoke of an unbelieving husband's being sanctified by a believing wife, but this was different. She would be going into a relationship as a believer, knowing from the beginning that Jack didn't share her faith. Samantha had seen firsthand the consequences of willful disregard of this particular counsel, had seen too many Christian husbands or wives whose spiritual beliefs had been either shaken or completely decimated, if not by the immoral lifestyle of an unbelieving partner, then by the lack of shared commitments and values. How could she consider embracing a life with someone who had no interest in the very things that were most important to her?

But she *loved* him! "Oh, Lord . . . how can I simply ignore my feelings? How do I dismiss the fact that I love him . . . and he loves me?"

Pray for him . . . and trust me. . . .

Startled by the clarity of the whisper in her spirit, Samantha caught her breath. It occurred to her that she wasn't quite sure *how* to pray for Jack.

"He doesn't know you, Lord, although sometimes I think he believes in you. But by his own admission, he's lived a life that must be anathema to you. Surely you don't want me to love a man like Jack. And yet I do! Dear Lord, help me; you know I love him. . . ."

And so do I, child. . . . So do I. Trust me with your beloved. Pray for him, and trust me.

Thoroughly shaken, Samantha squeezed her eyes closed as if to shut out her surroundings, forcing herself to see nothing, know nothing, but the silence. Scarcely breathing, fervently yearning for still more than she had been given, she waited, clinging to the one who had never failed her. And finally, little by little, she felt the darkness in her spirit give way to light. From the deepest recesses of her being came an all-encompassing calm, a singing peace that flowed and filled her until she could no longer keep silent.

And finally she was able to pray. She prayed for an indeterminate time, prayed for the man who called himself an infidel, the man who only tonight had vowed his love and protection to her. She prayed for the divine pursuit of Jack's soul, the redeeming grace fered by a suffering Savior. She prayed for deliverance for th she loved. And she prayed for the courage to love him rig to entrust him to the only one who could heal him and whole.

Uptown on Thirty-Fourth Street, Jack Kane paced the floor in his bedroom. The room was shadowed, its only light the dying fire and an oil lamp on the bedside table. The house was quiet and cold, the streets below deserted.

Earlier he had donned his smoking jacket in the expectation of relaxing by the fire, perhaps reading for a time before going to bed. Such optimism had been foolish, he admitted sourly to himself. For hours, thoughts of Samantha had filled his mind like swarming bees. He had thought of nothing else, had done nothing else since arriving home except to walk the floor and think. Think about Samantha.

She had come close to admitting that she loved him tonight. His heart rose to his throat every time he recalled that admission, inadvertent though it had been.

And he had kissed her, there was that. And even though she hadn't actually kissed him back, neither had she resisted him.

Best not to dwell on that, he told himself firmly. Still, he couldn't quite stop the thought of how she had looked at him after he released her, not with the revulsion he had half dreaded, but with her magnificent eyes still shining from the tears that had filled them earlier, and a softness he hadn't seen in them before—at least not for him.

Unwillingly, he also remembered the utter despair that had clouded her features when she told him of the beating that had killed her unborn child, the terrible anguish in her voice when she revealed the bitter truth that she was now barren because of that same beating.

Jack knotted his fists at his sides and went to stand at the window. The night had cleared, the rain finally giving way to a sky studded with random stars and a bright half-moon. He stood looking out, staring into the night, seeing nothing but Samantha's lovely but tormented features. It was incredible to him that he had come to love her so fiercely when she in turn had done everything possible to discourage him. Even the wrenching awareness that marriage with her would never include children, that it would more than likely always see her haunted by the tragedy of her past, wasn't enough to turn him away from her.

Indeed, he couldn't imagine *anything* that could turn him away from her. Except perhaps Samantha herself. If she simply would not have him, if she refused to even consider making a life with him—well, then, what could he do?

There had to be something. Some way to finally make her his. There *had* to be!

He looked up to the pale wisps of cloud passing over the moon. For a long, still moment he watched the sky. Finally, he brought one clenched fist to his mouth, pressing it against his lips so hard he tasted blood. And then for the first time in years, he addressed an unknown Deity he wasn't even sure he believed in—but one in whom Samantha most definitely *did* believe—with an utterance of desperation that began in the very depths of his spirit.

"If you're as real as she believes you are," he grated out, "if you're really out there and as all-powerful as she seems to think you, then show me how to help her. How to heal her. Let me, the make up for all the pain she's suffered. Show me how the kind of a man she deserves, the kind of a man she can there me, mind—but for her. Just—do it for her."

Feeling suddenly self-conscious in spite winds in th wasn't another soul within earshot, Jack ing up pockets of his jacket and started to w But then he stopped and turned bac as he added, "I do love her, you know. More than I ever thought I could love anything or anyone, and that's the truth. I'll take care of her, I promise you. I'll cherish her. And I'll never hurt her, or let anyone else hurt her, not ever again. My word on it."

21

David's Search

I stood beside the couch in tears
Where pale and calm she slept,
And though I've gazed on death for years,
I blush not that I wept.

RICHARD D'ALTON WILLIAMS

David Leslie had never agonized over a patient as he agoni~
over the suffering young woman named Terese.

He had been excruciatingly close to losing her m~
but each time she had surprised him by clinging~
nacity he wouldn't have thought possible in ~
gerously ill. He could actually *see* her fighti~
of death that seemed to hover in the ro~

David had witnessed similar strug~
experience had led him to wond~

ged, valiant spirits who battled so fiercely. So great was the ordeal taking place in this room that he now found himself laboring along with his patient, as if by his own efforts he could somehow facilitate hers.

It had been over a week since Madog Wall had brought her to the mission, and so far there had been no improvement; if anything, her condition had worsened. Most of the time, she drifted in and out of consciousness, and for the past three days, she hadn't been coherent for more than a couple of minutes at a time. David knew she couldn't possibly last much longer if she didn't turn for the better soon.

He fretted that there must be someone he ought to notify, but he had no idea where to look. He hadn't been able to get anything out of the little girl, Shona, and as for Terese, although she had muttered the same word two or three times in the throes of her delirium, David wasn't sure what she was saying or even if it was a name at all. It sounded like "Gaven," but when he questioned Shona, she merely shook her head, obviously as much in the dark as he.

He *did* know that he had become too involved emotionally. Against everything he had been taught—and even against his own intincts—he had allowed himself to make a kind of *attachment* to young woman that was neither professional nor practical.

wasn't only that he was spending too much time at her bed-
He was also sacrificing the few precious hours at night when
et have been taking his own much-needed rest to dig into
ical text he could find, in hopes of discovering some-
ht have missed, some new treatment he didn't know

that he had come to care too much. He knew
re of the pitfalls of becoming emotionally in-
had actually known physicians who had suf-

fered the consequences of ignoring this counsel. He'd never thought it would happen to him. Certainly not with a perfect stranger, one swollen with child, and one with whom he had scarcely exchanged a reasonable conversation.

But it had happened before he'd realized, and now he wasn't quite sure how to extricate himself, how to step back and regain some semblance of emotional distance. And yet he knew he must.

Even if she survived—and the thought that she might not wrenched his heart—there was more than likely a husband waiting somewhere, worrying about her, wondering what had happened to her. David knew his own part in this ought to be limited to treating her condition and trying to learn anything he could that might lead to that husband, or at least to a member of her family.

The thing was, he didn't even know where to start. He supposed he could always go and speak with Madog Wall, see if the man could think of anything at all that might help. But he was fairly certain it would be a waste of time. Wall claimed he had never seen either Terese or Shona before the day he brought them to the mission.

A soft moan from his patient jarred David back to his surroundings. He put a hand to Terese's forehead, and the heat from her nearly scorched him.

On the other side of the bed, Shona sat, silent and watching David. He forced a smile but could see she The child had something almost painfully *unchild* that was disconcerting to say the least.

But then, from what David had seen of t Ireland, most of them, children included kind of adversity and tragedy that tende one survived at all. The little girl acro dured more affliction in her few years than most adults could even imagine. There was no telling what she . . . and Terese . . . might have gone through up till now.

And, sad to say, he seemed incapable of making things any better for them.

***

When David finally found time later in the day to pay a visit to the *Vanguard,* he found Madog Wall lying on his back, working on the underside of one of the newspaper wagons. The big man hauled himself up, wiping his grease-smeared hands down the sides of his trousers as he mumbled a greeting.

It would have been easy to feel threatened by the big, lumbering Irishman's size and battered features. But David had come in contact with Wall on other occasions and by now knew that he wasn't the mean-spirited thug he appeared at first glance. Mostly he saw in Madog Wall a rather shy giant who thought slowly and spoke haltingly, but almost certainly wasn't vicious or cruel. Wall *was* said to be fiercely protective of his employer, the notorious Black Jack Kane, but David didn't necessarily think that was a character flaw.

Today, however, he was surprised to sense a certain evasiveness in the man as he inquired about Terese and Shona. Madog seemed almost defensive, insisting that he knew nothing—"nothing a'tall" about the girls.

"Didn't I already tell you everything I know, Doc?" he said, still rubbing his large hands against his thighs. "They showed up on a Sunday, they did, lookin' half starved and poorly. When the older one didn't knotted away, I brought them to the mission house. I done the only sense to do, don't you see?"

"You did the right thing, Madog," David assured him. "I'm simply trying to find out if by any chance they have relatives or friends here in the city. Terese—the older of the two—is seriously ill. I was hoping she might have said something to you, anything at all, that might help me to locate a family member." He paused, studying Wall for a moment. "You're quite sure there was nothing?"

The other frowned and looked away. "It's as I said, Doc, I don't know nothin' else. The older girl, she passed out almost as soon as they showed up."

Still, David couldn't shake the feeling that Wall was concealing something. Perhaps it was only because he'd had his hopes disappointed. There seemed no reason for the man to dissemble, after all.

"Well, then—if you're sure—" He gave a nod, turned, and started to go.

"Doc?"

David turned back. Wall seemed to be squirming where he stood. His small eyes went over David's face as if he were trying to gauge whether or not he ought to say more.

"What is it, Madog? Did you think of something?"

The big man shoved his hands down into his pockets. He pursed his lips together, watching David. After a frustratingly long time, he finally replied. "Well, there was one thing—and mind, I'm that certain the girl wasn't tellin' the truth—but she did keep goin' on about how Mr. Kane was 'expecting' them."

David's frowned. "Mr. Kane? *Jack* Kane?"

Wall nodded, his mouth twisting with disapproval. "I didn't pay her any heed, of course. Sure, and Mr. Kane wouldn't be acquainted with two poor immigrant girls such as them, now would he?"

David stared at him. "Did you tell Mr. Kane about this, Madog?"

Wall shook his head. "He wasn't here at the time, and '

didn't seem to be no need to bother him with it. Then after a day or so I just forgot." His expression changed to a troubled frown. "Now that you come askin', though, I wonder if I did wrong."

Wall was clearly seeking for reassurance, but David's mind had begun to race. "Tell me exactly what the girl said, Madog. Try to remember everything."

Wall took his hands out of his pockets and wiped one over his bald head. "Well, let me think now. She was set on finding out Mr. Kane's home address. Said he was *expecting* them—her and the little lass. Is she all right, by the way, Doc—the little girl?"

David gave a nod. "She's fine. Go on, Madog. Please. What else do you remember?"

Wall shrugged. "Just that she was set on seeing Mr. Kane. *Right away,* she kept saying. She was a pushy one, she was."

"Anything else? Think carefully, Madog."

Wall shook his head. "No, sir. That's all there was." He cast another uneasy look at David. "Should I have mentioned it to Mr. Kane, do you think, Doc?"

"Well . . . yes, actually, Madog. I believe you should have told Mr. Kane. It might be important."

"But I'm that sure Mr. Kane wouldn't have had nothing to do with that girl's . . . condition, Doc! She isn't the sort he'd traffic with. Mr. Kane is an *important man.*"

David was beginning to feel some pique at Wall's adulation of his employer, whose reputation couldn't have been much more deplorable. He reminded himself that Wall was obviously rather slow-witted and slavishly loyal. There was no call to be impatient with the man.

"Well, what's done is done," he said. "The important thing is that you tell Mr. Kane now. You need to tell him exactly what you've told me without delay."

Wall's face underwent an immediate transformation. David supposed it spoke leagues about the infamous Jack Kane if a man like Madog Wall could be intimidated by the mere thought of his displeasure.

Almost in the same instant, however, the thick features seemed to relax. "Can't do that, Doc. Mr. Kane is away."

"Away? For how long?"

Wall shrugged. "A day or two more, I expect. He and that young Mr. Sheridan went up to Albany to some sort of a big political conference and a—a *banquet*. Whatever that might be," he added.

The thought went through David's mind that a day or two might be too late. "Is there anyone else who might have information about this, Madog? Someone who works with Mr. Kane, perhaps?"

Wall frowned, rubbing a hand over his chin. "Well, there's Mrs. Harte, of course."

"Mrs. Harte?"

"Aye, Mrs. Harte—the lady who sometimes works for Mr. Kane. Real nice lady, Mrs. Harte. Mr. Kane seems to admire her a lot." Wall gave a knowing smile—not a leer, but more a pleased expression, for his employer's good judgment. "Now that I think of it, seems to me she's been helping Mr. Kane and young Mr. Sheridan with some kind of a newspaper story about the people coming across."

A thought struck David. "You don't mean Mrs. *Samantha* Harte, by any chance, do you?"

"That's her. Do you know Mrs. Harte, then, Doc? Isn't she a fine lady?"

David gave a distracted nod. He had met Samantha Harte several times, actually, most often in response to a summons for medical attention for one of the immigrant families in the area. She had

could see what the doctor had meant when he'd described her as "seriously ill."

She saw something else as well. Watching David Leslie, there was little doubt that he had formed an emotional attachment to his patient. He couldn't seem to drag his eyes away from the stricken young woman, even as he replied to Samantha's questions.

The girl *was* lovely. Despite her grave condition, there was no mistaking her comeliness. Her strong, arresting features had been ravaged by disease and, probably, the extreme privation so common to the Irish immigrants. But in a better time she must have been positively striking.

Samantha was almost relieved that Cavan wasn't here to see his sister's condition. She could just imagine what it would do to him to see her in such a state.

After another moment, she turned her attention to the child who sat on the other side of Terese Sheridan's bed. She'd been aware of that bright, intense gaze ever since her arrival at the mission and several times had ventured a smile of reassurance. Invariably, however, she received only a solemn, blue-eyed gaze that seemed to hold an entire lifetime of sorrow.

Samantha sensed that this child had had no reason to smile for a very long time, if ever. The thought brought her an immeasurable sadness.

She went around the bed to the little girl, who watched her with the guarded stare of a stray kitten. "You must be Shona," she said gently, waiting for some acknowledgment from the child.

When none came, she tried again. "I'm Samantha, Shona. I want you to know how sorry I am that no one was at the harbor to meet you. There was some confusion, and we didn't know you'd arrived. We should have been there." She paused. "Your brother, Shona? Didn't he come with you?"

The little girl's lip trembled. "He died. Tully died at the hospital." The look of bewilderment and pain in the child's eyes cut through Samantha like a scream of grief.

David Leslie had been watching them. "What hospital is that, Shona?" he asked gently.

The girl hesitated, her gaze going to Terese. "She said it was called 'Tompkinsville.'"

Samantha sucked in a quick breath. So they had been caught up in that terrible place after all! "Oh, Shona, I'm so sorry! I know all this has been awful for you. But we're going to help you now, I promise."

The girl turned slowly back to face Samantha, and that small, thin face with the haunted eyes again tore at her heart. This child, who could not be more than nine or ten years old, surely, wore a look of wretchedness and defeat that made Samantha want to gather her into her arms and comfort her. Yet she sensed the gesture would be rebuffed. This was a child who almost certainly would not dare to trust such a show of emotion.

So she simply stood there, hurting for Shona Madden and Terese Sheridan, at the same time painfully aware of her own helplessness and inadequacy. After another moment, she shrugged out of her coat and turned to David Leslie. "What can I do to help?"

He looked at her with something akin to relief. "Would you mind staying for a while? I need to tend to some of the other patients."

Samantha loosened the cuffs of her shirtwaist and briskly rolled up her sleeves. "Of course, I'll stay. But I'd like to get a message to Mr. Kane as soon as possible." She nodded to Terese Sheridan. "He and her brother are in Albany."

David Leslie looked at her. "So she *does* have family here! I was hoping there would be someone."

Samantha dipped a cloth in the basin by the bed. "Not only does she have her brother, who's going to be absolutely thrilled to find her, but she's also under the sponsorship of the *Vanguard*. That's where I come in." She glanced at the little girl who seemed to be watching her every move. "And she has her friend, Shona, of course. I know how much that must mean to her."

David Leslie gave a wan smile, and Samantha noticed again how tired he looked. It was obvious that Terese Sheridan had a highly dedicated doctor looking after her. That, along with the love and concern of her brother, and the resources of Jack's newspaper as well, would make it seem that she had a great deal in her favor.

But as she turned back to the suffering girl on the bed, she wondered if anything would really make a difference.

❧❦❧

Samantha was aware of Shona's close scrutiny throughout the evening as she tended to Terese Sheridan. The child scarcely moved, except once to go downstairs to eat, and even then one of the women volunteers had to coax her.

She returned in scarcely no time, sitting down on the same bedside chair to resume her vigil. Other than shifting her gaze from Terese to Samantha periodically, she remained quiet and unmoving. If Samantha attempted to draw her into a conversation, she would make an almost inaudible reply, then again fall silent.

Samantha ached for the child's misery. With her entire family lost to her, she was apparently all alone except for Terese Sheridan. She seemed such a forlorn little thing, with those sorrowful eyes and solemn demeanor. Samantha wished she could think of something to brighten those pinched features, but she felt at a loss to manage more than a consoling smile every now and then. This was a very sad little girl, badly in need of affection and attention. But the only person left to whom she was likely to turn now lay hovering between life and death, according to David Leslie.

Samantha felt Shona watching her. For a moment their eyes met, and she realized that in addition to the sadness brimming in the child's gaze, there was also a sharp glint of fear lurking there.

She knew a moment of dismay and even anger, that any child should have to feel so abandoned and so utterly alone. Without warning, her thoughts went to Jack. From what she knew, he couldn't have been all that much older than Shona Madden when he arrived in New York, still a boy, with the sole responsibility of a younger sister and a baby brother.

As hard as it was to picture Jack ever being frightened of *anything,* it occurred to her now that he must have been terrified. Cast onto the shores of a foreign country, in a strange city, with no one to meet him, no one to turn to for help—how could he *not* have been frightened?

Her heart softened even more toward him as she tried to picture that unyielding chin and hard-set mouth, the restless dark eyes and strong, always busy hands on the person of a bewildered fourteen-year-old boy. A boy with no parents, no home, no friends or family waiting for him—only a sprawling, noisy city teeming with hidden dangers and unknown terrors.

She wondered how much of that boy still lingered in the man—a man who could go cold and stonyhearted in an instant, whose rage unleashed was the stuff of outrageous gossip and whose very name had become synonymous with power and notoriety.

How much of what Jack had become had begun with that frightened, lonely boy who had entered the city with nothing but the clothes on his back and the will of a titan?

She could have wept for them both, for the little girl sitting across from her and for the man she sometimes thought she really didn't know at all. Who could say which of the two had actually suffered most?

She looked back at Shona Madden, who had taken Terese's hand between both her own and was rubbing it gently, over and over again in a kind of insistent rhythm, as if to will her return to consciousness.

Again Samantha knew a fierce urge to reassure the girl, to tell her she was no longer alone and that everything was going to be all right very soon now.

To her sorrow, she didn't think the girl would believe it. In truth, she wasn't sure she believed it herself. And so she kept silent as she went on trying to cool the raging fever of the girl who lay delirious, seemingly losing the battle for her life, while the child with the pain-filled eyes willed her to survive.

23

Long Night's Vigil

Have mercy, Heaven, on feeble clay—
Hear Thy stricken people pray.
RICHARD D'ALTON WILLIAMS

It was after nine o'clock the next night before Jack and Cavan arrived at Grace Mission. Samantha was still there. She hadn't left Terese Sheridan's bedside except to eat in the mission kitchen and take a brief rest the night before. The child, Shona, had slept only sporadically; for the most part she, too, remained seated by the bed, watching over the older girl with a steady, solemn intensity.

Samantha knew she must appear altogether disheveled by now, but for once she didn't care how she might look to Jack. Her only thought was one of overwhelming relief when he and Cavan Sheridan walked in.

Nor did it occur to her to be in the least surprised that Jack would accompany his young reporter on so personal a quest. She never questioned but what he would come, once word of Terese Sheridan's condition reached him. Not only did he hold Cavan in high regard, but Samantha suspected that he had also developed a kind of protective, big-brotherly affection for him. At times she wondered if Cavan Sheridan hadn't in some way helped to ease the absence of Jack's younger brother, Brady.

She rose at the sight of them, catching her breath at the anguished expression on Cavan's face the moment he saw his sister. Jack must have noticed, too, for he grasped the boy's shoulder as they approached the bed.

Samantha couldn't begin to imagine what must be going through Cavan's mind as he gazed down on his sister—his only surviving family member—for the first time in years. Like Jack, he had left Ireland years ago, when he was still a boy, so Terese would have been only a child at the time. Indeed, she was scarcely more than a child now, despite the fact that she was carrying a baby of her own.

Jack gave her a long look, releasing Cavan's shoulder as they came to stand on the other side of the bed from Samantha and Shona. "How is she?" Jack asked, his expression skeptical after another glance at Terese.

Trying not to alarm Cavan, Samantha chose her words carefully. "There's been . . . no change as yet. She's still very ill."

Jack searched her gaze for a moment, then stood watching as Cavan dropped to his knees beside the bed.

Samantha could have wept for the stricken look on his face as he knelt there, staring at his sister, who lay as still as death itself, except for her harsh, labored breathing.

Cavan's eyes held utter torment as he covered his sister's hand with both of his. His gaze traveled the length of her form, linger-

ing only a second or two on the swollen mound of her abdomen
beneath the bed linens. Samantha saw him shudder, then bring
Terese's hand to his lips.

His voice sounded hoarse and strangled as he murmured to her.
"Oh, *alannah, alannah,* I should never have left you behind. What
have I done to you?"

Again Jack reached to grasp his shoulder. Samantha was surprised at the strained expression that settled over him all of a sudden. He had the look of a man who had suffered a great blow. His
usually dusky complexion was strangely pale, and as he stood gaz-
ing down on Terese Sheridan, he was perspiring as though the
room weren't almost uncomfortably chill. As she watched, his gaze
swept the dormitory room like that of a man seeking escape. Yet
he remained with Cavan, one large hand gripping the other's
shoulder.

As for Cavan, he seemed unaware of anyone else in the room as
he bent even closer to his sister, tears streaming down his cheeks.
He went on crooning to her, now in the strange tongue Samantha
had come to recognize as Gaelic. Across the bed her eyes met
Jack's, and he gave a small nod of his head to indicate they should
leave the two alone.

❦

The corridor outside the room was dimly lit, the building hushed
with the stillness of night except for an occasional outcry from one
of the women in the dormitory.

For a moment Jack stood staring back into the room, and
Samantha thought he seemed vastly relieved to have left it. Finally,
he turned to her. "You said David Leslie is taking care of the girl?"

Samantha nodded. "Do you know him?"

"Only by reputation. He's said to be a fine doctor."

"Oh, he is, I'm sure! But . . . I wonder just how much he can do. She's *very* ill, Jack."

"Aye, so it would seem. We came none too soon, I'm thinking." He paused. "I wonder if she shouldn't be moved to the hospital."

Samantha expelled a long breath. She was only now beginning to feel the signs of a dragging fatigue and a kind of numb inability to think clearly. "I don't know if it would make any difference, but I suppose we could ask. Doctor Leslie said he'd be back around ten."

She looked up to see him watching her, his dark eyes sharp with concern. "You look exhausted," he said bluntly. "How long have you been here?"

Samantha evaded his question. "I'm all right. I thought I should stay, at least until Cavan got here."

"Well, he's here now. I'm going to take you home."

"No, not yet," Samantha told him firmly. "Didn't you see his face? He shouldn't be alone . . . if something happens. I believe I'll stay awhile longer."

Impatience sparked in Jack's eyes but quickly subsided. "If you must," he said. "I'll stay for a bit, too, then. I'd like to see what the doctor has to say."

Samantha was too tired . . . and too grateful for his presence . . . to argue. The truth was that she *wanted* him to stay. She felt the need for the strength and steadiness he seemed to impart simply by being in a room. And at the moment, she feared they were going to need all that and more as the night wore on.

Yet at the same time she puzzled over the strange mood that had come over him. He seemed restless—even agitated—as though something more than sadness for Cavan and Terese Sheridan were gnawing at him. Now that she thought of it, he had been peculiar since he first walked into the room.

"Jack—is there something wrong?"

He shook his head in reply, not quite meeting her gaze. "No, nothing's wrong. I'm a bit tired is all."

Samantha could almost see the shutters slam closed over those dark eyes. She supposed it was possible that her own turbulent emotions and exhaustion were simply playing tricks on her, but she didn't think so. Still, there was no point in thinking he would explain. She had seen the hard set to his mouth, heard the edge in his tone that plainly spoke of barriers that would not be breached.

At least not until she was willing to risk more of her own heart, her *self*, than she had ventured so far.

Back inside the dormitory, Jack could feel Samantha watching him. He stood leaning against the wall nearest the door, while she stood beside Sheridan at his sister's bedside. He hadn't meant to be short with her, but there was no explaining what had come over him at the sight of the Sheridan girl.

He didn't understand it himself; he certainly hadn't *expected* it. But one look at her, lying there, so tragically young, so dangerously ill—so obscenely *violated*—had sent a wall of bitter memories crashing over him like an avalanche.

She didn't look a bit like his mother, this girl. She wasn't dark or delicate, instead appeared tall and almost lanky. Her hair was a copper blaze, where his mother's had been black as jet. And she was younger, this unfortunate lass—quite a bit younger than his mother had been . . . at the last.

He supposed it was her pitiful condition: the illness, the delirium, the pregnancy, the utter *tragedy* of what had happened to her. The savage assault and its bitter consequences.

No, Samantha couldn't possibly understand, couldn't beg comprehend how the sight of the poor girl on the bed h through him like a reaper's scythe, tearing through years of grief and a suppressed rage that even he knew to be irrational. He had no way, no words, of making her understand why the sight of a victimized girl he had never seen before tonight should suddenly threaten to undo him.

But she had seen the change in him, Samantha had, and was troubled by it.

Her eyes had been filled with questions, questions he couldn't answer. He couldn't explain this, not even to Samantha. No one knew the secret that ate at him. No one. Not even Rose or Brady.

Especially not Brady. After all, it was because of Brady he had bottled up the pain and kept his silence all these years, even though there had been times when his insides virtually *screamed* to tell someone the truth.

He glanced around the room, his attention caught by the child who had been sitting beside the Sheridan girl's bed all this time. The little Madden tyke, Samantha had explained. The hollow-eyed wee girl had lost everything—parents, home, brother—and now it seemed she was in danger of losing the one familiar face left to her, the one person who at least knew her and perhaps could relate to her.

His thoughts went to Rose, his own younger sister. She must have been about the same age as the little Madden girl when he'd brought her and Brady across. No doubt she had been just as frightened, too, although at least she had had a big brother to turn to.

His mouth twisted in remembrance. *A big brother indeed!* He had been all of fourteen and as terrified as his younger sister and baby brother—Brady—had been, though he had steeled himself to conceal his fear from them. With nothing but the clothes on their backs and a pittance in his pocket, he had led them out of the harbor into a veritable nightmare.

New York. A city teeming with strangers who spoke in unknown languages. Dogs and pigs running rampant in the streets, rooting through heaps of rotting garbage and waste. Painted women crooking their fingers at him despite his youth and the two wee wanes clutching at him. Filthy street urchins diving in and out among the bustling crowds, shoving and shrieking and begging.

The stink of the sprawling city had seemed like the stench of hell itself, and the angry voices and jostling bodies pressing in on them might have been a legion of demons, so terrifying had they appeared to them that day. Jack had wanted nothing so much as to turn and run, to bolt back onto the ship with his siblings and head home.

But of course by then there had *been* no home.

Somehow they had survived, at first on the squalid streets, then later in the sordid warrens of the Five Points—ah, now *there* was a place that could easily be construed as a demons' den.

He knew what was said about him, now that those ugly years were all in the past: that he'd built an empire with nothing but Irish brass and the devil's luck. In truth, he had built it all from a boiling well of rage and an equally fierce resolve to never again be at the mercy of another human being.

But somewhere inside him, buried so deep he had thought never to confront it again, there had always been the memory of what had driven him here in the first place . . . and a sense of dread he had never admitted to another soul.

And tonight it had taken but a brief glimpse of another's misery to newly ignite his own.

He looked at Samantha and found her watching him. Quickly, he glanced away, but not before he had seen the questions . . . and the hurt in her eyes. And suddenly, for the first time in a *long* tim he found himself wanting—*needing*—to unburden himself, as much to break down any remaining barriers between him and Samantha as to purge himself, at least once, of the dark secret that had driven him out of Ireland, only to ride his soul for all the intervening years with the relentless ferocity of a bloodthirsty vulture.

But this wasn't the time—and certainly not the place. The people in this room had their own pain, their own dark agonies, to deal with. He had come to help, if he could, not to add to their misery. They already had more than enough of their own.

He hesitated for only an instant, then pushed himself away from the wall and started toward the lonely-looking little girl beside the bed.

24

A Meeting in the Mission House

There should be more than trials and tears
For those of young and tender years.
ANONYMOUS

Samantha watched with growing curiosity as Jack went to stand beside Shona. From all appearances, he was managing to carry on a conversation of sorts with the little girl, although the tone of his voice was so low that from the opposite side of the bed one couldn't make out more than a few words of what they were saying.

The child's face was lifted toward Jack, her countenance just as solemn and intent as ever, though perhaps slightly more animated than before. Jack, on the other hand, was smiling: a different kind of smile for him, one with not even a hint of cynicism, no sardonic twist of the mouth, no mocking glint in the eye. There was a gentleness about him now, a softness in his eyes rarely seen.

It occurred to Samantha, with a twinge of guilt, that she really ought to be reassuring Cavan rather than trying to eavesdrop on Jack and the little Madden girl. But Cavan seemed to have withdrawn to a private place occupied only by himself and his sister, and Samantha almost felt that to speak to him at this time would be to intrude. He and Terese had been separated for years, after all, and in spite of the grim circumstances, this had to be an extremely momentous occasion for them . . . and one not necessarily meant to be shared.

Besides, she couldn't help but be intrigued by the scene on the other side of the bed. So she moved away a little, and Jack, seeing her, gave her a smile and gestured that she should come around the bed and join him and his new friend.

⁕

She was a sober little thing, the Madden tyke, but then she had reason to be, given all that she had likely endured in her few brief years. The child was so gossamer thin that Jack fancied she would snap like a butterfly's wing under the slightest amount of pressure.

He recalled Brady's writing that the girl was ten years old, but she might have been two or three years younger, so small and fragile was she. She had a cloud of flaxen hair, so fine it might have been spun silk, and the biggest, most sorrowful blue eyes Jack had ever seen, eyes that seemed enormous in that thin little face. For some incomprehensible reason he suddenly found himself wondering if those eyes had ever lighted with a childish delight instead of the fear and the unhappiness that now looked out at him.

What would it take, he thought, to coax a smile from such a child as this, a child who looked as if she might never have known what it *was* to smile?

"You've met Shona, of course?" Jack said to Samantha as she came to stand beside him. "She's ten years old, it seems, and comes from Limerick."

Samantha smiled at the girl, who ducked her head down as if confused by all this attention. She would have been quite a lovely child had she not been so thin and pale as to appear unhealthy. Even in her malnourished state, with her fair hair in tangles and her face all sharp planes, there was a winsomeness about her that tugged at Samantha's heart.

She was surprised to realize that the child had apparently evoked a similar response in Jack. She looked from one to the other. Jack had stooped over to reduce the distance between himself and the little girl, who was watching him closely with something akin to awe—and perhaps a measure of fearfulness as well. It occurred to Samantha that to one so small, Jack must appear a veritable giant, and a somewhat dark, forbidding one as well.

"Do you understand who we are, lass?" he asked the child, his tone as quiet and as solemn as Shona's countenance.

Shona stared up at him, studying him as if bewildered by his attention. "Mr. Kane."

Jack nodded. "That's exactly right, just as I told you. And this is Mrs. Harte, my . . . good friend and one of the editors from the newspaper." He paused. "Do you know what that is, Shona—a newspaper?"

The child shook her head, her gaze never leaving Jack's face.

Interesting, Samantha thought, that Jack had realized right away that a child like Shona would very likely have no conception of something as common as a newspaper. Not many would have thought of such a thing, herself included.

"Well then, we shall have to bring you a copy whe

again," said Jack cheerfully. "A newspaper is a little like a book, you see—though with not as many pages. People read it to learn what's going on about the city and perhaps find stories of particular interest to them. The name of my newspaper is the *Vanguard,* by the way."

He motioned toward Cavan. "The lad there with your friend, Terese, is her brother, Cavan. They haven't seen each other for a number of years, did you know that?"

Shona glanced across the bed to watch Cavan and Terese for a moment but made no reply.

The exchange went on like that for several minutes, almost entirely between Jack and the child, with Samantha merely looking on and nodding her agreement every now and then as called for.

She supposed she should have found it curious, how Jack seemed to have managed to win over the girl—if not her trust, exactly, at least her interest—in such a short time. Yet watching the two, his rapport with the child seemed so easy, so natural, that anyone who didn't know better would have assumed he was an old hand at dealing with children, that he almost certainly had a family of his own.

Samantha knew, of course, that he had raised his younger brother and sister almost entirely single-handedly; that might account for the ease with which he communicated with the Madden child. Still, she couldn't help but remember how quick he had been to insist that he could accept a marriage without children, once he'd learned that she was barren.

As she stood there, watching him with the forlorn little girl, a sudden wave of sadness rose in her. The painful realization of what she would be cheating him of, should she ever agree to his proposal, nearly doubled her over, and she had to struggle to keep from bolting from the room.

But in the same instant she told herself she was fretting over nothing, because she *wouldn't* agree to his proposal; she couldn't even *consider* it.

"Samantha?"

She looked up to find him watching her with a question in his eyes. Samantha shook her head a little to clear it. "I'm sorry?"

"I was telling Shona that perhaps one day soon she could come and have supper with us. Would that be all right with you?"

Samantha looked from one to the other, barely managing a smile. "Yes, of course. I'd . . . like that very much."

She deliberately avoided looking at Jack. "Perhaps I could have you both to my place for a meal," she said with forced enthusiasm. "We'll have to make plans."

Jack seemed to be caught off guard as much as Samantha by the child's reply. "Thank you very much, but I'd want to wait until Terese is well enough to come, too, please."

Samantha didn't know what to say and looked to Jack for help. He straightened, taking his time to answer. "I'm sure your friend, Terese, wouldn't mind if you came just once without her," he said carefully. "Later, we'll all of us celebrate your arrival in proper fashion."

Samantha turned to look at Cavan, who had risen to his feet and now stood staring down at his sister. She despised herself for giving in to the pessimism that had been lurking at the edges of her mind all evening, but at this moment it was difficult to believe that Terese Sheridan . . . or Cavan either . . . would be likely to have cause for celebration in the near future.

Unwilling to give in to her own dismal thoughts, she walked quickly around the bed and took Cavan by the hand. "Would you like me to pray with you?" she asked him. His eyes filled as he nodded, and Samantha squeezed his hand. She wished she could do more, but at this point she believed the most important thing she could do for Cavan or Terese Sheridan was to pray, and pray unceasingly.

As she and Cavan knelt beside the bed, she saw that Shona had followed their lead and was kneeling, hands folded, looking up at Jack as if she clearly expected him to join them.

He looked at the child, then at Samantha, but merely stood aside, his jaw set in a stubborn line, his gaze carefully averted from Terese Sheridan.

By the time David returned to check on Terese, it was after ten. He stopped just inside the room, surprised by the contingent surrounding her bed. Samantha Harte and a young man were kneeling, obviously praying, as was Shona, while a startlingly tall, dark-haired man in a well-tailored overcoat stood watching them.

The man locked eyes with David for an instant, then returned his attention to Samantha Harte, still deep in prayer. Although David suspected that the young man kneeling beside Terese's bed might be her brother, he couldn't think who the other man might be. After another moment, he bowed his own head and added a fervent request to that of the others.

Afterward, Samantha Harte introduced him to Terese Sheridan's brother, a likable young fellow who was obviously devastated by what had happened to his sister. David wished there were something he could say to alleviate Cavan Sheridan's fears, but under the circumstances false reassurance would be worse than nothing at all.

The dark, imposing man he'd noticed on entering turned out to be Jack Kane—*the* Jack Kane. Upon their introduction, David had all he could do to conceal his surprise. From everything he had heard about the publishing giant, he would hardly have expected

Kane to show up here on behalf of an immigrant Irish girl. Of course, Kane was thoroughly Irish himself, and it was his newspaper that was funding a number of immigrant resettlements. Even so, it seemed more than a little peculiar to find him making a personal call at a mission house.

For that matter, Jack Kane himself wasn't at all what David might have expected. Oh, it was easy to sense a certain . . . hardness in the man, a self-confidence, perhaps, even a kind of arrogance, not to mention the unmistakable aura of power that seemed to vibrate in the very air around him. There was no mistaking the fact that this was a man accustomed to having his own way; he wore authority like an outer garment. Yet there was an openness about Kane when he shook David's hand and looked him square in the eye that seemed to instantly draw him in and include him as an equal.

It soon became apparent to David as well that Jack Kane's concern for Terese was wholly genuine, if unexpected.

"I was wondering what you would think," Kane inclined his head toward Terese, "of moving her to the hospital."

"I've considered that, and frankly, I think it might be treacherous to move her just now," David replied. "Besides, in my opinion, nothing can be done for her at the hospital that isn't being done right here."

David found it necessary to actually look up to Kane—an uncommon occurrence for him, since he was nearly six feet himself. It seemed to him that Kane's expression projected no hint of condescension nor any suggestion that David might be inadequate. To the contrary, he felt the man was merely exploring all the possibilities for helping Terese—which, of course, was what David himself wanted, too.

Kane studied him for a moment, then nodded. "You're reputed to be an excellent doctor. Do you agree with that?"

David lifted an eyebrow but had to smile a little at Kane's directness. "Of course," he said dryly. "How else would I have attained such a lucrative practice?"

It was Jack Kane's turn to quirk an eyebrow.

"Yes, Mr. Kane," David went on, "as it happens, I do consider myself a good doctor."

Again Kane gave that short, expedient nod. "Yet you work almost entirely with the poor."

David glanced at Samantha Harte, who stood watching the two of them. "It's where God put me," he said matter-of-factly. "I expect Mrs. Harte would understand what I mean."

David felt himself being measured under Jack Kane's scrutiny and had to make an effort not to squirm a little. The man was almost disturbingly *intense.*

"Here's the thing, Dr. Leslie," Kane said brusquely. "If you say she shouldn't be moved, I'll accept that. But I expect you to do everything you can for the girl. If there's any question of money, you've only to ask. I—my newspaper—will be paying her expenses, for however long it's necessary. I'd like her to have the very best of care, whatever it takes."

David bristled a little at his tone. "I give all my patients the best care I can manage," he said shortly.

"No doubt you do," Kane said in the same clipped tones. "I'm simply asking you to make Miss Sheridan a special case."

David studied the man, but Kane's expression was now unreadable. Whatever warmth he might have imagined he'd seen earlier had given way to a shuttered, flinty stare. Only slightly annoyed, David decided that this was simply Jack Kane being . . . Jack Kane.

What Kane couldn't know, of course, was that Terese Sheridan had already become a "special case" to David. A very special one indeed.

Samantha could see nothing in David Leslie's face that gave reason for encouragement, no sign of any change for the better in Terese. Her heart ached for Cavan, who hovered nearby, watching the doctor closely, almost fearfully.

Finally, Dr. Leslie asked them to step out of the room so he could examine Terese. Shona made no move to go, as though the decision had already been made for her to stay.

Cavan followed Samantha and Jack out of the room with obvious reluctance. In the hallway, he turned to Samantha. "Mrs. Harte? Is there a chance, do you think?"

Samantha delayed her reply. The truth was that she held little optimism for Terese Sheridan's recovery. Yet Cavan was obviously pleading for some remnant of hope, no matter how slim, and she couldn't quite bring herself to disappoint him.

She felt Jack's hand on her shoulder as if to steady her. "Cavan . . . I don't know what to think," she ventured. "Terese's condition is . . . critical, as you know. It seems to me that all we can do for her right now is to keep praying."

"Aye," Cavan said dully, his expression bleak. "I know she's in a bad way, all right." He stopped, and in that instant something like anger flared in his eyes. "'Tis a hard thing to grasp, why God would allow such a bitter blow to fall to her. So much suffering, and her so young. There's no telling all that she's gone through, and now this—"

He stopped, turning abruptly to walk off as if he could not get away quickly enough.

Instinctively, Samantha reached out to him, but Jack stayed her hand. "Let him go, Samantha. He might do well to be alone for a time. Besides, you can't help him. No one can help with a grief so great."

Samantha turned to look at him. Something in his tone of

voice—a kind of weary knowing, a sad but certain conviction—caused her to study him carefully.

She saw in his face a look of raw anguish, and she was struck by the inexplicable sensation that, for a very long time now, Jack had burned with some sort of agonizing pain that the tragic incident with Terese Sheridan had somehow rekindled.

"Jack? What's wrong?"

He didn't answer, instead looked away, as if staring off into a great distance. The past, Samantha wondered. Was he remembering whatever had happened to cause him such despair?

"Jack?" she prompted gently. "Can't you tell me?"

He turned back to her, searching her eyes, the pain in his still unabated. "Do you really want to know, Samantha?"

"Yes, of course I do."

"Why?"

"Because you seem so sad," she said directly. Unable to stop herself, she put a hand to his face.

He caught her hand and held it to his cheek. "The only time I am sad these days," he said softly, "is when I'm away from you."

For an uneasy moment, Samantha thought he was about to revert to his more typical role of the seductive rogue. It was a role she found increasingly difficult to reconcile with the great gentleness of which she knew him to be capable, and the kindness and genuine compassion he could display when least expected.

For the most part, Samantha had learned to look past the masks he was given to donning. The man behind those masks, after all, was the man she had come to know . . . and love.

The thought froze in her mind. There it was again, that unbidden admission of her feelings for Jack, feelings that both thrilled and terrified her. Heart hammering, she tried desperately to cage the thought, but she might as well have given actual voice to the words, might as well have *shouted* them down the corridor, so clearly and insistently did they continue to echo in her heart.

In any event, she must have been wrong about his intentions, at least for the moment. Although his dark gaze was piercing and almost intimate, it seemed to hold nothing but a surprising tenderness and the same searching question that had been there before.

Slowly, then, he released her hand. "Perhaps I *will* tell you, *mavourneen.*" His voice was a low rumble in the hushed hallway. "But not here, not tonight. There is already enough darkness afoot in this place. I'll not be dredging up still more. For now, why don't you go back inside while I go and see about the boy?"

Samantha studied him for another moment, but she sensed he was right. Their responsibility here tonight was to Cavan and his sister, not to each other.

God willing, there would be another time and place to learn just what lay behind the pool of sorrow in his eyes.

25

Through the Eyes of the Beholder

The Lord sees not as man sees; man looks on the outward appearance,
but the Lord looks on the heart.

1 S A M U E L   1 6 : 7

THE CLADDAGH, IRELAND, LATE NOVEMBER

The afternoon was cold and dreary, with a soft rain that showed no signs of abating soon. Brady had covered his parcels well with three thicknesses of canvas, but even so, by the time he reached the Claddagh, the weight felt damp under his arm.

He half ran up the path to Gabriel's house, stopping at the door to pull in a couple of deep, fortifying breaths before knocking. As he'd expected, it was Gabriel who answered. The big fisherman showed no sign of pleasure at the sight of Brady. That, too, was to be expected.

From the look on Gabriel's face, Brady knew he would have to talk fast, and so he plunged right into his discourse. "I apologize for dropping by unannounced like this, Gabriel, but I'll be leaving soon, you see, and wanted you to have these before I go."

He shifted the paintings to both hands, holding them out to Gabriel. The big fisherman glanced from Brady to the paintings, then back at Brady. The bright blue eyes remained cold, the craggy features implacable.

"They're portraits," Brady explained, pushing them at Gabriel with such persistence it would have been awkward for him *not* to take them. Even so, the other made no move toward acceptance.

"They're portraits," Brady said again. "One of each of you—Roweena, Evie, and yourself. I did them some time ago, with the intention of making them Christmas gifts. Since I've decided to leave before then, I thought I'd go ahead and bring them by. Won't you take a look at them?"

Gabriel Vaughan's face, Brady reflected, would have foiled Michelangelo. The man might have been chiseled from granite, so resolute and unyielding was that bearded countenance. With the pronounced aquiline nose and the deep blue eyes so piercing they could have shattered an iceberg, the big fisherman never failed to remind Brady of one of the ancient clan chieftains—a *warrior* chieftain, at that.

At the moment, he had all he could do not to squirm under Gabriel's narrow-eyed scrutiny. He could see the play of emotions flitting across the giant's features: surprise, skepticism, suspicion, and finally what appeared to be a reluctant desire to accept the proffered gifts.

"Step in, then," said Gabriel after a noticeable hesitation. There was no mistaking the grudging tone in his invitation.

Brady would have liked nothing better than to accept, but to do so would mean going against the casual air he hoped to convey.

"I'd really like to, Gabriel, but I have an appointment. I just wanted to drop these off while I had the chance."

That said, he finally managed to press the paintings into the other's hands. "I hope you like them."

Gabriel studied him. "You say you'll be leaving soon?"

Brady nodded, giving a quick, somewhat rueful smile. "Afraid so. I still have a lot of territory to cover."

"When will you go?"

"Oh, not for a couple of weeks yet. But I'm going to be pretty busy in the meantime. I still have some things to finish up in the city before I leave. I'm going to head north, to Westport, then on to Sligo."

Gabriel nodded, regarding him thoughtfully for a moment. "You might as well come in and say your good-byes, then. Since you'll be leaving soon." He paused. "If you want."

Brady pretended to hesitate. "Well, all right. Perhaps for just a moment. I do have to be on my way soon, though."

He saw Roweena the instant he walked inside the cottage. She was stirring something in the large black pot hanging inside the hearth. She gave no smile, merely a furtive, quick glance and a nod before turning back to her work.

Evie, however, came trundling across the room in a rush. "What's this, Brady Kane? What have you brought us? And where have you been?"

As always, she piped his name in her childish singsong voice as if it were but one word: *Bradykane*. Brady smiled at her and gestured toward the paintings, which Gabriel was laying out on the table.

"Here, Gabriel, let me help you with those," he said, pulling the canvas wrappings off the one on top, which was the portrait of Evie.

He held it up to the child, and she slapped both hands to her cheeks, her eyes going wide, her mouth pursing in a circle of surprise and delight. "'Tis *myself!*" she cried, bobbing up and down. "You made a painting of *me,* Brady Kane!"

"It is you, indeed," Brady said, laughing at her antics. "Mischievous imp that you are."

The next portrait was of Roweena. Brady held it up for their admiration—in his own estimation, this was his finest work to date—but Roweena hung back, clearly feeling awkward and badly flustered. Color stained her cheeks as she finally approached, and she kept looking from the painting to Gabriel—but never at Brady.

"Ohhh, Roweena!" cried Evie. "See how beautiful you are! Didn't I tell you? Didn't I?"

Roweena only blushed even more furiously as Gabriel shushed the child. Brady discreetly refrained from making any observations about the portraits, especially Roweena's. But in truth he thought he *had* managed to capture her delicate beauty, her fragile grace, as well as the high spirits that sometimes flared in those magnificent eyes when least expected.

Now he uncovered the painting of Gabriel. The big man was clearly discomfited by what was, Brady felt with no small amount of pride, an impressive likeness, if not entirely realistic. The force of the man, the strength and power so evident in every move he made, had somehow come through. But even Brady recognized the fact that something was either askew or lacking; his rendering of the stubborn black hair, the proud nose, the flashing eyes, the rugged jaw—although technically true to form—failed to capture the elusive essence of the giant.

There was something about Gabriel Vaughan that simply could not be contained by a piece of canvas. Perhaps that accounted for the puzzlement in Roweena's eyes—and in Evie's, too, to some extent—as they studied the portrait of Gabriel. Both of them kept stealing glances at Gabriel as though trying to identify just what was different from the man in the painting.

For the most part, Brady's stay was gratifying. Although Roweena never looked at him directly or said a word to him, Brady sensed that she was pleased by the portrait, if self-conscious about all the attention that accompanied it. He also suspected that the mere fact of Gabriel's allowing him entrance had given her some satisfaction.

As for Evie, the child didn't quit chirping about her "par-tret" the entire time Brady was there. And Gabriel, although obviously at a loss about his own likeness, did seem taken by the girls' portraits, from which he could not seem to tear his eyes away.

All the way back to the city, Brady could scarcely contain his elation. No mistake about it, his plan was working just as he'd hoped.

Soon now—very soon—he could play his trump card.

By evening, only Evie seemed to have lost interest in the portraits. She had propped her likeness against the corner wall of the kitchen and gone outside to empty the washbasin. She would not return for several minutes, Roweena knew—not until she had "followed the first stars," as she liked to say, and dawdled a bit in the yard.

In the meantime, Roweena sat at the table where the *faideog* flickered in the draught. The wick was nearly too short for the tray of oil and would soon have to be replaced. From time to time she stole a glance at Gabriel's portrait, dappled in the glow of the firelight. Ignoring his protests, she had positioned his likeness on top of the dresser, where it could be seen from any place in the room.

As to her own image, she would have tucked it away behind the curtain if Gabriel had not insisted that it remain where he had placed it, resting against the hearth wall. She watched him for a moment, sitting in his chair beside the fire, seemingly lost in thought entirely and oblivious to her presence in the room.

Just as well, for she would not have him notice how his portrait drew her gaze. It was not merely the fascination his strong, rugged features held for her, although in truth she had always found Gabriel pleasing to look on—unobserved, of course. But what most commanded her interest in the painting was the obvious difference in how she saw Gabriel as compared to how *Brady Kane* apparently saw him.

For the life of her, she couldn't fathom how Brady could be so blind to Gabriel's true appearance. No matter how closely she searched, she could find no trace of the kindness, the wisdom, the dry humor, the *gentleness,* so much a part of Gabriel's nature. There was no light in the eyes, no tenderness about the mouth—no softening whatsoever of the rough-hewn countenance she knew by heart.

The face in the portrait was more that of a hard, unyielding man, perhaps even a sour-tempered man. A man who had never known a sunset or a song, who had never rescued a baby bird from the bushes, never tended to a child's scraped knee or carried that same child, laughing, on his sturdy shoulders.

Ah, no, the man with the cold, relentless visage in the painting wasn't Gabriel. Not *her* Gabriel.

Her Gabriel . . .

Roweena caught her breath at the effrontery of her own thoughts. How had such irrational musings gained a foothold on her mind?

She had no right to think of Gabriel in such a way, had no right to think of him in *any* way other than in the role in which he had placed himself—the role of her guardian. Clearly, that was how he saw himself in relation to her, and so must she.

Even so, she could not comprehend Brady Kane's apparent inability to see Gabriel as he really was.

This much she knew: Gabriel might not be to her all she would wish. But she *knew* him, knew his heart, his spirit—knew the good things, the noble things that made him the man he was.

Brady Kane had rendered only a shell of the man she knew, and she somehow resented him for it almost as if he had stolen something from Gabriel.

Gabriel could not seem to drag his gaze away from the portrait of Roweena, now bathed in the flickering glow from the hearth fire. It was inconceivable to him how Brady Kane could have captured her likeness with such clarity and perfection. He seemed to have missed not the smallest detail, not the slightest aspect of her loveliness. Even the tiny imperfections—the slight rise at the bridge of her nose, the almost imperceptible way one corner of her mouth would lift higher than the other when she smiled, the small birthmark just below her left ear which time had nearly faded to nothing—had been caught by the American's considerable skill and depicted with uncanny accuracy. Kane had missed nothing, it seemed. So lifelike, so compelling was his portrait of Roweena that it almost seemed to breathe under one's scrutiny.

But it wasn't the realism of the portrait that confounded Gabriel. What had set his mind to spinning had little to do with the exceptional ability of the artist or even the stunning, true-to-life resemblance of the painting to Roweena. It was something much more elusive, something another might have missed.

But Gabriel had practically raised her from a child, had cared for her over the years, day after day. Living in such close proximity for so long a time, it would have been impossible *not* to know her, and

From the light pouring into the room, he thought it must be nearly noon. His head began to clear, slowly at first, until he remembered what day it was. The sudden recognition was like downing a full pot of strong black coffee all at once.

Thursday. Tonight was the night.

He lay unmoving, his heart still racing, his breath coming in ragged gasps. His head felt like a blacksmith's anvil, and his mouth was as foul as a pigpen. He'd practically drunk himself into a stupor the night before, finally stumbling into bed a couple of hours before dawn.

In spite of his good intentions, he had been drinking for two days almost without letup. He wasn't sure why. Some of it had to do with today's affair, of course. He was tense, had been all week.

He hadn't been able to work for days now, and that in turn caused him even more tension. At this point, he was so far behind in his assignments for Jack, he'd be lucky if he didn't get a furious summons home.

Added to that was the fact that he was running out of funds. The initial payment to Biller and Robuck had set him back a pretty penny. If he didn't post a story and a new recommendation as to some immigrants for Jack to sponsor soon, he was going to land himself in a real fix.

No wonder he needed a drink now and then to steady his nerves.

Now and then?

He ignored the uneasiness lurking at the edge of his mind. This was no time for self-examination. Besides, once today was over with, he'd be able to concentrate again. Get back to work. Redeem himself with Jack, knock off the drinking, and get some much-needed work done. It was just the anticipation of tonight that had him rattled, that was all.

As he lay looking around his rented room, arms locked behind his head, he felt the beginning of the need for a drink to start the day, even though he was still slightly high from the night before. Only the chill of the room and the sickening pounding of his head kept him from getting up to retrieve the bottle on the desk.

He swallowed down the vile taste in his mouth and stretched a little. He ought to get up, have some breakfast, get himself together. But he was still shaken by the nightmare, still disoriented.

He refused to give a stupid dream any credence. It had just been the liquor and maybe some anxiety about tonight, nothing else.

He wouldn't think about it. Better to think about Roweena instead. Just for a minute or two.

After tonight, he was pretty sure he wouldn't have to resort to dreaming about her. If everything went as planned—and why wouldn't it?—then he'd be able to see her out in the open whenever he wanted.

With Gabriel's blessing.

He smiled, then winced as his lips cracked from the dryness. He needed to clean himself up a bit. Get a haircut and a shave. Have his landlady press some clothes. Needed to look presentable tonight, even though he'd get roughed up a little in the fray.

Not much, of course. He'd warned those two uglies to have a care when he appeared on the scene. He didn't want any broken bones for his trouble. In fact, he didn't want any more pain than absolutely necessary. They were to push him around just enough to make things believable, no more.

He wished he didn't feel so uneasy about those two. Especially Robuck. They were both bad business, but something about Robuck literally gave him the creeps.

Well, what did he expect? It wasn't exactly a job for missionaries. Besides, he'd seen the way their eyes bugged when he quoted the price. Money was everything with their kind. They would do the deed, he'd pay them off, and that would be the last he'd ever see of them. And good riddance.

This was worth a few risks, after all.

Roweena was worth a *lot* of risks.

He let his mind wander, imagining what it would be like with her once Gabriel took the cuffs off and they had a chance to be together.

Roweena was a total innocent. She had never been with a man; he was sure of it. No way a man would have ever gotten past Gabriel.

His mouth twisted at the sudden, unbidden image of the big fisherman, beefy arms crossed over that massive chest of his, standing guard with a scowl.

But not for much longer, he reminded himself. It would all be different after tonight.

He was going to be good to her. He really was. He would court her in grand fashion, make her head swim, make her wild for him. He'd gain her trust, win her over entirely. And eventually . . . soon . . . she'd be warm and willing in his arms.

This time, though, it was going to be different. *Roweena* was different, a different kind of girl. She was everything he could ever want. He had never felt this way about a woman. Never.

This time, he wanted more than just another quick fling. He was going to change, change for Roweena. He'd be different with her. She was so good, so innocent—so trusting. He would be the kind of man she'd look up to. She'd be crazy in love with him, and he would cherish her. Even Gabriel would approve.

Eventually . . . who could say? He might even marry her.

He wasn't so sure he'd ever go back to the States, at least to stay. He was Irish now, thoroughly Irish. And Ireland was where he belonged.

There was still Jack to be dealt with, of course. He had to figure a way to keep big brother from disowning him until he could support himself. He might want to live in Ireland, but he had no intention of living *poor.*

Ah, well—he could handle Jack. Hadn't he always?

For now, he needed to get on with the day. This was the day that was going to change everything.

He pushed himself up, slung his feet over the side of the bed, grabbing his head with both hands when the pain slammed down on him. His eyes went to the bottle on the desk, and he decided to have just one quick drink. Just one. To settle his stomach, ease the headache.

After all, he had to be in top shape for the day ahead.

In another minute, he got to his feet and headed for the desk.

27

An Ill Wind over the Claddagh

How sad to see eyes clouded, dim . . .
Eyes meant by God to mirror Him.
ANONYMOUS

Gabriel took the streets at a brisk clip, his coat buttoned all the way up, the scarf Roweena had knitted him drawn snugly about his throat.

Early in the evening, a raw wind had blown up, cutting across Galway and the Claddagh with a wintry chill. The sea tossed and heaved like a bad-tempered behemoth roused too soon from its nap. In deference to the weather, the village lanes were nearly deserted. The Claddagh's fishermen were huddled by the hearth fire tonight, their children shut safely indoors against the wind. Gabriel himself had issued a caution to Eveleen not to get her "feathers blown off" by dawdling in the yard, as was her custom this time of day.

No one had yet forgotten the Big Wind that had caught all Ireland by surprise January past, nor was it likely that anyone would forget it for a long time to come. Memories of animals and entire houses blown out to sea by the savage storm were still all too vivid in the minds of mothers and fathers, daughters and sons. Loved ones had been lost, homes destroyed, lives devastated. Ever since, each time a strong wind stirred the thatch on a roof, all Galway looked to the sky with apprehension.

Gabriel's haste was not born of fear, however. He had endured enough winds in his time to recognize tonight's as nothing more than an ordinary blow that would subside without wreaking any real damage. What had him pounding the cobbles in such haste at this hour was the message from Ulick, delivered late in the afternoon. Immediately after reading his friend's hastily scrawled note, he sent word to the other men that he would not join with them to pray this night, as was his custom, that instead he had another obligation to see to.

He was to meet Ulick at the house of his cousin, near the priory. Gabriel didn't question why his friend simply didn't come to his home. Those who knew Gabriel Vaughan best also knew that he was adamant about keeping men's business removed from his personal life. Because of Roweena and the child, he exercised every caution; he had never allowed much tramping in and out of his house, even by those with whom he had a long-standing friendship.

The thought of Roweena and Eveleen alone at the house made him pick up his stride still more. They were used to his Thursday night absences for prayer meeting, and tonight he had left the house even earlier than was his habit. But for some reason, he was exceedingly anxious to get the meeting with Ulick over and done with—not only because he was eager to hear whatever information the man might have for him, but also because he was uneasy about leaving Roweena and the child alone.

Perhaps the wind had unnerved him more than he'd realized. He looked up at the sky, totally bereft of moon and stars. It seemed that the wind had already died. The dark streets had fallen silent, with an unnatural stillness hanging over the entire Claddagh. An unaccountable shudder seized Gabriel as he turned onto the lane that led to his destination. He felt chilled through, but not as a result of the night air. It was more the unexpected calm that had spooked him, he realized.

Like most fishermen, he had experienced firsthand the strange, singular quiet that often preceded a storm. As he trudged up to the front door of the small, mud-walled cottage where Ulick was waiting, he caught himself holding his breath, as though bracing himself before yet another blast of December wind could come shrieking down upon his head.

Ulick threw open the door only a second or two after Gabriel knocked. The mouth beneath the drooping mustache was set in a thin, hard line, and the uncommonly pale eyes met Gabriel's with a look that seemed to hold something more akin to dread than welcome.

In that moment, Gabriel feared that he was about to be caught up in more than one storm this night.

⁂

Clive Robuck shifted his bulk and stepped back a little deeper into the shadows, accidentally tromping Biller's foot.

An oath from the smaller man brought an indifferent shrug from Robuck. "Get yourself some proper boots, why don't you?"

"I'll be getting myself a hot water bottle and a roaring fire after this night, I can tell you," Biller groused.

"Aye, and for me a warm-blooded woman as well. This infernal weather has me near frozen. I wish the little chit would come out so we could get on with it."

"'Tis still early," Biller reminded him. "I can't help but wonder why Vaughan left before his usual time. You don't think there's something wrong?"

Robuck turned to eye him. "You worry too much. You'd worry yourself witless if you had any to begin with."

"Seems to me there's a fair measure to worry about with such a stunt as this," Biller muttered.

"Are you cracked, man? We couldn't have found a softer job! We scare a wee girl for a bit and let the man who's paying us come to the rescue. Nothing could be easier, it seems to me."

Still scowling, Biller continued to dig a crater in the mud with his toe. "Unless something goes wrong."

"What could go wrong?" Robuck snapped, out of patience with his cohort. "Any *gawm* could pull this one off. Even you." Without turning away, he spat on the ground, then added, "Quit your bellyaching. You saw for yourself, the big man is gone—just as Kane said he would be. What does it matter if he left a bit early? The girl will show any time now, and when she does, we'll get this—"

Biller fastened a hand on his arm and jerked his head in the direction of Vaughan's house. Robuck turned to see a dark-haired tyke trundle out the door, a basin in hand. She stopped just long enough to clumsily pull the door shut with her other hand, then went around to the side of the house, where she tossed the contents of the basin onto the ground.

As Kane had predicted, the chit clearly meant to dawdle awhile in the yard. For a moment, she stood unmoving, looking idly about at her surroundings. After a time, she tucked the empty basin under her arm and did a few skips and a couple of hops around a piece of bare shrubbery growing near the house. She stopped long enough to pull her bulky sweater more tightly around her, then headed toward the back of the house, all the while staring up at the sky as she went.

Robuck lifted a hand to Biller to signal that they would move in a moment. On instinct, he pulled his pistol out of his back pocket.

"What are you doing?" Biller hissed behind him. "The American said no weapons! And we agreed!"

Robuck whipped around. "Shut your gob!" he ordered in a harsh whisper. "You want to give us up?" He palmed the gun and aimed it square in Biller's face. "This isn't a weapon. 'Tis insurance, is all. Weren't you just the one fretting that something might go wrong? This is to make sure nothing does. Now come on before she—"

They stopped, turning to look as the door was flung open with a bang and another girl—no, a woman, this one—stuck her head out and called, "Evie! Eveleen—come inside now!"

Robuck thought her voice peculiar, as if she had a sore throat or was perhaps hoarse from a cold.

She couldn't see the little one from the doorway, of course. And the mischievous tyke stood unmoving, her shoulders hunched, one hand over her mouth as if she were enjoying her fun altogether.

Robuck looked from the wee girl to the woman, who now stepped outside the door and once again called to the child. She waited only a moment before ducking back inside, then returning with a lantern in hand.

In the lantern's faint glow, Robuck could see that she had a full mane of dark hair and, though slender, was a fine, well set-up woman. Something stirred inside him as he watched her look about the front yard, then start toward the side of the house.

"What's this?" Biller rasped behind him. "Kane made no mention of anyone besides the child!"

"This," Robuck whispered, taking a step forward and gesturing that Biller should follow, "is clearly more than we bargained for. Indeed, I'm thinking this job comes with a bit of a bonus."

"Wait! We're not to move until Kane is in place. That was the plan."

But Robuck was already moving. Gun still in hand, he went at a crouch, as quickly and quietly as a mountain cat.

"Kane be skunked. I have my own plans," he said under his breath, heading for the house.

Brady went at a run, his heart banging against his chest wall. He stumbled once on a loose cobble, righted himself, and hurried on. He'd meant to be in place well before now, to make certain that Gabriel had indeed left the house and that the two thugs had actually showed up. At the last minute, however, he'd delayed just long enough for a quick drink, to fortify himself.

He should have left earlier . . . shouldn't have stopped. . . .

He tried to reassure himself as he rounded the corner. He still had time, after all. In fact, he was exactly on time.

The wind had blown up again after a brief break, stinging his face as he ran. But he picked up his pace still more as he spotted the old oak tree directly across the road from Gabriel's cottage. He'd chosen the tree as his "station"; from there he could see both the front and the side of the house, as well as Robuck and Biller when they made their move.

His chest was burning, and the pounding in his head matched the slamming of his heart as he reached the oak tree. He stopped, gasping for breath, looking around.

He saw Roweena first, holding a lantern, then Evie, hunched down at the side of the house. He snapped his gaze right and spotted both Robuck and Biller.

Everything seemed to happen at once. Without warning, his carefully scripted plans spun out of control, and he was left reeling.

He had never considered the possibility that Roweena might come outside too. Not once in all the times he had watched the house to study their routine had she ventured outdoors with Evie.

Until tonight.

Suddenly, Robuck and Biller started to move, going at a crouch but going fast. Brady knew he had to think, had to do something.

Instead he froze. His mind was as leaden as his feet. Even as he watched the two take off—Roweena turning and starting for the side of the house, calling Evie as she went—he realized that Evie was oblivious to it all, at least in that moment. He watched the men split, with the bullish Robuck heading for Roweena while the smaller Biller lunged at Evie. Even knowing what was about to happen, Brady couldn't move, couldn't stop his mind from spinning.

He didn't dare break in on them yet—he would ruin everything. He would have to explain himself to Roweena, and then she'd know that he was behind it all. Everything would be spoiled.

But what if things got out of hand and Roweena got hurt? Could he trust Robuck not to get rough?

Trust him? Of course, he couldn't trust him! He hadn't trusted him from the beginning. The perpetual sneer on his face, the hooded, calculating set of his eyes, his obvious contempt, had set Brady on edge the moment they met.

But that was to be expected. He was just another roughneck. That didn't mean the two wouldn't carry off the job as planned. Roweena complicated things by showing up as she had, but

Robuck could keep her at arm's length long enough for Brady to make his stand.

He wouldn't dare to hurt her. To him and Biller, this was nothing but another job. A work for hire. The only thing they'd even questioned him about was the money, and he'd agreed to their price. They wouldn't do anything to risk the rest of their payment.

And he wouldn't delay his part. No, he'd actually move it up a little. He'd wait only a few minutes, just long enough for his "rescue" to have the desired effect.

For an instant, the irrational desire for some sort of weapon seized Brady. Maybe he should have brought something along, just in case. A gun.

But he'd never used a gun in his life. Besides, he didn't need a weapon. Robuck and Biller wouldn't have weapons. He'd been dead clear about that.

He reminded himself that the two toughs he'd hired were just that—common thugs. Not killers.

Everything had been orchestrated, right down to the last detail. They would do their part as planned, and he would do his.

Brady's hands were shaking, his entire body trembling so violently that pain shot through him like a volley of grapeshot. He steeled himself, trying to stay calm. But the throbbing in his skull sent a surge of nausea exploding up in him, and try as he would, he could not rid himself of the panic that jolted through him at the sight of the two men—men he had hired—heading directly for Roweena and Evie.

28

A Darkness in Heaven

What that fate may be hereafter
Is to us a thing unknown.
"A SOUTHERN" FROM THE
SAMUEL B. OLDHAM COLLECTION

At the corner of the house, Roweena stood for a moment, looking about. It was a dark night entirely, with no lights of heaven overhead. The wind that had died earlier had renewed itself over the past few minutes, and she pulled her thin shawl more closely about her shoulders.

She lifted the lantern a little higher as she started around the side of the house, stopping the instant she saw Evie, hunched down, laughing as if her sides would split.

The child *did* test her patience at times. "What . . . are you doing? Don't you know . . . you frightened me?" she scolded.

Evie straightened, her smile still in place but somewhat more tentative now, as if she saw that Roweena was in no mood for her foolishness.

"I was only having fun with you," she said, speaking slowly so that Roweena could make out her words in the dim light from the lantern. "I was playing hidey-seek."

"There is no fun . . . in being thoughtless!" Roweena snapped. She knew she was being shrewish—perhaps she was making too much of little—but in truth she *had* been frightened. There were no stars for the child to "follow" this night, and with Gabriel away she didn't like her roaming about in the darkness for any length of time.

Evie's puckish features pulled into a fierce pout, and she stood scuffing the toe of her shoe without looking at Roweena.

The child invariably melted most of her attempts at sternness, but Roweena tried to keep a firm tone. "Inside with you now, do you hear? Gabriel will not be pleased to learn of your little joke."

Evie finally looked up and started toward her, and Roweena lifted the lantern to illumine her steps. When the child suddenly stopped in midstride, Roweena renewed her warning. "Eveleen, if you don't come inside with me right now, you will not play outside again for another week!"

Evie's gaze lighted on Roweena for only an instant before deflecting to something behind her. Suddenly, the child's eyes grew wide, and her mouth pursed in a circle of surprise.

"Evie?"

Without warning, a look of fear spread over the girl's features, sending a crawling sensation along Roweena's spine.

She felt the blood drain from her head. A gust of wind lashed at her face, whipping her hair over her eyes, nearly obscuring her vision. Her pulse racing, she started to turn to see what had spooked

Evie so. But at the same moment, the dark form of a man leaped out of the shadows and grabbed Evie.

Roweena cried out and lunged forward, but before she could reach Evie, a heavy arm came around her own neck, another around her waist, trapping her.

Panic and the foul scent of body odor and stale tobacco induced a surge of nausea that lodged in her throat and threatened to strangle her. She gagged for breath and tried to scream, but the thick arm pressing against her windpipe choked off her air and smothered her voice.

Stunned, Roweena felt herself hauled back against a large, solid body. She stumbled, trying to twist free, only to be seized in an even more vicious, bruising grip.

In a blinding blaze of horror, she saw Evie struggling to break free of a small, wiry man with a kerchief over the bottom half of his face. Even though her ears were deaf, Roweena could hear in her mind the child's terrified screams.

At the sight of Evie in such a state, her own fear gave way to a fury so intense that something inside Roweena snapped. She flailed her arms like a wild thing, striking out, meeting nothing but air, trying to wrench herself free as her futile attempt to scream was once again choked off and the arm about her waist tightened to the point that she thought she would be sick.

Then the night itself exploded into madness.

Brady stood, frozen in rising panic and confusion. It was happening too fast. Everything was going wrong. Evie screaming, then silenced by Biller's hand over her mouth. Roweena struggling, thrashing and pounding her feet like a wild woman in an insane dance of terror.

And Robuck—holding her, shouting and swearing at her, spewing vile obscenities that seemed to contaminate the very air around her, even though Roweena wouldn't be able to hear a word he was saying.

Brady's own insides were screaming, and for an instant he thought he had cried aloud, then realized his protests were only in his head.

His ears thundered as his pulse sped out of control. His mind began to spin, groping for reason, scrambling to think of what to do.

The scene erupted before him like a nightmare exploding into reality. A raging wave of guilt and self-revulsion crashed over him as he stood watching the horror he had unleashed.

He was trapped between desperation and indecision, shocked into near paralysis by the catastrophe he himself had set in motion.

***

Gabriel made his way through the narrow lanes of the Claddagh with a blind eye to almost everything around him.

The wind that had seemed so ineffectual only minutes ago now seemed to carry a slicing edge that slashed his face and an angry roar that filled his head.

The vague sense of apprehension that had been rising in him all evening was now a shaking, hammering dread, driving him home in a fever, pressing him on despite the feeling that he was dragging a ball and chain around his ankles.

Ulick's words virtually shrieked inside his skull with every step he took, and he could not take the darkened streets quickly enough. In the moments since he had left Ulick, his earlier uneasiness about leaving Roweena and Evie alone had spiraled into a taut coil of tension.

Perhaps he was merely being foolish or reacting to the wildness of the night; Ulick's startling revelation had left him badly shaken, after all. But whatever the reason, whatever the anxiety squeezing at him, he had to get home, and as quickly as he possibly could.

He was almost running now, the blood thundering in his head, his heart pounding from the exertion.

The only thought his mind would hold was what he had learned from Ulick this night. Of everything he might have expected to hear, never in a lifetime would he have expected what he *did* hear.

But thank the gracious Lord that he *had* heard it, before disaster could strike.

Unbelievable—*incredible*—that something which had happened so long ago, so far away in the past, could still reach out across the years and touch today, that one night of savagery could possibly alter the lives and even the destinies of two or more generations.

They had to be told, but how he dreaded the telling. Yet it would be a dangerous folly entirely to keep such a secret from the two of them.

But *was* it a secret? Roweena, of course, knew that she was the result of a brutal attack on her mother. Gabriel had told her what he knew, once she was old enough to understand. Then, too, she actually remembered bits and pieces of the past: the convent where she and her mother—badly deranged by then—had lived when she was only a wee girl. The fire that had destroyed the convent and killed her mother. The years she had lived with Gabriel's parents, then later his uncle—until finally Gabriel himself had assumed her guardianship.

But what about Brady Kane? Was it possible he had never been told? Or, if he knew, did he simply not grasp the significance, not realize what it might mean to him? And to Roweena?

An unbidden thought of the portraits Kane had painted struck

Gabriel, and he stopped for an instant where he was. He remembered how the likeness of Roweena had disturbed him, the sense
of something . . . sick, even obsessive, behind the artistry. Had he
really seen what he thought he had, or had the *wrongness* of the
portrait merely been a kind of warning?

Sick at heart, anguished in spirit, but more anxious than ever to
reach home, Gabriel finally broke into a full run, his heavy boots
slapping and pounding the cobbled streets that only minutes before had been silent.

29
Encounter with Evil

Men of the same soil placed in hostile array,
Prepared to encounter in deadly affray.
ROBERT YOUNG

Roweena fought against the man's effort to turn her about, to make her face him. Perhaps a part of her thought, irrationally, that to see him face-to-face would only make him more real—more dreadful. But her strength was as nothing compared to his.

He turned her easily, roughly. He was a big man—not tall, but thickset with massive shoulders and a barrel chest. His hair was a dull shade of red, worn long and heavy. Like the other, he wore a kerchief covering his mouth, but even as she watched, he lifted a hand to tug it down, letting it fall around his neck, as if he *wanted* her to see his face.

His eyes were the worst: close set and hooded, they held the flint of a mean spirit and the coldness of one who would inflict pain without so much as a second thought.

Only a deliberate act of will empowered her not to scream in his face as he lifted his free hand and passed it back and forth in front of Roweena, bringing it so close he almost touched her.

He had a gun.

Unwilling to let him see her fear, Roweena tried to avert her gaze. But he pressed the cold barrel of the gun under her chin to tilt her face, forcing her to look directly at him.

He was speaking to her. Roweena had all she could do to concentrate on the cruel line of his mouth, to try and read what he was saying. For some reason, she did not want him to know about her deafness, for fear he would somehow use it as an advantage. His words came too fast, though, and she managed to make out only fragments of his speech.

". . . careful . . . you do. Me and you . . . inside . . . have ourselves . . . fun. . . . Behave yourself . . . neither you nor her . . . get hurt. . . ."

No . . . oh, dear Lord, no . . . not that . . . not the evil thing that had been done to her mother . . . please . . . blessed Savior . . . not that. . . .

He looked past her, to the other man holding Evie. Again Roweena tried to read his lips.

". . . shut that brat up! And keep . . . out here until. . . . Won't take long. . . ."

Roweena managed to half turn to see Evie draw her leg back and kick her captor on the shin, hard. In retaliation, the man hauled her up against him, holding her like a rag doll. Flailing her arms, twisting and kicking, she intensified her fierce, but futile, attempt to escape his clutches.

Roweena saw that she was calling out for Gabriel almost with every breath until the man slapped a hand over her mouth. Wide eyed, she held out her arms to Roweena in supplication.

Roweena could bear no more. She squeezed her eyes shut, only to be yanked roughly about to face the redheaded man again. This time he pressed the gun up against the side of her head. His eyes held fire, his mouth twisted into an ugly scowl as he harangued her with obscenities, then, ". . . I'll blow . . . brains out and hers as well if you don't do as . . ."

No, not Evie . . . she could not let them hurt Eveleen. . . .

"Please—make him let her go!" she begged him. "She's . . . little more than a babe! Please!"

She had no way of knowing if he answered, for he merely pushed her around and began shoving her toward the house. Roweena's legs threatened to give way beneath her, but she forced herself to go on, hoping that by doing what he wanted she might be able to protect Evie. And yet she knew that her sanity—perhaps her life and Evie's life as well—depended on her *not* going inside the house. At least out here there was a chance that someone would hear . . . someone would see. . . .

Even with the thought, she knew her hopes were in vain. Everyone was inside on a night like this, and the wind would no doubt swallow all their pleas for help.

She choked down her panic, digging deep inside herself for some semblance of calm. She sensed that her captor was an angry, impatient man. If she fell to pieces entirely, there was no telling what he might do.

Gabriel . . . where was Gabriel? Shouldn't he be back by now?

Her mind began a desperate litany as she stumbled and her captor shoved her on, the gun prodding her in the back. *Oh, God, have mercy on us. . . . Christ, have mercy on us. . . . Mercy, please, Lord, have mercy. . . .*

Reason deserted Brady when he saw Robuck put a gun to Roweena's head, then begin to push her toward the house.

But there wasn't supposed to be a gun! They had agreed—there would be no weapons! And he couldn't let him take her inside the house! She'd be trapped there with Robuck!

His stomach wrenched.

Oh, God, what have I done? What have I done?

At that moment, Evie let go a volley of blood-chilling shrieks. He saw that Biller had picked her up like a sack of flour in one arm and was trying to silence her with his other hand.

A storm exploded in Brady's mind and propelled him into action. He shot forward, sprinting across the road, shouting until he thought his lungs would burst as he went. He twisted his ankle on a protruding stone, stumbled, gasping with the pain, but kept on going, driving into the yard and storming toward Robuck and Roweena.

Robuck whirled around, one burly arm wedged under Roweena's throat, the gun barrel pressed against her temple as he used her to shield himself.

"That's far enough! Back off, or I'll plug her!"

Brady stopped, fury scalding him, pouring through him, nearly blinding him and filling his ears with a deafening roar. "Let her go, Robuck! What in blazes do you think you're doing?"

Robuck's lips curled back over his teeth in a feral grin. "Whatever I want, Yank. Whatever I want. You going to stop me—you and your . . . 'no weapons'?"

Brady's mind raced. Roweena was facing him, her eyes wild with fear. Out of the corner of his eye, he saw Biller set Evie to her feet, not releasing her but trapping her by the neck of her sweater.

Brady couldn't think. Roweena could read his lips, but even if she were too terrified to make out what he was saying, Evie would hear. She would know he'd had a part in this. A big part.

Somehow he had to salvage his plan, without either Roweena or Evie getting hurt. But how?

"Let her go," he said, his voice a low threat. "You can't get away with this."

Robuck continued to sneer. "I already have. Get lost, Yank. Come back in a few minutes, when I've finished with her. Then you can "rescue" the both of them!"

He gave an ugly laugh, then jerked Roweena around and, as if Brady presented not the slightest threat, turned his back on him and renewed their trek toward the house.

Suddenly Brady's *plan* no longer seemed important. It didn't matter whether Roweena knew what he had done. The only thing that counted was saving her. And Evie.

His head cleared, and he felt almost weightless as he launched himself at Robuck's back like an arrow shot from a bow.

But Biller shouted a warning, and the big man turned just in time, yanking Roweena around with him. With one beefy arm locked around her throat and the gun leveled at her head, he stood, legs outspread, his entire bearing a challenge.

"She's dead if you don't back off, Kane! You know I mean it!"

Brady saw the wildness in his eyes, the tears of terror in Roweena's. He took a step backward, then another, and as he did, Robuck's sneer broadened.

"That's better, Yank" he said, waving the gun toward Brady. "Now then, you get yourself right over there, where Biller can keep an eye on you until I've finished my business with the lassie here."

Brady wasn't sure what happened next. Roweena must have thought Robuck was distracted to the point that she could free herself, because she gave a violent wrench, crying out with the effort, pitching herself forward. But Robuck apparently had the strength of a bull and yanked her back by the neck. She collided against him with such force that she screamed in pain.

At the same instant, out of the corner of his eye Brady saw Evie shrug free of her sweater, leaving Biller holding it by the neck, empty. The child took off running, shrieking as she went, but suddenly stopped dead, directly between Brady and Robuck.

She whirled around toward Brady, then toward Robuck and Roweena, clearly uncertain as to what to do.

Brady saw the danger and called out to her, waving her off. "No, Evie! Go back! Go back!"

She gaped at him, then again turned to look at Roweena. She stood there as if transfixed, staring at Robuck who now raised the gun and with an oath aimed it directly at her.

"Robuck!" Brady shouted, waving his hands. "No! You hurt her—you *touch* her and the deal is off, you hear me? No deal!"

Robuck looked at him, narrowing his eyes as if calculating his options.

"No deal," Brady repeated again, his voice low and threatening. "And so help me, I'll see you hang."

Still the big man eyed him, seemingly unmoved, showing no sign of taking the gun off Evie. Roweena was staring at Brady with an expression of total shock and something else . . . something terrible, something so wounding that it pierced him through, cutting right into his very soul.

Finally, Robuck looked back at Evie and waved the gun toward Brady. "Over there with your pal, chit. And stay put, or I'll hurt this beauty in ways you've never heard tell of."

Still Evie hesitated, whipping around first to Brady, then to

Roweena, who shouted at her to run. For some reason, this seemed to infuriate Robuck. He slapped Roweena, hard.

At that point Brady went mad.

✦❊✦

Gabriel had just slid in behind the elm tree on the rise back of the house when he saw Roweena try to twist free of her captor, only to be hauled back against him.

He knotted his fists, struggling against a near mindless fury as she cried out in pain. At the same moment, wee Evie *did* manage to break free.

Gabriel held his breath as the child ran to the ground between Roweena and Brady Kane and stood, looking from first one to the other, as if trying to decide which way to run.

He took it all in: Kane's uncertainty and indecision. The girls' terror. The small wraith of a man now standing off to the side, looking as if he'd rather be anywhere else than where he was.

As he listened to the exchange between Brady Kane and the man with the gun, he realized that Kane had apparently orchestrated this whole thing.

But *why?*

He clenched his hands so hard that his nails dug blood from his palms. His ears drummed, and his stomach twisted with sick fear as he stood in the darkness, waiting for the right moment.

Suddenly Roweena screamed at Evie, and the child took off running toward Kane. At the same time, the man with the gun slapped Roweena in the face.

The last shred of Gabriel's self-control snapped, and rage rose up in him like a deranged monster unbound.

He pushed away from the tree and went roaring down the yard, heading straight for Roweena and the man with the gun.

The sight of Gabriel hurling himself across the yard, rushing toward them, elicited a cry of almost delirious relief from Roweena. At the same instant, she saw Brady Kane break into a run, right behind Gabriel, while the smaller man who had held Evie captive took off running into the night.

But her relief was short lived. The man with the gun suddenly pushed her away. She staggered, swaying on her feet, as she saw him sweep the pistol toward Gabriel.

In that instant, Roweena realized what was about to happen.

She never hesitated but lunged forward, bolting madly toward Gabriel, her feet scarcely touching the ground in a desperate attempt to reach him before the bullet did.

"Roweena—no!" Gabriel saw her fly toward him and called out to her as he ran, hoping to block her from the path of the gunman's bullet. At the same time, Brady Kane, running toward them, shouted a warning.

But Roweena kept running, fairly leaping over the ground toward Gabriel, throwing herself in front of him as the gunshot exploded and shattered the night into pieces of despair.

At first Brady didn't even realize that the screams being ripped from someone's throat were his own. He saw Roweena fling herself wildly at Gabriel, saw the look of a love in torment fade from her face as Gabriel caught her in his arms and lowered her to the ground, saw the crimson stain blossom quickly over her shoulder and down one side of her chest—and all the while he kept on screaming.

The raw anguish in the giant's face hit him like a blow. For a moment he stood numbly, watching Gabriel cradle Roweena against him. Then Gabriel looked at him, and Brady saw the dreadful *knowing* in his eyes.

When the racking clarity of what had happened finally registered, he swung around toward Robuck and, heedless of the gun the man held trained on him, charged him like a bear gone mad with blood lust.

A shot rang out, and he felt a blast of pain tear through his shoulder. But he threw himself at Robuck, pounding him with his fists, cursing him—and himself—with all the fury that been unleashed by the sight of Roweena lying limply in Gabriel's arms.

They grappled for the gun, and another white hot slam of pain ripped through Brady, this time in his side. Nausea swept through him, and the night rushed in on him as he felt himself thrown off Robuck and slammed onto the ground, on his back.

He caught one brief glimpse of Gabriel hurling himself at Robuck, hammering a mighty fist at the man's head, and saw the gun go flying out of Robuck's hand as the man fell to his knees, then facedown in the mud.

⚜

Brady thought he must have drifted in and out of consciousness for a time, but for how long he had no way of knowing. He glanced over at Robuck. The man was still lying in the mud. Apparently, he was unconscious, not dead, for Gabriel was trussing his hands and feet behind him.

Biller was nowhere in sight.

There were others milling about now, a few men, mostly women. Probably neighbors who had finally heard the commotion and ventured out. They spoke in hushed tones, standing back, watching.

Brady lifted a hand to Gabriel, groaning at the pain that scalded his side with the effort.

"Roweena . . ."

For a moment, Gabriel stood staring down at Brady in silence. Finally, he gave a terse reply. "She's alive," he said. "Evie is with her. I will see to your wounds in a bit, but not until after I take care of Roweena."

"But she'll be all right?"

Gabriel didn't answer, merely stood looking down at Brady in stony silence.

"Get her a doctor, Gabriel," Brady urged, reaching up for the big man's sleeve, but missing it when the pain again shot through him with a vengeance. "I'll pay. Whatever it costs. She needs a doctor."

"I *am* a doctor," the big fisherman said dully. Slowly, he shrugged out of his coat and knelt to one knee to cover Brady with it. Brady shrunk inwardly from the terrible sorrow in the big fisherman's eyes.

"What have you done here tonight, Brady Kane? And why have you done it?"

Brady couldn't bring himself to look at him. "I . . . didn't think. . . . No one was supposed to get hurt. . . . I only meant to bolster your opinion of me. It was all put-up."

He could feel Gabriel's eyes boring into him. "Why, man? Why would you do such a thing?"

"For Roweena," Brady said, shame flooding him like a fever as he turned his gaze back to Gabriel. "But it all went wrong . . . so terribly wrong. Roweena wasn't even supposed to come outside . . . only Evie. I thought, by pretending to save Evie . . . I could get in your good graces and you'd not fight Roweena's seeing me. . . . I never thought . . . I never wanted anyone to get hurt."

Brady stopped to catch his breath. The sky overhead was beginning to spin, and he felt sick, so sick. . . .

"It's you she loves, Gabriel. . . . Did you know? Roweena . . . she loves you. . . . I saw it in her face when she was running toward you, . . . and I knew I had done it all . . . for nothing. I almost got her killed . . . for nothing. . . . She meant to die for you. . . ."

For a long, terrible moment, Gabriel looked at him. Dazed, weakness sucking him in, Brady saw the other's anger and surprise fade, to be replaced by a patent look of contempt.

"You poor, pathetic fool," Gabriel finally said, an inexplicable note of sadness edging his words and making Brady cringe. "So you didn't know."

"Know what?" Brady muttered, feeling the ground beneath him start to whirl, along with the sky.

"You need to be told, I suppose, though I should not have to be the one to tell you."

Gabriel's voice sounded farther and farther away, as if he were retreating into a dark, winding tunnel. "Roweena and you—" he said, "there is every possibility that you had the same father."

Brady struggled to keep his eyes open. "You're mad," he said, attempting a weak laugh but failing.

"I'm not mad. Roweena's mother was violated by a drunken British soldier. Revenge for a raid by one of those infernal secret societies Ireland is forever spawning. There were three women tortured and raped that same night. All Galway women." Gabriel paused. "Your mother was one of them."

"You *are* mad," Brady mumbled. "My father was Sean Kane."

Gabriel shook his head. "No. Sean Kane was your brother's sire. And your sister's. But not yours. Your father was one of a band of soldiers—an Englishman."

Brady pushed at him, as if by pushing him out of his sight he could also drive Gabriel's words out of his hearing. "I don't believe you. . . ."

"'Tis the truth," Gabriel said, getting to his feet. "But I will waste no more time with you for now. I must get back to Roweena." He paused, staring down at Brady. "When you are strong enough, you write to your brother in America, Jack Kane. *John* Kane—*Sean,* in the Irish. Named after *his* father, so it seems. You write and ask him to tell you the rest of the story. Just know for now that Roweena may well be your half sister. There is no way of knowing for certain she is *not.*"

That said, Gabriel walked away.

A long, keening wail ripped from Brady's throat. Then he turned his face into the mud and retched.

PART THREE

On an Altar of Ashes

We went through fire and flood. But you brought us
to a place of great abundance.

PSALM 66:12, NLT

30

A Subtle Threat

Wherefore do ye pause
Before the rich man's dwelling? Will your woes
Avail to move his pity, or to touch
One chord of feeling in his hardened heart?
ELIZABETH WILLOUGHBY VARIAN

NEW YORK CITY, DECEMBER

The plan had begun to take shape in the back of Jack's mind the night before. So suddenly had it come—and so clearly could he imagine its success—that by the time he left his office late in the afternoon on Monday, he decided to go directly to Grace Mission and speak with Terese Sheridan.

During previous meetings, he had sensed a number of contradictions in the girl, and he knew that any doubts or uncertainties she might have would only work to his benefit. If a vague uneasiness tended to plague him on the way to the mission house, he told himself it wasn't because he meant to take advantage; to the contrary, he would be doing her a great favor. Not only would his plan considerably ease the way for her, but at the same time he would be able to give Samantha something he believed she wanted more than almost anything else.

If he was right, then he was convinced that she would finally agree to marry him.

He had not realized that Samantha could be so exasperatingly stubborn. Without fail, every time he had raised the subject of marriage over the past month, *she* had raised the subject of their differences—most particularly the fact that Jack didn't share her faith—almost always followed by a mention of her inability to give him a child.

No matter how adamantly he insisted that he would do whatever he could about their religious differences, and that a childless marriage was far preferable—at least to him—than no marriage at all, she remained unconvinced.

Yet Jack no longer questioned her feelings for him. The few times—and they *were* few—that she'd allowed him to embrace her, he had sensed an unmistakable depth of emotion, even passion, in her response, although she clearly tried to suppress it.

But hang it all, she wasn't fooling him, and the frustration of knowing that she did in fact care for him but was unwilling to do anything about it was driving him over the edge.

He was desperate to make her see things his way, to find something that would turn the battle to his advantage.

Now that he thought he had found just the thing, he was almost in a fever to get on with it.

※◎◎◎※

It seemed to Terese that she woke up a few minutes at a time, day by day, until the vast sea of sickness finally lay behind her.

In the days that followed the first step of her healing, she couldn't seem to keep her eyes open. She slept night and day. When she did rouse, it was like waking from one dream only to enter another. Her surroundings were veiled, her mind a fog-obscured maze. She couldn't manage to hold onto a logical thought more than a few seconds or remember what happened from one hour to the next.

Yet now, more than three weeks later, she could still recall her first glimpse of Cavan on the night that had marked the turning point in her recovery.

She hadn't known him at first—indeed, hadn't even remembered where she was or how she got there. It had seemed to require a monumental effort just to force her eyes open, and when she did, she'd been startled by the sight of a figure sitting in the shadows, close beside her bed. But at her quick intake of breath, he had moved to clasp her hands in his, calling her by name and whispering, over and over again, "Glory be to God. . . . He has spared you, little sister!"

He had wept the first time Terese called him by name, and she had also wept, out of her weakness, but more from the incredulity of being reunited at last with her brother, the only family left to her.

In the days that came after, she often awakened to find him sitting beside her bed, holding her hand tightly, as if he feared that he might lose her again. Little by little the years between them began to fall away as her memories of the brother she had not seen for so long a time faded into the reality of the man he had become. A *good* man, she sensed, a man of gentleness and integrity.

They talked much, but never once did he question her about the babe or show shame for her condition. As for Terese, she avoided as much as possible any mention of his job, for the thought of his connection with Jack Kane, Brady's brother, never failed to trouble her.

Mostly they filled in the blank spaces of their years of separation, sharing their mutual grief for the father who had died not long after coming across and the mother and sisters who had perished in the heartless poverty and hunger of an island winter. As Terese grew stronger, they sometimes talked for hours, almost always speaking in the Irish, unless others were in attendance—as was often the case.

There was Shona, of course. Little solemn-faced Shona, whose quiet presence was as dependable as the sunrise. It seemed the only time the child left Terese's side was at mealtimes and during evening vespers.

And Mrs. Harte—*Samantha,* as she insisted Terese call her—was the loveliest and, as both Terese and Cavan agreed, surely the *kindest* lady one could hope to meet, with a smile that seemed to warm the entire sickroom and great dark eyes where flecks of light sometimes danced, but where more often than not a hint of old sorrows seemed to brim.

She was a real *lady,* Samantha Harte was: delicate and slender with thick, glossy hair neatly wrapped in a twist at the back of her neck, skin the color of fresh cream, and soft hands with delicately manicured nails. So quietly did she move that her skirts gave hardly a rustle, and always, she seemed to smell like flowers.

Yet, on the very next day after Terese regained consciousness this elegant lady with the fine manners and educated speech had rolled up the sleeves to her dainty shirtwaist and bathed Terese as gently as if she were a wee babe. She had even washed her hair and put a ribbon in it. And all the while she had continued to speak in that soft and gentle voice, telling Terese that she was "lovely," that her cropped hair was "magnificent," and that everyone was "thankful and relieved" that God had granted her so great a healing.

As the days passed, Samantha Harte had continued to come,

sometimes tending to Terese's most personal needs, but also offering her a kind of womanly companionship unknown to Terese before now. She even read aloud to her, mostly from the Holy Scriptures. One in particular had caught Terese's attention and had quickly become her favorite, so much so that she would ask Samantha to read it over and over again, relishing the way it sounded in her new friend's refined way of speaking:

"For I know the plans I have for you, says the Lord, plans for welfare and not for evil, to give you a future and a hope."

She would smile then, Samantha would, and assure Terese that God did indeed have a plan for her, and that it was for good, and she must keep her hope. Terese wanted to believe her, but at times she couldn't help but question whether such a promise was truly meant for her. She was beginning to wonder if, because of her sins, God hadn't given up any plans he might have had for her and turned his back on her altogether.

She appreciated the way Samantha spoke of the babe: as if it were a *good* thing, not a burden to be borne or a problem to be solved. The baby was a *gift,* Samantha would say, an image that more and more appealed to Terese. As far as she was concerned, the child she carried was the only good thing to come out of her relationship with Brady, other than the passage to America.

She liked it best when Samantha came alone, but on occasion Jack Kane accompanied her. Terese felt awkward entirely around Brady's older brother. He was a formidable man, even frightening. He reminded Terese of a dark and dangerous mountain cat with his unfathomable gaze that seemed to bore right through her soul and the hard mouth that could no doubt say cruel things when provoked.

Part of the reason she felt so miserably uncomfortable with him, of course, was the lie Brady had propagated about the baby's being the issue of an "unknown attacker." But now that she had actually met him, Terese thought she better understood Brady's reluctance to incur his brother's displeasure.

Other than an unmistakable similarity in appearance, the two obviously shared little in common. Jack Kane would be no dreamer, no lighthearted jester or careless rogue who indulged himself in soft living. Brady's brother was clearly a hard man. Even when he smiled, those granitelike features gentled not a bit.

Terese wished he would just stay away, but being her *benefactor*—the word was bitter on her tongue—she supposed he had every right to come as often as he wished.

The one visitor she *did* look forward to each day, even more than Samantha Harte, was Dr. Leslie. If evening arrived without a sign of him, Terese would grow restless and disappointed. But when he finally walked into the room, her dark mood would instantly flee at the sight of his slightly crooked smile and soft but decidedly warm greeting.

She had never known a man as kind and seemingly good-natured as the lean-faced physician who, according to Samantha, had cared for Terese "tirelessly." Something in his gentle treatment of her, his infinite courtesy toward her—and that somewhat shy, heart-squeezing smile that always seemed especially for her—evoked an unfamiliar longing in Terese. It was a desire to be different—*better*—than what she was.

Yet even as she yearned to be a *lady*—someone like Samantha Harte, for example, worthy of a man's respect and admiration—she knew a terrible, aching shame that made her want to hide herself from David Leslie's gaze. No doubt he would despise her if he knew the truth.

As for Jack Kane, he would probably toss her out into the street if he were ever to learn that the child she carried was the result of a clandestine affair with his younger brother.

Given the churning state of her emotions, it was small wonder that her head began to swim in confusion when the two men directly responsible for her turmoil walked into the room together.

⚜

"Ah, Terese. How are you this evening?" Dr. Leslie reached her first, smiling as he took her hand and, as he always did upon entering the room, proceeded to check her pulse.

Jack Kane stood behind him at a slight distance. He neither smiled nor frowned but merely stood watching, his eyes shuttered, his expression inscrutable.

"A bit stronger," Terese answered honestly. "I sat in the chair by the window for quite a long time this afternoon. And I was actually hungry for supper."

"Excellent! Well, then, tomorrow, if you feel up to it, we'll let you begin walking in the corridor instead of just tiptoeing about your room."

Terese had been moved into a room by herself nearly two weeks past. According to Samantha, the change of rooms had been at the specific request of Jack Kane, who insisted Terese would rest better in quieter surroundings. Although Dr. Leslie had agreed, Terese couldn't help but wonder if the move hadn't been precipitated more by Kane's obvious discomfort with the dormitory, where the other women often moaned or wept aloud in their distress.

The doctor released Terese's hand and straightened. "And where is your faithful shadow this evening?"

"Shona? She went down to vespers."

"That's where I'm headed as well. Terese, Mr. Kane would like to speak with you if you're up to it."

Terese looked from the doctor to Jack Kane, whose quick smile wasn't reflected in his eyes. "I won't stay long," he offered in that deep, strangely quiet voice that still held more than a hint of his Irishness. "A few minutes, no more."

"Yes . . . of course," Terese managed, trying not to sound as grudging as she felt.

"Very well, then," said David Leslie. "I'll leave the two of you to your visit."

He turned to go, promising to look in on her later. Terese had all she could do not to call him back. Jack Kane's dark presence unsettled her when others were in the room; the prospect of being alone with him for any length of time unnerved her entirely.

Kane stepped closer to the bed. "May I?" he said, pulling up a chair and sitting down before Terese could answer.

"I won't tax you with small talk, Terese," Kane said. "I just want to say that I'm sorry for your troubles. All this has been very difficult for you, I know, but Dr. Leslie assures me that you're making good progress these days."

"Aye . . . yes, I'm . . . feeling much better now."

The cat seemed to have taken her wits along with her tongue. Unsettled by his close scrutiny, Terese glanced away.

"I'm glad to hear it," Kane said in the same flat tone of voice that made Terese think he wasn't glad at all, that indeed, he didn't much care one way or the other how she was doing.

"Mrs. Harte visits you often, does she?"

Terese turned back to him. "Almost every day. She's been kindness itself."

"Yes, she's a remarkable lady, isn't she? And of course you'll want to heed any suggestions she might have for you. She'll be instrumental in helping you to get settled." He paused. "Your brother hasn't been the same since you arrived, by the way. We seldom see him without a smile on his face these days."

Kane also cracked a smile, which quickly fled.

Terese was beginning to wonder why, exactly, he had come. Certainly he didn't *want* to be here; he looked almost as if he couldn't wait to take his leave.

"I'd like to ask you about *my* brother," said Kane.

Terese's heart slammed against her chest. "Your brother?"

He nodded. "Brady. I haven't wanted to disturb you with this, but since you say you're feeling stronger, I thought you wouldn't mind if we had a chat."

"No—I mean, that's fine, sir."

"Brady made the arrangements for your passage, isn't that so?"

Terese gave a nod, not trusting her voice. Her mind raced in alarm. Had he somehow learned the truth about her and Brady—about the baby?

"The thing is, I haven't heard from him in some time, you see, and I thought perhaps you'd at least be able to tell me how he was when you last saw him, before you came across."

Only slightly relieved, Terese caught a breath to steady herself. "Oh . . . well, he seemed quite . . . fit to me, sir."

Kane was still watching her as he framed his next question. "Did you know Brady well?"

Terese's pulse accelerated again. *Careful,* she warned herself. *Be careful. . . .*

"Oh . . . no, hardly at all. Though he was . . . a great help to me—and the children."

The room was close, and Kane moved to unbutton his topcoat and take off his gloves. "Yes. I was sorry to hear about the little Madden boy, by the way. Too bad, that." He hesitated, then went on. "So then—I don't suppose you'd have any idea why my brother has been so out of touch of late? In truth, I'm somewhat concerned about him. Not that he was ever the great communicator."

Terese felt suddenly cold, so cold she had to steel herself against the chattering of her teeth. "I can't imagine, sir. I'm sure you'll be hearing from him soon. He's probably just . . . busy."

Kane's eyes were so dark—almost black—they seemed to hold no light at all. It was impossible to even begin to sense his thoughts. Moreover, the man seemed to almost never blink, giving his gaze even more intensity.

"Well—let's hope you're right." He paused. "I trust he took good care of you—and the children?"

Terese's mouth had gone dry. "Sir?" She cringed as she heard her voice crack.

"Brady—I hope he saw to everything you needed for the passage."

"Oh . . . aye, he did." Terese could not resist adding, "Though I expect he made payment for more than we got."

Kane frowned. "How's that?"

"As I understood it, your brother—he took what your newspaper sent and paid for second-class passage for the three of us. But we were put in steerage."

A dark crimson flush spread over Kane's features. "You traveled in steerage?"

"Yes, sir. But I don't mean to sound ungrateful."

His mouth twisted downward. "You needn't apologize. I know all about steerage, as it happens. I came over that way myself. A wretched experience entirely."

Terese found it impossible to imagine this big, brooding man, in his fancy attire and daunting air of confidence, trapped in steerage like any ordinary peasant.

Kane brushed a hand down the side of his face, and his expression seemed to clear a little. "I regret that you had to go through that. I can't think how it happened. Didn't my brother see you onto the ship?"

Terese hesitated. She mustn't tell him, of course, that his precious brother couldn't be rid of her soon enough, once the arrangements were made.

She had to be that careful of what she said. She didn't want Kane asking too many questions.

Even so, her response nearly stuck in her throat. "He . . . your brother said he had other business to attend to. A lady from the orphan home—where Shona and her brother had been staying—saw us to the ship. But she wasn't allowed on board with us."

"I see." Kane's mouth was a thin, unyielding line. "Well, there's no undoing it now. Nevertheless, I'm sorry it happened."

He didn't *look* sorry, Terese thought. He looked almost as if he had no feelings at all. She also noticed that he was no longer meeting her eyes but seemed to be considering how to phrase his next words as he lightly slapped one glove against the palm of his hand.

"So then—what are your plans for the child?"

"My . . . plans?" Terese was startled by his directness. Men didn't refer to a woman's delicate condition unless they were family—and even then, only if it were absolutely necessary; it was unheard of.

But perhaps Jack Kane considered himself above the proprieties. Perhaps he figured he could say and do whatever he pleased.

"You'll not be keeping it, surely." His tone made this no question, but a statement of fact.

Suddenly furious with the man's presumption—never mind that he was her *benefactor*—Terese pushed herself up from the pillows. "I will indeed be keeping my child!"

He never so much as blinked but merely crossed his arms over his chest, still not quite meeting her gaze. "And how, exactly, will you manage?"

"Why, I intend to work! I'll not be asking for charity once I'm well again."

He raised an eyebrow. "That's very commendable, I'm sure, but perhaps not altogether practical. What sort of a position do you expect to find with a babe in arms?"

He sat there, so large and intimidating—so confident in himself and his money and his . . . control over her—that Terese knew a sudden stab of fear. The truth was that at this moment, at least, Jack Kane *did* have control over her, even had the power to keep her—and the babe—from going hungry.

And he knew it, perhaps was even flaunting it.

Then she remembered Cavan, and relief came rushing over her. "I don't know just yet what sort of work I'll be finding, sir. But as soon as I'm able, I'll be looking for a position. Until then, I expect Cavan will take care of me and the babe. He's already assured me that he would look after us."

Kane traced his dark mustache with a finger and nodded. "Cavan's a fine young man. And of course, he'll not see you go without. In fact, he'd likely assume full responsibility for you and the child." He stopped. "If you were to allow it."

Now he did look directly at Terese, his eyes narrowing as he did so. "But perhaps you can see that you'd be making things impossibly difficult for both you and your brother if you were to burden him in such a way. Cavan is scarcely more than a boy himself. It doesn't seem quite fair to put so great an obligation on the shoulders of one so young."

Silent for a moment, Kane continued to slap a glove against his hand. When he again spoke, his tone was thoughtful, even mild. "You might want to consider the fact that Cavan is only beginning his own career. And though he's a talented lad, he has a long road to travel before he'll be making the kind of wage it takes to support an entire family. I have every intention of helping him to further his education and gain as much experience as possible, but he'll need to apply himself. I'm afraid your brother will have little time for anything but work in the next few years if he's to be as success-ful as he hopes to be—and as successful as I think he *can* be."

Terese stared at him in dismay, too confused and uncertain to form a reply. She hadn't thought of being a burden to Cavan. In truth, she hadn't thought much about the future at all. She had been too ill, too overcome by her circumstances to do much more than simply exist from day to day.

Consequently, Jack Kane seemed to think she was nothing more than a useless, idle girl who would need to be dependent on some-one else for an indefinite time. She groped for something that might convince him otherwise, convince him that she could be—*would* be—responsible. Self-sufficient.

But he gave her no chance for argument, instead rose to his feet. "We needn't speak of this right now," he said, buttoning up his finely tailored overcoat and slipping on his gloves. His tone was al-most friendly as he added, "I promised Dr. Leslie I wouldn't stay long, after all. For the most part, I simply wanted to drop by and make certain you have everything you need. We'll talk again soon. When you've had more time to think."

With that, he gave a quick nod and turned to go, leaving Terese more confused and troubled than ever.

She had expected to dislike Jack Kane, given Brady's intermina-ble grousing about his brother. She had not, however, expected to be *frightened* of him, indeed hadn't thought of feeling *anything* to-ward Kane other than a grudging acceptance of his help in getting out of Ireland and making it possible for her to start over here in the States.

But she *was* frightened. Kane's voice had been quiet, his manner smooth and even solicitous at times. Nonetheless, the man had threatened her; she was sure of it.

But threatened *what?* What could a man like Jack Kane possibly want from her so much that he would employ threats to obtain it?

Shaken, Terese began to tremble, only a little at first, then more violently. She was no match for such a man, and she knew it. Her mind went to Cavan. There had been something in Kane's tone when he spoke of Cavan—something veiled, something too subtle to decipher—but it had been there all the same.

Her stomach gave a sudden wrench at the reminder that Kane was Cavan's *employer.* And Cavan, although he admitted to not being blind to Kane's shortcomings, fiercely admired the man. More than that, however, he loved his job. The job that Jack Kane had made possible for him.

She wouldn't dare mention to Cavan what had just transpired. He might get angry, do something foolish and spoil his standing with Kane, even lose his position. No, no matter how badly she wanted to tell him, she would have to keep her silence.

Samantha. Samantha would know what to do.

But almost as quickly as she considered it, Terese dismissed the possibility. There was something in Samantha's eyes when she looked at Jack Kane, something in her tone of voice when she spoke about him, that left little doubt as to her feelings for him. Terese had seen it more than once and puzzled over it, wondering how a woman as fine and good as Samantha Harte could be taken with the likes of Jack Kane.

But that she *was* taken with him, Terese had no doubt.

Come to think of it, Kane's grim features seemed to soften when he was with Samantha. He became—less forbidding. Perhaps he fancied *her,* too. Perhaps they even had an understanding.

No, she couldn't tell Samantha either. It seemed she couldn't tell anyone.

Throughout the rest of the evening, Terese went back and forth with her suspicions, struggling to convince herself that she was wrong, that she was being foolish and had only imagined any covert threat in Jack Kane's demeanor.

But her alarm only grew, so much so that by the time David Leslie returned from vespers she was too distracted and tense to enjoy his company.

If Jack felt a nagging uneasiness, even a measure of self-disgust, after his visit with Terese Sheridan, he quickly brushed it aside as he rode home. He was too gripped by his plan, too stirred by the possibilities and what they might mean to his relationship with Samantha to allow any misplaced sense of guilt to spoil his mood.

Clearly, the girl had been shaken. If nothing else, he had set her to thinking. And his instincts told him that Terese Sheridan was smart enough and enough of a survivor to reason things out to her own benefit.

Also, it was evident that she cared deeply for her brother. She wasn't likely to do anything that might go against Cavan.

He would give her a few days—three or four at the most—then pay her another call. This time he would put his offer on the table.

Unless he had misjudged the girl entirely, by then she would have seen the logic in his idea and would be ready, even eager, to accept.

Only once before he reached home did he fully consider the enormity of what he was about to set in motion. He actually had to bite down hard on the sudden surge of guilt and self-reproach that rose up in him, bringing with it the temptation to abandon the idea altogether. But the thought of Samantha and what he held in his power to give her was all he needed to suppress any doubts he might have had.

Samantha was worth any price he had to pay, certainly worth more than Terese Sheridan's foolish notion of raising a child on her own.

31

Before the Storm

I it is who shall depart,
Though I leave with heavy heart.
GEORGE SIGERSON

By the time Samantha and Jack left Maura Shanahan's flat, evening had drawn around the city, wrapping it in the deep, gray iron of a lowering sky and a bitterly cold wind that held the threat of snow.

Their breath misted the air inside the cab, and Samantha tugged the fur lap robe more snugly about her. It had been a good day, she thought with satisfaction as the cab neared her apartment. Earlier in the afternoon, Jack had sent a message with the news that the case against Maura Shanahan had been dropped, and would Samantha like to be at the jail when she was released? They would then see the woman safely home.

After leaving Maura—still slightly dazed by her good fortune but vastly relieved to be reunited with her children—Samantha had spent most of the ride back trying to thank Jack for his intervention. Although he pretended to dismiss her effusive gratitude as excessive and unnecessary, Samantha was convinced she was right: Maura Shanahan would never have gained her freedom if Jack hadn't taken a personal interest in her case. Instead, she might well have been swallowed up in a justice system that was at best unpredictable and often corrupt.

He had gone out of his way to help a woman he scarcely knew, and if Samantha wasn't mistaken, he had done it, not so much for Maura Shanahan, but for *her*—because of her own personal desire to help the unfortunate woman. Admittedly, Jack seemed to have a genuine fondness for Maura's son, Willie, who he insisted was one of his "spunkiest" newsboys. But there was no denying the fact that he'd first become involved in the Shanahan case primarily because of Samantha. How, then, could she *not* be grateful?

"I think perhaps I may start calling you 'Sir Jack,'" she said teasingly.

He lifted an eyebrow. "Well, now, I've been called many things, Samantha, but certainly that's a new one. To what do I owe such a radically inappropriate moniker?"

"It seems that you've been spending rather a lot of your time lately rescuing damsels in distress."

"Ah, I see. A knight in tarnished armor."

"I'm not so sure about that."

"Badly tarnished, Samantha. Take my word for it."

Samantha studied him, thinking he did indeed wear a kind of "armor" much of the time. His way, she had learned, of keeping others at a safe distance.

"I can't help but wonder," she said, "why you are so intent on making yourself out to be such a blackguard."

One corner of his mouth quirked, but his expression was without humor. "Just living up to my reputation, Samantha. I have a certain image to protect, you know."

"Not with me, you don't. And I'm not sure I give much credence to your so-called reputation anyway. I'm beginning to think you may just perpetuate the myth so people won't know that you're actually a very decent man."

He gave a small whoop of amusement. "Now there's an original thought! I declare, Samantha, you ought to try your hand at writing. With your imagination, you'd trounce my other reporters."

"Oh, do stop it, Jack!" she scolded him. "You don't fool me anymore. Just look what you've done for Maura Shanahan. Going to the trouble of hiring your own attorney for her, accompanying me to the jail and the meetings with Avery Foxworth—even driving her home after she was released today. And what about Terese Sheridan?" she went on. "Your protection of that poor girl hardly qualifies you as a scoundrel. Not to mention little Shona Madden. The child thinks you're ten feet tall!"

He didn't smile as she'd expected, instead sat tapping his fingers on the handle of the door. "That woebegone wee tyke would no doubt adore anyone who happened to throw a crumb of attention her way. Samantha—"

He stopped, his expression turning even more solemn as he faced her. "Samantha, I only wish you were right. I wish I *were* a better man than I appear to be, better than I'm presumed to be. I'd like nothing more than to be the kind of man you might *wish* me to be. But the truth is, I'm not, and you mustn't delude yourself into thinking otherwise."

He waved off her attempted objection. "Don't try to paint me as something other than what I am, Samantha. We both know I'm on my best behavior with you because I'm set on making you my wife. And I meant what I told you the night I first asked you to marry me: I'll devote myself to winning your trust and to being a good husband. But I'll not attempt to deceive you nor allow you to deceive yourself."

Samantha sensed that this declaration was absolutely sincere. And doubtless she ought to heed it, word for word. But it wasn't quite that easy, given the fact that she had come to love Jack Kane—loved him in spite of his questionable past, in spite of his less than admirable qualities, and in spite of his harsh opinion of himself. It was too late to go back, now that she knew—and loved—not the facade he presented to the world, the man he was presumed to be, but rather the heart he had opened to her, the man he was.

"Samantha?"

She tried not to look at him, for he would surely see more in her eyes than she wanted him to. But he was not to be put off. With one hand, he gently but firmly turned her about to face him. "Do you understand what I'm saying?"

Something flickered in his eyes, and Samantha saw again that he was altogether serious and, moreover, that he was determined to make her accept this uncompromising depiction of himself.

"You won't permit me to even give you the benefit of the doubt?" she said, trying for a lighter tone.

His eyes searched hers, and for a moment Samantha thought there was something more he wanted to say to her. But then he blinked, and his features cleared.

"Not a bit of it," he said, matching her tone. "Though if you're inclined to show me a measure of mercy now and then, I wouldn't be too proud to accept it."

He released her, and a heavy silence hung between them for several minutes, with nothing to be heard except the jangle of harness and the clop of the horse's hooves on the street.

"Here we are," he said, rousing Samantha from her thoughts as they pulled up in front of her apartment building. "I don't suppose you're going to invite me in," he said.

"You know very well I won't, so why do you always ask?"

"My image, remember?" He grinned at her, a return to his earlier sardonic humor. "Outrageous womanizer that I am, I have certain standards to maintain."

"Yes, well, not with me, you don't."

"Very well," he said. He gave a long, dramatic sigh—known as an "Irish sigh," according to Jack, because "didn't we perfect the art?"

His gaze went over her face with such a depth of tenderness and unmistakable longing that Samantha thought he would surely kiss her. Instead, he merely lifted her hand and brushed his lips over her gloved fingers.

Samantha didn't know whether she was relieved or disappointed. Perhaps a little of both.

He left her at the door, again lifting her hand to his lips before making his quick little bow and returning to the cab.

Samantha stood and watched the cab until it disappeared into the night. Was he right? Was he really the awful man he made himself out to be, the infidel others rumored him to be? Was she merely blinded by her love for him, too foolish, too stubborn to get away from him while she still could?

Oh, Lord, she prayed silently, *you told me I should pray for him and trust you . . . and I have . . . but nothing's changed—no matter how much I pray, nothing seems to change—including my feelings for him. . . . What am I to do, Lord? What am I to do?*

She stood there for a long time, praying for Jack and about what she was to do, but the night—and her spirit—refused to give up the silence. Finally, chilled and heavyhearted, she went inside.

For the first time since their arrival, Terese had been able to talk Shona into playing with some of the other children at the mission house. She stood watching them now, a small circle of little girls, all as thin as Shona and just as shabbily dressed, moving the wooden pieces of a puzzle around the floor of the hallway downstairs.

Even in play, Terese observed, the girl's face was solemn and intent, as if set firmly on some grave purpose. But she was a generous and good-natured child, if unnaturally quiet, and seemed to be getting on well with the others.

When the front door opened, the children scarcely noticed. But Terese felt her heart give a small leap as David Leslie walked in.

His doctor's bag in hand, his sand-colored hair ruffled by the wind, he smiled at Terese and came directly to her. "I can't tell you how glad I am to see you and Shona downstairs!"

Terese felt her face flush at the way he was looking at her—as if he truly *was* glad to see her. Quickly, she reminded herself that he was her doctor, after all. It was only natural he would be gratified to see any improvement.

Yet at times she sensed it was more than that, that his interest in her perhaps went beyond that of a physician for his patient. Why that would be so, however, eluded her. By now she was heavy with the child; she could not possibly be attractive to him or any other man. Still, the way his eyes seemed to brighten when he looked at her, and the way he could not seem to drag his gaze away from her, made her wonder.

More than once of late, she had caught herself wishing she could have met him at another time . . . before Brady, before the foolish, sinful dallying that had brought her to her present state.

Her hand instinctively went to her abdomen. But David Leslie seemed not to notice. He brushed a stray strand of hair away from his forehead, still smiling at her. "It's good to see Shona with the other children. I've tried to coax her to join them, but with no success. You're very good with her."

"She only agreed because I promised to watch," Terese told him. "She's terribly shy and unsure of herself."

"And reluctant to leave you as well, I've noticed. But she looks content enough for now. Why don't we go to the kitchen and see if there's any coffee left from supper? I'm chilled through."

Without waiting for a reply, he went to Shona, leaned down and said something to her, gesturing toward the hallway, then came back to Terese. "We have permission to excuse ourselves," he said, pressing her arm to turn her toward the doorway.

In the kitchen, they sat across from each other at the table—a large, badly scraped, makeshift affair around which the matrons and volunteers took their meals. David Leslie insisted that Terese have a glass of milk while he drank his coffee. "Only milk for you until the baby is born, young lady," he said with mock sternness.

Terese made no reply. He seldom mentioned her condition, hardly ever referred to the baby itself, and when he did she felt a wretched sense of shame and embarrassment course through her.

"Terese?"

She looked up to find him watching her.

"I know it's probably difficult for you, but I think perhaps we ought to talk about the baby. Have you thought about what you'll want to do after the child is born?"

Terese tried to take a drink of the milk he had set out in front of her, but it stuck in her throat. She set the glass down, avoiding his gaze. "I . . . don't know as yet what I'm going to do."

"I understand," he said gently. "You've been too ill to make any kind of decision. But keep in mind that you're not alone in this. Since you and Shona are both under the *Vanguard*'s sponsorship, it's not as if you're without means, you know. Samantha Harte will do everything possible to assist you."

His mention of the *Vanguard* sent a chill down Terese's spine. She could still see Jack Kane's face as it had been when *he* asked her about her plans.

"Mr. Kane doesn't think I should keep the baby," she said bluntly, lifting her face to watch his reaction.

He stared at her, his brows knitting in a frown. "What?"

"Mr. Kane," Terese repeated, unable to keep the anger out of her voice. "He made it perfectly clear he doesn't think I'm fit to care for a child."

David Leslie's lean features tightened still more. "Did he say that?"

Terese shrugged. "Not in so many words, he didn't. But he made his meaning clear enough all the same." She paused, the anger and apprehension Kane had evoked in her still all too real. "Do you agree with him? Do *you* think I ought to give away my baby?"

David Leslie studied her in silence. When he finally replied, his tone was quiet but firm. "What you do about the baby is your decision, Terese, no one else's. Certainly, given the circumstances, no one would fault you if you decided *not* to keep the child. But I must say, I've had the impression all along that you want to keep it."

"I *do!*" she cried. "I wouldn't be giving it up for anything!" She leaned forward, her hand brushing against the glass of milk. "But Mr. Kane—"

David Leslie reached to steady the glass, then covered her hand with his own. "No one is going to make you do anything you don't want to do, Terese. I'm sure Jack Kane didn't mean to insinuate that you should give up your own child. After all, he's committed the resources of his newspaper to helping you resettle. You must have misunderstood him."

Terese glanced at his hand covering hers, and he quickly released it.

She had *not* misunderstood Jack Kane. The more she thought about the encounter, the more certain she was that for whatever reason, the man had been telling her not to keep the baby.

". . . Kane would have no reason to care one way or the other, after all," David Leslie was saying.

He went on, but Terese no longer heard him. A sudden jolt of fear sent the blood rushing to her head at a dizzying speed. There was the puzzle, right enough: why *should* Jack Kane care what an unmarried Irish immigrant girl decided to do with a child that he doubtless assumed to be unwanted entirely?

More to the point, if Kane thought her unfit to care for the child of an unknown attacker—what would he do if he knew the baby had been sired by his own brother? If he was this dead set on her giving up the child when he knew nothing of its father, then dear Lord have mercy, he would probably take it from her himself if he knew it was of his own bloodline!

Terese almost strangled on the thought. It was as if someone had looped a noose around her neck and suddenly tightened it.

David Leslie was watching her, she realized, his expression questioning. "Excuse me," she mumbled, drawing away from the table. "I mustn't leave Shona alone any longer."

In her haste to get away from the doctor's searching gaze, she nearly knocked over her chair as she got clumsily to her feet and fled the room.

≈✦≈

David stood, watching her go, dismayed that he must have somehow upset her still more when he had only meant to reassure her. For a moment he had actually thought she was about to faint, so quickly had she paled and begun to tremble.

He called out to her once, but if she heard him, she pretended not to. She made her way to the door, swaying a little when she reached it, then steadying herself with one hand on the frame before starting off down the hall.

Obviously, this business with Kane had unsettled her more than he'd realized, though probably for no just reason. Kane surely couldn't have meant to frighten her.

But she *was* frightened, that much was clear. What in the world could the man have said to unnerve her so completely?

One thing was certain: she would have been at a grossly unfair disadvantage with him. Kane *was* rather formidable, after all. He could easily overwhelm someone in Terese's tenuous position.

On the other hand, he did not think that Terese Sheridan would be easily cowed. To the contrary, one of the things that had first drawn him to her was the strength he had sensed in her, the seemingly indomitable will that, even in the worst of her delirium, had often surfaced and blazed, if only for a brief moment.

No, he decided, even taken unawares, Terese would somehow manage to dig in and stand her ground if the situation required it.

In any event, David resented Kane's apparent lack of sensitivity, even if his intentions had been totally without malice. Besides, he couldn't be absolutely certain that Kane had meant Terese no ill will. Jack Kane was legendary for his ruthlessness; if the rumors were not overblown, he had destroyed more than one businessman who dared to go against him. Look at that series of articles he'd done some time back about the prominent citizens who doubled as the landlords of brothels and gambling dens all over the city. Kane had pulled no punches, had actually named names and cited their abhorrent practices one by one.

Even though David had silently applauded the articles, the act itself could be pointed to as an example of Kane's cold-bloodedness.

Whatever the man's intentions, David thought he would probably raise the issue of his interest in Terese's unborn child next time they met. She was his patient, after all, and still recovering. He had the right to inquire into whatever might have occurred to unsettle her so.

But even as he tried to convince himself, David knew his concern was something more than a natural desire to protect a patient. For a moment there he had been absolutely furious with Jack Kane at the mere thought that he might have somehow, even inadvertently, intimidated Terese.

He swallowed against an unfamiliar tightness in his throat, wondering not for the first time what he was to do about these increasingly disturbing feelings for his lovely young patient. The entire situation was unthinkable. He was a good deal older than she, for one thing; even though she was in the advanced stages of her pregnancy, she was little more than a girl. He had learned that she was from a radically different culture, a primitive, remote place—one of the Aran Islands it. More than likely only a handful of people in the States had ever heard of it. In addition, she was only now recovering from a precarious illness and still had a long way to go before she fully regained her health.

The rest of it was that she probably had no interest in him whatsoever except as her physician.

David raked a hand through his hair in frustration—frustration with himself and with the situation as a whole. If he were to be completely honest, he would simply admit the fact that he was a fool and stay well away from Terese Sheridan.

Very well, he was a fool. But as for staying away from Terese—he already knew he would do no such thing.

What he *would* do, however, was to try to think of a way to help her gain a measure of independence rather quickly. He admired her for wanting to keep her baby, indeed would have been disappointed if she had *not* wanted to keep it. If for some reason Jack Kane *did* mean to see that she gave it up because of her precarious circumstances, then the best thing *he* could do for her was to find a way by which she could support herself and the child.

As it happened, by the time he reached his office under the stairway, an idea had already begun to form.

32

Suspected Enemies

There is something here I do not get,
Some menace that I do not comprehend.
VALENTIN IREMONGER

A winter storm greeted New Yorkers just before noon Thursday and didn't pass until it had deposited several inches of snow on the city. A vicious wind blustered most of the day, whipping snow in the eyes of the horses as they ploughed through the streets with their various vehicles and forcing pedestrians to hunch their shoulders and bow their heads against its fury.

By late afternoon the snow was still falling. City streets were treacherous, and merchants and office managers began to close shop and send their people home.

At Grace Mission, Terese Sheridan sat in a chair by the window, watching the wind-driven snow spiral around the iron fence that ringed the building. The sky was the color of gunmetal, but the ground was totally white, its brightness relieving much of the gloom that ordinarily settled over the city this time of day.

Shona was perched on the bed, cutting out snowflakes from a page of newspaper, an activity learned from one of the other children. From time to time she glanced up, as if alert to Terese's glum mood.

Terese pretended not to notice. She was too preoccupied, too embroiled in her own worries to reassure the child.

At another time she might have enjoyed watching the curtain of snow whipping about the grounds. Earlier, when the storm first settled in, the children had scurried up and down the corridor, darting from one window to another to watch the drama taking place outside. Even Shona had seemed excited at first, later settling into a kind of quiet contentment as she occupied herself.

Perhaps it was natural to experience a sense of serenity and well-being while watching the wintry world from a safe, warm place inside. But for Terese, the wail of the wind and the sight of the heavy, congested sky emptying itself onto the city only served to darken her spirits still more.

If Samantha had come, Terese thought, perhaps this black mood would have passed by now. And, in fact, she *had* promised to come by today with new books for both Terese and Shona. But of course no one would venture out in weather such as this if it wasn't necessary, so the afternoon promised to drag on with no surcease from the monotony.

The attacks of dread that had seized Terese since the encounter with Jack Kane had become more frequent over the past two days. No matter how much she tried to suppress her fears, she couldn't seem to bury them altogether. She worried over the health of the child in light of her long, drawn-out illness and the brutal ship crossing. She worried over how long it might take her to recover from the birthing itself. She worried over the money she would need to make some sort of a home for herself and the child.

And she worried about Shona, for she had already decided she would not let the child go to strangers if she could help it. There was no telling what it would do to the girl to be ripped away from the one familiar person in her life, and this after losing her parents and brother, all in such a short time.

Terese had lived with dread so long that it seemed she couldn't remember a time when her chest didn't ache with it. But it was worse now than ever. Before, she had had only herself to fend for, and she had always been strong and able to manage, even in the harshest of circumstances.

But now she had the added responsibility of a baby. She drew a weary sigh as yet another blast of wind-driven snow lashed the side of the house. What would it be like, she wondered, to be Samantha Harte or Jack Kane, to be permanently secure in the knowledge that you had a roof over your head and food in the larder and adequate means to care for yourself and your family? Did their kind have any inkling of what it was like to live in fear of hunger or the cold, always at the mercy of another's whim or act of charity . . . when the very meaning of existence could be summed up in one word: *survival?*

Perhaps one of the reasons she so admired David Leslie was the way he seemed to devote himself to making survival possible for others less fortunate, obviously sacrificing his own comforts in the process.

Terese stared out into the storm, shivering, not so much from the cold as from the thought that she could just as easily be on the other side of the window, trudging through the snow in search of a place to sleep where she and her unborn babe would not freeze to death. At least here, thanks to David Leslie, she could count on a clean bed and enough to eat.

Which was more than she'd been able to count on most of her seventeen years.

The babe gave a strong kick just then, and Terese pressed a hand against her stomach. "It will be better for you," she murmured. "It *will*. Somehow, some way, I'll see to it that you don't have to scratch and scrape just to survive, I promise you."

When an ugly whisper insinuated itself at the corner of her mind as to how, exactly, she expected to keep such a rash promise, Terese brushed it aside.

She *would* keep it, no matter what it took. In her heart of hearts, she was determined to find a way.

***

"Turner Julian has finally made good on his threat, Jack. He's bringing suit against you. Along with three of the other business-men he claims you 'defamed.' They're filing a joint suit."

Avery Foxworth tapped his fingers on the arm of the chair, watching Jack closely.

They had met at the *Vanguard* for a change, rather than at the at-torney's office; considering the weather, Jack was just as glad.

He shrugged and made a dismissing gesture with his hand. "Julian is the instigator, I take it?"

Foxworth nodded.

"Besides my scalp, how much does he want?"

"Half a million."

Jack whistled softly. "The man does carry a fierce grudge, now doesn't he?"

"I warned you, Jack. Julian has been verbally filleting you ever since the exposé you published on the brothels—your . . . . 'Harlots and Hypocrites' piece." Foxworth wrinkled his nose as if he'd caught a whiff of a particularly vile odor. "I told you that you were asking for trouble when you ran it."

The exposé Avery Foxworth was referring to was an entire series Jack had done some time back on crime in general and prostitution in particular—and on those who helped to perpetuate the vice running rampant in the city. It was hardly a secret among the newspapermen—and the police force—that quite a few of the city's bawdy houses and gambling dens, not to mention some of the most abominable tenement buildings in New York, were owned by certain wealthy, "upstanding" citizens.

One of those citizens was the society physician, Turner Julian—a man Jack knew to be a consummate bigot, a hypocrite of the first rank, and, as a doctor, little more than a charlatan. In his editorials accompanying the exposé, Jack had applied a number of scathing epithets to Julian—"Fifth Avenue medicine man," for one—as well as an entire slate of allegations, which he had carefully documented. In addition, the series itself listed specific "business establishments" and other properties—some of which were virtual death traps—owned by Julian and his cronies under the cover of a middleman.

Admittedly, there was more to it on Jack's part than some sort of high-minded desire to expose the crooked shenanigans of Turner Julian and his kind. What Avery Foxworth didn't know—nor did anyone else, for that matter, except for Rufus Carver—was that to this day Jack was convinced that Turner Julian was directly responsible for the worst of Martha's suffering and final humiliation during the last days of her life, before the cancer finally claimed her.

Julian had made no secret of his contempt for the Irish, had shown Martha not a shred of mercy as the vicious disease ravaged her body and stripped her dignity from her day by day. When Jack persisted in trying to get the condescending physician to do something to ease her pain, Julian had dismissed him with unthinkable callousness, telling him that if he "wanted miracles, then call a priest."

The next day, however, the insufferable physician had gone on to perform—and totally botch—a hasty surgical procedure that caused Martha more agony than ever. When Jack realized what had happened, he went after Julian like a madman. If Rufus hadn't pulled him off the terrified doctor, Jack would probably have murdered the man in the middle of the hospital hallway.

He had bided his time in the intervening years, determined that he would not only expose Julian for the quack he was but for his shady business practices as well. Finally, after accumulating all the evidence he needed, he published everything he had in the *Vanguard*.

Since then, he'd heard from various sources that Julian's practice had suffered considerably in the wake of the exposé. Of course, Julian was old money—as was his wife—so financial ruin was never a real consideration. No doubt what galled the man most was the besmirching of his precious family name and the aspersions cast on his competence.

"Tell me again exactly what sort of proof you have." Avery Foxworth's prodding yanked Jack back to his surroundings.

"I have more than enough," Jack assured him. "Signed statements from some of the newsboys who also work as bagmen for Julian's 'managers,' and others from a couple of his former landlords. Copies of the deeds Julian holds—the man wasn't clever enough to reassign them. And, as I believe I told you before, I also have a sworn account from a former prostitute who used to work in one of his brothels and whom Julian himself patronized on several visits—before he beat her almost to death." Jack paused. "She was fourteen at the time."

Again Foxworth made a face of distaste. "The . . . young lady in question—did she give a statement to the police at the time?"

Jack twisted his mouth. "She was little more than a child—and a prostitute, Avery. Of course she didn't go to the police."

"But she talked to you?"

Jack shrugged. "Money will buy almost anything, as you undoubtedly know. Even the truth." He studied his attorney. "You seem annoyed, Avery. Anything in particular?"

Foxworth pursed his lips. "You don't seem to be taking this quite as seriously as I think you ought to."

"Now there you're wrong, Avery. I take being sued very seriously. Very seriously, indeed. But I don't see how Julian can hurt me. I'm not fool enough to go public with a fire-baiting story unless I have the means to put out the blaze. My own character may be a bit questionable, but I wouldn't risk the integrity of the paper."

Avery seemed to consider that for a moment. "No, I'm sure you wouldn't. Well, I trust you have all your documentation under lock and key, because we're likely to need it before this is over and done with."

Jack nodded, jerking his head toward the safe behind his desk. "It's all there. Don't fret yourself."

Foxworth stood, slipping on his fine leather gloves and smoothing them one finger at a time. "Very well, then. I believe I'll be getting along while the streets are still passable. It's getting nasty out there."

Jack got to his feet and came around the desk. "Thanks for coming by, Avery," he said, shaking his attorney's hand. "You'll be in touch?"

Foxworth gave a nod. "I'm going to prepare some sort of informal reply to the suit first thing. Just a letter, you understand, expressing the proper indignation and perhaps a veiled threat or two. It will get us nowhere, of course, but I want to go through those papers you have before we do anything else." He paused. "I don't suppose I could take them with me?"

Jack thought about it but didn't like the idea. "No offense, Avery, but I'd feel better keeping everything here for now."

"Never trust an Englishman, eh, Jack?"

Jack merely smiled as he opened the door to the hallway. "I never trust *any* man, Avery."

Foxworth left, shaking his head as he went.

Jack went to the window that looked out on the street and stood watching for a moment. He was tempted to change his mind about going to the mission house yet this afternoon. From the looks of it, the snow wasn't going to stop anytime soon.

But his plan had been burning a hole in his gullet for three days, and he was simply too impatient to put it off any longer. Besides, he had already sent Cavan Sheridan up to Albany, just as a precaution. This storm ought to keep the lad there over the weekend, at least. If the girl should get too wrought up, she might be tempted to confide in her brother, and Jack didn't want to have to deal with the both of them at once. He was fairly certain he could bring Cavan around without any great difficulty, but one problem at a time for now.

It was almost two-thirty. He would go to Grace Mission yet this afternoon, then come back and work for another two or three hours.

No point hoping to see Samantha tonight, after all; she wouldn't be venturing out in this kind of storm. He might as well finish the piece on the Harrison-Tyler ticket and get started on tomorrow's editorial.

Outside, he found Madog Wall shoveling off the stoop. The man tipped his hat to Jack and made way for him.

"You're not drivin' yourself home, are you, Mr. Kane?"

Jack pulled his topcoat collar a little higher around his throat. "Not yet, Madog. I thought I'd take the paper wagon over to Pearl Street. I figure it will get me there and back with less trouble than the carriage."

Madog looked appalled. "But, Mr. Kane—the way this is comin' down, you'll be soaked clear through by the time you get there! And half froze, to boot."

"Nonsense!" Jack waved off the man's concern and headed for the wagon. Given half a chance, Madog would fuss over him like a nervous granny. "A little snow isn't going to hurt me. I rather like the stuff. But I'll have your cap if you don't mind."

The burly Irishman looked altogether bewildered. "Sir?"

"Your cap, man! Lend me your cap if you're so worried about my staying warm!"

Madog stared at him as if he'd taken leave of his senses, but, always obedient, grabbed the cap off his head and tossed it to Jack. "'Tis good and clean, sir. Practically new, it is."

Jack laughed at him as he perched the wool cap on his head and hiked himself up on the bench of the wagon. "You're a good man, Madog!"

He clucked his tongue a couple of times, and the sturdy gray started off through the snow.

33

A Procession of Visitors

Hope, like the gleaming taper's light,
Adorns and cheers our way.
OLIVER GOLDSMITH

By the time Samantha reached Grace Mission, she realized she
might have made a mistake by venturing out into the storm. But
she had said she would come today and hated not to keep her
word. Besides, she had new books for Terese, as well as a lovely doll
for Shona, made by one of the ladies at church.

The cab she had taken was small and far too light for such a
heavy snowfall. Twice on the way they had gotten stuck, another
time nearly tipping over when they rounded a corner. Samantha
didn't relish the thought of the return trip in the same vehicle, but
she might not be able to hire anything else. Given the way the
snow was coming down, she had no intention of staying more than
a few minutes, so she asked the driver to wait for her outside the
mission.

The street was nearly deserted and desolate in the storm, the afternoon almost as dark as late evening. Snow sliced her skin, and the wind brought tears to her eyes as she hurried up to the front door.

Inside, it was more cheerful. Some of the children, no doubt aided by the volunteer workers, had made paper snowflakes and other winter decorations, hanging them from the banisters. A fire blazed in the grate in the front room, and from the direction of the kitchen came the sound of voices and pans rattling.

As Samantha started up the stairway, she heard the familiar sounds coming from the "sickroom"—the dormitory that housed the women and children who were seriously ill. The faint moans and cries never failed to tear at her heart, and ordinarily she would have gone there first, before visiting Terese and Shona. There was little she could do except to walk among the beds, inquiring after each patient or clasping a hand to offer reassurance. Sometimes she would hold one of the infants or toddlers for a while so that its mother could take a much-needed rest. Sometimes she could do nothing at all but pray for them.

Today, however, she went directly to Terese's room. She found Shona perched on the bed, making cutouts, while Terese sat by the window, watching the snow. Their obvious pleasure when she walked into the room warmed Samantha's heart, and now she was glad she'd made the effort to come.

She explained that she could stay only a few minutes. "I've left a cab waiting for me because of the storm. But I wanted to at least come by and give you these."

She gave Shona the doll and was rewarded to see the child's entire countenance light up with delight. After only a moment's hesitation, she received a hug from the girl, who then sat holding the doll in her arms as if it were the most precious, wondrous thing she had ever seen.

"What will you name her?" asked Samantha, smiling.

Shona looked up, seeming to consider the question with great care. "Her name is 'Samantha,'" she said solemnly.

Samantha blinked quickly, for an instant overcome with emotion. "Well," she finally managed, "I have never had a doll named after me, Shona. Thank you."

Terese's eyes also brightened when Samantha handed her the parcel of books. Included were a copy of Dickens's *Pickwick Papers* and a collection of Mr. Irving's regional stories. The books actually came from Samantha's own small library, but she chose to keep this information to herself.

Samantha had been surprised at how well Terese could read. So many of the immigrants she worked with—the Irish in particular—were either illiterate when they arrived or at best had only a rudimentary grasp of the English language; many from the more remote regions in western Ireland spoke only Gaelic. But both Cavan and Terese had been extremely fortunate in that their father, schooled in the basics by a Catholic priest, seemed to have passed on a love of reading to his children.

Shona was another matter. The child had obviously received very little in the way of education, a situation Samantha hoped to eventually remedy.

Watching Terese, Samantha sensed that in spite of her pleasure at the new books the girl seemed distracted, perhaps even troubled. There was a tension about her that hinted of some concern.

"Terese? Are you not feeling well?"

The girl looked at Samantha, then quickly glanced away. "No, I'm fine," she said, the reply coming perhaps a little too quickly.

Samantha didn't want to pry, but she couldn't shake the feeling that there was definitely something wrong. "You're quite sure?" she prompted gently.

The smile Terese gave seemed a little forced. "'Tis the snow, perhaps. It makes me feel a bit . . . edgy somehow."

Samantha studied her. "You *do* know, don't you, Terese, that if you ever have a problem, I'm here to help. I hope you wouldn't hesitate to ask."

The girl smiled again, this time more naturally. "You're very kind to us, Samantha. But please don't fret yourself about me. I'm perfectly fine. Truly, I am."

Samantha was hesitant to leave so soon but knew she must. "Well, then, I should go, I suppose. The storm is getting worse by the minute. Oh—I almost forgot. Cavan wanted me to tell you that he had to go out of town but will be back in a day or two. Mr. Kane sent him to Albany—that's the state capital—to gather some information for the paper."

Terese frowned. "Cavan went away in such a storm? Will he be all right?"

"Oh yes, he'll be fine! You mustn't worry about him. He's already there by now, and I'm sure if the storm gets too bad he'll simply stay over until the worst has passed."

Terese didn't look altogether convinced, but she said nothing more.

Still reluctant to go, Samantha drew on her gloves with deliberate slowness. Finally, after another hug from Shona and an extended good-bye to the two of them, she left.

The blast of icy snow and wind that greeted her as she stepped outside made her suddenly anxious to get home and stay there.

<hr/>

David Leslie seldom found himself at a loss for words with a patient.

But then, Terese Sheridan was no ordinary patient.

He hesitated at the door to her room, feeling as ill at ease as a callow schoolboy—not altogether because of what he was about to suggest but more because he knew how disappointed he would be if Terese turned him down.

But then why would she, he reasoned? This could easily be—indeed, would certainly appear to be—at least a partial solution to her concern about how she was going to support herself and her baby.

Ever since their conversation of the day before, David had been mulling over a number of possibilities as to how he could help her. He thought he might have finally settled on an idea that would relieve her mind somewhat about the future.

And what might it mean to *his* future, a sly voice whispered at the back of his mind? He could hardly pretend this was entirely for Terese, now could he?

By now David was thoroughly annoyed with himself for his own ambivalence. At the worst, she wouldn't be interested. He could still offer.

He drew in one long steadying breath, cleared his throat, and walked into the room.

⁂

Snow swirled like thick fog all about Jack. Madog had been right; he *would* be wet clear through by the time he reached the mission. His topcoat was already soaked.

This was no ordinary snowstorm; that much was certain. It was more of a blizzard. He had thought he was prepared for the worst, but he was beginning to wonder if he might have been a bit of a fool for hopping onto an open wagon in such a storm. The wind was ploughing up the street, shrieking like a banshee, hurling the snow full force as it came. Jack wouldn't have been all that sur-

316

prised to find himself lifted off the wagon and tossed into the street.

He kept his head down, his shoulders hunched, but there was no real protection for his stinging skin or burning eyes. He caught a breath, sucking in a blast of snow and choking on it. Everything was white, the very air a heavy curtain of ice and snow blowing wildly in the wind.

He considered turning back, but he was over halfway there by now. Besides, by tomorrow the streets might be well nigh impass-able.

The decision made, he swept his woolen neck muffler up over the bottom half of his face as a kind of mask and kept going.

Terese looked up when David entered, and he was unreasonably pleased at the way her eyes lighted when she saw him.

He had half expected to find Shona with her, perhaps had even been *hoping* she would be here, to give him an excuse for delay.

"Dr. Leslie," she said quietly.

David stopped just inside the room, transfixed for the moment by the sight of her. Even in the dusky room, with only the gray light from the window framing her, her hair was a cloud of fire. Cropped as it was, it still curled softly around her face. She was dressed in a faded hand-me-down garment donated by one of the church benevolent societies. Even in this, and noticeably swollen with child, she somehow managed to strike a bearing of uncom-mon loveliness.

And she *was* lovely. This pregnant, seventeen-year-old girl with the haunted eyes and the slightly cynical smile literally took his breath away. He was in love with her, no doubt about it: hopelessly, helplessly in love for the first time in his life.

317

Almost thirty-five years old and he had suddenly turned into an awkward, lovesick fool. David sighed. Was there anything more pathetic, he wondered, than a wretchedly shy bachelor in love for the first time?

"Would it be terribly difficult," he said, walking the rest of the way into the room, "for you to call me 'David'?"

Terese looked surprised but then smiled. "Not so terribly difficult, I suppose . . . *David.*"

He savored the sound of his name on her lips. "That's better. So—how are you feeling?"

"Stout," she said dryly. "A bit like a bloated whale." The next instant she blushed, as if she had only then realized that her response might be indelicate.

David laughed, hoping to relieve her embarrassment. "I assure you, you don't in the least resemble one. Where is your shadow, by the way?"

"Shona? She went downstairs to show off her new doll, I expect. Samantha brought it for her."

"I'm surprised Samantha would venture out on such a day. But no doubt you're glad she did."

She nodded, and he pulled up a chair directly in front of her. "I had an idea I wanted to discuss with you," he said. "Are you up to a chat?"

Again she gave a nod, watching him.

"Terese, I know you're concerned about the future," he began somewhat awkwardly. "About how you're going to manage with a new baby to care for."

She frowned, a guarded look rising in her eyes.

"I've been thinking about you—your situation, that is—ever since we talked yesterday. And I believe I may have a solution. One that could benefit both of us." David paused, then decided to just get on with it. "I'm wondering if you might consider staying on here—after the baby is born I mean—as an employee?"

She stared at him, clearly bewildered. "I don't understand."

David undertook to explain. "Like most of the missions in the city, we depend almost entirely on volunteer assistance, and we've been fortunate in that respect. The churches and some of the immigrant societies have been wonderful in helping us as much as they can. But as it happens, we've grown too large to continue without at least a few full-time employees." He stopped. "I—was thinking that perhaps you might be interested in a position with us."

Her mouth dropped open a little. "A position? What sort of position?"

"I'm in rather urgent need of someone to help care for the children, you see. They don't get nearly enough attention, as you may have noticed. You're awfully good with them, Terese—I've watched you from time to time. The children take to you."

"Why . . . I like them, too, sure, but how much help could I be—"

"Oh, I don't mean right away," he hurried to assure her. "Naturally, you can't take on anything of the sort until after the baby comes. But I was hoping that, later, you might consider a job here."

She was still frowning, but David thought she also seemed interested.

"But surely that wouldn't be a real job—taking care of the children," she said.

He laughed a little. "Actually, it would probably take a great deal more time and effort than you might expect. But even if it didn't, I could use your help in other areas. Didn't you tell me you'd done housework and even a bit of nursing for a woman back in Ireland?"

She nodded slowly. "Aye. Jane Connolly. She was in a bad way,

Jane was. I kept house for her and helped tend to her personal needs as well."

David laced his fingers together on one knee. "That kind of experience would be awfully helpful to me. Would you be willing to do the same sort of thing here at the mission? I realize it would be menial work, but it's important work, all the same."

Her chin lifted a little. "I'm not above doing for others, if that's what you mean."

David smiled at her. "No, I didn't think you would be. Now I'll be perfectly honest, Terese: the salary wouldn't be all that generous. I'm trying to build a staff here and at three other mission houses in the city, so there's not a great deal of money available. But you would have a small wage, plus a room of your own for you and the baby—and your meals, of course."

He could definitely see a glint of excitement in her eyes now. "You're serious about this, then?" She leaned forward a little. "You'd do this for me?"

"No, Terese, I'd actually be doing it for *me,*" David emphasized. "I'm rather desperate for help."

She studied him with an intensity that made David squirm a little.

"But why *me?*" she asked. "No doubt you could get another woman right away, someone who's not going to be—indisposed—for a time. Why would you wait for me?"

He should have known she was too sharp witted to simply grab at the idea without questioning his motives. He expelled a long breath, holding her gaze, although he could feel a bit of a flush creeping up his face. "I might just as well be honest with you, I suppose. I *do* need the help—that's no exaggeration. But the rest of it is that I . . . ah . . . I really don't want you to leave."

Her eyebrows lifted slightly.

David's palms suddenly felt clammy, and he knotted his hands into fists on top of his knees. "I'm not very good at this sort of thing, Terese. Haven't had much practice, you see. What I'm getting at is that I . . . ah . . . find you attractive, and I like . . . being with you."

He gave a helpless shrug. "I'm not saying this very well, am I?"

She was looking at him with unconcealed disbelief. "You think me . . . *attractive?*"

Had he not been so ill at ease—or so intent on convincing her—David might have laughed at her incredulity. "Only a blind man wouldn't find you attractive, Terese. But it's much more than that. I—*like* you. Very much, actually. And I don't want you to go away."

She straightened a little, her hands gripping the arms of the chair. She sat in silence for a time, seeming to consider his idea. "Shona? Would she be staying, too?"

"Oh—well, of course, she can stay as long as need be. I suppose later Samantha Harte will try to locate a family who will take her in—even adopt her—if Shona is agreeable. But until then, naturally she can stay right here with you."

He could almost see her uncertainty warring with a growing interest in his proposition.

"You don't have to decide now," David offered. "I just thought . . . it might relieve your mind a bit to know you have a job waiting—if you want it."

A shadow of something touched her face. A sinking feeling struck David. Perhaps he had put her in an untenable position by admitting his attraction to her, and she simply didn't know how to reject him without spoiling her chances for the job.

He rose, suddenly anxious to get out of the room before she turned him down altogether. "I should be going," he said, his words spilling out in a rush. "I haven't finished my rounds yet. As I said, I don't need an answer from you right away. Just . . . take your time. And, Terese—"

She looked up, her expression unreadable.

"I want you to understand," he said awkwardly. "The job is in no way connected to my . . . interest in you. I mean, I wouldn't want you to think that you'd have to suffer my . . . attentions . . . just because you took the position. If it happens that you don't return my feelings, that wouldn't affect your employment in any way, I assure you."

He turned, then, almost stumbling in his haste to flee the room before she could reply.

⁂

Terese watched him go, her emotions rioting in his wake. She was stunned by what had just occurred. The offer of a job would have been wonder enough—it was like a gift from heaven—but that a man of David Leslie's stature would take a fancy to her, and in her condition at that, was nothing short of astounding!

Bitterly, she reminded herself that he knew virtually nothing about her, indeed believed her to be an innocent girl victimized by an unknown assailant. No doubt if he knew the truth about her—and the baby—he would change his tune entirely.

But in the meantime he had thrown her a lifeline, had given her a means of escape from a situation that only hours ago seemed utterly hopeless.

Now if the great Jack Kane came sniffing around with his prying questions and subtle threats, she need not cower. She had the promise, not only of a job, but a roof over her head and safekeeping for her baby.

As for the other—David's interest in her—she need not deal with that now. It was enough that he had offered her a position—and with no strings attached.

He was a good man, a kind man, and she was drawn to him, no denying it. But she must not for one minute allow herself to believe that anything could ever come of it. He would not want her if he knew the truth, and she would not deceive him, if ever it came to that.

She had had quite enough of deceit. If she ever managed to extricate herself from the web of lies and deception that she and Brady had initiated by their own actions, she would never tolerate anything less than the truth again, not in herself or in another.

But for now she would take comfort in the knowledge that perhaps God had not deserted her after all. She had begun to fear she might have imagined his forgiveness. From the day she had dropped to her knees in the middle of a mean, squalid street in Galway City and begged in desperation for his mercy, she had tried to hold fast to the belief that there was hope for her and her child, after all, in spite of her sin. But during the nightmare voyage across the ocean and all that came after, she had found it difficult, nearly impossible, to hold onto that hope.

Now she somehow felt as though her hope had been renewed. For the first time in months, the burden of fear dropped away, and relief washed over her like a fountain of goodness.

"Perhaps God has not forgotten us after all," she murmured, touching her abdomen where the babe rested within her. "Perhaps he truly *has* given us a future and a hope."

***

Jack pulled the wagon as close as he could get to the curb, which because of the drifting snow wasn't very close at all. Tugging Madog's cap down over his ears, he turned his coat collar up about his throat, then leaped off the wagon bench and hitched the gray to the post in front.

Inside, he glanced into the front room, pleased to see the little Madden girl playing with a group of the other children. As much as he enjoyed the child, today he wanted Terese Sheridan alone.

He took the steps two at a time. At the door to her room, he stopped. She was sitting in a chair by the window. She looked to be asleep, and Jack hesitated, but only for a moment before pulling the cap from his head and walking into the room, not bothering to knock.

※◎◆◎※

Terese had dozed after David left, but she roused the instant Jack Kane stepped inside the room.

He had caught her off guard, and for a moment she was somewhat disoriented. The light squeezing in through the window was gray and weak, casting the room in shadows. But she could see Kane clearly enough, and at the sight of him a wave of black fear swept through her.

Clad in an obviously expensive topcoat with a white posy in the lapel, he looked every bit the city gentleman. But Terese was not fooled: Jack Kane was no gentleman. Brady's brother, by Brady's own definition, was a shark.

His dark features were set in a hard, unyielding look. He raked a hand through his hair, never taking his eyes off her as he walked the rest of the way into the room.

Every muscle in Terese tensed. But then she remembered that, thanks to David Leslie, she need not fear this man. She straightened, lifted her chin and braced herself for whatever was to come.

34

Eye of the Storm

The winter is cold,
the wind is risen.

FROM COLLOQUY OF THE ANCIENTS,
THE FENIAN CYCLE

"Terese," Jack said with a quick nod. "How are you keeping today?"

"Very well, thank you." The unmistakable note of caution in her voice was reflected in her eyes.

Without waiting to be asked, Jack crossed the room and took the chair opposite her, close to the window. "Quite a storm we're having," he said, gesturing toward the window.

She made no pretense at casual conversation, nor did she attempt to conceal her suspicion as she sat watching him.

"You'll want to know that Cavan is out of town for a day or so," Jack offered conversationally. "He's in Albany, on assignment. I expect he'll be back in a couple of days, if he doesn't get snowbound."

"Aye, Samantha told me."

Jack frowned. "Samantha was here?"

She nodded. "She left a short while ago. Half an hour, perhaps. She was anxious to get home because of the storm."

"She came by cab, I suppose?"

"She did, yes."

Jack was as irritated as he was surprised at the thought of Samantha traipsing about in such beastly weather. She could be the most *headstrong* woman at times.

His attention returned to the Sheridan girl. He hadn't missed the fact that she'd referred to Samantha by her given name, rather than as "Mrs. Harte." He supposed that shouldn't surprise him. Samantha wasn't one to stand on formalities, and she'd spent a great deal of time with Terese Sheridan—and with Shona as well—over the past few weeks. He had already observed that a kind of unlikely friendship had developed.

Samantha did have a deucedly soft heart when it came to those less fortunate, and she seemed particularly drawn to Terese Sheridan. That being the case, he should probably take care not to antagonize the girl too much; he wouldn't want to give her a means of unduly influencing Samantha against him.

As she might be tempted to do. Especially after today.

Watching the girl, he caught the same sense of something he had glimpsed before: a strength of will not usually seen in one so young. There were times when her countenance took on a look of challenge, a defiance that brought to mind the words *Irish proud,* as he tended to think of it—the often irrational obstinacy and hardheaded willfulness that he sometimes thought must characterize a major part of the Irish race, and that unchecked often proved to be their undoing. Brady displayed it in strong doses. And if truth be told, he himself had been afflicted with a goodly measure of it as well.

He was dealing with a girl, or rather a proud young woman, who might not be so easily brought to heel if she were not almost entirely dependent—at least for now—on his support. A part of Jack could not help but admire her spirit, even the way she was glaring at him at the moment in spite of her ashen appearance and the profound effort it was undoubtedly taking to reveal no sign of unease in his presence.

He had not come to match wills or wits, however. In the long run, if the girl were even half as clever as he suspected her to be, she would concede. What choice did she have, after all?

He did not like himself very much at this moment, indeed felt slightly ashamed of the way he meant to take advantage. But this was for Samantha, he reminded himself.

And ultimately, for Terese Sheridan as well. He couldn't imagine what she must be thinking, to believe that she could support herself and a child, given her present circumstances. On her own, she was utterly destitute, still severely weakened by her extended illness, and entirely without resources, aside from whatever the *Vanguard* chose to provide and the small stipend her brother could perhaps manage. She had no income, no position, and perhaps an extended lying-in period ahead of her yet. What could she hope to offer a child but more of the same poverty from which she herself was trying to escape?

Originally he had planned to allow young Cavan and his sister to live above the stable in back of his house. He had even gone so far as to partition it and make an extra room. But that was before he decided to pursue his present plan, to gain custody of the child. Of course, if the Sheridan girl cooperated, the rooms would still be available to her and her brother if they were interested.

He still believed that, although Terese might not see it his way until a long time hence, he was actually offering her the opportunity to make a new beginning without the encumbrance of a child. Eventually, she would realize what he had done for her and even be grateful to him. Until then, however, he would have to suffer her resentment and what was almost sure to be a great deal of anger.

He realized he'd been woolgathering then and looked across at her to find her watching him with a wary, inquisitive expression.

"We talked the other day about your plans for the future," Jack said. "I thought we might continue the conversation, if you're up to it."

He saw her tense even more. The hands on the arms of the chair were white knuckled by now, and her features, always sharp, grew taut and almost unpleasant.

She didn't care for him; that much was clear, Jack thought with a touch of grim amusement. But then, why should she? Certainly, he had given her no reason to feel much of anything toward him except distrust and dislike.

But he would give the girl credit: she didn't blanch, didn't flinch, didn't even blink under his scrutiny. If he unsettled her at all, she wasn't about to give him the satisfaction of seeing it.

Ah, well, the Irish always did like a worthy opponent. "Have you thought any more about the possibility of giving the child up for adoption?" he said with no further preliminaries.

She paled. "No! As I told you, I will be keeping my baby."

"And I will ask you again, how do you plan to manage?" Jack said mildly.

Her eyes blazed and she threw her answer back in his face with an ill-concealed note of triumph. "I have a job, as it happens. A job with room and board."

Caught off guard, Jack studied her for any sign of dissembling. His deliberately moderate tone was in direct contrast to her obvious agitation as he replied. "I see. Well, now—you seem to have accomplished a great deal in three days. May I inquire as to the nature of this—position?"

She smiled at him, a catlike smile that was both sly and defiant at the same time. "Dr. Leslie has offered me a job with the mission. I'm to have a room for myself and the baby, as well as wages."

Jack had not for a minute anticipated this, but he was careful not to react. "Good of him, I must say. But what happened to your idea of letting your brother take responsibility for you and the child?"

Anger sparked in her eyes. *"I* will take responsibility for *myself*—and for my child!" She paused, shooting Jack a look of transparent dislike. "As you were so quick to point out to me, Cavan should not be burdened at this stage of his own career. Now I won't have to depend on him. Or anyone else."

Jack was having a difficult time keeping his own anger under control. He wasn't sure whom he was most aggravated with—the Sheridan girl or David Leslie. He detested being caught unawares, being put at a disadvantage—especially by a seventeen-year-old immigrant girl.

He had come here prepared to be fair, even generous, thinking he knew exactly the strings to pull that would disarm Terese Sheridan and put her on the defensive. Now he apparently would have to rethink his strategy.

So be it. He was convinced that in spite of her obvious satisfaction with herself, she could still be turned easily enough.

As he'd told Avery Foxworth earlier, money would buy just about anything.

***

Samantha was dismayed to see how the street conditions had worsened since she'd first left home little more than an hour ago.

Now she was stuck in the cab, sandwiched between a freight

wagon in front and a carriage behind. They had been sitting here for several minutes. The horse was pawing the ground and snorting from the cold, while Samantha's breath steamed the air inside the cab. They had covered only two blocks from the mission when they came to a stop, but it seemed as if it had taken forever to gain even that.

She was cold and growing more and more restless, but there was absolutely nothing she could do except to sit and shiver, waiting. All around them, other drivers and passengers were either out of their vehicles, checking to see what the delay was, or shouting impatient barbs at one another.

When they finally began to move again, Samantha breathed a long sigh. She couldn't reach home soon enough. But her relief was short lived. As they rounded the corner onto Beckman, the wheels skidded, throwing the cab into a skid. One wheel must have hit a deep rut, causing the cab to careen. It swayed, shuddered, and then pitched sideways.

Samantha cried out as she was thrown hard against the side of the cab, wrenching her shoulder. It took her a moment to realize that she wasn't actually hurt, merely stunned.

There was silence for a few seconds, then she heard the loud whinnying of the horse and voices approaching the cab. The nervous driver hurried around to help her out.

Outside, Samantha found the horse still standing, but the cab seemed lodged with one wheel embedded in a treacherous rut and the other severely bent. Clearly, she would be going no farther in this vehicle.

Some of the people in the crowd expressed concern for her, but after Samantha assured them that she was all right, they began to dissipate.

She stood in the middle of Beckman Street, which was hopelessly rutted and dangerously icy, trying to decide what to do. She decided it would be foolish to try her luck with yet another cab, and the chances of getting one of the rare conversion sleighs or a cutter were probably next to nothing in this part of town. She considered her situation for another moment. Fortunately, she had worn a pair of sturdy boots and her warmest coat and gloves. She wasn't all that far from the mission; the most practical thing would be to return.

If David Leslie was there, perhaps he could manage to see that she got home somehow. If not—then she supposed she would have to spend the night there.

Her decision made, she brushed herself off, secured her hat, and started walking in the direction from which she had come.

<hr/>

She would not let him see so much as a hint of fear in her—she would *not!*

Terese sat waiting for Jack Kane's next remark; clearly, he had not finished his business with her yet. She cautioned herself against feeling too much satisfaction at this point, even though his surprise upon learning about her job offer had been obvious. She knew little about Brady's powerful older brother, but she had seen enough to know that Jack Kane was not a man who appreciated being outfoxed. She must be careful. It would be foolish entirely to deliberately antagonize this man, no matter how her blood boiled at his insufferable bullying.

So she continued to watch him carefully, determined to stay calm and coolheaded in anticipation of yet another barrage of unpleasant questioning.

It wasn't long in coming.

"No doubt the good doctor's proposition seems like an excellent solution to your future," Kane said in a tone that sounded almost friendly. "A job, a place to stay—a place with which you're already familiar—and a small wage for pocket money. I'm right in assuming it would be a *small* wage, am I not?"

Terese made no reply but simply gripped the arms of the chair a little more tightly.

"But I would suggest that you think about this at some length, girl. What about later? Will you be satisfied to stay here indefinitely, working for a pittance, never striking out on your own, never being more than a drudge—and raising your child in the midst of sickness and despair? Is that all you want for yourself—for the child?"

Terese clenched her teeth, determined not to let him shake her. "It would not be forever," she said tightly. "Just for a time, until I decide what I want to do." She paused, choosing her words carefully. "I should think you would approve. Sure, it must be an expensive venture, bringing so many to America and paying for our keep indefinitely. Wouldn't you prefer that we earn our own way instead of being dependent on you and your newspaper?"

He regarded her with a look that made Terese go cold inside. Those black eyes of his gave no hint of what he might be thinking, but his hard mouth had thinned until it was little more than a slash.

"Despite what you may have been led to believe by my brother," he said slowly, his tone still smooth and unperturbed, "I have no intention of supporting you or anyone else 'indefinitely.' As a matter of fact, should you fail to cooperate, to keep up your part of the arrangement, I can always arrange to have you sent back to Ireland."

Terese's heart slammed hard against her chest. At the same time the babe kicked, as if the womb itself had been shaken by Kane's threat.

"Why are you doing this?" she choked out. "Why are you so—set against me?"

He stood, his lean frame looming tall and dark in the dreary room. "I'm not against you, Terese. To the contrary, I'm trying to

332

help you. But since you're so determined not to *accept* my help, it occurs to me that I should approach this as I would any other business matter, one in which we can both benefit."

He began to tap his gloves lightly against the palm of one hand. "The simple fact is that you have something I want," he said quietly, his eyes glinting like black fire. "And I have the means to make your life either considerably easier or—much more difficult." With that he turned away, leaving Terese to stare at his back.

Her throat burned as if she had swallowed acid. "What—could I possibly have that a man like you would want?" she asked him warily.

He had been looking out the window, but now he turned and gave her a cold, unpleasant smile. "I think you already know the answer to that, Terese," he said, his voice a low rumble in the stillness of the room. "I want your child, of course. And I'm willing to pay you a handsome price for it."

⁂

She looked up into his face, her own countenance going ghastly white. *"Why?"*

Jack debated about what, exactly, to tell her, then decided it might work to his advantage to simply tell her the truth. "For Samantha," he said quietly. "She can't have children of her own, you see. I want to marry her, but she feels that she would be—cheating me, because she can't give me a child. I don't care about that, but she *does*. And, to put it bluntly, Terese, I happen to believe that at this particular time in your life, you wouldn't be nearly as good a mother as Samantha."

A flush of anger suffused her features, but Jack went on, giving her no chance to interrupt. "You're young, girl. Some would say *too* young to shoulder the responsibility a child brings. Be that as it may, you have your entire life ahead of you—you'll have plenty of time to bear all the children you want. Right now, this baby that you're carrying will be more burden to you than blessing. But it can make all the difference in the world to Samantha."

"And to you," she said with an ugly twist of her mouth.

Jack nodded. "Exactly." He drew in a long breath. "Terese, you can't fight me. As I see it, you really don't have a choice. If you go against me, you'll regret it. If you cooperate, I'll see that you—and Cavan—are well taken care of for years to come. Be reasonable, girl. You like Samantha. You know she'd be a good mother. Do this for her, and you'll have my gratitude."

"And if I don't?"

Jack lifted his brows. "Do you really want me to answer that?"

Jack saw the sudden blaze of fury in her eyes, only to be replaced almost instantly by fear, and at that moment he disliked himself more than he had for a very long time.

He was deliberately baiting and intimidating a vulnerable young girl, a girl who had already suffered a brutal assault, who carried a *child* because of that assault, a girl who had left her own country to begin anew in a strange city in a strange land—with the help of the newspaper he owned. He was the one individual committed to helping her—and instead he was manipulating her.

Suddenly, something stopped him, riveting him as he stood staring at her. He remembered the night he had seen Terese Sheridan for the first time, how it had affected him. He had nearly gone weak at the excruciating memories she had evoked in him with her critical illness, her weakness, the seeming hopelessness of her situation.

That night there had been no sign of the dauntless will, the inner strength, the fiery spirit that by now he had come to recognize in the girl. He had not yet encountered the brashness that dared to challenge him, the stubbornness that, at least in one more mature and more experienced, might well have presented a fair match for his own bullheaded resolve. He had not yet caught a glimpse of her fundamental *toughness*. But he saw it now, and he thought he saw something else as well, something that didn't quite add up: this girl was no ordinary *victim*. He had known his share of victims—those who had suffered bitter, sometimes devastating abuse or trauma. And while many eventually overcame the worst of the effects, it had been Jack's experience that it almost always took years—as was most definitely the case with Samantha, who still showed evidence of her ill treatment. And in some cases, like his own mother's, healing never came at all.

When his mother was brutalized, it had destroyed her health—and nearly her mind as well. Jack had been old enough at the time to be only too aware of her suffering; she had never been the same after her agonizing experience. Ever after, she had lived in a kind of invisible cage, frightened of living, often uncertain, and always watching . . . watching everyone and everything. Jack was fairly certain that she never again experienced so much as one night of unbroken sleep. In her nightmares, she suffered the attack over and over again until the day she died giving birth to Brady.

The girl who sat glaring up at him was no doubt frightened, but her fear seemed more to fuel her determination than to cower her. She feared, not him, exactly, but more the threat he represented. And she was willing to fight him. This girl was not weak, not faint-hearted, in mind or in spirit. In short, she simply gave little sign—other than the pregnancy itself—that she had been beaten or violated. Terese Sheridan, he sensed, was not so much a victim as a survivor.

His every instinct suddenly engaged and went on the alert. *What if she hadn't been assaulted at all?* What if she were lying about some clandestine affair, using the *Vanguard*'s resettlement program to flee her past and improve her circumstances? Or what if she had been promiscuous and gotten herself trapped by her own indiscretion? She didn't seem the type, but then there was often no telling the "type."

At the back of Jack's mind, he recognized that his present line of thinking might be nothing more than an attempt to rationalize his own heartless behavior, and again he felt an uncomfortable dart of self-disgust. Nevertheless, he decided to test his suspicions.

"Forgive my bluntness, Terese," he said. "But I confess I might have made the assumption that you wouldn't mind giving up the child all that much, considering the experience that brought about your condition in the first place. Perhaps I even thought you'd be relieved." He paused, ignoring her attempted protest. "It isn't such a rare thing, after all, for an unwanted infant to be put up for adoption."

"But my child is *not* unwanted!" she shot back at him, half rising from the chair. "And you're not talking about adoption. You're trying to buy my baby!"

Jack took his time in answering, raking her with a speculative gaze. He deliberately remained standing, keeping the advantage. "I suppose you might see it that way," he finally said. "But I tend to think of it more as giving you your freedom."

"I don't *want* to be free of my own child!"

Jack continued to feel his way. "Yes, I'm beginning to understand that. And I must say that while your . . . commitment to your attacker's child might be admirable, it's also passing strange. I should think you'd find it very difficult, if not impossible, to feel any sort of affection for a child that was forced upon you through such a heinous experience—and one over which you had no control."

He waited, watching her closely. For the first time he thought he detected some confusion in her and perhaps a measure of uncertainty.

He saw her swallow with noticeable effort. "'Tis not the child's fault, what was done to me," she said, her eyes averted.

"Of course it wasn't," Jack agreed amicably. "But the fault was not yours, either. And yet you seem to feel obligated."

He let the words hang, unfinished, not quite a question, yet not quite a statement either.

"'Tis not obligated I feel," she said after a noticeable hesitation. "The child is a part of me, after all."

"How did it happen, Terese?" he said quietly.

She looked up at him, her eyes slightly wild. "Please don't—ask me to talk about it," she stammered out, quickly lowering her gaze to her lap. "I can't possibly."

"I see. Because it's still too painful?"

"Yes, of course it's painful!" she said, her words shooting out like bullets. "Besides," she added, her voice lower and slightly unsteady, "it's not—seemly, to speak of such things with you, a man I scarcely know. I—don't want to speak of it at all, not ever again!"

Jack said nothing, deliberately waiting. When she refused to look at him, he stepped a little closer to her. "This . . . unspeakable act that was perpetrated on you—where did it happen?"

She looked up. "What?"

"Where did the attack occur? Where were you?"

"I—in Galway," she stammered. "Galway City."

She was rattled, Jack could tell. He sensed it was time to press. Hard. "At night?"

"Night—yes, it was at night." She frowned at him. "Didn't I say I don't want to speak of it?"

"What were you doing alone in the city at night?"

She was clearly confounded by the way he was baiting her. "I—I had an errand. I was doing an errand for Jane Connolly. My employer."

"An errand you couldn't attend to during the day?"

"If I could have seen to it by day, wouldn't I have done so?"

"Did you know the man?"

She stared at him, not answering.

"The man who assaulted you," Jack said roughly. "Did you know him?"

"N-no, I did *not* know him! And I will not discuss this any further with you! It—shames me!"

Jack jumped on that. "But why should it shame you, when you were entirely innocent? You *were* innocent," Jack said, pausing. "Weren't you?"

She glared at him with all the scalding hostility he suspected she was capable of and something else, something Jack had seen in the eyes of other adversaries whom he had outmaneuvered: the quick fury at being found out, followed by panic and a desperate attempt to maintain the lie.

"What are you saying?" Her words were little more than a harsh whisper, and Jack suspected that the insolence in her tone was nothing more than an attempt to shield herself.

Jack no longer gambled, not at the gaming table. But the old instincts that had once made him such a formidable opponent remained keen. He was responding to those instincts now, convinced that Terese Sheridan's anger and indignation rang patently false.

The girl was lying through her teeth or he would be a salmon marching.

<hr />

As Samantha approached Grace Mission, she saw the newspaper wagon parked in front of David Leslie's chaise and drew a sigh of relief.

She tried to walk faster, but the depth of the snow made if virtually impossible to hurry. She hadn't thought of Jack stopping by to
visit Terese on a day like this, but she was grateful he had. Apparently he had decided the newspaper wagon would be more sensi-
ble than a carriage. A wise decision, she thought, considering her
experience with the cab.

His being here meant that she would almost certainly have a
ride back to her apartment. And the thought of driving through a
snowstorm in an open wagon was still more appealing than being
stranded away from home overnight.

The heavy snow sucked at her feet, rendering her boots nearly
useless as she trudged the rest of the way up the street. In her haste,
she stumbled and nearly fell when she turned onto the walk leading to the mission building. Righting herself, she conceded that at
one time she might have tried to pretend that her eagerness had
nothing to do with seeing Jack, that she was simply anxious to get
out of the storm. But in truth she *was* eager to see him; these days,
that seemed to be the case more often than not.

She was also exceedingly pleased that he had ventured out in
the middle of a snowstorm to visit Terese Sheridan. No doubt he
would minimize any mention of it, but to Samantha it was one
more example of the kindness she knew to be a part—albeit a
well-concealed part, much of the time—of his nature.

She was almost at the front door before she realized she was
smiling like a schoolgirl.

⁂

Jack was angry now, too, his temper suddenly stoked by the
thought that he had, for a time, almost fallen for her scheme. But
now that he knew she was no different from any of the others—most of them far older and a great deal more shrewd—who

at one time or another had tried to dupe him, the last shred of sympathy for the girl drained away and he dropped all pretense of consideration for her feelings.

"You know exactly what I'm saying." He slung the words at her with blistering contempt. "You had yourself a tawdry little affair and then didn't quite know how to deal with the consequences, wasn't that it? You've been lying all along, haven't you? You thought you'd play me for the great fool: wangling free passage to the States for yourself, taking advantage of a program meant for those genuinely deserving of it—and then what would it have been, eh? Living on the *Vanguard*'s dole as long as you could pull it off, you and your—"

She hauled herself to her feet, the chair scraping the floor with a loud screech. Her eyes blazed with a poisonous rage, and she actually raised a hand as if to strike him.

But Jack merely gave her a cold look and launched his final volley with deliberate scorn. "No doubt it was easy enough to hoodwink my brother into buying your story. It never did take much for one like you to wrap Brady around her little finger. He always was a fool for a cheap skirt, especially if she could work him for a bit of sympathy in the process."

A sound like that of an animal in torment ripped from her throat. The cords in her neck stood out as if she were strangling, and her features, admittedly striking even in the advanced stages of her pregnancy, now contorted with hatred, taking on a dark, ugly flush of crimson.

She raised both arms as if to dive at him, and for a moment Jack thought she actually would attack him.

"'Twas your good-for-nothing, deceitful brother who got me into this fix, I'll have you know!"

35

Truth and Betrayal

And I hardened my heart
For fear of my ruin . . .
I hardened my heart,
And my love I quenched.
PADRAIC PEARSE

Jack reared back as if she had struck him. Indeed, she *did* lunge for him, but he caught her wrists between his big hands, easily trapping her.

A thunderous pounding worked its way up his skull as he stared down at her, holding her captive. "What are you talking about?"

She twisted and bent backwards, trying to loosen his hold on her, but Jack had her in a merciless grip, and she couldn't shake him. Shock mingled with fright in her eyes, and he saw that she was as appalled by her outburst as he was. The look of utter horror on her

341

face sent a cold blade of dread twisting through him, a warning that what was to come would be nothing he wanted to hear.

But surely this was more of her lies!

"Tell me!" Jack shouted at her. "And I'll have the truth this time, you little slut!"

The fear in her eyes suddenly faded, and she was now one furious pyre of hatred. She bared her teeth like a wildcat and screamed at him. "I'm no slut, but if I am, 'tis your brother you can thank for it! *He* sired the child I carry!"

"I don't believe you!"

"Believe me or don't believe me, but it's the *truth* I'm telling you! That's what you wanted, wasn't it? The truth?"

"You were attacked—*raped!* Brady told me the whole ugly story in his letter."

"Brady *made up* the whole ugly story, man, don't you see? He got me with child by leading me to believe I *meant* something to him, playing me for the foolish green girl I was, and then after using me, he sent me packing. To *you!* But not until after he put up the lie he knew would get me here!"

She disgorged the words as if she were spewing poison at him, her face a crimson, enraged mask of pure fury. "'Twas your precious *brother* who gave the lie, not me! I only did what he told me to do, in order to keep my child! Your darling Brady would have had the babe cut from my womb entirely, but I couldn't bring myself to do it! I could not do away with my own child even if its father *is* a worthless dog!"

A murderous, black rage rose up in Jack. His ears roared with it, his head swam with it. He began to shake, violently, like a man with the palsy. Fury possessed him, like a great dark beast unleashed from a pit somewhere deep inside him.

He wanted to strike her, to slap her face until her neck snapped, to inflict on her the depth of pain she had settled on him. The same malevolent force that had overtaken him so completely in the past that had almost driven him to violence now surfaced in him again, and he knew that the last shred of self-control was all but lost to him.

He looked at her, then grasped her shoulders and gave her a vicious shove, tossing her away from him with a force that knocked her backwards into the chair. She shrieked at him and would have scrambled to her feet, but Jack raised a warning hand to her, and she sank back against the chair, the anger rapidly fading from her eyes, giving way to a rising fear.

"Don't . . . say . . . another word!" he warned her.

"It's the truth and I can see you know it!" she countered in an unexpected blast of defiance.

"Shut up, you little baggage! Shut up!"

The room seemed to echo with their shouting, that and the sound of his own harsh breathing. Jack knotted his fists at his side until pain darted up both arms, but it was nothing compared to the pain of betrayal that threatened to unman him. *Brady's betrayal.*

She looked up into his face, and she was as still as death except for the tears beginning to pool in her eyes. And Jack knew, knew beyond all doubting, that the girl had spoken the truth. And yet he could not seem to take it in.

He saw that she was shivering, whether from the cold of the room or fear of him, he didn't know or care. He had no pity in him for her now, no shame for his treatment of her. He was still caught in the grip of a darkness that felt as if he would explode with it, and there was no room for anything but the wild, savage fury that threatened to take his mind, his sanity.

"Why?" he choked out. "If you're telling the truth—and mind, I will find out if you're not—if it's so, then why the deceit?"

She hugged her arms to herself, rubbing her shoulders as if they ached. "He—Brady—said it was the only way. That you would—disown him and throw me out into the streets if you knew the truth." She glared at him as if she had no doubt whatsoever that Brady had been right.

Jack studied her, still struggling for some semblance of control. "He refused to marry you? He wanted you to get rid of the child instead?"

"He used me!" she fairly hissed the words at him. "He pretended to care for me, but all the time he was only trifling with me! And myself fool enough to believe I mattered to him!"

Something occurred to Jack, and he hurled the charge at her. "You thought to trap him with the child, didn't you? You *let* it happen, thinking to hold him."

To his surprise, she seemed to falter. As he watched, some of the defiance faded from her eyes. "At first, I may have meant to do just that," she said, her voice trembling but quieter now. "I wanted to get away so desperately, don't you see, that I admit I would have done most anything! But later—" She stopped, squeezing her eyes shut for a moment. Then she opened them and went on. "Later, I came to care for him, and I truly thought he—"

She broke off, shaking her head as if dazed. Her eyes were dark with despair, and she began to sob, her shoulders heaving. But Jack scarcely saw.

"I will have the child," he said with a bleak, hard coldness. "You know that, don't you? Perhaps my spineless brother didn't want it, and you, my girl, most assuredly cannot afford it. But if you have finally spoken the truth, then the child you carry is of my blood."

He stopped, yanking the chair in which he had earlier sat roughly off the floor, then slamming it down with a shattering blow. *"And make no mistake, I will have it!"*

Without another word then, he turned and charged blindly from the room, leaving the sound of her anguished weeping behind him.

❧❀❧

Samantha heard the voices the minute she stepped inside. Bewildered at first, she stood in the entryway, looking around.

When she realized where the sound was coming from, she approached the stairway, then hesitated. Her heart seemed to skip a beat when she recognized Jack's voice, raised in what was plainly a fit of anger.

Then she heard Terese scream. She was screaming at Jack. In that moment, Samantha knew something terrible had happened.

Heart pounding, she grasped the banister and started up the steps, stopping dead when a heavy thud shook the floor above her. Samantha heard Jack shout something, followed by the sound of Terese weeping.

She gathered her skirts and took the steps at a run, halting at the top when she saw Jack come lurching out of Terese's room, his dark features distorted and forbidding with unmistakable rage.

He stopped in the hallway at the sight of her, close enough to Samantha that she could see the searing blaze of fury in his eyes. A shock of black hair had fallen over his brow, and his face was an angry crimson. He stood there, legs astride, his black topcoat hanging open, his eyes wild, his face a dark thunderhead.

For the first time, Samantha was afraid of him.

He closed the distance between them in two wide steps, coming to stand directly in front of her. "Did you know about this?" he grated out in a tone Samantha had never heard from him before. *"Did you?"*

"Know about what? Jack—what's wrong?" Instinctively,

345

Samantha reached a tentative hand to his arm. He shook her off with a violence that stunned her and left her trembling.

At that moment, David Leslie came up the stairway, taking the steps two at a time.

He hesitated at the top when he saw Samantha and Jack. "Samantha?" He looked from one to the other. "What's happened?"

Jack ignored him, his eyes boring into Samantha. "I asked you if you knew," he said again with the same raw bitterness in his voice.

"Knew *what?* Jack—"

Suddenly, he uttered a low sound in his throat and shoved his way past her. When David Leslie would have stopped him at the top of the steps, Jack hurled him aside with such force Samantha thought the young physician would surely go hurtling down the stairway.

She cried out Jack's name, but he was already barreling down the steps.

David Leslie turned toward her, his dazed expression mirroring Samantha's own state of shock and bewilderment. At that instant, a long, chilling wail shattered their inertia and sent them rushing toward Terese's room.

36

Darkness and Deception

Why is it effects are greater than their causes . . .
And the most deceived be she who least suspects?
OLIVER ST. JOHN GOGARTY

It took well over an hour for Samantha and David Leslie to get the entire story of what had transpired between Jack and Terese. A large part of that time was spent simply trying to calm Terese enough that she could tell them *anything*.

She seemed caught in the grip of near hysteria when they reached her. Indeed, Samantha feared that the girl might have suffered a kind of emotional breakdown. Although David seemed inclined to reserve his opinion, Samantha could tell that he, too, was deeply concerned.

Because of the baby, he didn't administer a sedative, but instead relied merely on smelling salts and a cold cloth. And prayer.

Samantha quickly learned that David Leslie was one physician who relied as much—perhaps even more—on divine power as he did on his own medical skills, exceptional as they seemed to be. He bade Samantha to pray as he worked over Terese, and clearly he was praying too. In truth, Samantha sensed he had not ceased praying since they entered Terese's room.

At first, much of the girl's account had been almost unintelligible, even irrational. But after David finally got her to bed, applied the salts, and soothed her with a continuous stream of reassurances, she began to make herself understood. Even so, her disjointed, fragmented story seemed almost unimaginable.

What Samantha did manage to glean left her reeling in confusion and disbelief. Much of it made no sense, but as she stood at the foot of the bed, watching David with Terese and listening to the girl's ranting, she slowly, little by little, began to fit the pieces together.

Whatever had transpired between Terese and Jack had obviously been ugly, even violent, and had left Terese convinced that he meant to take her baby away from her, once it was born. If she was to be believed, Jack had made a number of particularly vile accusations during the heated exchange, had even threatened her.

As much as Samantha wanted not to believe what she was hearing, she had seen Jack's face for herself. The man who had come charging out of Terese's bedroom had been enraged, capable of anything.

Incredibly, it seemed that Terese had not been assaulted after all—there had been no rape. Jack's brother had evidently fathered the child during the course of an affair, and together the two of them—Brady and Terese—had woven a web of deceit that had fooled everyone, including Jack.

But now that he knew the truth, he was threatening to take the child.

Again Samantha found herself hard pressed to credit Jack with such unthinkable cruelty. And yet . . . there were the old stories, the rumors of his ruthless business dealings, his relentless and often merciless pursuit of anything he wanted. The men he had ruined. The corruption that shadowed him. And always, his vicious, fearful temper.

Samantha could not forget the look in his eyes: the wildness, the explosive rage she had seen there when he confronted her on the landing. By now, she was more than bewildered and shocked by Terese's account: she was heartsick and terrified that everything the girl had told them might be true.

Without warning, Terese suddenly pulled Samantha back to her surroundings, pushing herself up from the pillows and, her eyes still glazed but more lucid now, calling out to her. Samantha hurried around to the side of the bed and took her hand. For a moment, she feared the girl was going to lapse into yet another fit of mindless weeping. Instead, she seized Samantha's hand and began to repeat the same thing over and over again, like a frenzied litany: *"He's going to take my baby, Samantha! He's going to take my baby away from me!"*

When Samantha tried to reassure her, Terese lifted herself even more, grasping Samantha's arm and pleading, "Help me, Samantha! Please! You have to stop him!"

Overcome by pity for the girl and her own feelings of helplessness, Samantha again attempted to comfort her. "Terese, I'm sure Jack didn't mean anything he said—he wouldn't—"

Terese clutched at Samantha's arm. "No, Samantha, you don't understand! You didn't hear him. He wants the babe for *you!* He *told* me so. He told me how you—can't have children. He means for you to have my baby! He says you'll marry him then. Oh, Samantha, please—don't let him do this! Don't let him take my baby!"

Samantha stood staring at Terese Sheridan. So great was her shock, so brutal the pain that knifed through her, that she thought her heart would surely shatter to pieces.

At the same time, a terrible anger began to surface in her. "Jack . . . actually said that? That he wants the baby for *me?*"

Terese nodded. She was weeping again. "And when he found out about Brady and me—it only made things worse! He was furious! He was like a crazy man!"

Terese's hand tightened still more on Samantha's arm. "You can reason with him, Samantha," she said, her voice lower but her eyes still burning with desperation. "I'm nothing to Jack Kane! He doesn't care what happens to me. But he *does* care about you, Samantha! Please—don't let him do this!"

The weight centered in Samantha's chest grew even heavier. She patted Terese's hand absently, all the while feeling as if she would be sick at any moment. She glanced at David Leslie, saw him watching her with something akin to pity.

"It will be all right, Terese," she managed to say, her voice sounding distant and strangled in her ears. "Just . . . you rest now. I'll . . . take care of this. No one is going to take your baby from you."

Then she turned to David Leslie. "David—your buggy . . . may I use it, please?"

He gave her a blank look. "My buggy?"

Samantha nodded.

"Well . . . of course, you can use it, but, Samantha, you can't take a buggy out alone in this storm!" He stopped, glanced at Terese, and added uncertainly, "I don't think I ought to leave—"

"No, of course, you mustn't leave. I can drive myself. Really," she insisted at his dubious look. "I drove my mother's buggy all the time when I was still at home. I'm quite capable."

"But it's already dark, Samantha! It's far too treacherous. At least, wait until tomorrow—"

"David—please. I'll walk if I must, but I have to do this. I have to see Jack tonight."

He studied her, then, with obvious reluctance, gave a nod of assent. "I wish you wouldn't, but—please, Samantha, be careful."

But Samantha was already halfway across the room, stopping only long enough to gather her coat and hat from the chair.

❧❧❧

Jack sat hunched over his desk, the dim light from the oil lamp on his desk casting shadows over the blank piece of paper in front of him. He was making no pretense of working. He could think of nothing else, indeed had thought of nothing else since leaving Grace Mission, but Brady's betrayal.

He had no doubt but that Terese Sheridan had finally spoken the truth. He had known it the instant the words left her mouth, in spite of his initial attempt to deny it. He hated admitting it, even to himself, but he knew that Brady was just irresponsible and selfish enough to be guilty of the girl's accusations. It both infuriated him and sickened him that his brother had not been man enough to admit to his own child, had instead allowed the girl he had wronged—scarcely more than a child herself—to not only shoulder the entire burden alone, but to live a lie in the process.

Not that the Sheridan girl was innocent. Apparently, she had been a willing enough participant in the affair itself. But as for the rest of it, he tended to believe her insistence that Brady had spun the lie, and she had simply gone along with it, not knowing what else to do by then.

Jack shook his head. "Blood tells," 'twas often said, and perhaps it was truer than anyone thought. Perhaps his younger brother was merely displaying the same craven willfulness of the British soldier who had sired him. For whatever the man had been who forced himself on their mother—and God only knew how many other women that hellish night—he had above all else been an ignoble, spineless brute. Was it possible for such a thing to be passed down from one generation to another?

He expelled a harsh, ragged sigh. Perhaps he had been wrong all these years, to keep the truth from Brady. He wondered now if it would have made any conceivable difference, had he told him everything from the beginning.

He had thought to give the boy an untroubled mind, to protect him from the painful truth about the vicious assault on their mother—the assault of which Brady was the fruit. Had he erred, then, in concealing the fact that his brother was not, after all, the son of Sean Kane, an allegedly fearless—or would that be *foolish?*—rebel leader, that he was in fact the seed of a drunken soldier of the Crown, bent on revenge? Revenge for a night raid led by Sean Kane and some of his cohorts. A raid for which their mother, God rest her soul—and others—had paid a terrible, obscene price.

Would the truth somehow have made Brady stronger, more careful of his actions and their consequences? Or, as Jack had feared, would it have made him even wilder and more reckless than he was?

If he were altogether honest, he would have to concede that Brady's parentage was not the only unpleasantness from which he had shielded the boy over the years. Indeed, he was beginning to think he might have shielded his brother from too much, too long.

When Brady got into trouble with the nuns at school, Jack had invariably intervened, playing on their sympathy for the "poor, motherless boy," whose only home life consisted of a too-busy older brother and a housekeeper. And those times when Brady's gambling debts soared above what his monthly stipend could cover, Jack had never permitted the thugs to take it out of his hide, but instead bailed him out, the only punishment a stern lecture—which was promptly forgotten—and some menial jobs about the house, which were likewise either forgotten or ignored.

There had been a girl or two as well—summarily condemned by Jack as fortune hunters before he paid them off and sent them packing.

Not so different a scenario as what he had thought to enact with Terese Sheridan, he thought guiltily.

He had been holding a cigar between his fingers, unlighted and forgotten, and now he crushed it in his hand and tossed it onto the floor. After a moment, he propped his elbows on top of the desk and put his head between his hands, squeezing his temples in an attempt to blunt the brain-splitting headache that had begun on the frenzied drive back to the office.

The pain in his head, however, was nothing as compared to the immense black pain in his soul. He felt as if the center of his being had been bayoneted, brutally ripped through.

He would have thought he had known despair before tonight, but the raw, gaping hole that now opened somewhere inside him was as agonizing as any desolation he had ever suffered. He felt as if it might well tear him asunder before the night was done.

And Brady's deceit was only a part of it. Jack could still see the stark lines of terror engraved upon the Sheridan girl's face, and the awful thing of it was that for a moment he had actually reveled in her fear of him.

But the worst had been Samantha: the way she had looked at him, the unmistakable horror in her eyes that, at least at that moment, had not even moved him.

By now the Sheridan girl would have told Samantha everything. No longer would she doubt the unsavory stories, the rumors that dogged him; from this night on, she would believe them and even worse.

And she would be justified entirely. Oh, he had improved his behavior some over the years, modified his dealings to some extent, even played at being respectable. After meeting Samantha, he had taken his efforts even more seriously. But had he ever actually believed he could change?

Perhaps for a time. A very *brief* time. No doubt that accounted for his rash promise to Samantha that he would attempt to be the kind of man she deserved, the kind of man she wanted him to be. A man she could trust.

But while he might have been able to fool Samantha, he had never once managed to deceive himself. Inside, tenuously concealed, lurking just behind the facade he had erected, was the same man he had always been, the man he was reputed to be.

Samantha knew by now that his promises were false. Unreliable. Worthless.

His heart was as black and as cold as the pit itself. For a moment his mind raced back to the evening in Philadelphia when he had met with Edgar Poe. He remembered the decadence he had sensed about the man, the abhorrent *darkness,* and how shaken he had been when he realized that perhaps the reason Poe evoked such a conflict of feelings in him—feelings that ranged all the way from a reluctant sort of fascination to a chilling kind of dread—was the fear that the same darkness resided in *himself.* So eager had he been to get away from the man, to return to Samantha—the brightness and the goodness of her—that he had been almost rude.

His light had been Samantha, and she was lost to him. Now there was no light left to him, only darkness.

The old black melancholy draped itself over him like a shroud.

At the back of his mind, he was aware that he was sinking quickly into a disgusting state of mawkishness. Only his fierce aversion to self-pity kept him from sliding the rest of the way down into the loathsome swamp of Irish despondency.

At least he could do the humane thing for Terese Sheridan. He would go back to the mission tomorrow and put the girl's fears to rest. There was no reason to terrorize her any longer. Without Samantha, why would he want someone else's child—even his brother's?

No, Terese could keep her baby, and the *Vanguard* would keep the resettlement agreement intact. After all, the girl had been duped by a master, he thought bitterly. Brady was nothing if not the consummate confidence man.

He would make sure she and the child were taken care of; that much, at least he could do. There would be Cavan to deal with, of course. The lad knew nothing as yet. Once his sister had bent his ear, no doubt he would leave the *Vanguard*'s employ. But he was a good enough reporter and writer to land a job on any other news-paper in the city—with or without a reference from Jack, though he would surely give him a sterling one if need be.

It occurred to Jack that he would miss Cavan Sheridan, and he was saddened by the realization. Strange entirely, the things one recognized when it was too late.

As for Brady . . . Jack glanced down at the blank paper in front of him, then reached for a fresh cigar. After lighting it, he took up his pen and began to compose a letter to his brother. It struck him that he didn't even have a current address. He supposed he would sim-ply post it to the one in Galway in hopes the young fool had at least taken measures to have his mail forwarded, wherever he was.

Jack had once thought that, should he ever decide to tell the boy the truth about his brutal beginnings, he would tell him face-to-face and be prepared to help him deal with the shock. But he was now convinced he had waited too long as it was, had protected Brady to a fault, perhaps had even inadvertently encouraged his lack of character. He would write him this very night with the whole story and let him take the blow on his own, to deal with it however he could.

He would, of course, tell him he knew about the affair with Terese, the baby, and the lie Brady had fostered. He would also make it clear that from now on Brady would have to earn his keep—and he meant exactly that: he would earn it, whether from the *Vanguard's* payroll or somewhere else. He would do the job, or there would be no pay.

He would also suggest that, as long as he was being paid by the *Vanguard*, Brady would apply a portion of his salary to his child's support.

But Jack knew even as he wrote that he could not bring himself to do the one thing Brady apparently feared: he could not completely reject his brother. He was still Brady, the boy he had raised more as a son. And the bitter truth was that Brady's deception, painful as it was, somehow seemed no worse than his own.

37

I Would Give You
the World. . . .

This heart, fill'd with fondness,
Is wounded and weary.
FROM WALSH'S IRISH POPULAR
SONGS, 1847

Half an hour later, Jack finished the letter, sealed it in an envelope, and stuffed it inside his waistcoat pocket for posting.

He stood, easing his shoulders and wishing he had a powder for the pain in his skull. He walked over to look out the window, but there wasn't much to be seen. It was still snowing, though the wind seemed to have died some. The street was all but deserted, except for Whitey and Snipe. The two newsboys typically slept under the steps of the bindery across the street but at the moment stood warming themselves at one of the trash barrels.

Jack shoved his hands down in his pockets, watching the two.

When the weather was as brutal as it was tonight, he sometimes allowed a few of the lads to sleep in the hallway downstairs or in the horse barn, which they seemed to prefer.

The city teemed with homeless children—a fair number of whom were newsboys. They slept wherever they could, ate whatever they could beg or steal usually, and some even grew up to be respectable. But to New York's shame, many died from exposure or hunger before they had the chance to grow up at all.

He turned and looked around his office, small and cluttered and dark, and decided he would spend the night here, on the sagging sofa across the room. He already knew that sleep wasn't likely to come tonight, so why brave the snowstorm to reach home?

He went back to his desk and put out his cigar. He moved to snuff out the lamp but decided first to call down to the newsboys and tell them to come inside if they wanted. Just then he heard footsteps on the stairway. He stopped where he was, frowning. There was no one here this time of night, except for Madog Wall, and the big Irishman would not be so light footed on the stairway. The presses were shut down for the night, the workers gone.

One of the newsboys? Not likely. They knew they weren't allowed past the door unless Jack offered.

As a precaution, his hand went to the top right drawer of the desk, where he kept his gun.

The drawer was locked. He glanced across the room at the door. It was closed, but through the frosted window at the top he could make out the vague shape of someone standing outside. Quickly, his eyes still on the door, he fished in his pocket for his keys, then quietly unlocked the desk drawer and withdrew the pistol.

He stood waiting, the gun leveled directly at the door as it opened.

Samantha was almost certain that, in the heat of his rage, Jack would come here, rather than going home—not only because he'd been driving the newspaper wagon, but because, if she were not badly mistaken, the *Vanguard* was more home to Jack than the sprawling mansion on Thirty-Fourth Street. This was where he spent most of his days and, by his own admission, a good many of his nights.

She had been to Jack's office only once before, and then in broad daylight. The building seemed eerily quiet and dark this time of night, but a dim light could be seen through the frosted glass of his office door.

She hesitated, her hand gripping the doorknob, realizing now that it had probably been the worst kind of foolishness to come here. Because of the snow, it had taken her more than twice as long as it should have just to get here, and she'd held her breath most of the way, praying the buggy wouldn't hang up or overturn.

It occurred to her that she didn't even know what she intended to say to him. Nevertheless, she was here, so finally, with a shuddering breath, she turned the doorknob and prepared to face him.

The door creaked open, and she stepped inside to find him standing behind his desk, pointing a gun directly at her.

The office was dim and gloomy and reeked of cigar smoke. The light flickered in the draft, casting Jack in shadows, making him appear more a dark and menacing stranger than the man she knew.

Or the man she had thought *she knew . . .*

Samantha was too stunned to speak, much less cry out. She could do nothing but stand and stare at Jack and the gun in his hand.

"*Samantha!*"

In an instant, he lowered the gun and came round the desk.

"What are you *doing* here?" He virtually shouted at her, making it more an accusation than a question.

Samantha opened her mouth to speak, but the gun was still in his hand, albeit lowered to his side, and her mind seemed unable to get past the sight of it.

As if he had read her thoughts, Jack glanced from her to the gun in his hand, then turned and went back to the desk, shoving the pistol inside a drawer.

"Sorry about the gun," he said. "I couldn't think who might be in the building this time of night."

Samantha made no reply. He came around the desk again, not taking his eyes off her. This time when he spoke his voice had returned to its earlier sharpness. "I hope you didn't come here alone."

Before Samantha could answer, he said, "You *did*, didn't you? What on earth possessed you?" He looked thoroughly put out with her, which for some reason did nothing but anger Samantha.

She found it incredible that he would have the presumption to show impatience with her after what he had done. "Don't concern yourself with how I got here," she countered. She heard the chill in her voice and realized that it was merely a weak reflection of the cold fury she felt toward him at the moment.

"Samantha—"

He had come to a stop a few feet away from her, and he stood now, hands clenched into fists at his sides, looking at her. Samantha was momentarily caught off guard by how utterly drained and exhausted he appeared.

Something tugged at her heart, but she forced herself to ignore it. "I came here because I have to know one thing," she said, cringing at the tremor in her voice.

He took a step toward her, repeating her name, but Samantha quickly raised a hand to stop him. "Just tell me if it's true: Did you threaten to take Terese's baby away from her?" She paused. "And did you really tell her you wanted the baby for me? *Did* you?"

His eyes searched hers, and for a moment Samantha could see him hesitate, as if he might be trying to arrange his thoughts exactly right.

"The truth, Jack," she said, raising her voice. "There's been quite enough lying."

She saw him expel a long breath, but he didn't try to avoid her gaze. "I'd not be the one to argue that. All right, then, Samantha: aye, it's true. I did tell the girl I meant to have the child, and that I wanted it . . . for you."

Samantha tried to swallow, nearly choking on the dry knot in her throat. "How *could* you? That girl is supposed to be under your protection! You're committed to helping her, and instead you *terrorize* her! And then try to excuse your unforgivable behavior by claiming you did it for me!"

"But it *was* for you, Samantha, and that's the truth."

Samantha heard the sudden thickening of his Irish accent as he visibly grew more agitated.

"Surely you can believe that much, at least. Why else would I want the child?"

"Don't you *dare* to use me as an excuse for your bullying!" Samantha hurled the words at him with enough force that he actually blanched as if she'd struck him.

She almost faltered, surprised at the intensity of her own anger. But she couldn't stop what she had begun. "Did you ever once think to question how I might feel about such an insane idea?" she railed on. "But, no, of course, you wouldn't. *You* decided what was best for me, and that was that, wasn't it? You just naturally assumed that I would consent to whatever you decided. Because you're Jack Kane! It doesn't matter how cruel or obscene your behavior happens to be; if you want a thing done, then that's the start and finish of it! Jack Kane takes what he wants, no matter who gets hurt or destroyed in the process. That's just how it is with you, isn't it, Jack?" She stopped to catch a breath. "Well, *isn't* it?"

He stood there, saying nothing, his hands now unclenched and hanging limply at his sides, his face dark—not with anger, Samantha sensed, but with pain.

But his pain didn't move her. Not now. She wouldn't allow it.

"Why?" She choked out. "Why would you do such a terrible thing to that girl? To me?"

A hint of the old mocking smile curved his lips when he answered her. "As you said, Samantha, there was something I wanted. I simply did what needed to be done in order to get it. Aye, you're right: that's my way. Always has been. And what I wanted this time was you. As my wife. So I set about to make it happen."

Samantha gaped at him in utter astonishment. "You couldn't possibly believe I would marry you after you did such a deplorable thing to Terese."

He merely lifted one dark eyebrow.

Samantha felt ill. "You did," she said slowly, her voice trembling. "You actually thought you could . . . buy me! With a child."

A cold vise closed around Samantha's heart as she stared at him in horrified disbelief. "I can't believe you did this," she said brokenly. "I thought . . . I knew you—"

"And didn't I try on more than one occasion to convince you that you *didn't* know me, Samantha?" His voice cracked like a whip in the quiet of the room. "Didn't I try to warn you I wasn't the man you seemed bent on making me out to be? *Didn't* I?"

He had, of course. And she had blindly tried her best to ignore him, to see him as she wanted him to be instead of how he really was.

She should have listened to him. . . . She should have believed him. . . .

Slowly, he walked toward her, stopping directly in front of her, only inches away. His eyes burned into Samantha, but he made no move to touch her. She saw that he looked ravaged and drawn. But she closed her heart against him. She *had* to.

When he spoke again, his voice had gentled. "Whether you believe me or not, Samantha, I regret what I did. My actions were despicable; that's true. For whatever it's worth, I will tell you that I have every intention of making amends to the Sheridan girl—however I can."

He paused, his shoulders slumping slightly. "Something tells me, however, that there's nothing I can do to make amends to *you*, and for that I am sorrier than you can possibly know."

Samantha looked away before she could allow herself to soften toward him. "I simply do not understand . . . how you could do such a thing. I never would have believed it of you, Jack. Never."

"Samantha? Samantha, look at me."

She did and instantly regretted it. Her mind insisted that he had betrayed whatever trust she had begun to hold for him, that he had done a terrible thing, and she must bury any feelings she might have ever felt for him. But her heart reminded her that he was still Jack, still the man from whom she had known great kindness and gentleness and . . . affection. He was still Jack—the man she loved. And something in her spirit made her hesitate to turn completely away from him.

So she faced him, waiting.

As he began to speak, his fingers kneaded the lapel of his coat. Samantha could not help but notice that his hand wasn't all that steady.

"'Tis not likely I can make you understand, Samantha. In truth, I'm not at all sure I understand myself. But I do know this much, wrong as I may have been: I wanted to give you something,

Samantha, something to make up for what had been taken from you, so that you wouldn't mind so much . . . your childlessness."

When Samantha would have interrupted, he lifted a hand to stop her. "You seemed so intent on not marrying me—for two reasons: the fact that you couldn't give me a child, and also be-cause—as you put it—I could not share your faith. Well, it seemed to me that there was little I could do about the faith. But there *was* something I could do about a child. And so—" he gave a light shrug—"I set about doing it."

Something seemed to open in Samantha, just enough that she could glimpse the truth behind Jack's words. *Oh, God, he really did do it for me, didn't he? But it was still wrong, Lord . . . so very wrong!*

Samantha felt her heart squeezed nearly beyond endurance as Jack went on. "You're absolutely right to be furious with me. I should never—*never*—have presumed to do such a thing and ex-pect that somehow you would sanction it. I must have been a little mad to even conceive of it."

His voice had grown hoarse, deeper, the brogue even thicker. "Samantha . . . will you try to believe this much, if nothing else: I . . . love you, as I have never loved another woman."

As if anticipating her protest, he again raised a hand to silence her. "Even Martha, though I did love her well. Quite frankly, *mavourneen*, I would have done almost anything . . . to make you mine."

Watching him, Samantha could see the difficulty with which he swallowed, as if trying to choke down the bitterness of his own words. "Instead . . . I've turned you away. And for that, I will never forgive myself."

He gave a lame attempt at a laugh. "What a fool I've been. I set out to be the kind of man you could love—and only managed to prove to you that I'm not."

O, Lord, what am I to do about this man? What?

Samantha blinked back the unshed tears that had begun to scald her eyes while he spoke. "You're right," she said softly, her own voice now thick with emotion. "You *have* been a fool. You didn't have to do anything to make me love you, Jack! I already *did* love you!"

As she watched, he squeezed his eyes shut for an instant. When he opened them, he took a step toward her, then stopped. *"Did,* Samantha? And what about now?"

Samantha saw the agony in his eyes, saw his need, his unspoken plea. *Oh, God—what do I do?*

She knew that she could do nothing less than tell him the truth.

"I do love you, Jack," she said simply. "I wish I didn't. But, God help me, I do."

He reached for her, but Samantha lifted her arms as a shield. "No—don't. Please."

He held out his hands to her, turned palms-up in a gesture of supplication. "At least say you can forgive me, Samantha."

Could she? How could she *not?* Christ forgave, didn't he, had forgiven her and so many others, would forgive Jack as well if he would only ask. How could she dare to withhold her forgiveness from the man she loved more than anyone or anything in the world?

She supposed she could view what he had done as a measure of his love for her. But it was still wrong. Terribly wrong. And so horribly unfair to Terese.

"I . . . don't know. You'll have to give me time, Jack."

"Woman," he said, his voice raw, his gaze steady upon her, "I would give you anything you asked of me. I would give you the very *world,* if I could. Don't you know that by now?"

His words struck Samantha like a blow. She realized then that she *did* know it, *had* known it for some time. And she also knew in that moment that whether she could trust anything else about Jack or not, she could trust the fact that he loved her.

But somehow, it wasn't enough.

She looked at him, saw his eyes, bruised by fatigue, his features, world-weary and dispirited. She wanted to touch him, to reach out to him and comfort him.

She wanted to *change* him, and she knew she was on dangerous ground. No one was going to change Jack. She could not hope for such a thing. Nor could he change himself. Only God held it in his power to change a heart, to heal a soul.

Please, God . . . I know you love him enough to help him. . . . Please, somehow . . . make him the man you want him to be . . . the man he seems to believe he never can be. Not for my sake, Lord, but for his good . . . and for your glory . . . change him.

He was watching her with an expression of such tenderness . . . and such sadness . . . that Samantha thought he would break her heart.

"Samantha, I can't—"

He broke off as the quiet of the room was shattered by a long, screeching wail.

They both froze in stunned confusion. Samantha saw Jack tense, a frown crossing his face.

"Jack?"

He closed the distance between them in one long stride, grasping her arm and pulling her to his side as the blood-chilling screech again pierced the night.

He spun around, dragging her with him toward the door.

"Jack, what is it?"

"The *Vanguard*'s fire whistle," he said, his eyes reflecting Samantha's bewilderment and sudden surge of fear.

38

In the Crucible

When you walk through fire you shall not be burned,
and the flame shall not consume you.
ISAIAH 43:2

Before they even reached the door, he heard Madog Wall come roaring up the steps. *"Mr. Kane! Fire! There's a fire in the pressroom!"*

The moment they reached the open door, Jack smelled it—the acrid, scorching odor his cigar smoke must have earlier masked.

He and Samantha almost collided with Madog at the top of the stairway.

"How bad?" Jack saw the fear in Samantha's eyes, the spark of panic in Madog Wall's, and deliberately kept his voice calm and all business.

"'Tis bad, Mr. Kane! Blowin' up fast, it is. You and Mrs. Harte have to get out of here! Now!"

Jack's mind went into a spin. He glanced from Madog to

Samantha, then handed her off to him. "Take Mrs. Harte out. You see her safely outside, and don't come back into the building! I have to see what I can do."

"Oh, Jack—no! You have to come with us!" Samantha cried out.

Already the smell of smoke had sharpened. Jack tightened his grip on her arm. "I won't be long. I have to see if there's any way I can save the presses, Samantha! Go on now—go with Madog! I need to know you're safe outside!"

To his amazement, she pulled back, clutching at his arm. "No, I'm not leaving you in here alone!"

Jack looked at her, then glanced over her head to Madog with a look the big Irishman quickly grasped. As Jack freed himself from Samantha, he set her carefully but firmly back, away from him and into Madog's sturdy arms.

"Is there anyone else in the building?" Jack shouted as Madog led Samantha to the top of the stairway.

"No one but yourself, sir, so look lively! Will the fire station hear the whistle, do you think?"

"We can hope. More likely one of the fire spotters will sound the alarm. As soon as you get outside, start pumping. Use the buckets from the horse barn." Jack stopped, then added, "And yell for help!"

Jack watched them go partway, Madog holding on to Samantha, trying his best to reassure her as they went. "It will be all right now, Mrs. Harte. Mr. Kane, he'll be out directly. For now, though, it's for me to get you out of the building."

Back inside his office, Jack fumbled with the combination on the safe until the door sprang open. His hand was shaking a little as he retrieved the envelopes that held the evidence for the exposé, along with a couple of other packets he couldn't afford to lose.

The odor of smoke was much stronger now, and he knew he had to get to the pressroom without waiting any longer. With a last glance around the office, he started for the door, stopping only long enough to grab his coat off the sofa, where he'd tossed it earlier.

He sprinted down the steps, throwing on his coat and shoving the documents from the safe in his pockets as he went. At the bottom he veered right and took off at a run down the narrow hallway that led to the pressroom. He could see small clouds of smoke floating under the door and out into the hall.

He was almost there when a roar sounded from inside the room and the door exploded open, unleashing a roaring burst of flame and churning smoke. Jack could actually feel the heat. He stopped, stunned by the force of the treacherous blaze. His eyes were already tearing, and his chest burned from the thick fumes of the smoke.

For a moment he could think of nothing but the new steam press—his pride above every other piece of equipment in the pressroom. Then his mind went to all the flammable materials stored inside that room, and he realized the entire building was surely doomed.

Dense smoke and flames were pouring out the door into the hall. There was no way he could get into the room, and if he didn't move fast, the flames would overtake the hall as well, trapping him.

He would not allow himself to think of what the fire would take from him. One thing he was determined it would *not* take was his life.

He turned then and, with the flames beginning to snake along the floor behind him, raced down the hall toward the outside door. His chest was burning as if the fire had exploded inside *him,* and the bitter, black taste of smoke filled his mouth. As he charged out the door and into the street, his eyes sought and found Samantha, watching Madog ply the pump. Jack leaped over a frozen pool of ice and came to stand in front of them.

Samantha's eyes went over him as if to make certain he was all right. There was something else there, too, but Jack had no notion of what. He couldn't think of anything except the *Vanguard*'s going up in smoke, although he realized his hopes weren't entirely dead when he caught himself listening for the sound of the fire wagon.

Madog paused long enough to give Jack a quick glance. "Thanks be you're all right, sir!" he said, then resumed his pumping.

Jack wiped a hand over his forehead and, glancing at it, saw that it was black with smoke.

"Is it bad, sir?" said Madog.

Jack stood staring at the building. "It's bad," he said quietly.

The words were no more out of his mouth than he felt Samantha tug at his arm. "Jack! Look! Up there!"

Jack glanced at her, then turned to look where she was pointing. His blood chilled at the sight of a small face framed in the upstairs window of his office. A closer look revealed a boy, gesturing wildly. Although they couldn't hear the child's screams through the closed window, there was no mistaking that he was crying for help.

Madog had dropped the pump handle and now stood staring up at the window. "Merciful Lord, 'tis Whitey!" he cried out.

The little newsboy whose only home was under the steps at the bindery.

"What's he *doing* up there?" Jack groaned.

Madog stood, shaking his head. "Snipe is probably in there somewheres too. You don't see one without the other. I'll bet the two rascals let themselves in to get out of the snow."

Jack had never known the boys to come inside without permission, but perhaps the storm had made them bold.

He tried to think, but his mind seemed frozen on the sight in his office window. He couldn't stop the image of the way the fire had blasted through the door of the pressroom and gone rolling down the hall. By now the blaze had surely cut off the landing of the stairway.

The boy was probably trapped.

***

Samantha looked from the terrified child in the upstairs window to Jack. His face was set in a hard mask, his eyes narrowed as he scanned the *Vanguard* building. She could almost see his mind working, considering the options—of which there seemed to be none.

"Could he jump, do you think?" asked Madog Wall.

Jack hesitated, then shook his head. "Even if he managed to break the window, we'd never catch him. We've nothing to stop his fall."

Suddenly there came the sound of several explosions. Samantha screamed as windows shattered and smoke began to billow through to the outside.

She felt Jack's arm go around her as he started to drag her backwards. "Madog, get her away from here!" he shouted, thrusting her toward Madog Wall. "The two of you, go over to the bindery!"

Indecision crossed the big Irishman's face. "Please, sir, I'll be going after the boy! You stay with Mrs. Harte!"

"No!" Jack roared at him. "No offense, man, but I can move faster! You see to Mrs. Harte—I'm going back in!"

Samantha reached out, grasping his arm. "Jack! No, you can't!"

He turned to look at her, his gaze softening for an instant before he turned back to Madog Wall. "Pour that bucket of water over me, man! Be quick!"

Madog didn't hesitate but picked up the bucket he had just filled and doused Jack with its contents.

Samantha shivered at the sight of his head and topcoat drenched in the bitter cold.

Suddenly in the distance they heard the sound of bells clanging furiously.

"There they come, sir!" shouted Madog. "The fire wagons are coming! There's help for the lad now!"

Others from surrounding buildings had begun to gather as well: newsboys and factory workers who had heard the commotion. Samantha felt a quick surge of hope for the first time since they'd seen the child in the window.

Jack stood, listening to the fire bells, then shook his head. "They'll never get here in time! I'm going after him! Now get away from here—both of you!"

He paused, his eyes hard on Madog Wall. "You're a good man, Madog, and I'd trust you with my life. But right now I'm trusting you with *Mrs. Harte's* life, and hers means a great deal more to me than my own. I don't want you to leave her side, not for a minute, no matter what happens. You understand? If that fire begins to move, you take her and get her a safe distance away. I want your word on it!"

Madog hesitated but after a second or two nodded his head in agreement. "Aye, sir. You have my word."

Again Samantha tried to stop Jack, but he pulled free and went tearing up the walk to the building.

She saw him come to a halt at the entrance door, glance inside, then step back to look up at the second story. She followed the direction of his gaze and saw that the boy was no longer at the window.

At that same instant, the window where the child had been standing only moments before suddenly exploded, shattering glass and blowing debris high into the night sky. Sparks and cinders sprayed the darkness like fireworks.

For the first time, Samantha realized the snow had stopped.

But not the wind.

For a moment she and Madog Wall stood staring in horror at

the burning building. Then the big Irishman swept her to his side and propelled her across the street.

From their watching place at the side of the bindery, Samantha saw Jack disappear inside the *Vanguard* building.

She cried his name softly to herself and began to pray.

⁂

When Jack saw no trace of the newsboy in the window, he took a tentative step inside the building, then another. He might as well have stepped into a nightmare.

Heat like that of a furnace smacked him full in the face. The stairway was engulfed in flames, the hall leading to the pressroom completely cut off by a curtain of smoke and fire. To his right, the hallway was still clear, but he knew it wouldn't be long before the blaze spread the length of the building.

Already the heavy dark smoke was searing his lungs and scalding his eyes. He was trying to decide which way to move when a scream sounded above him. He looked up and saw the newsboy standing at the top of the stairway. The lad's eyes were wild with terror, his incessant screams nearly choked off by the smoke and roaring flames.

"*Mr. Kane! Help me, Mr. Kane!*"

Jack saw that the blaze would catch the boy up at any second and waved him away. "*Get away from the stairway, boy! Move back!*"

At first the lad made no attempt to move but simply stayed where he was, screaming his head off.

Again Jack shouted up at him. "*Whitey! Get away from the steps! That way—*" he flung out his arm motioning the boy to the hallway on his right. "*Go to the back of the building, boy! I'll meet you there!*" A thought struck him. "*Whitey—is Snipe in the building too? Where is he?*"

The boy stared at him, then shook his head. "He—Snipe was in the pressroom."

Jack knew with a sinking feeling that there was no getting the other boy out, not if he was in the pressroom.

"All right, son—you go on now! As fast as you can, you hear!"

Relief flooded him when he saw the boy finally break and run. Taking time only to swab his handkerchief against his wet coat and cover his mouth with it, Jack leaped around the flaming wall and took off down the hallway.

At the back of the building, he saw that although the smoke was thick and heavy, already coiling around the ceiling and windows, the old iron steps that wound up to the second floor were still clear.

He took the steps two at a time, his boots clanging loudly on the metal. At the top, however, there was no sign of the boy.

"Whitey!" He started off down the hall, shouting the boy's name as he went, then came to a dead stop. Between him and the top of the main stairway, which by now was a blazing pyre, the hall that he had prayed would be clear was instead blocked by a veritable barricade of smoke and flames.

Jack looked up and realized that the pocket of fire must have been kindled by the flames snaking along the ceiling and partway down the door frame, reaching the crates and boxes stacked high outside the archives room.

His gaze traveled downward. To his horror he saw the prone figure of the little newsboy lying on the opposite side of the wall of fire separating them.

⁂

Across the street at the bindery, Samantha and Madog Wall stood watching the inferno that had been the *Vanguard*. Samantha refused to let herself dwell on the enormity of the loss this would be to Jack. She could do nothing for now except to pray God's protection around him and the little newsboy.

The thought of her last few minutes with Jack in his office, the harsh words, the painful scene between them, struck her like a heavy fist, and she nearly doubled over with the memory.

Oh, Lord, to think that only moments ago I was asking you to change him! Now, all I can think of, all I can pray for, is that you'll save him! Lord, put a wall around him and the child—a barrier between them and the flames! Carry them through the fire, Father! Just . . . lift them up in your arms and carry them through the fire!

Lord, you know how much I love him! Right or wrong, I can't seem to help myself, even after everything that's happened. Please, Father, in your mercy and in your love, please save Jack! Save him for me . . . and save him for you! Even if we can never be together, please get him safely out of that building! Please!

She gasped aloud in relief as two fire wagons, bells clanging, finally rounded the corner and pulled to a stop in the middle of the street.

"Thanks be," muttered Madog. "And about time, too."

Their relief was short lived. At the chilling sound of glass shattering, Samantha looked up to see that the whole building now appeared to be ablaze, with smoke and flames pouring from the windows and rising from the roof.

Beside her, Madog Wall added what might have been a fervent petition to her own earlier prayers when he said, in a choked voice, "Lord, have mercy! Only you can save them now!"

With tears stinging her eyes, Samantha again took up her desperate plea in Jack's behalf, now praying the promises of God for him and the child he had gone to rescue.

<hr />

Jack's chest threatened to explode along with the windows as he dropped to his belly and began to crawl closer to the blazing pocket between him and the unconscious child.

"Hold on, son!" he muttered to himself as he stopped, poised on all fours while he tried to gauge the best way around the fire. There looked to be a fraction more room on the outside wall, but if he went that way and the window blew, he was sure to be caught in a storm of fire and glass.

He opted for the side nearest the wall and started in that direction, again keeping as close to the floor as possible. Even in the space of a few seconds, the flames had fanned out, coming toward him at an incredible speed. In no time the boy would be past reaching.

He was fighting for breath now, his lungs raw and burning from swallowing too much smoke.

He stopped at the very edge of the fire and saw there was scarely an inch of floor space that wasn't aflame. He knew what he had to do, and he also knew that he was going to get burned, he and the boy both. But his one chance to get Whitey out of the building was to keep low and move far enough into the fire that he could make a grab for the boy and yank him back to himself, quickly enough that neither of them got caught up in the blaze.

Head down, he paused to steel himself before inching any farther. Flames lapped out at him, and for a minute he lost his nerve. He couldn't imagine anything much worse than death by fire. If he turned back now, he could still save himself.

Through the veil of smoke he saw the boy flinch slightly, saw the small, fair head twist a little to the side, and knew he was still alive.

He couldn't just leave him. But he was more frightened than he'd ever been in his life. Still he hesitated, staring into the hellish wall of fire that separated him from the boy.

Suddenly, without warning, it was as if somebody had crawled alongside him and whispered a warning. In that instant he knew he couldn't do what he had to do on his knees. He would have to use his long legs for more than slugging about the city for once and jump—far and high.

He hauled himself upright. The handkerchief he had pressed against his mouth was useless now, dry and smoky. He tossed it aside and stood staring into the fire.

"He will cover you with his pinions, and under his wings you will find refuge. . . ."

Jack looked around, startled. Now where did that come from? It was Scripture, he knew that much, having heard Martha refer to it during the last days of her agony. What, then—a memory?

He let out a long puff of breath, flexing his legs and knotting his fists. In spite of the blistering heat, he suddenly felt cold and began to shake.

But only for an instant. He felt his shoulders clasped by strong, steadying hands as another whisper sounded. From behind him? Or in his head?

"When you walk through fire you shall not be burned, and the flame shall not consume you. . . ."

He turned to look. There was nothing behind him but smoke, thick and oily, nothing in front of him but a wall of fire.

". . . the flame shall not consume you. . . ."

Jack took in as much smoke-filled air as he dared and leaped through the fire, sweeping the boy up in his arms and hurling himself and the child into—and out of—the flames, then on down the hall to the back stairway.

He knew. He didn't know how, he didn't know why, but he *knew*. He knew his escape had had nothing to do with *him*. Nothing.

He ran, and with every step, inside his head he was chanting one word, a word that was both plea and prayer: *God!*

God!

God!

And in his soul he knew that in losing everything . . . he had gained even more.

He made it outside with the boy in his arms, then collapsed in the snow.

39

Second Chances

The Cross is the hiding place of the hopeless and brokenhearted,
The meeting place for all those who seek a second chance.

CAVAN SHERIDAN,

FROM *WAYSIDE NOTES*

THE CLADDAGH, CO. GALWAY, WESTERN IRELAND, CHRISTMAS EVE

Roweena uncovered the spiced beef, pressed in between two plates, where she had left it to set overnight. After marinating for over a week and simmering most of yesterday, Gabriel's favorite Christmas dish now filled the entire cottage with its piquant aroma. They would enjoy it tonight, cold, along with potato cakes, which were ready to bake, and her own special barm brack, already cooling on the table. Today, as was their custom on every Christmas Eve, they had fasted, but tonight they would break the fast with the late supper she had spent most of the day preparing.

She straightened, watching as Evie added some additional ivy and bay leaves to the mantel above the fireplace. The child was fairly dancing by now with excitement, and Roweena was grateful that Eveleen, at least, seemed determined to display a measure of the season's cheer.

The days leading up to Christmas had been a solemn time this year. Right up to today, there had been no real sign of merriment or festivity, except for wee Evie's brightness and anticipation of the hours to come.

Of all the things that might account for Gabriel's quietness and restraint these days, Roweena hoped that worry for her was not one of them. She was recovering nicely, after all, thanks to his expert care and healing skills. By now her wound required nothing more than a small bandage and a quick examination each day. She had not regained much use of her arm as yet, but Gabriel said that was only a matter of time and proper exercise.

It was not unusual for Gabriel to be somewhat contemplative during the season of Christmas, of course. It had always been a time of reflection for him, a time of much prayer and meditation. Each year during Christmas week, it was his custom to go off by himself for a bit each day, to be alone with the Lord and the Scriptures. Even afterward, he would often seem quiet and somewhat distracted throughout the evening.

This year, however, his times away from the cottage had been more frequent and longer in duration, his moments of preoccupation more often than not marked by deep-creased frowns and eyes clouded with what appeared to be a faint sadness, even a kind of brooding.

He had performed the yearly preChristmas tasks as usual: making repairs and patching the cottage, discarding any dross that had gathered inside and out over the preceding months, cleaning the outbuildings and applying whitewash where needed. He had even helped Roweena and Evie scour the furniture with sand, scrub the hearth, and clean the fireplace.

Yesterday he had gone to the *Margadth Mor*—the Big Market—to "bring home the Christmas," just as he always did. In fact, Roweena thought he must have emptied his pockets in the process, for he had returned bearing a fine, plump goose and a more than ample supply of dried fruits, spices, and tea.

Evie had practically swooned at the sight of the delicacies. But when Roweena commented that "Sure, and you've brought home a feast for the kings," Gabriel had merely smiled somewhat absently and gone to sit by the fire.

Any departure from custom had been so slight as to be negligible—except for his uncommonly grave demeanor. Roweena could not help but wonder just how much of his behavior had to do with Brady Kane. She suspected that Brady's betrayal still troubled him greatly, as it did her.

But for herself, it wasn't the actual betrayal she found most painful—although, sure, Brady had done a shocking, terrible thing. What she could not seem to put out of her mind was the stunning revelation that she and Brady might actually be half brother and sister.

There was no way of knowing for certain, of course. According to Gabriel, there had been many soldiers drunk on the whiskey and mad with the blood lust that horrible night. But even the possibility that the same man might have fathered both herself and Brady, no matter how incredible it might seem, could not be ignored.

When she remembered the feelings Brady had once stirred in her at the beginning, when they had first met, a wave of sick shame invariably washed over her. Those feelings had always been confusing and troubling to her, and in truth they had weakened and died long before she'd ever learned of the possible blood tie between herself and Brady. Even so, Roweena still bitterly regretted the fascination he had once held for her.

Every time she looked at Gabriel, she wondered how she could have ever misplaced, even for a moment, her affections. Once she faced the truth about her feelings for *him,* there had been no emotion left for Brady, except a kind of sad fondness, the same sort of hopeless affection she might have felt for a wayward friend.

Or brother.

It was Gabriel she loved. It would *always* be Gabriel, despite the fact that he could not see her as anything but a defenseless child.

In any event, she was concerned about his unusual behavior and decided that when he returned later today she would speak with him about it.

For weeks, Gabriel had heard the rumors about Brady Kane but had steeled himself not to listen, not to care. Whatever happened to the deceitful young American, he had only himself to thank, with his profligate ways, his scheming, and his lies.

It was said in the marketplace and elsewhere that the Yank was drinking himself to death, that in fact Kane lay drunk most every day and night. Gabriel hardened his heart to the stories. If the young fool was indeed intent on killing himself with the drink, then let him have at it.

He was resolved not to feel anything for the boy, not to care even a little about what happened to him. Kane had dug his own hole; let him lie in it.

For a time he had almost succeeded. What man could not harden his heart, after all, if he set his head to doing so?

But it seemed the Spirit had a different idea. At first the nudging was gentle, more a whisper. But when he remained obdurate, the holy whisper became a shout; in the dead of night, at the break of day, when he worked, when he walked, he felt the urging upon his heart until he could no longer ignore what his God would apparently have him to do.

And so he had gone to the city. He had gone grudgingly at first, on the pretense of tending to the boy's wound, which was, in fact, festering badly and in desperate need of attention. Brady was already far more ill than he would have been had he had proper medical care on an ongoing basis. That fact alone had pricked Gabriel's conscience rather sharply.

The rumors about Kane's drinking had not been exaggerated. Each time Gabriel stopped by, he found the American in his cups. It soon became clear that the lad was never sober. His physical condition had deteriorated badly. He had lost a great deal of weight in a very short time, and his skin was tinged with the unhealthy, puffy appearance of the malnourished drunkard.

At first he fought Gabriel, trying to ward him off with a volley of abusive language and self-pitying protests. But finally, seeing that Gabriel would not be turned away, he took to whining about his pain, his wastrel ways, his brother's deception—all the while fueling a poisonous, self-centered hatred.

He seemed particularly fond of insisting that he was hopeless. Forsaken. Lost.

"No man is truly lost unless he chooses to be," Gabriel would counter.

Kane's reaction was to turn suddenly hostile, even angry.

Late one afternoon, Gabriel entered the flat—never locked—and knew an instant of alarm when he thought the boy had died. Sprawled across the bed, clad only in his underclothing, Kane gave no indication that he still breathed.

When Gabriel tried to rouse him, there was no response whatsoever, although by now he knew the lad was still alive. He glanced around the cluttered bedroom and saw several whiskey bottles scattered about, all empty. At first, he was merely disgusted, then angry. He shook Kane hard, not really caring if he hurt him. At last, however, he realized that this was no ordinary drunken sleep: Brady Kane was unconscious.

He flew into action, tugging him over to the pump and splashing cold water over his head. Other than a slight moan, there was still no response.

Gabriel charged out of the flat, taking the steps two at a time, frightening Meg Hannafin, the landlady, nearly out of her wits when he charged into her front room, demanding, "Hot tea or coffee at once!"

For almost two hours he forced strong tea down Brady's throat, doused him with cold water, chafed his arms and legs to get his blood moving, and walked him back and forth through the flat until finally he roused him out of his stupor. Kane awoke in a foul temper and sick with a thunderous headache—but for all that, he was alive.

The next day, Gabriel hired Murtagh Molloy to move in with Kane temporarily. The lad's indignant shouts of protest had bounced off the buildings in Galway City for two days. He stopped raving only because he finally lost his voice.

Big Murt, as he was called, was even larger than Gabriel. Molloy was, in fact, huge, a veritable colossus who never failed to make Gabriel think of a rampaging Norseman. But the man fell into the role of both warden and steward with surprising ease. Of course, considering what he was paying him, Gabriel thought Molloy should perhaps do the wash and feed the geese as part of the bargain.

First thing, the two of them set about clearing every bottle of the drink out of the flat. Within the hour, they had the place as whiskey-free as a nun's prayer closet. And dry it remained. They also took care to remove the young American's clothing, all but his night wear, as well as his room key.

Gabriel put out the word that any man selling the Yank whiskey would answer to both himself and Big Murt. At the same time.

It took nearly three weeks. Kane shouted, he cursed, he pounded the walls until they shook; other times, he cried and took on like a motherless babe. But at last he was sober and reasonably stable.

And with a little help from Big Murt and Gabriel, he had remained so.

But it was time now for the lad to make it on his own, and Gabriel could not help but be concerned for what might happen.

He had gone to Kane's flat again this afternoon with the thought of trying to talk some common sense into that thick head and perhaps even convince him to go back home to his brother.

He found the lad at the desk, head in his hands, staring at what appeared to be a fairly lengthy letter spread out in front of him. Kane looked up when Gabriel entered, but only for an instant before turning back to the vellum sheets on top of the desk.

Gabriel looked at Murtaugh and jerked his head toward the door. The big man gave a nod and stepped outside.

Gabriel waited, and finally, after a long enough time to make the silence awkward if not downright rude, Kane acknowledged his presence. "Making our daily rounds to check on the prisoner, are we?"

Gabriel ignored the jibe. Some days the lad took refuge in sarcasm. Other days he was almost civil. "Good day to you, too, young sir," he said, going to sit down, uninvited, on the only other chair in the room, a lumpy affair by the window.

Once seated, he studied Kane and saw with some concern that the American's eyes were red rimmed, his countenance patently haggard. More troubling still was the noticeable trembling of his hands.

"Not bad news, I hope?" Gabriel ventured, inclining his head to the letter at Kane's fingertips.

The lad's smile was bitter. "Oh, indeed not! It seems that for reasons of his own, my esteemed big brother has finally decided to tell me the charming story of my ever-so-humble beginnings."

His words fairly dripped acid, but Gabriel could hear the pain behind the anger.

"I see."

Kane's eyes were slightly wild as he continued in the same cutting tone. "Yes, apparently Jack's had a recent attack of conscience—a surprise, that, since I was unaware that he even possessed such a burdensome thing—and decided to come clean with the whole ugly truth. I can scarcely wait to write back and tell him that you stole his thunder."

Gabriel remained silent. He found himself hurting for the young American. Why, he wondered, had the brother waited until now? How much better it would have been to tell the lad face-to-face, not in a letter when they were an ocean apart.

"He kept the secret for my own good, of course," Kane said, his voice even harder now. "You have to understand, Gabriel, that my brother is always doing something for my own good. Jack always knows best. About everything."

"Well—at least he has told you the truth, finally," Gabriel said, knowing the words to be rather lame. Given the young American's state of mind, he was hesitant to ask the next question but wanted to know. "And . . . does he mention the Sheridan girl? Did she arrive safely, then?"

As he watched, Brady Kane seemed to shudder. When he spoke, his voice had dropped considerably. "She had a difficult time of it, apparently. But she's all right now." He passed a hand down the side of his face. "Jack knows everything," he said. "About me and Terese. About the lie. He knows the baby is mine."

Gabriel frowned. "What lie is that?" What sort of a story had the young fool concocted, he wondered?

Brady looked at him, seemed about to answer, then apparently thought better of it. "Nothing. It's nothing. I don't want to talk about Jack," he said firmly. "Or Terese. And I especially do not want to talk about my illustrious *pedigree,* if you don't mind! Whether you realize it or not, it's no easy thing to find out that not only was your father not the man you believed him to be, but worse yet, he was an *Englishman.* And a rapist to boot."

Gabriel shrugged. "There are good Englishmen and bad. The same could be said of the Irish. But in truth I know a little of what you mean, being a foundling myself."

Kane turned toward him, his eyes widening in surprise. "You?"

"Aye. I never knew the identity of my natural parents. I was set out in a basket at the door to Lynch's Castle on a summer's night. Fortunately for me, I was taken in and adopted by an aging couple who treated me as their own." He looked at the troubled young man across from him, studying him for a moment. "Is your brother a bad man, then?"

Kane glanced away, then shook his head. "No, not a bad man. Just—a stiff-necked one."

"Nevertheless, I'm sure he thought he was doing right by you, lad. Don't be too hard on him."

Gabriel stirred himself back to the reason he had come. "So, now—how are you feeling, lad?" Gabriel asked.

Brady scowled at him. "Do me a favor, would you, Gabriel? Stop being so blasted nice to me! I know you hate my guts, so stop pretending you don't! What has all this been about, anyway? A matter of your Christian duty?"

"In the first place, Brady Kane, I don't hate you at all," Gabriel said mildly. "'Tis only you, hating yourself, that would seem to be the problem. And as for my Christian duty, aye, that's a part of it, no doubt, but not the whole."

Kane curled his lip. "No preaching today, Gabriel. I'm not up for it."

Gabriel crossed his arms over his chest. "Perhaps you'd rather talk about what you plan to do next. Will you be going back to the States?"

Brady laughed—an ugly sound. "I haven't the faintest notion what I'm going to do next, but I'm most assuredly not going back to the States. I don't know that I ever will. Jack made one thing perfectly clear, however."

He feigned a stern frown and a harsh tone that Gabriel assumed was meant as mimicry of his brother. "I will earn my own keep from this time forth. From now on, there will be no monthly wage unless I *earn* it."

"That would seem fair enough," Gabriel replied. "'Tis how it is with most men, after all."

"Yes, well, in that event, perhaps I can convince you to give me back my clothes and my wallet," Kane shot back sarcastically. "I can hardly go about the business of earning my own keep until then."

Gabriel studied him. The face, a handsome one when it was not contorted in anger or bitterness, was leaner than it had been when they'd first met. And there had been lines added, he noticed now, lines that gave at least the appearance of maturity. The lad no longer looked like a boy—which indeed he wasn't—but a man. A man who had lived hard and perhaps foolishly, but a man all the same.

"I did what I did to save your life, you know. There was no meanness in it," Gabriel said, hoping it was the truth.

To his surprise, Kane gave him no argument. Instead, he sat quietly, regarding Gabriel with a curious expression. "And perhaps you *did* save my life. Even I know I would have destroyed myself if I'd kept to the same road. But if you don't mind my asking, man, why did you do it? Why did you bother?"

"I thought you were worth saving," Gabriel said simply. "As did the Lord, I'm sure."

"I said no sermons, Gabriel." Kane stopped, glancing away for a moment. When he turned back, his expression had cleared some. The anger and bitterness were no longer evident. In their place was a look that might have been genuine curiosity. "You've gone out of your way to help me, and you took a great deal of abuse from me in the process. Yet you didn't have to do *anything* for me. So why did you?"

Why, indeed? Gabriel wondered. He had asked himself the same question many times. With no real answer, except for one.

"I merely saved your hide, boy, to buy you time for the Lord to save your soul."

"Am I supposed to understand that?"

Gabriel shrugged. "It would be to your benefit to try, I expect."

Brady waved a hand as if to dismiss the subject. "No more talk of saving me, Gabriel. We both know I'm hopeless."

"I know nothing of the kind. 'Tis as I told you, no man is hopeless unless he chooses to be."

"Better stop it, Gabriel," Kane said with a sly look. "Your harping at me only makes me thirsty for a drink."

"Far better that it make you thirsty for a cup of God's grace."

Kane looked at him. "You told me yourself that you're a doctor, but I declare, Gabriel, you do sound a whole lot more like a priest."

Gabriel smiled a little. "'Tis true that I'm a doctor. But I am no priest."

389

Brady studied him with a quizzical expression. "You really are a doctor, then? But you have no practice."

Gabriel gave a shrug. "My practice is the Claddagh. I care for many people there. Whoever needs me. I simply do not refer to myself as a physician. 'Tis not a title that gives worth to a man, only the good he does."

"Did you *ever* have a practice?"

"I was a doctor on the mission field for a time. I made the choice not to return."

"Because of Roweena." It was a statement, not a question.

Gabriel narrowed his eyes.

"Oh, come on, man! You're in love with her, and don't deny it! But why did you feel it necessary to give up your career?"

Gabriel hesitated, then saw no reason to answer. "It was a choice I made. Roweena was but a child then, and she needed a guardian. She had lost everyone in her world, you see. I could not take a frightened child to the mission field, and I could not bring myself to leave her behind. She had no one. So I stayed."

Gabriel got to his feet. "I should be going. But there is something I would ask you first. 'Tis one of the reasons I came." He paused. "I thought perhaps you might want to join us for Christmas dinner tomorrow."

40

Wise Men and Kings

The Lord has sought out a man after his own heart.
1 SAMUEL 13:14, NLT

From the look of utter astonishment on Brady Kane's face, Gabriel
might just as well have asked him to charge into a sea of fire blindfolded.

"You can't be serious!"

"I am entirely serious," Gabriel assured him. "I'll admit that I'm
speaking on impulse, without asking Roweena first. But I know
her well enough to know she will not mind. To the contrary, she
will probably be pleased. She has been fretful for some time now
about the state of your health and your heart. And in case you've
wondered, she bears you no ill will for what you did."

It was true. They had talked, the two of them, and he had not
been surprised to realize that Roweena's only thought for the

American was one of concern for him—and even a kind of sadness that he would stoop to such dishonorable behavior.

Even so, there was something here that needed saying, and he commenced to do so. "Your dangerous and foolish scheme might have ended in a terrible tragedy, which you have no doubt realized by now. As it was, your betrayal caused Roweena much pain, in addition to the physical injury she sustained. Nor was wee Eveleen unscathed by your treachery. The child was terrified. She had nightmares for weeks afterward."

Kane's expression was one of abject misery, but when he started to speak, Gabriel stopped him. "To their credit, neither bears you any grudge. Roweena's heart is a forgiving one, as is the child's."

Kane shook his head, as if to clear it. "I—don't know what to say."

"Well, whatever you might want to say, it would be best said to Roweena and the child, I'm thinking. We will set an extra place. If you decide to come, you will be made welcome."

He turned as if to go, then stopped. "There was one other thing—"

Kane, his expression still somewhat stunned, gave a distracted nod.

Gabriel was suddenly uncertain as to whether he should even ask. But he had to know. He had to.

"The night . . . you were shot. You said something—"

Again he stopped, unable to get the words out.

Kane was watching him, one eyebrow raised in a question.

"You said . . . that Roweena—that you saw her love for me in her face. You said that she loved me, that she meant to die for me—"

Again Kane nodded, his gaze raking Gabriel's face. "You honestly didn't know, then? You had no idea?"

"No." Gabriel looked away. "And I can scarce believe it, despite what you seem to think—"

"Gabriel," Kane said softly, "I know what I saw. And you'd see it, too, if you would only open your eyes. Roweena is no child for you to watch over. She is a woman, and make no mistake, man, she's in love with you."

Gabriel finally managed to expel the breath he'd been holding. He looked at Brady Kane, half expecting to see a sneer. Instead he saw something that could have almost been taken for a kind of affection.

"I must go," he said again, now somewhat embarrassed and anxious to get away. "You think about tomorrow. It will be awkward for you at first—for all of us, no doubt—but it will be all right. If you want to come, that is."

"Gabriel—"

Gabriel turned back to him, waiting.

"I suppose I should thank you. For everything."

Gabriel could not stop a smile. "That would seem to be in order."

"But I still don't pretend to understand why you did it," Kane said. "Roweena . . . Evie . . . they could have been killed. You as well. Because of me. You could have had me prosecuted! Yet you didn't. I don't see how you . . . how *any* of you . . . can possibly forgive what I did. And I certainly don't understand why you went out of your way to help me. No one would have blamed you if you had just let me die."

"I expect the Lord God would have made things sorely miserable for me if I had done that. I don't know what to tell you, lad. There is no disputing the fact that you are a thickheaded, self-indulgent, reckless young fool."

He saw Kane wince, but there was no easy way to say this. "I'll not deny that at first I tended to you somewhat grudgingly. I wasn't at all convinced that you were worth my efforts. In truth, I believe I was more inclined to snap your neck than lend you a hand. But for some reason known only to him, God had other ideas, and he pressed me until I simply had to obey. Now that is the only answer I can give you, whether you understand it or not. I expect God merely used me to keep you from destroying yourself, so he might yet have his way in your life."

Brady shook his head. "Gabriel, Gabriel—you are a study! Why would you even think the Almighty would want anything to do with the likes of me? I'm sure he prefers to deal with a better class of fellow than myself, and who would blame him?"

Gabriel tried to think, tried to pray at the same time. *Lord, there must be some way to penetrate that thick skull and that cynical heart. Show me, for I am at my wit's end with this boy.*

Something occurred to him, and he leaned against the door frame, considering. "There was a man," he finally said, "who, if truth were told, more than likely could have matched you sin for sin, Brady Kane. Indeed, in many ways, I would say there is much resemblance between the natural man in each of you. Like you, he was a man of the arts: a singer, a writer of songs, a fine musician. He was also a sensual, passionate man, at times to his own destruction.

"This man, he probably didn't miss much when it came to mucking up his life. He lied when it was expedient. At times he manipulated, at least when it was in his best interests. He even feigned madness," Gabriel went on, with a slight shake of his head, "in order to extricate himself from a nasty piece of business. He was also a murderer. He slaughtered men by the thousands and ten thousands. Perhaps worst of all, he sent one of his own men—a good man, it would seem—to his death . . . just so he could seduce the man's wife."

"Even *I'm* not that bad," Brady muttered, cracking a sardonic smile.

Gabriel didn't answer his smile. "He did all that and other terrible things as well, this man. And yet, the Lord God, didn't he call him 'a man after my own heart' in spite of his sinfulness? He loved this man. He treasured him. He prospered him, even made him a king. And through this man—this philandering, scheming, often devious, bloodstained man—God established the lineage of his only beloved Son, Jesus the Christ."

Gabriel stopped. "Perhaps you've heard of him? He was David, son of Jesse. Writer of the Psalms. King of Israel. And in many ways, a man like you, Brady Kane. Only wiser."

He stopped, aware of the other's now unwavering attention. "David, don't you see, was wise enough to know that no matter how far he ran or how grievously he sinned, he could not escape the love of his Father God. He was human, and so he sinned. But he was loved with a divine love, and so he was forgiven. And always, *always,* he was wise enough to accept his God's forgiveness and begin anew."

Gabriel looked at the young American long and hard. "That is the mark of a real man, I'm thinking. A man of strength and wisdom will not spurn his Creator's love and forgiveness. He will not lightly reject the divine opportunity to begin anew. And if you would once take the time to read that copy of the Scriptures I left lying on your desk some weeks ago," Gabriel said, inclining his head toward the desk where Kane sat, "you would find instance after instance of other men who gained such wisdom only after reaching the point where all seemed lost and hopeless."

He turned then and opened the door, but Brady Kane's voice stopped him before he could step outside.

"Gabriel?"

He turned back. The American was standing now, a faint, wry smile softening his features. "So long as we're speaking of wisdom, I have to submit that a true man of wisdom would surely recognize the love of a woman when he is faced with it day in and day out."

Gabriel stared at him, not knowing whether to berate him for his Yankee insolence or salute him for his boldness, given the tenuous state of their relationship. He did neither, instead merely lifted a hand in farewell, saying, "'Tis Christmas Eve, Brady Kane. I wish God's peace on you."

Then he left for home.

After Gabriel had gone, Brady stood staring at the closed door for a long time. He felt as edgy as a cornered cat, and he wanted a drink in the worst way. Yet he knew that if he weakened and somehow found the means to acquire a bottle, there would be no help for him this time. Gabriel had done more than any other man would have done. He wasn't likely to find another savior next time around.

Besides, he hated the thought that he couldn't lick this on his own. He had always prized his independence—or at least what independence Jack had allowed him. What did it say about him if he let himself become enslaved to something as crude as a bottle of whiskey?

He began to pace the room, thinking. Thinking about Gabriel Vaughan, who had never known his birth parents but apparently hadn't let it influence his life. He thought about Jack, who had tried his best to keep him from learning the truth about *their* parents. Yet even in the face of his still raw bitterness and shock, he knew that Jack had only meant to shield him.

Finally, he thought about a man named David, who seemed to

have broken all the rules and yet had apparently been given more than his share of "second chances."

Was that what Gabriel had been trying to do for him, Brady wondered? Give him a second chance?

He stopped in the middle of the room, clenching his fists. He still felt as if every nerve ending in his body was screaming in pro- test at his hard-won sobriety. But that was one thing he *wouldn't* think about. He didn't dare.

Just then, his hulk of a jailer—"Big Murt"—let himself back into the flat. He was carrying a piece of Brady's luggage, and, without so much as blinking, walked up to Brady and set it down at his feet.

"Gabriel told me I should give you back your belongings now," he said. At the same time, he handed Brady the key to the flat. After a moment, he smiled, saying, "Well, then, I expect I will be on my way now. Best of luck to you, Brady Kane."

The only sound in the flat seemed to be that of Brady's ham- mering heartbeat as he stood contemplating his sudden solitude. The key in his hand felt as if it were burning his skin. He looked from it to the door, then turned, crossed the room to the desk, and placed the key on top of it.

After a moment, he sat down and, with slow and precise move- ments, folded Jack's letter and returned it to the envelope, tucking it inside the desk drawer for now. He would think about his brother later.

Along with a lot of other things.

For a moment, he sat staring at his hands, which were trembling slightly. Finally, he stirred, and, picking up the small, worn Bible ly- ing where Gabriel had placed it, began to thumb through its pages.

41

Christmas Eve in the Claddagh

I follow a star
Burning deep in the blue,
A sign on the hills
Lit for me and for you.
JOSEPH CAMPBELL

That evening they lit the three-branched candle, to commemorate the Holy Trinity. Later they would also light the large Christmas candle, which would burn through the night to show the Christ child that he was welcome in this house.

They took their time over their food, and when they had finally finished, Gabriel pulled away from the table, smiling contentedly. "I'm thinking 'tis a good thing altogether that we do not indulge ourselves like this more than once a year," he said, pulling back a bit from the table and thumping his stomach. "Else I would no longer be able to squeeze through my own doorway."

Roweena returned his smile, thinking that she could not remember a time when Gabriel had weighed a pound more or less than he did today.

He had returned late, too late for any discussion before the supper. But to Roweena's relief, he had seemed more himself this evening, teasing Eveleen and offering frequent and high praise for the food.

As he had at the beginning of the meal, Gabriel now led them in a prayer, this time an evening blessing. He kept his head up, to make certain Roweena could read his lips:

"In thanks we came to this table, sweet Lord and Savior. . . . In thanks we rise and ask your angels round our hearth, your spirit in our heart, your blessing on the heads of all who love and serve you in this house."

Roweena rose immediately to remove the dishes, but to her surprise, Gabriel lifted a hand to stop her. "Let it wait for a time, and I will help you later."

Roweena scarcely knew what to do. She never allowed Gabriel's help in the preparation of a meal or in tidying up afterward. It simply was not done.

As she stood there, watching him in confusion, he turned to Evie. "I would speak with Roweena alone now, lass. Why don't you go along and ready yourself for bed?"

The child thrust out her chin, but he forestalled any attempted protest. "Later, you may share a last cup of tea with us, and we shall look for the Christmas star. But only if I hear no grumbling in the meantime."

Wee Evie looked at him, seemed to consider her options, then smiled. "Aye, but may I ask you first, Gabriel—"

He gave a nod, his expression tolerant and indicating that he already knew what was to come.

"Do you think," said the child, "that the animals will kneel at midnight? To worship Baby Jesus?"

Roweena smiled at the tender look that crossed Gabriel's rugged face. Evie had asked this same question every Christmas Eve since she could string words together—at least three years now. And every year, Gabriel could be depended upon to give the same answer.

"Why, I do not know, child," he said, taking Evie onto his lap. "Though some say such a thing does happen. 'Tis a secret, is it not? But what I *do* know, and this is no secret, is that one day the world itself shall kneel before the Christ and confess him King."

Satisfied, Evie locked her arms around his neck and kissed him soundly on his bearded cheek, then hopped down and scurried off to the back of the cottage, disappearing behind the curtain.

For just a moment, Roweena's heart swelled with love for the two of them. Then she realized that she was still standing, doing nothing, and habit again urged her to clear the table. She actually reached for a platter, but Gabriel caught her hand in restraint. "Sit down, lass. I want to talk with you."

Confused by his behavior, Roweena sank down onto the chair directly across from him, waiting. She wanted to speak with him, too, after all, so perhaps this would be her opportunity. But she would have been more comfortable waiting until her work was finished.

Gabriel sat watching her for a moment before he spoke. Her faint smile looked a bit uncertain, and her hands were clenched on top of the table as if she didn't quite know what to do with them. With some amusement, he realized the reason for her discomfort and, giving her a teasing smile, said, "This table will not quake beneath a few dishes left unwashed, lass."

She returned his smile with a sheepish one of her own.

"First, tell me how it goes with your shoulder today," he said. "Has it troubled you much?"

"Not a bit. Though won't I be glad when my arm is no longer so useless?"

"Once you increase the exercises, you'll see a marked improvement," he reassured her.

He dragged his gaze away from her slender hands for a moment to study his own but remembered to lift his face before he spoke again, so she could read his words. "Roweena—if I have seemed somewhat—preoccupied of late, I wanted you to know that it's nothing to be concerned about. In any event, I thought perhaps I should explain."

She leaned forward a little, obviously intent on what he was about to tell her. So she had been worried after all. He should have told her sooner; he knew that now. But he hadn't been at all sure how she would react, and he didn't want to trouble her, as the injury to her shoulder . . . and the one to her heart . . . had not yet healed.

"First, I would like to ask you something," he continued. "'Tis about Brady Kane, though if you would prefer that we not speak of him, I'll understand."

She tilted her head in a puzzled expression. "I don't mind . . . talking about Brady. I seldom think about the . . . trouble he brought upon us. In my heart, I still feel sadness, but I have forgiven him. But what is it, Gabriel? Has something happened?"

Gabriel chose his words with great care, determined not to distress her. "I thought, at least for a time, that perhaps you had . . . feelings for him. I even asked you as much, if you recall."

A sudden flush spread over her face, and she quickly looked away. Fearing that he had embarrassed her, Gabriel again touched her hand to get her attention. When she looked at him, he went on, as reassuringly as possible. "'Tis all right, lass, if that's the case. There was no way you could have known—about the other. The two of you are young, after all, and Brady Kane is a well-favored young man. And you, Roweena, you are a lovely . . . young woman. It was a natural thing entirely if you were taken with him, and him with you. But now that you know—that there could be the same blood between you, well, you mustn't reproach yourself for anything you may have felt before you knew. Tell me you aren't, lass."

She looked at him, then shook her head. "No . . . not so much now. At first I felt . . . ashamed, you know? But in truth, my . . . feelings for Brady were so short lived and so fleeting that these days when I think of him at all, I usually try to think of him—I hope you don't mind my saying this, Gabriel—but I try to think of him as my . . . brother." She stopped, then added, "And it seems he could be."

Gabriel studied her, not for the first time greatly touched by the gentleness of her spirit, her forgiving nature—her honesty. He squeezed her hand a little. "Well . . . that's fine, then. So long as you have peace with it all. He is doing well now, by the way. I thought you'd want to know."

She brightened a little. "You've seen him?"

He told her then what had transpired in the preceding weeks, told her everything, leaving out only the coarser details. Her gaze scarcely left his face during the entire account.

Only when he had finished did Gabriel realize that he was still holding her hand. He made no move, however, to release it until he saw that tears had pooled in her eyes. Dismay clenched his heart, and he immediately got up and went around the table and sat down next to her on the bench.

"Oh, lass, don't, now! Don't cry. He will be all right. I have surrendered Brady Kane to the Lord's hands, and so must you. It's for God to take care of him now."

Awkwardly, he patted her shoulder. He was surprised by her reply when it came.

"But, Gabriel, I'm not weeping . . . for Brady Kane! I'm weeping because you are such . . . a kind, good man! To think that all this time . . . I have been worried for you, thinking that you were off somewhere . . . because you were troubled . . . and instead you were busy taking care of a man . . . who betrayed your trust!"

Gabriel could not seem to manage a proper response to that, indeed could not seem to do anything except continue the ineffectual patting of her shoulder. "Well, now . . . it will all work out in the end. I'm sure."

"Oh, it will, Gabriel! I know it will, thanks be to God—and thanks to *you*."

It struck him then that there would likely be no better time than this, while they were close . . . and alone . . . to speak his heart. Gently, he took her by the shoulders and set her just far enough away from him that she could read his lips . . . and he could see her eyes. "Roweena—there is something else I would ask you."

She was looking at him in absolute trust, and Gabriel knew a sudden moment of utter panic. What if he was wrong? What if Brady Kane had been wrong? What if he somehow destroyed the bond between them, the good and pure affection that had grown throughout the years? Did he really want to risk that?

"Gabriel?"

At her quiet prompt, he searched her eyes, hoping desperately for a glimpse of whatever it was that Brady Kane had claimed to see. But her gaze on him was, as always, warm and trusting, and fond, too, there was that. But love?

And then Gabriel realized that he did not exactly know what love looked like in a woman's eyes.

"I—in truth, I am almost fearful of asking you—what I had intended to ask," he stammered.

Her delicate brows knit in a frown. "But you can ask me anything, Gabriel. What is it?"

He took so deep a breath he almost strangled on it. He seemed to have lost both his wits and his speech, all at the same time. "Roweena—what about your feelings for *me*, lass? Have you ever thought . . . what I mean to say is, how do you . . . think of me?" He felt a fierce rush of color spread over his face and could have trounced himself for being such a great *gommel*.

He dragged his gaze back to her and saw that her cheeks, too, were flushed with color. But where he was cringing, she was smiling.

"Oh, Gabriel . . . are you sure you really want me to answer that?"

His hands on her shoulders were trembling like those of a palsied old fool! He hadn't the courage to look at her, instead fastened his gaze on the candle in the middle of the table. "If you'd rather not, Roweena, I understand."

Oh, Lord, give me the courage to hear the truth, for I know her well enough to know she will not speak anything less. Unless—out of some misplaced sense of obligation, she might try to say what she thinks I want her to say. No, not that, please, God, I would rather she despise me than be . . . grateful . . . to me. . . .

"Gabriel?"

He glanced back at her, almost fearfully. Her enormous gray eyes seemed to have caught the firelight as she studied him. Then she moved toward him, catching him entirely unawares as she lay her head against his chest.

Gabriel hesitated, then slowly slipped his arms around her in an awkward, uncertain embrace. He was fighting for every breath, it seemed, and lost the battle entirely when she said, her words muffled against his chest so that he had to strain to hear, "I think of you with love, Gabriel. 'Tis the only way I've *ever* thought of you, the only way I know *how* to think of you."

The knot in Gabriel's throat increased by half. He cupped the back of her head and tipped her face up toward his. "What are you saying, then, lass?"

"What are you *wanting* me to say, Gabriel?"

He gave everything over, then: his pride, his common sense . . . his heart. "I expect I am wanting to hear you say that you . . . could love me, Roweena. As a woman loves a man. That you could love me in that way, at least a little."

"And what if I . . . love you more than everything, Gabriel Vaughan? What if I always have?"

He squeezed his eyes shut for an instant, then opened them. "Is that the truth, lass?"

She smiled at him, and he could see the firelight flickering in her eyes, and he saw something else as well, and wondered how it was that he had not seen it before this moment, for it was as bright and shining as a star. He saw her love for him.

He traced the sweet line of her cheek with his fingertips, marveling at the sheer perfection God had made of her face. "As for me," he choked out, "it seems I have loved you forever. I have loved you since you were a wee lass, holding on to my hand and trying to match my wide steps. I have loved you as a brother and as a friend. But, oh, *mo chridh, mo chridh,* if it pleases you, I would love you from this time forth as a husband and a lover."

She eased back from him, only a little. "Are you asking me to marry you, Gabriel?"

"Indeed, I am, lass," he said, finally managing to cross the vast ocean of uncertainty and go where his heart had long wanted to be.

The firelight in her eyes began to dance the instant before she came into his arms again in a rush of softness and sweetness. "Then I am saying yes," she murmured against his heart, leaving Gabriel slightly startled . . . and infinitely thankful.

He might have held her forever, just as they were, had not wee Eveleen peeped out from behind the curtain, dark eyes snapping with impatience. "Gabriel? *Now* can we go looking for the star?"

Holding Roweena with one arm, he opened the other to the child, who immediately came bolting across the room to complete their circle. "Aye, *alannah,*" he said. "The three of us, we will go searching for the star together."

42

Out of the Ashes

Out of the ashes of broken trust,
The rubble of failure and dreams burned to dust,
Out of the ruins of human deceit,
The pain of betrayal, the shame of defeat,
God sifts the gold from this worthless debris,
Lifting the good only his eyes can see,
Then turns the wheel of his sovereign design
And changes the dross of life to the divine.

B . J . H O F F

NEW YORK CITY

It was Christmas morning, and Wall Street was almost entirely deserted. The light snow that had fallen the night before glistened beneath a light glaze of ice. There was no wind, leaving the city blanketed in a white stillness.

Jack Kane stood in front of the ruins of the building that only days before had housed the *Vanguard,* formerly one of the largest, most influential newspapers in the state.

His newspaper. His dream. His greatest success.

His life.

Or so he had once thought.

He smiled grimly to himself, partly to relieve the pain, but more because, no matter what else he felt, there was no mistaking the irony of it all. What had taken him nearly two decades to build had been reduced to a heap of bricks and ashes in one night by a couple of homeless newsboys. Sadly, one of those boys had died in the very fire he helped to ignite.

Had Whitey, the younger of the two, not lived to tell the tale, Jack might never have known the ones responsible. But Whitey *did* live and was only too eager to name the man who had paid him and his now deceased cohort, Snipe Jenkins, to set the blaze. The reason for Whitey's eagerness, of course, was Jack's promise, in exchange for the information, to do what he could to keep the boy out of the lockup.

The man who had set the two little miscreants to their dirty work was already gone. Avery Foxworth had hotfooted it out of the city before the police—or Jack—could get to him. Most likely he was on his way back to where he'd come from.

It still made Jack's blood boil that his former attorney would not have to pay the piper for his treachery. Bu it was done, and if he were altogether honest he supposed that throwing Foxworth's black hide into a cell wouldn't have helped much, if at all, to ease the hurt. So let the British have him then, and good riddance.

But Turner Julian and his corrupt pals who had hired Foxworth to double-cross Jack—well, now, that might be another story entirely. Granted, one frightened newsboy's word wasn't much. But it was a start.

Had they really thought he would quit if they burned him out? He doubted it. More than likely their main intent hadn't been so much to ruin him—surely they knew he would be heavily insured—but more to destroy whatever evidence he held against them, to foil any chances he might have against their lawsuit in the courts. By razing his building, they would also slow him down considerably, just in case he tried to retaliate in print.

Well, they might have accomplished that much at least. But they wouldn't stop him. There would be no end to any of this until he saw Julian and the others behind bars. He still had the evidence of their dubious dealings in prostitution and other questionable "business" practices. And he would have Whitey's testimony. If that wasn't enough—then somehow he would just have to find more.

Meanwhile, the documents they had sought to destroy in the fire were now safely stored in his desk at home.

But that was for another day. Today was Christmas, and he still had gifts to deliver. He was going to Grace Mission later in the morning, no matter how unpleasant it might turn out to be.

That it *would* be unpleasant he didn't doubt.

Still, he had taken the first step to making peace with Terese Sheridan days before. In truth, the girl had been decent enough about it—more so than Jack had a right to expect. Once she realized he was in earnest and meant to bully her no longer, that in fact he was even hoping to help her and the child, financially or otherwise, she had accepted his apologies, albeit somewhat coldly.

True to form, she had gone on to let him know that since she had a *position* now, she would not be needing his help. Nevertheless, Jack intended to find a way around her stubbornness. That baby she was carrying shared his blood, after all.

As for her brother—it would be a very long time, if ever, Jack suspected, before Cavan would be able to even tolerate the sight of him, much less grant him the grace of forgiveness. Jack understood, but even so, the loss of the boy's respect and admiration grieved him more than he would have anticipated. But as Rufus had reminded him, there were always bitter consequences to a man's sins.

The most bitter of all, of course, was the loss of Samantha. Not that she had ever been his to lose. Everything he had tried in order to win her had failed, even before the night of the fire. But what he had tried to do to Terese Sheridan had finally and irrevocably marked the end of any relationship they might have had—even their friendship.

He still thought about trying to see her at some point, though not in hopes of redeeming himself with her—he knew when he was defeated, after all. If he couldn't convince her to marry him when he could have still offered her . . . *everything* . . . he certainly had no chance whatsoever now. But he wanted at least to tell her how sorry he was, how deeply he regretted what he had done.

He had made no attempt in that direction, however, at least not yet. He still needed time: time to try to make some sense of what had happened to him inside that burning building two weeks ago. What had happened—and what it meant.

All he really knew for certain at this point was that he was different. He had come out of that fire changed in a way he would have never thought possible.

Rufus had tried to help him sort through it during the days that followed, was still helping him, one step at a time. God bless the man, he had accepted Jack's story at face value, never once questioning its veracity or its plausibility. Of course, Rufus being Rufus, he had practically been beside himself with joy for Jack and what he emotionally referred to as "finally, the answer to ten years of storming heaven for the most hardheaded man in the city!"

Jack wasn't sure he would ever find the courage to face Samantha, no matter how much time passed. He had no reason to hope she would even agree to see him, much less believe anything he told her. Worse still, there was always the possibility she would think it just another scheme on his part to wear her down and convince her to marry him.

Unable to bear the pain that the thought of Samantha still brought to him, he shoved his hands down inside his pockets and took a last look at the remains of what had once been the most important thing in the world to him.

On impulse, he walked around the rubble to see if he might spot anything worthwhile, anything that might still be usable. He was stooped over, sifting through the ashes surrounding a ruined piece of metal from one of the old presses, when the sound of a buggy coming to a stop made him turn and look toward the street.

What he saw brought him to his feet, heart pounding.

Samantha, in David Leslie's buggy, was pulling up in front of the building—the little that was left of the building, that was. Too stunned to move, Jack stood watching as she stepped out of the buggy and began to walk toward him.

She had never looked lovelier, her face rosy from the cold and framed in the black velvet hood of her cape. A touch of lace could be seen at her neck, above the fastenings of her wrap, and as she picked her way carefully toward him, he caught a glimpse of highly polished black boots.

The sight of her struck him like a blow, taking his breath.

She slowed her pace when she saw him watching her, as if she might be reluctant to reach him. But she didn't stop until she came to stand in front of him, only inches away.

"Samantha." He heard the strangled sound of his own voice, as if the cold air had snatched the word up and blown it out across the debris of the building.

"Hello, Jack."

He was somewhat surprised that she would meet his gaze so directly. When he thought about seeing her again, he almost always figured she would turn away from him—if not *run* away from him.

Instead, she stood there, searching his face as if she were looking for something.

Jack forced himself to meet her gaze, making no attempt to conceal his feelings as he did so.

She had not seen him since the night of the fire, and as she faced him, Samantha was shocked to see how he had seemed to age in so brief a time. She was almost certain there had not been so much silver along his temples before, nor had his deep-set eyes ever looked so shadowed. Those were new lines bracketing his mouth, and his face looked even leaner than she remembered.

The softness in his eyes was new, also, as was the utter lack of defiance, and even the old, bristling arrogance seemed to have disappeared. But it was more than that. Even though he definitely looked rather the worse for wear, he seemed to have acquired a kind of . . . stillness about him that had never been there before.

He glanced at the street, at the buggy parked there, and his mouth quirked a little. "Have you stolen the good doctor's buggy for good, then, Samantha?"

Samantha smiled. "No, but he does tend to be excessively generous with it. I promised not to take advantage of his good nature any more after today. It's just that I . . . wanted to see you, to tell you how sorry I am about—everything." She inclined her head toward the ruins behind him, her heart aching for all he had lost.

She was relieved to see that he didn't seem nearly as devastated—or as angry—as she would have expected him to be. "How are you, Jack?" she finally asked, somewhat lamely.

"Well enough."

"Have you thought about what you're going to do? About the paper?"

He glanced over his shoulder, then back to her.

"Rebuild, of course. Right here."

She almost smiled at the decisiveness that was so much a part of his nature. "Yes, I thought you would."

"I'm glad you came, Samantha. I've—wanted to see you. Just hadn't worked up the courage as yet."

His faint smile was somewhat shaky, Samantha thought.

Suddenly, she couldn't remember anything she'd come here to say. Only that she had to see him, had to see for herself that he was all right. It was Christmas, after all, and he had lost so much.

More than anything else, however, she had to see for herself if it was true, what Rufus had told her.

And it was. She saw it in his eyes now, and for the first time in a long time, the stone lying heavy on her heart began to lift.

"You said you wanted to see me," she ventured. "Was there—something special?"

Jack wished he could simply blurt out the truth: *Because I'm dying without you in my life! Because I need you more than I need anything else in the world! Because I love you beyond all telling!*

Instead, he merely stood there gaping at her like a colossal fool. "I wanted to tell you how sorry I am—for what I did," he finally managed. "For all of it."

She was looking at him with a peculiar expression. "Actually, you *did* tell me. The night of the fire."

"Yes, well, there's—something else, something that happened later, that I wanted you to know." He pulled in a deep breath, and the cold air burned his lungs.

"I do know."

Jack stared at her. "You know—what?"

"I've talked with Rufus," she said, not quite meeting his gaze. "He told me . . . everything. I hope you don't mind. He thought you might want me to know, but he wasn't sure you'd tell me; he was afraid you might be too—"

"Hardheaded?" Jack offered.

"I believe that was the word he used, yes," she said, turning back to him with a faint smile. She stood there, as if she wanted to say more but wasn't sure she ought to.

"Well, for once, Rufus is wrong. I would have told you—if I'd thought you'd see me, that is—but I wanted to wait until I'd thought it through more carefully. I had to know it was—real."

"And?"

"Well—I don't pretend to understand it, not all of it. But it seems to me that it's real." Jack paused. "And I'm fairly certain you had a hand in it."

She gave him a questioning look, but something told Jack she knew exactly what he was talking about.

"That night, when I was still inside the building, you were praying for me the entire time. Weren't you?"

Her look was guarded, but he could see the flare of curiosity in her eyes as she nodded. "How did you know?"

Jack thought about how to answer her, decided there *was* no answer. Not really. "I didn't, at least not then. Not until later. What I *did* know was that I didn't get myself or the boy out of that building on my own. I was—well, Rufus says I was *delivered* out of the fire."

"And what do you think?" she asked softly.

He cracked a ghost of a smile. "Did you ever try to argue with Rufus?"

She returned his smile. He had been so hungry for one of her smiles, Jack realized now. Starved for it.

"Actually, no," she said. "I don't believe I would want to match wits with Rufus."

"Then you take my meaning. Besides, I could no more deny it than explain it. Rufus is right: I was delivered out of that fire. Something—no, *Someone*—literally picked me up, the boy and myself, and carried us out of that building. That's what I believe happened, and I'd be the poor fool altogether if I were to try to convince myself that anyone other than the Almighty himself could pull off such a feat."

She was studying him with such intensity that Jack felt as if his very soul had been laid bare to her scrutiny. But somehow that didn't bother him now, not as it might have before. He wanted no more secrets in his life, especially where Samantha was concerned.

Samantha couldn't stop herself from searching those dark, disturbing eyes. But for the first time since she'd known Jack, the gaze she had more often than not found unfathomable—shuttered tightly against her and the rest of the world—now looked back at her with an unwavering directness that stole her breath.

There was a kind of freedom in that look she had never sensed before today. It was almost as if the man behind that gaze had been imprisoned and was now unbound.

Oh, my Lord . . . it's what I prayed for, isn't it? It's what I've begged you for all this time!

She realized she had missed whatever he said. "I'm sorry?"

"I wasn't burned. There isn't a mark on me or the boy." His

words came faster now and fired with a kind of passion she could see reflected in his eyes. "I *heard* him promise me that I wouldn't be burned. And I wasn't. It was as if the fire never even touched me. But it *did*. There was no way it could *not* have touched me."

Samantha had all she could do to look at him. She was strangling to keep from bursting into tears.

Thank you, Lord! Oh, my wonderful, all-powerful Lord—thank you!

"Samantha?"

She looked at him, still fighting back her tears.

"Do you believe me?"

"Oh, Jack! Of course, I believe you!" It was all she could do not to close the brief distance that lay between them and take his hand, touch his face. She wanted . . . needed . . . to touch him.

She saw him drag in a deep, ragged breath. He closed his eyes for just an instant, then opened them. "Samantha—I promised myself I wouldn't do this. I have absolutely no right—but now that I see you, I have to ask. Samantha, is there—can there ever be any chance—for us?"

A raw, tearing pain knifed through Samantha's heart at the thought of walking away from him now. He *had* changed, she didn't doubt it for a moment. So strongly could she sense the Lord's working in his life that she no longer feared she might be in opposition to God's Word by marrying him.

Jack had changed.

But had *she?*

"You're afraid," he said quietly, never taking his eyes off her. "Of what, Samantha? The past? Because of what happened with Harte? Or are you afraid of me, afraid to trust me?"

The tenderness in his eyes was almost Samantha's undoing. Only now did she become aware of how close together they were standing.

When had he moved? Or was it *she* who had moved?

She shook her head. "I'm not sure. Both, I suppose."

"Do you know what I think, sweetheart?" he said, his voice low and slightly hoarse as he took her by the shoulders.

Samantha refused to meet his eyes.

"It strikes me," he went on without waiting for her to answer, "that a God who can carry a man and a child through a burning building and bring them out completely untouched can most likely take away any scars the past might have seared upon your spirit." He stopped, then added, "And in the process, perhaps he might even help you find a way to trust a hardheaded but somewhat wiser Irishman. What do you think?"

His hands tightened on her shoulders as he gently pulled her closer to him. "Samantha?"

He tipped her chin to make her look at him, and when she did, when she drank in the strong features and the depth of feeling in his eyes, she realized with a sudden, startling clarity that he was right. She had to trust the God who had saved Jack from the fire—and saved him from eternal death—to now enable her to trust *Jack*.

Her throat seemed swollen shut. She could only manage a small nod as he pulled her into his arms. He held her, his chin resting on top of her head for a moment, neither of them saying a word.

"Jack?" she said, finally stirring.

He dipped his head to look into her eyes.

"The last time you asked me to marry you, you told me not to give you an answer just then, to wait."

Something glinted in his eyes as he watched her, waiting.

"I'd like to give you my answer now, if that's all right."

His arms tightened around her, and Samantha lifted her face for his kiss.

"Is that your answer?" he said afterward, smiling into her eyes.

"Well—first I have a request."

He looked at her.

"I think I understand now what you were trying to do—about Terese's baby," Samantha said carefully.

A quick flash of pain and remorse crossed his face. "Samantha—"

She put a finger to his lips to silence him. "No, wait. I know now that you did what you did out of love for me. As wrong as it was, I understand what was behind it. And I forgive you."

He expelled a long breath. "Thank you, sweetheart."

"But I was wondering—"

His dark brows lifted.

"I never wanted Terese's baby—"

"Ah, I know that, Samantha. It was foolishness entirely on my part—"

Again she touched his lips. "I want Shona."

He blinked, and Samantha went on. "If you really want to give me a child, Jack, I would like it very much if Shona could be that child."

His eyes narrowed a little as he regarded her with just a trace of his old speculative scrutiny—and the hint of a smile. "Shona, is it?"

"Don't you see? She has no one else but Terese. And with the baby coming, it might be difficult for Terese to give Shona as much attention as she needs."

He seemed to consider the idea. "That's true. Of course, the lass would be needing *two* parents, it seems to me, not just a mother."

"Yes," Samantha said softly. "That's what I had in mind."

Somewhere across the city, Christmas bells began to ring with the ancient glad tidings and great joy . . . and the promise of peace for all who believed.

Epilogue

❊

Be very careful never to forget what you have seen the Lord do for you.
Do not let these things escape from your mind as long as you live! And
be sure to pass them on to your children and grandchildren.
DEUTERONOMY 4:9, NLT

Samantha and Jack were married in May of 1840. Shortly after
their wedding trip, they adopted Shona Madden. In the years that
followed, they adopted two other children, both Irish immigrants
who had been orphaned: Donal, adopted at age four, and Molly,
adopted at six months.

Jack rebuilt the *Vanguard,* which eventually became one of the
largest and most influential newspapers in the country. He and
Samantha labored throughout their marriage to found several immigrant aid societies. They also established two city orphanages.

Until his death, Jack Kane pioneered a number of reforms for the immigrants flooding America in the 1800s. The questionable reputation that once shadowed him eventually faded into the past, and he became known instead as a man of great faith and compassion, as well as one of true vision for the role of the Irish in America's future.

To celebrate their fifteenth wedding anniversary, Jack and Samantha journeyed to Ireland, where he was reunited with his brother, Brady.

Gabriel and Roweena became man and wife during the summer of 1840. In addition to Eveleen, whom they raised as their own daughter, they became the parents of four children: three sons, Matthew, Brian, and Connor; and one daughter, Aisling. Throughout most of the years of their marriage, they opened their home and their hearts to children who had nowhere else to go.

Terese Sheridan married David Leslie a year after giving birth to her son, Kieran, whom David later adopted. In time they allowed Jack Kane to share in Kieran's life as his uncle, along with Terese's brother, Cavan. They also had a daughter named Nessa, after Terese's mother.

Terese worked alongside David in the mission houses of New York City and continued her efforts even after David went to be with his Lord.

Brady Kane never returned to the United States but spent his life in Ireland. He became an artist of some renown, recognized especially for his landscapes of rural Ireland, Galway in particular. For most of his life, he struggled between a hard-won faith and a tendency toward alcoholism. He never married, nor did he ever meet the son he fathered with Terese Sheridan. He remained friends with Gabriel and Roweena Vaughan until his death at the age of forty-nine.

Cavan Sheridan rose to prominence as a reporter and a journalist, eventually reconciling with his friend and employer, Jack Kane, for whom he established a nationwide news service. In addition to his *Wayside Notes,* he also published several other books of poetry and essays with the Kane publishing houses. At the age of twenty-nine, he married Selia Ryan, a young Irish immigrant from County Clare, who bore him eight daughters and one son.

The descendants of the Kanes, the Vaughans, and the Leslies carried on the faith of their parents, passing down God's Word and his love to succeeding generations on both sides of the Atlantic.

B. J. Hoff is one of the CBA market's most widely recognized authors of fiction and devotional works. Her novels and inspirational collections have captured a worldwide reading audience. In addition to her best-selling Emerald Ballad series and *Winds of Graystone Manor,* she is the author of *The Penny Whistle,* the Daybreak Mysteries series, and the popular devotional books *Thorns and Thrones* and *Faces in the Crowd.* Among her works are a winner of *Christianity Today's* Critics Choice Book Award for Fiction, a Gold Medallion Award finalist, and numerous winners of Excellence in Media Silver Angel Awards. A former church music director, B. J. and her husband live in Ohio and are the parents of two grown daughters.